T0072542

PENGUIN CLASSICS

TALES OF SOLDIERS AND CIVILIANS
AND OTHER STORIES

Ambrose Bierce was born in Miegs County, Ohio, in 1842, but he grew up in northern Indiana. Bierce briefly attended the Kentucky Military Institute, where he apparently studied surveying and mapmaking. When the Civil War broke out, he enlisted as a private in the Indiana Ninth Brigade and eventually rose to the rank of lieutenant and served as regimental cartographer. He was present at some of the fiercest battles in the war—Shiloh, Chickamauga, Missionary Ridge, Pickett's Mill, and others—and his war experience later provided the background for his most important war stories and for several autobiographical essays and sketches. After the war, he served as an aide for the Treasury Department in Alabama and later joined a fact finding expedition to the west. Eventually, he settled in San Francisco, and it was there he committed himself to the literary profession. He was a columnist and editor for various newspapers, including William Randolph Hearst's *San Francisco Examiner*. In 1871 he traveled with his wife to England and remained there for three years, writing for the British periodicals *Figaro* and *Fun*; his first three books were published in England. After he returned to California, Bierce continued to work as a journalist, but, particularly in the 1880s, he also devoted much of creative energy to writing short fiction. He published his collection of war fiction, *Tales of Soldiers and Civilians*, in 1892, and a volume of tales of the supernatural, *Can Such Things Be?*, in 1893. He also continued to work on his wry and sardonic definitions and collected them in his notorious *The Devil's Dictionary* (1911). Bierce's lacerating wit and devilish satire earned him the epithet "Bitter Bierce." After 1899, Bierce lived in the East, and the last years of his life were largely devoted to preparing a handsome twelve volume set of his *Collected Works* (1902–12). That work complete, he revisited the battle sites of his youth and then traveled westward to El Paso. In December, 1913, he entered Mexico, presumably to accompany Pancho Villa's army. He was never heard from again.

Tom Quirk is Professor of English at the University of Missouri–Columbia. He has written on several American authors, including

Hawthorne, Poe, Melville, Twain, Wallace Stevens, Jean Toomer, Willa Cather, Joyce Carol Oates, Langston Hughes, and others. He is the author of *Melville's Confidence Man, Bergson and American Culture, Coming to Grips with Huckleberry Finn*, and *Mark Twain: A Study of the Short Fiction*. He is the editor or co-editor of several books, including *Writing the American Classics, American Realism and the Canon, Mark Twain: Tales, Speeches, Essays, and Sketches, Biographies of Books*, and *The Viking Portable American Realism Reader*.

TALES OF SOLDIERS
AND CIVILIANS

AND OTHER STORIES

———————

AMBROSE BIERCE

EDITED AND WITH
AN INTRODUCTION AND NOTES BY
TOM QUIRK

PENGUIN BOOKS

PENGUIN BOOKS

Published by the Penguin Group
Penguin Putnam Inc., 375 Hudson Street,
New York, New York 10014, U.S.A.
Penguin Books Ltd, 27 Wrights Lane,
London W8 5TZ, England
Penguin Books Australia Ltd, Ringwood,
Victoria, Australia
Penguin Books Canada Ltd, 10 Alcorn Avenue,
Toronto, Ontario, Canada M4V 3B2
Penguin Books (N.Z.) Ltd, 182–190 Wairau Road,
Auckland 10, New Zealand

Penguin Books Ltd, Registered Offices:
Harmondsworth, Middlesex, England

First published in Penguin Books 2000

ISBN 978-0-140-43756-0
ISBN 0 14 04.3756 8
(CIP data available)

Set in Stempel Garamond

CONTENTS

INTRODUCTION   vii
SUGGESTIONS FOR FURTHER READING   xxvii
A NOTE ON THE TEXT   xxix

from IN THE MIDST OF LIFE

Soldiers

A Horseman in the Sky   5
An Occurrence at Owl Creek Bridge   11
Chickamauga   20
A Son of the Gods   26
One of the Missing   32
Killed at Resaca   43
The Affair at Coulter's Notch   49
The Coup de Grâce   57
Parker Adderson, Philosopher   63
An Affair of Outposts   69
The Story of a Conscience   78
One Kind of Officer   85
The Mocking-Bird   95

Civilians

The Man Out of the Nose   103
The Man and the Snake   110
The Boarded Window   117

from CAN SUCH THINGS BE?

Can Such Things Be?

Moxon's Master   127
A Tough Tussle   136
A Resumed Identity   143
The Night-Doings at "Deadman's"   149
The Realm of the Unreal   157
The Damned Thing   164
Haïta the Shepherd   172

The Ways of Ghosts
  Present at a Hanging 179
  A Wireless Message 181

Soldier Folk
  Three and One Are One 185

from NEGLIGIBLE TALES

Negligible Tales
  A Bottomless Grave 193
  Jupiter Doke, Brigadier-General 200
  The City of the Gone Away 209
  The Major's Tale 215
  Curried Cow 222
  A Revolt of the Gods 228

The Parenticide Club
  My Favorite Murder 233
  Oil of Dog 241

from ANTEPENULTIMATA

  A Bivouac of the Dead 247

from THE OPINIONATOR

The Controversialist
  The Short Story 253

EXPLANATORY NOTES 261
GLOSSARY OF MILITARY TERMS 269
BATTLE SITES AND BATTLE LEADERS 271

INTRODUCTION

Herman Melville once complained that he would likely be known to posterity, if at all, as the man who had lived among cannibals. The substance and interest of his fiction insured him against such a fate. Ambrose Bierce has not been so fortunate. He is popularly known as the man who in old age walked into Mexico to accompany Pancho Villa's army and was never heard from again, only incidentally known as the author of *The Devil's Dictionary* and several exquisite short stories, and hardly known at all as a prolific writer whose collected works filled twelve substantial volumes. His final, and presumably fatal, gesture is romantic, I suppose, but it is also absurd. Besides, no one really knows where and how Bierce died. He might well have been engineering one last literary hoax; some scholars think so, and he was capable of such deception. The mystery of his last days is at least vividly obscure, but it has tended to eclipse the steadier certainties of the life he did lead.

The final image of him is ridiculous; he becomes something of an inverted Don Quixote—a seventy-one-year-old asthmatic huffing and puffing through the Mexican deserts chasing after an army whose politics, if he ever considered them, he would have deplored, more intent on putting himself in harm's way than tilting at windmills, to be sure, but perversely idealistic nonetheless. But Ambrose Bierce was not a ridiculous man, and the life he lived was more interesting and more substantial than its flamboyant and perhaps imagined conclusion. Though his fiction is not autobiographical in the way that Melville's is, Bierce's actual life does shed light on the themes and techniques of his imaginative writing. For that reason, it is worthwhile to linger over his biography before commenting on the achievement of his short fiction.

It was Gen. William Tecumseh Sherman who observed that "War is Hell." Ambrose Bierce, who had seen much of the same war and often closer at hand than Sherman himself, defined the subject somewhat differently in *The Devil's Dictionary*: "War, *n.* A by-product of the arts of peace. The most menacing political condition is a period of international amity. . . . War loves to come like a thief in the

night; professions of eternal amity provide the night." The authority of Sherman's remark, we must suppose, derives from sad experience. Bierce's is founded on the jaundiced coupling of abstractions
uttered in a tone of weary urbanity and says a great deal more about
the persona of the cynical lexicographer than it does about war or
peace. This is to be expected of a man who has acquired (among
other sinister sobriquets) the title "Bitter Bierce."

Despite ample and fine biographical treatment of the man, Ambrose Gwinett Bierce remains, and will perhaps always remain,
something of a mystery. It is not at all clear, at any rate, how much
of his supposed bitterness was temperamental and how much contrived, and it is easy to overestimate the depth of his resentment.
We know, for example, that, apart from his devotion to his brother
Albert, Ambrose was not particularly attached to or even fond of
his family. We know as well that in his *Collected Works* he reserved
a section of one volume for stories gathered together under the title
"The Parenticide Club." Whether these two facts, taken together,
make a third is less certain. Judging from the tone of the two stories
from that section and included in this volume ("My Favorite Murder" and "Oil of Dog"), the thought of parenticide provided the occasion for tall tale humor and grisly fun and nothing more. And as
the reader will soon discover, much of the shock and affecting
pathos of his serious short fiction derives from the loss of some
family member—a wife, a twin brother, a father, a mother. Bierce
knew how to play to his reader's sensitivities, even though he did
not necessarily share them himself.

Though the narrator of "My Favorite Murder" is accused of
murdering his mother, his legal defense is that that crime pales in
comparison with the way he murdered his uncle. This is purely antic fiction, and we know, as yet another fact, that Ambrose preferred his successful and relatively worldly uncle Lucius, to his
pious and bookish father, Marcus, and certainly bore his uncle no ill
will. Lucius Versus Bierce had come west to Ohio from Connecti-
cut in 1815, and his younger brother Marcus had followed him a
few years later. He had almost immediately embarked on plans for
self-improvement, adventure, and self-advancement. He partici-
pated in the illegal Patriot's War to rescue Canada from British
domination and thereafter was known as "General Bierce." He escaped conviction for violating U.S. neutrality laws and, in fact, was
eventually elected the mayor of Akron.

The writer's father, Marcus Aurelius Bierce, by contrast, came
west to a religious settlement known as "Horse Cave" in Meigs
County, Ohio, and it was there that Ambrose was born on June 24,
1842. While the uncle enjoyed a flamboyant popularity, the father
eked out an obscure living on farms, first in Ohio and, after 1846, in
Indiana. It is not surprising that Ambrose might attempt to emulate
the uncle and scorn the father.

Bierce attended a poor country school in Indiana and apparently
from an early age rejected the dour religious conviction of his family and surrounding community. Many years later he would define
faith as "belief without evidence in what is told by one who speaks
without knowledge, of things without parallel." However, in his
youth he had neither the opportunity nor the literary sophistication
to express this sort of contempt. His uncle paved the way to both,
perhaps, when he sent his nephew to the Kentucky Military Institute in 1859, for the curriculum there was a demanding one and the
previously recalcitrant boy proved to be an able student.

Like another supposedly rebellious spirit, Edgar Allan Poe, with
whom he is so often compared, Bierce seems to have responded
to—even liked—soldierly discipline and decorum. Surely it was at
the military institute that he acquired the military bearing that char-
acterized him for the remainder of his life. It appears that he also
received more than adequate training in topographical engineering;
the surviving maps that he made during the Civil War reveal either
a natural talent for or thorough training in draftsmanship. In either
case, Bierce's alert responsiveness to natural contours and spatial re-
lationships, so necessary to mapmaking, would serve him well in
the war and also in his short fiction.

Bierce returned to Indiana from the military institute later the
same year. He was eager for the sort of adventure and experience
that was unavailable to him there, however, and spent his time
performing odd jobs with little enthusiasm. A national emergency
supplied him with a personal opportunity. When the Civil War
broke out, the young man enlisted as a private in the Indiana Ninth
Brigade for three months' service, ample time, it was believed, to
put down the insurrectionists to the south. His entrance into the
conflict does not seem to have been prompted by a principled political interest in preserving the Union so much as by the sort of fiery
idealism that motivated his uncle to "liberate" Canada. Even so,
during his first brief tour of duty, which consisted mostly of skir-

mishes or minor battles, Bierce established his courage by risking his life to rescue a fallen comrade.

After the three-month term had expired, the Ninth Brigade was reorganized for a three-year tour of duty (the revised estimate of the time necessary to end the war) and Bierce reenlisted as a sergeant. His brigade returned to the Cheat Mountains of western Virginia, where he again saw minor action. When his brigade was assigned to the Army of the Ohio, Bierce was destined to experience the horror of battle on a grand scale. The Army of the Ohio, under the command of Gen. Don Carlos Buell, was ordered to join Grant's Army of the Tennessee for assault on the Confederate railroad center in Corinth, Mississippi. However, the Confederate General A. S. Johnston launched his own offensive against Grant on April 6 at Pittsburg Landing, Tennessee, a day before the Army of the Ohio arrived. The engagement became known as the Battle of Shiloh, after the name of a small chapel in the area. In an essay, "What I Saw of Shiloh," Bierce remarks upon the irony: "The fact of a Christian church . . . giving name to a wholesale cutting of Christian throats by Christian hands need not be dwelt on here; the frequency of its recurrence in the history of our species has somewhat abated the moral interest that would otherwise attach to it."

As the war progressed, Bierce rose through the ranks, eventually to first lieutenant, and he was present at many of the fiercest engagements of the war. In the Battle of Shiloh, the Ninth Indiana alone lost 170 men. The total figures are staggering: Federal soldiers killed or wounded, 13,047; Confederates, 10,694. Other engagements in which Bierce saw action were at least as brutal. The Battle of Stones River (January 1863): Federal soldiers killed or wounded, 9,532; Confederates, 9,239. The Battle of Chickamauga (September 1863): Federal soldiers killed or wounded, 16,170; Confederates, 18,454. He was also present at other bloody encounters, as violent if not so epic: Missionary Ridge; Pickett's Mill (which he later described as "criminal" for its mismanagement); much of Sherman's campaign for Atlanta, which, as the army moved southward, produced a steady torrent of death (in a single month, over twenty thousand men from both sides were killed); a skirmish at Kennesaw Mountain (where Bierce himself received a near fatal injury from a sniper's bullet requiring three months' convalescence); and the Battles of Franklin and Nashville.

Bierce had entered the war a boy of nineteen. When it was over he was still young; though, as his Civil War memoirs repeatedly lament, he had also left his youth somewhere behind him. He had witnessed the grotesqueries of war, but he had also observed the fear, spite, arrogance, and stupidity of human conduct, alongside transcendent acts of valor and self-sacrifice. He had dutifully followed orders from on high, though he at times privately thought them ill informed or misguided. He had been seriously wounded, and, briefly, he had been a prisoner of war. He acquired a lifelong respect for Generals Buell and William Hazen, under whom he had served and who in Bierce's estimation had been unfairly rebuked, and something less than respect for Generals Sherman and Grant, who enjoyed the nation's favor.

And he had experienced the unthinkable. In the Cheat Mountains of western Virginia, for example, he witnessed an event that would find its way into the disturbing tale "The Coup de Grâce." One day his column passed the repulsive bodies of fallen soldiers, "their blank, staring eyes, their teeth uncovered by the contraction of lips." The next day, they passed the same bodies, which seemed to have altered their positions, to have shed part of their clothing, and to have lost their faces. They had been eaten by pigs. In the fiction, Bierce describes the scene this way: "Fifty yards away, on the crest of a low, thinly wooded hill, [Captain Madwell] saw several dark objects moving about the fallen men—a herd of swine. One stood with its back to him, its shoulders sharply elevated. Its forefeet were upon a human body, its head was depressed and invisible. The bristly ridge of its chine showed black against the red west. Captain Madwell drew away his eyes and fixed them again upon the thing which had been his friend." The point to be made here is that the macabre quality of Bierce's imagination often consisted in humanizing the unimaginable, not in adding contrived or ghastly detail to his fictions.

After the war, Bierce found employment but he remained without occupation. It would be years before he resolved to become a writer, but he seems to have already acquired one of the indispensable requirements, which he would declare in his essay "To Train a Writer" (1899): To the aspiring writer "a continent should not seem wide, nor a century long. And it would be needful that he know and have an ever present consciousness that this is a world of fools and rogues, blind with superstition, tormented with envy, consumed with vanity, selfish, false, cruel, cursed with illusions—

frothing mad!" The peace at Appomattox, it would appear, had not abolished the depravity of his species.

For a time Bierce served as an aide for the Treasury Department in Alabama, having the unenviable duty of seizing and protecting southern cotton that the government had decided was federal property. Though evidently blameless himself, Bierce saw several instances of roguery, opportunism, and venality among his northern colleagues, and he continually faced the possibility of retributive justice of one sort or another from resentful and frustrated southerners.

Along with a deepening cynicism, he acquired at this time the asthmatic condition that plagued him for the rest of his life. For these and other reasons, Bierce may have welcomed the unexpected opportunity to join General Hazen in Omaha for a fact-finding expedition of the west. Besides, the offer carried with it the promise of a captaincy. Through no fault of Hazen's, the commission eventually offered him was for a second lieutenancy, but by the time Bierce received this news he was in San Francisco. Bierce indignantly refused the commission and left the army for good, but he was to remain in California for many years.

He took a job as a night watchman at the Sub-Treasury building in 1867, and it was about this time that he undertook to transform himself into a professional writer. Bierce approached the project with the sort of discipline he would years later advise in "To Train a Writer"—reading widely, especially in the classics, sharpening his perceptions and attempting to think clearly, and, if any were left to him, "dispelling his illusions and destroying his ideals." His literary debut was the publication of a poem in the *Californian.* Though he continued to write poetry for the rest of his life and published two volumes of satirical verse, *Black Beetles in Amber* (1892) and *Shapes of Clay* (1903), he concluded early that his métier was not as a poet and directed his energies toward the writing of prose.

Apart from the novel, which Bierce considered a "short story padded," he proved to be capable in a variety of genres—the essay, the sketch, the fable, the satire, the tall tale, and of course the short story. He was soon publishing pieces in local periodicals, and when he was offered the opportunity to edit *The San Francisco News Letter* he gave up his job at the Treasury and began to write the "Town Crier" column. Later, he offered Bret Harte some of his essays that were rather more serious than the satiric journalism he was contributing to the *News Letter.* They were published in *The Overland*

Monthly, and it was in that periodical that Bierce published his first piece of short fiction in 1871. It was in that year, too, that he married Mollie Day, the daughter of a prosperous miner.

In a relatively brief time, Ambrose Bierce had found his calling, trained himself as a writer, infiltrated San Francisco literary circles, and married above his station. For a man who, by all odds, should have lived out his days as the village atheist of Elkhart, Indiana, Bierce had succeeded mightily. His "Town Crier" column had acquired some reputation as far east as New York and London, his popularity in Britain rivaling that of Bret Harte and Joaquin Miller. This was propitious, for the bride's father promised to send the newlyweds to England as a wedding present. Bierce resigned from the *News Letter* and the couple left the city in the early spring of 1872.

He instantly became so fond of the mother country, and perhaps of the English fondness for him as well, that he remained there for three years. Often using the pen name "Dod Grile," he wrote for *Figaro* and *Fun.* Bierce began to socialize with the Fleet Street crowd and established a close friendship with the humorist Tom Hood. Bierce's first three books were published in England—*The Fiend's Delight* (1873), *Nuggets and Dust* (1873), and *Cobwebs from an Empty Skull* (1874)—and the first two of his three children were born there. His expatriation, in other words, was altogether agreeable, and he might have remained in England indefinitely, but his wife, who had returned home for a visit, wired him that she was pregnant with their third child. Somewhat reluctantly, he sailed for America in September 1875.

Now a father with three children, Bierce was faced with beginning to build a career once again, and he seems to have taken a more calculated interest in the project than he had when he first arrived in San Francisco. He became the associate editor of the *Argonaut,* a periodical with a definite political agenda in mind, and to write his "Prattle" column, which sometimes contradicted the purposes of the owners. Under the pseudonym "William Herman," Bierce and T. A. Harcourt published *The Dance of Death* (1877), which purported to condemn the waltz on moral grounds, but did so in suggestive, almost lurid detail. Whether this literary hoax was intended to succeed in commercial as well as antic terms is unclear, but it became something of a best-seller, and Bierce himself helped sales along by damning the book in the *Argonaut.*

In 1879, Bierce abruptly retired from the literary life and removed to the Black Hills of the Dakota Territory. Perhaps his move can be explained because he did not get along with Frank Pixley, the founder of the *Argonaut*; perhaps it was because the San Francisco of the 1870s had become in the words of his biographer Carey McWilliams "magnificent, dull and empty"; or perhaps it was because Bierce, with three young children to support, was seeking a more stable financial future. In any case, he served as a mining engineer in Rockerville and planned to have his family join him there in the not-too-distant future. This undertaking ought to have been immensely profitable to Bierce and to the company for which he worked, but ineptitude, spite, and knavery worked together to spoil the venture. Despite charges of corruption and mismanagement, Bierce, as he had done in Alabama after the war, performed his duties honestly and honorably. According to Paul Fatout, who has exhaustively charted Bierce's experience in the Dakotas, he was the ablest businessman and miner in the entire company. For a man whose motto was "Nothing matters," it is nevertheless apparent that his personal sense of integrity mattered deeply to him. Whether Bierce's conduct proceeded from principled idealism or from a feeling for what he owed himself is not clear.

Back in San Francisco, or rather nearby, since his asthma troubled him there more than at higher elevations, the journalist worked five years for the *Wasp*, where he resumed his "Prattle" column. By 1886 he was out of work once again, however. The entrance into his life of the young publisher of the *San Francisco Examiner*, William Randolph Hearst, was fortuitous. Bierce suddenly had a regular income, a certain autonomy that allowed him to work out of the city, and, though the two men were often in decided disagreement, considerable freedom from editorial intervention. From 1887 until 1899, when he left to live in the east, Bierce worked for Hearst in, if not absolute contentment, at least productive stability.

Unfortunately, it was during this period also that his domestic life disintegrated. He separated from his wife in 1888; the next year his son Day was killed in a gun duel. How much or little the combination of hard-won professional success and personal disappointment and grief installed within him the productive tensions necessary for his art is impossible to say. Regardless, it is a fact that these same years saw the creation of much of his best work. He continued to fashion what would become his notorious *The Devil's*

Dictionary (1911), though it first appeared as *The Cynic's Word Book* (1906). More pertinent to this volume, Bierce wrote a remarkable number of short stories in a relatively brief time, enough, in fact, to publish two volumes in successive years. *Tales of Soldiers and Civilians* was published simultaneously in England as *In the Midst of Life* in 1892; his tales of the supernatural, *Can Such Things Be?*, was published in 1893.

The titles of these two collections are perhaps indicative of the high literary ambitions the author had for them. No doubt a British audience for his volume of Civil War stories would possess neither the fund of fairly recent memories of a national conflict nor a casual acquaintance with the place, occasion, or seriousness (both political and symbolic) of the war. It was likely for that reason that the English edition was published under the title *In the Midst of Life*, though it is unclear whether the change was the decision of Bierce or his publishers, Chatto and Windus. In any event, the phrase is taken from the funeral service in the Anglican Book of Common Prayer: "In the midst of life, we are in death." The change in title gave his volume of tales the force of spiritual parable and freed it from the historical associations it would have had for an American audience. His collection of supernatural tales, on the other hand, took its title from *Macbeth*. Shortly after the appearance of Banquo's ghost, Macbeth exclaims to Lady Macbeth:

> *Can such things be,*
> *And overcome us like a summer's cloud,*
> *Without our special wonder? You make me strange*
> *Even to the disposition I owe,*
> *When now I think you can behold such sights*
> *And keep the natural ruby of your cheeks,*
> *When mine is blanch'd with fear. (Macbeth 3.iv.)*

Whether or not the Shakespearean allusion also conveys something of the misogyny that is sometimes attributed to him, Bierce at least meant to suggest the moral dilemma that is implicit in much of his supernatural writing as well as to insist upon the literary merits of the genre.

Circumstances did not immediately conspire in favor of the author's ambitions, however. Though both collections of short fiction were favorably reviewed in America and England, the failures of publishing houses deferred at least in financial terms the success he may have anticipated. The reissue of an enlarged edition of *In the Midst of Life* in 1898 did something to correct the imbalance. Meantime, he enjoyed being the center of San Francisco literary circles. He gave a great deal of time and energy to aspiring young writers without compromising his severe critical standards; in return he typically received unqualified admiration from his pupils. In rather altered terms, Bierce occupied the position of a Dr. Johnson, whom he respected and admired, or a William Dean Howells, whom he did not. Still, the satisfaction he had once taken in the San Francisco literary life had diminished considerably by the end of the century. Bierce seemed to welcome the change Hearst provided by sending him east. He moved to Washington, where prior experience had demonstrated to him that he was relatively free from his asthmatic condition.

Bierce's duties there were not onerous, and he made several short trips to nearby cities, including New York where his remaining son lived. He moved in military circles now, and he visited more than once the Civil War battlefields he had known in an earlier life. The quality of feeling he experienced there is perhaps suggested in this volume by "A Bivouac of the Dead." When Bierce indulged himself in the memoir, and in dramatic contrast to his war fiction, he could become romantic. He concludes "What I Saw of Shiloh" in a tone of dismay and nostalgic grace: "Is it not strange that the phantoms of a blood-stained period have so airy a grace and look with so tender eyes?—that I recall with difficulty the danger and deaths and horrors of the time, and without effort all that was gracious and picturesque? Ah Youth, there is no such wizard as thou! Give me but one touch of thine artist hand upon the dull canvas of the Present . . . and I will willingly surrender an other life than the one that I should have thrown away at Shiloh." It is not so very surprising that Bierce should seek out one last battlefield, this time in Mexico, to throw away his life.

No doubt the debate about whether Bierce was suicidal will continue. It is rather more certain that in the beginning years of the new century he was contemplating final things. He was several times seriously ill and, it seemed, surrounded by death and sickness. His remaining son, Leigh, died of pneumonia in 1901; soon after, his daughter, Helen, contracted typhoid fever and nearly died herself; and his estranged wife, Mollie, died the same year. As for Ambrose Bierce, he was busily tying up loose ends. Thanks to the admiring support of the publisher Walter Neale, Bierce was able to bequeath to anyone who remained interested a handsome edition of *The Collected Works of Ambrose Bierce.* For four years, from 1908 to 1912, he worked diligently on what eventually became a twelve-volume set. He transferred his cemetery plot in California to his daughter in 1913 and soon thereafter announced to a friend in a letter, "I'd hate to die between two sheets, and, God willing, I won't." In October 1913 he left Washington. Once again he toured the battle sites of his youth and then moved on to New Orleans, San Antonio, Laredo, and finally El Paso. Apparently he acquired in Juarez the necessary papers that would permit him to accompany Pancho Villa's army (though this is by no means certain), and by late December he was in Mexico. He was never heard from again; this much is certain.

When we turn to Bierce's short fiction, it is wise to make some necessary distinctions. First, I have organized the selections in this volume in accordance with the organizing principle inherent in the tables of contents of his *Collected Works* because Ambrose Bierce did not make the sorts of confusions that some of his later anthologizers have. "A Tough Tussle," for example, though it takes place on a Civil War battlefield, is not really a war story. It was first published in *Can Things Be?*, and because he kept it in that volume in the *Collected Works*, we must conclude that he always considered it a tale of the supernatural. "Jupiter Doke, Brigadier-General" is not a war story, either, but a pointed comic satire, and one of his best in that vein. I do not pretend to know what Bierce had in mind when he grouped this and other stories together under the rubric "Negligible Tales," but Bierce was as capable of false modesty as he was of audacious and fierce independence. Finally, tales of the supernatural ("The Realm of the Unreal," for example) should not be confused with ghost stories (such as "An Arrest"). Again, I am not sure that I always recognize the distinctions he was making, but the perils of contradicting a man who insisted that he knew what he was doing and why remain long after the threat of his lacerating wit has vanished.

Ambrose Bierce was such a deliberate maverick that other distinctions that may not at first seem momentous or even real are also in order. As a critic, he was not critical but opinionated (as the title of Volume X of the *Collected Works*, *The Opinionator*, clearly indicates). In his essay "On Literary Criticism," he demonstrates just how little patience he has for those critics who "read between the lines," discover in this vacancy the author's true "purpose," and present it as a "problem" that the author has attempted to "solve." He had labels for such critics—"microcephalous bibliopomps," "strabismic ataxiates," and the like. (Is it any wonder that H. L. Mencken should find the man so appealing?) Bierce was not a humorist, either, but a satirist (though he freely acknowledged that a republican form of government could not sustain or encourage satire). He was not a comedian, but a wit (though his tall tales are sometimes extremely funny and his wit often more wry than biting). "Wit," he wrote, "may make us smile, or make us wince, but laughter—that is the cheaper price that we pay for an inferior entertainment, namely humor." So self-defined, he proclaims his superiority over and prohibits comparisons to men he knew and more or less liked—Bret Harte and Mark Twain.

Bierce professed to despise the novel and novelists. Following Poe, he argued that because a novel could not be read at a single sitting it could not achieve a single, unified aesthetic effect. Curiously, he held the romances of Scott and Hawthorne to no such standard. As for the novel, however, he believed that the legitimacy of the form died (depending on his mood) with Fielding and Richardson and surely survived no later than Thackeray. (By fiat, down go Howells and James.) More specifically, he had no use for realism and realists. He defined realism in *The Devil's Dictionary*: "The art of depicting nature as it is seen by toads. The charm suffusing a landscape painted by a mole, or a story written by a measuring worm." (Nevertheless, Stephen Crane and Ernest Hemingway responded to the disturbing realism of Bierce's war stories.) He was neither regionalist nor local colorist, though he sometimes acted as apologist for California writers and was capable of at least competent dialect writing. Still, he objected to the "corn-fed enthusiasm of the prairies" and thus dismissed Hamlin Garland with finality.

Bierce was American to his fingertips and trafficked in that national identity when he was in England, but he also announced that a " 'distinctively American literature' has not materialized, excepting in the works of Americans distinctively illiterate." He scoffed at the idea of originality and exalted excellence in established forms, but his own fiction is often rightly described as experimental, and he rang some interesting changes on familiar genres. Like so many

other writers of his day, Bierce was not above indulging in the
formulaic plot twists of O. Henry or the fantastic but dramatic
dilemmas of Frank Stockton. But he claimed to despise popular
magazine fiction and thought its highest function was to "stir up
from the shallows of its readers' understanding the sediment which
they are pleased to call sentiment, murking all their mental pool and
effacing the reflected images of their natural environment." He also
objected to the didactic in fiction, but this was easy for someone to
say who had at his disposal for most of his writing life a column in
which he could be as vituperative and as didactic as he pleased.

What are we to make of these snarled and snarling convictions,
and what is left standing once this freewheeling iconoclast is
done smashing the false idols of his day and of the next? Not
much, I suppose, but some awfully interesting fiction, interesting
and distinctive enough to make the adjective "Biercean" meaning-
ful. Besides, many of the idiosyncrasies of the man are not so
very perplexing. Like many, perhaps most, autodidacts, his self-
education was disciplined but not systematic, and he wears his eru-
dition a bit too gaudily at times. Having achieved such an exacting
style through severe training and determination, he could be as un-
forgiving as the recruit who has just made it through boot camp.
His mature prose is stately and polished to an almost Augustan
sheen. For that reason, perhaps, he could not resist publishing a
minutely prescriptive book of usage, intended mostly for journal-
ists and editors and rather indignantly called *Write It Right* (1909).
At all events, the verbal precision he eventually acquired was
brought into the service of the grotesque, the unreal, and the unthinkable, and the combination frequently resulted in superb
fiction.

In his essay "The Short Story," Bierce rebels against the laws of
realism, the laws "Cato Howells has given his little senate." Among
those laws is that of probability. In point of fact, he insisted, life itself is improbable—motives are impenetrable, occurrences unpre-
dictable and strange, moral imperatives perversely insufficient to
human emergencies: "It is to him of widest knowledge, of deepest feeling, of sharpest observation and insight, that life is most
crowded with figures of heroic stature, with spirits of dream, with
demons of the pit, with graves that yawn in pathways leading to the
light, with existences not of earth, both malign and benign—ministers of grace and ministers of doom." The fiction writer has no use

for probability "except to make what is related *seem* probable in the reading—*seem* true." This essay was published under the heading "The Controversialist." Of course Bierce's position here is deliberately contrary and, if nothing more, serves to authorize what he had already achieved in his short fiction.

Part of the author's special competence in creating the *seemingly* true probably derives from his training in topological engineering, in mapmaking, for he was capable of the dramatic rendering of spatial relations in ways that few writers of much greater talent would even attempt. The suspense and terror of "One of the Missing" or "The Man and the Snake," for example, are built up out of analogous situations. In both instances, the setting is soon organized around the fearful consciousness of a single (and supposedly fatal) focal point—the barrel of a rifle and eyes of a snake. Whether the protagonist is pinned down, as in the first instance, or transfixed, as in the second, the relation of hands, feet, furniture, and the like are depicted with the sort of minute precision that have led some critics, quite mistakenly, to label Bierce a realist. His imagination was vivid, but it was not realistic. He located the figures of his fiction in remarkably different environments with exacting attention, and he moved effortlessly from broad expanses to constricting human predicaments in ways that took the gothic out of doors or made suspense out of the stuff of sometimes accidental, sometimes providential operations.

In an autobiographical sketch that recounts his early experience of the war entitled "On a Mountain," Bierce wrote of his aesthetic appreciation of the Cheat Mountains of western Virginia. For a "flatlander" such as himself, who had grown up on the plains of Ohio and Indiana, "a mountain region was a perpetual miracle. Space seemed to have taken on a new dimension; areas to have not only length and breadth, but thickness." This same territory became the site for one of his most popular stories, "A Horseman in the Sky," and likewise depends on a talent for topographical rendering:

The country was wooded everywhere except at the bottom of the valley to the northward, where there was a small natural meadow, through which flowed a stream scarcely visible from the valley's rim. This open ground looked hardly larger than an ordinary door-yard, but was really several acres in extent. . . . Away beyond it rose a line of giant cliffs similar to those upon which we are supposed to stand in our survey of the savage scene, and through which the road had somehow made its climb to the summit. The configuration of the valley, indeed, was such that from this point of observation it seemed entirely shut in, and one could but have wondered how the road which found a way out of it had found a way into it, and whence came and whither went the waters of the stream that parted the meadow more than a thousand feet below.

Except for the self-consciously correct prose in which this scene is cast, it might have served as one or another actual report Bierce gave his commanding officers after a reconnaissance of the territory ahead. Into this picturesque fictional scene, however, Bierce introduces an improbable moral dilemma, once again related to patricide and specific to a drowsy Union sentinel named Carter Druse. The young sentinel shoots the horse of a mounted enemy soldier perched on a cliff across the way. The still mounted soldier plummets through the air into the valley below. This horseman in the sky supplies an image both for the reader and a Federal officer below that is at once horrifying and noble, as though this "equestrian statue of impressive dignity" were ushering in some "new Apocalypse."

Bierce's talents for mapping the territory of the imagination were combined with others. Those talents, too, perhaps derived from his experience in the war. The landscape he antiseptically charts with the detachment of an surveyor often takes a subjective turn and is typically colored by the limits of perception or invested with fear and dread. The war, at least as he remembered it when he came to write short fiction, was a world apart. "How curiously we had regarded everything! how odd it all had seemed!" he wrote in "A Son of the Gods." "Nothing had appeared quite familiar; the most commonplace objects—an old saddle, a splintered wheel, a forgotten canteen—everything had related something of the mysterious personality of those strange men who had been killing us." In "A Tough Tussle," he put it another way: In the soldier's nighttime vigil, "There are sounds without a name, forms without substance, translations in space of objects which have not been seen to move, movements wherein nothing is observed to change its place. Ah, children of the sunlight and the gaslight, how little you know of the world in which you live!"

At his best, Bierce is able to synthesize these two worlds—the precisely measurable and the uncertain and unnameable—with stylistic grace. A single, clear image sometimes conveys the tension: "This night was bright enough to bite like a serpent." More often,

he establishes an atmospheric apprehension. In "An Occurrence at
Owl Creek Bridge," the Confederate spy about to be hanged is invested with especially acute senses, so keen that they "made record
of things never before perceived": "He noted the prismatic colors in
all the dewdrops upon a million blades of grass. The humming of
the gnats that danced above the eddies of the stream, the beating of
the dragon-flies' wings, the strokes of the water-spiders' legs, like
oars which had lifted their boat—all these made audible music."

By contrast, for the child in "Chickamauga," the "haunted landscape" is vivid with light and color but eerily silent as well:
"Through the belt of trees beyond the brook shone a strange red
light, the trunks and branches of the trees making a black lacework
against it. It struck the creeping figures and gave them monstrous
shadows, which caricatured their movements on the lit grass. . . . It
sparkled on buttons and bits of metal in their clothing." "An Occurrence at Owl Creek Bridge" and "Chickamauga" are very nearly
perfect tales, and these descriptive passages, along with many others, serve simultaneously as clues to the final narrative disclosure
and as evocations of a mental world so vividly pictured that its mysterious reality is strangely compelling.

Bierce is masterfully adroit in his management of point of view
as well and carefully circumscribes how much or little he will or can
share with the reader. In "One Kind of Officer," the noise of battle
makes communication nearly impossible, and when a lieutenant
tries to convey some urgent information to his captain, we are told
in a unnervingly formal narrative voice: "His gestures, if coolly
noted by an actor, would have been pronounced to be those of
protestation." "A Son of the Gods" is subtitled "A Study in the
Present Tense" and takes a rather different narrative tack. It quickly
becomes a form of on-the-spot reporting, the narrative perspective
on a distant rider limited by his field glasses and a general uncertainty: "One moment only and he wheels right about and is speeding like the wind straight down the slope—toward his friends,
toward his death! . . . [H]e is down. No, he recovers his seat;
he has but pulled his horse upon its haunches. They are up and
away! . . . They are down at last. But look again—the man has detached himself from the dead animal. He stands erect, motionless,
holding his sabre in his right hand straight above his head. . . . It is a
sign to us, to the world, to posterity. It is a hero's salute to death
and history." In the voice of a ringside radio announcer (though

such an analogy would necessarily be obscure to the author), Bierce
has given a blow-by-blow narration in the present tense and yet before our very eyes he has converted the momentary bravery of a
"military Christ" into a tale of the "pitiless perfection of the divine,
eternal plan."

Bierce had a seemingly endless variety of points of view at his
disposal—one narrator has received his story secondhand; another
suffers from a lack of memory; another apologizes that he is "no
storyteller"; others, for one reason or another, cannot hear or see.
He sometimes prolongs moments and compresses eons. In "One of
the Missing," we learn that "it was decreed from the beginning of
time that Private Searing was not to murder anybody that bright
summer morning. . . . For countless ages events had been so matching themselves together . . . that the acts which he had in will would
have marred the harmony of the pattern." A few pages later, we are
immersed in Searing's perilous present. He is trapped beneath a col-
lapsed building, his own rifle barrel staring him in the face, the
reader held tight to the figure's tortured consciousness: "Here in
this confusion of timbers and boards is the sole universe. Here is
immortality in time—each pain an everlasting life. The throbs tick
off eternities."

For Bierce, the world of war is a disturbing mix of the chaotic,
random, and destructive events confronted by the ordered arrangements of military rank, decorum, and protocol. The combination
provides ample opportunity for irony. In many of his short stories,
for example, there is the drama of a conflict of duty, and in every
instance the observance of duty has its destructive consequences. In
"The Story of a Conscience," Captain Hartroy orders the immediate execution of a man who had once saved his life and then quietly
commits suicide. In "A Horseman in the Sky," the father commands his son to "do what you conceive to be your duty"; his duty,
it so happens, requires him to kill the father. In "An Affair of Outposts," Captain Armisted saves the life of the man who has made
him a cuckold, and as a consequence loses his own. Most affecting
of all, in "The Affair at Coulter's Notch," the artillery officer Captain Coulter complies with the command to fire upon his own
house; within are his wife and child. Related to these are stories of
false pride: of the witty stoic, Parker Adderson, who borrows his
courage from what he takes to be strict military observance; of
Lieutenant Brayle in "Killed at Resaca," a man "vain of his

courage"; or of Captain Ransome, whose wounded pride causes him to knowingly fire upon his own men, in "One Kind of Officer." These are rank offenses against the law of probability, to be sure, but they do not feel that way in the course of reading.

Bierce's tales of the supernatural, as well as his tall tale humor, are in this sense continuous, both tonally and morally, with his war fiction, and he sometimes bent existing comic forms to match his cynicism. More than once, he wrote in the mode of the condensed novel popular among the San Francisco Bohemians, including Bret Harte and Mark Twain. By reducing their "novels" to 500 to 2,500 words, complete with chapter titles, intricate plots, and thwarted love affairs, these humorists meant to burlesque the sentimental romance. Bierce used the same form, but he was not very much interested in parodic comedy. Instead he used chapter titles to deepen the irony of the events or to give them the effect of sinister parable. One chapter title reads, "How to Play the Cannon without Notes"; another advises, "When You Have Lost Your Life Consult a Physician"; yet another observes, "One Does Not Always Eat What Is on the Table," followed by a description of the local coroner examining a corpse.

Nor was Bierce the only California writer known for irreverence and verbal assault. Western journalism was notoriously fierce and coarsely comic, but his invective had little of the mischievous or the antic in it, and his comedy was so outlandishly grotesque (as in "Oil of Dog" or "A Revolt of the Gods") that it makes one a little bit ashamed to laugh. Bierce seemed intent on outdoing the competition, if only to maintain a cranky independence from the rest. He did not altogether succeed in keeping his admirers at bay, however. He disdained the role of humorist, but Mark Twain included several of his animal fables in his *Library of American Humor* (1888). He pilloried William Dean Howells, and when he learned that Howells had declared him one of America's three greatest writers, Bierce's acceptance of the compliment was less than gracious: "I am sure Mr. Howells is the other two." Nevertheless, Howells saw fit to include "An Occurrence at Owl Creek Bridge" in his *Great Modern American Stories* (1920).

At times Bierce even distanced himself from the terms of his own fiction, and of his own experience. In the 1870s, Bierce and Tom Hood made a pact, probably as a gesture of the depth their friendship, that the first to die should attempt to contact the other.

Shortly after Hood died in 1875, Bierce reported that he met the spirit of his old friend and had the "evidence of my own senses" as affirmation of the fact. A few years later, in the *Arognaut* he dismissed the experience by saying that "the senses fool one another," that "sight is translated into sound, or sudden and strong mental impressions are mistaken for tactual ones."

This brush with the world beyond would provide the basis for his story "The Damned Thing." However, there he gave yet another account of the presence of a spirit—the malevolent presence was of a color that the human eye is unable to discern. Bierce was fond of explaining his mysteries away by scientific or quasi-scientific theory, only to repudiate that explanation in its turn. In "A Tough Tussle," Second-Lieutenant Byring decides that his fear of the supernatural is not unusual; superstitious dread has been passed on generation after generation since the beginning of the human race and will require yet another ten thousand years to outgrow. But the final disclosure in the tale casts doubt on this view. In "Moxon's Master," Bierce uses Herbert Spencer's mechanistic definition of "Life" as the intellectual rationale for the creation of an automaton chess player, but that theory cannot quite explain why the machine is a sore loser.

Ambrose Bierce may have deserved every epithet applied to him—"wicked," "bitter," "cynical," and the like. I rather suspect he enjoyed his reputation, however; notoriety is for certain temperaments more fun than fame. He seemed to seize upon every opportunity for an irony, at any rate, as if it were some delicious morsel to be savored. He seemed to delight in his ability to make us squirm. If he preferred wit to humor, it was because he preferred to make his readers wince, not laugh. Of the pieces gathered together in this volume, only "Haïta the Shepherd" and "A Bivouac of the Dead" can be described as poignant. The others are shocking, horrifying, or unnerving; they are sometimes moving, but on the author's terms, not our own.

Despite all the disconcerting grotesqueries in his short fiction, composed it would appear with malice aforethought, I doubt we are ever tempted to think of Bierce as despairing. There is too much self-evident care and attention given to the style and cadence of his prose to really believe that nothing mattered to him, and there is too much fierce indignation for us to really believe he was beyond being morally offended. In keeping with his cynical persona, Bierce once defined happiness as "An agreeable sensation arising from contemplating the misery of another." Given the world he knew, or thought he knew, and the myriad ways he so vividly pictured that world for his readers, I suppose Bierce must have had his share of happiness.

SUGGESTIONS FOR FURTHER READING

Berkove, Lawrence. "Arms and the Man: Ambrose Bierce's Response to War." *Michigan Academician* 1 (1969), 21–30.

Davidson, Cathy N., ed. *Critical Essays on Ambrose Bierce.* (Boston: G. K. Hall, 1982).

———. *The Experimental Fictions of Ambrose Bierce.* (Lincoln, Neb.: University of Nebraska Press, 1984).

Fadiman, Clifton. *The Collected Writings of Ambrose Bierce.* (New York: Citadel Press, 1968).

Fatout, Paul. *Ambrose Bierce, The Devil's Lexicographer.* (Norman, Ok.: University of Oklahoma Press, 1951).

———. *Ambrose Bierce and the Black Hills.* (Norman, Ok.: University of Oklahoma Press, 1956).

Grenader, M. E. *Ambrose Bierce.* (New York: Twayne Publishers, 1971).

Joshi, S. T., and David E. Schultz. *Ambrose Bierce: A Bibliography of Primary Sources.* (New York: Greenwood Press, 1999).

Klein, Marcus. "San Francisco and Her Hateful Ambrose Bierce." *Hudson Review* 7 (August 1954), 393–407.

McWilliams, Carey. *Ambrose Bierce: A Biography.* (New York: A&C Boni, 1929).

Mencken, H. L. *Prejudices, Sixth Series.* (London: Jonathon Cape, 1927).

Morris, Roy, Jr. *Ambrose Bierce: Alone in Bad Company.* (New York: Crown Publishers, 1995).

Reed, Ishmael. "On Ambrose Bierce's *Tales of Soldiers and Civilians.*" In *Classics of Civil War Fiction,* David Madden and Peggy Bach, eds. (Jackson, Miss.: University Press of Mississippi, 1991), 37–43.

Solomon, Eric. "The Bitterness of Battle: Ambrose Bierce's War Fiction." *Midwest Quarterly* 5 (1963–64), 147–65.

Walker, Franklin. *San Francisco's Literary Frontier.* (New York: Alfred A. Knopf, 1939).

Wiggins, R. A. "Ambrose Bierce: A Romantic in the Age of Realism." *American Literary Realism* 4 (Winter 1971), 1–10.

Woodruff, Stuart C. *The Short Stories of Ambrose Bierce: A Study in Polarity.* (Pittsburgh, Penn.: University of Pittsburgh Press, 1964).

A NOTE ON THE TEXT

The texts for the selections in this edition are from the following volumes of *The Collected Works of Ambrose Bierce* (New York and Washington: The Neale Publishing Company, 1909–12): Volume II *In the Midst of Life (Tales of Soldiers and Civilians)*; Volume III *Can Such Things Be?*; Volume VIII *Negligible Tales, One with the Dance, Epigrams*; Volume X *The Opinionator*; and Volume XI *Antepenultimata.*

My thanks to S. T. Joshi and Charles Bradshaw for their help in preparing this volume.

From IN THE MIDST OF LIFE[1]

SOLDIERS

A Horseman in the Sky

I

One sunny afternoon in the autumn of the year 1861 a soldier lay in a clump of laurel by the side of a road in western Virginia. He lay at full length upon his stomach, his feet resting upon the toes, his head upon the left forearm. His extended right hand loosely grasped his rifle. But for the somewhat methodical disposition of his limbs and a slight rhythmic movement of the cartridge-box at the back of his belt he might have been thought to be dead. He was asleep at his post of duty. But if detected he would be dead shortly afterward, death being the just and legal penalty of his crime.

The clump of laurel in which the criminal lay was in the angle of a road which after ascending southward a steep acclivity to that point turned sharply to the west, running along the summit for perhaps one hundred yards. There it turned southward again and went zigzagging downward through the forest. At the salient[2] of that second angle was a large flat rock, jutting out northward, overlooking the deep valley from which the road ascended. The rock capped a high cliff; a stone dropped from its outer edge would have fallen sheer downward one thousand feet to the tops of the pines. The angle where the soldier lay was on another spur of the same cliff. Had he been awake he would have commanded a view, not only of the short arm of the road and the jutting rock, but of the entire profile of the cliff below it. It might well have made him giddy to look.

The country was wooded everywhere except at the bottom of the valley to the northward, where there was a small natural meadow, through which flowed a stream scarcely visible from the valley's rim. This open ground looked hardly larger than an ordinary door-yard, but was really several acres in extent. Its green was more vivid than that of the inclosing forest. Away beyond it rose a line of giant cliffs similar to those upon which we are supposed to stand in our survey of the savage scene, and through which the road had somehow made its climb to the summit. The configuration of the valley, indeed, was such that from this point of observation it seemed entirely shut in, and one could but have wondered how the road which found a way out of it had found a way into it, and

5

whence came and whither went the waters of the stream that parted the meadow more than a thousand feet below.

No country is so wild and difficult but men will make it a theatre of war; concealed in the forest at the bottom of that military rat-trap, in which half a hundred men in possession of the exits might have starved an army to submission, lay five regiments of Federal infantry. They had marched all the previous day and night and were resting. At nightfall they would take to the road again, climb to the place where their unfaithful sentinel now slept, and descending the other slope of the ridge fall upon a camp of the enemy at about midnight. Their hope was to surprise it, for the road led to the rear of it. In case of failure, their position would be perilous in the extreme; and fail they surely would should accident or vigilance apprise the enemy of the movement.

II

The sleeping sentinel in the clump of laurel was a young Virginian named Carter Druse. He was the son of wealthy parents, an only child, and had known such ease and cultivation and high living as wealth and taste were able to command in the mountain country of western Virginia. His home was but a few miles from where he now lay. One morning he had risen from the breakfast-table and said, quietly but gravely: "Father, a Union regiment has arrived at Grafton. I am going to join it."

The father lifted his leonine head, looked at the son a moment in silence, and replied: "Well, go, sir, and whatever may occur do what you conceive to be your duty. Virginia, to which you are a traitor, must get on without you. Should we both live to the end of the war, we will speak further of the matter. Your mother, as the physician has informed you, is in a most critical condition; at the best she cannot be with us longer than a few weeks, but that time is precious. It would be better not to disturb her."

So Carter Druse, bowing reverently to his father, who returned the salute with a stately courtesy that masked a breaking heart, left the home of his childhood to go soldiering. By conscience and courage, by deeds of devotion and daring, he soon commended himself to his fellows and his officers; and it was to these qualities and to some knowledge of the country that he owed his selection for his present perilous duty at the extreme outpost. Nevertheless, fatigue had been stronger than resolution and he had fallen asleep. What good or bad angel came in a dream to rouse him from his state of crime, who shall say? Without a movement, without a sound, in the profound silence and the languor of the late afternoon, some invisible messenger of fate touched with unsealing finger the eyes of his consciousness—whispered into the ear of his spirit the mysterious awakening word which no human lips ever have spoken, no human memory ever has recalled. He quietly raised his forehead from his arm and looked between the masking stems of the laurels, instinctively closing his right hand about the stock of his rifle.

His first feeling was a keen artistic delight. On a colossal pedestal, the cliff,—motionless at the extreme edge of the capping rock and sharply outlined against the sky,—was an equestrian statue of impressive dignity. The figure of the man sat the figure of the horse, straight and soldierly, but with the repose of a Grecian god carved in the marble which limits the suggestion of activity. The gray costume harmonized with its aërial background; the metal of accoutrement and caparison was softened and subdued by the shadow; the animal's skin had no points of high light. A carbine strikingly foreshortened lay across the pommel of the saddle, kept in place by the right hand grasping it at the "grip"; the left hand, holding the bridle rein, was invisible. In silhouette against the sky the profile of the horse was cut with the sharpness of a cameo; it looked across the heights of air to the confronting cliffs beyond. The face of the rider, turned slightly away, showed only an outline of temple and beard; he was looking downward to the bottom of the valley. Magnified by its lift against the sky and by the soldier's testifying sense of the formidableness of a near enemy the group appeared of heroic, almost colossal, size.

For an instant Druse had a strange, half-defined feeling that he had slept to the end of the war and was looking upon a noble work of art reared upon that eminence to commemorate the deeds of an heroic past of which he had been an inglorious part. The feeling was dispelled by a slight movement of the group: the horse, without moving its feet, had drawn its body slightly backward from the verge; the man remained immobile as before. Broad awake and keenly alive to the significance of the situation, Druse now brought the butt of his rifle against his cheek by cautiously pushing the barrel forward through the bushes, cocked the piece, and glancing

through the sights covered a vital spot of the horseman's breast. A
touch upon the trigger and all would have been well with Carter
Druse. At that instant the horseman turned his head and looked in
the direction of his concealed foeman—seemed to look into his very
face, into his eyes, into his brave, compassionate heart.

Is it then so terrible to kill an enemy in war—an enemy who has
surprised a secret vital to the safety of one's self and comrades—an
enemy more formidable for his knowledge than all his army for its
numbers? Carter Druse grew pale; he shook in every limb, turned
faint, and saw the statuesque group before him as black figures, rising, falling, moving unsteadily in arcs of circles in a fiery sky. His
hand fell away from his weapon, his head slowly dropped until
his face rested on the leaves in which he lay. This courageous gentleman and hardy soldier was near swooning from intensity of
emotion.

It was not for long; in another moment his face was raised from
earth, his hands resumed their places on the rifle, his forefinger
sought the trigger; mind, heart, and eyes were clear, conscience and
reason sound. He could not hope to capture that enemy; to alarm
him would but send him dashing to his camp with his fatal news.
The duty of the soldier was plain: the man must be shot dead from
ambush—without warning, without a moment's spiritual preparation, with never so much as an unspoken prayer, he must be sent to
his account. But no—there is a hope; he may have discovered nothing—perhaps he is but admiring the sublimity of the landscape. If
permitted, he may turn and ride carelessly away in the direction
whence he came. Surely it will be possible to judge at the instant of
his withdrawing whether he knows. It may well be that his fixity
of attention—Druse turned his head and looked through the deeps
of air downward, as from the surface to the bottom of a translucent
sea. He saw creeping across the green meadow a sinuous line of figures of men and horses—some foolish commander was permitting
the soldiers of his escort to water their beasts in the open, in plain
view from a dozen summits!

Druse withdrew his eyes from the valley and fixed them again
upon the group of man and horse in the sky, and again it was
through the sights of his rifle. But this time his aim was at the horse.
In his memory, as if they were a divine mandate, rang the words of
his father at their parting: "Whatever may occur, do what you conceive to be your duty." He was calm now. His teeth were firmly

but not rigidly closed; his nerves were as tranquil as a sleeping babe's—not a tremor affected any muscle of his body; his breathing, until suspended in the act of taking aim, was regular and slow. Duty had conquered; the spirit had said to the body: "Peace, be still." He fired.

III

An officer of the Federal force, who in a spirit of adventure or in quest of knowledge had left the hidden *bivouac* in the valley, and with aimless feet had made his way to the lower edge of a small open space near the foot of the cliff, was considering what he had to gain by pushing his exploration further. At a distance of a quarter-mile before him, but apparently at a stone's throw, rose from its fringe of pines the gigantic face of rock, towering to so great a height above him that it made him giddy to look up to where its edge cut a sharp, rugged line against the sky. It presented a clean, vertical profile against a background of blue sky to a point half the way down, and of distant hills, hardly less blue, thence to the tops of the trees at its base. Lifting his eyes to the dizzy altitude of its summit the officer saw an astonishing sight—a man on horseback riding down into the valley through the air!

Straight upright sat the rider, in military fashion, with a firm seat in the saddle, a strong clutch upon the rein to hold his charger from too impetuous a plunge. From his bare head his long hair streamed upward, waving like a plume. His hands were concealed in the cloud of the horse's lifted mane. The animal's body was as level as if every hoof-stroke encountered the resistant earth. Its motions were those of a wild gallop, but even as the officer looked they ceased, with all the legs thrown sharply forward as in the act of alighting from a leap. But this was a flight!

Filled with amazement and terror by this apparition of a horseman in the sky—half believing himself the chosen scribe of some new Apocalypse, the officer was overcome by the intensity of his emotions; his legs failed him and he fell. Almost at the same instant he heard a crashing sound in the trees—a sound that died without an echo—and all was still.

The officer rose to his feet, trembling. The familiar sensation of an abraded shin recalled his dazed faculties. Pulling himself together he ran rapidly obliquely away from the cliff to a point distant from its foot; thereabout he expected to find his man; and thereabout he naturally failed. In the fleeting instant of his vision his imagination had been so wrought upon by the apparent grace and ease and intention of the marvelous performance that it did not occur to him that the line of march of aërial cavalry is directly downward, and that he could find the objects of his search at the very foot of the cliff. A half-hour later he returned to camp.

This officer was a wise man; he knew better than to tell an incredible truth. He said nothing of what he had seen. But when the commander asked him if in his scout he had learned anything of advantage to the expedition he answered:

"Yes, sir; there is no road leading down into this valley from the south'ward."

The commander, knowing better, smiled.

IV

After firing his shot, Private Carter Druse reloaded his rifle and resumed his watch. Ten minutes had hardly passed when a Federal sergeant crept cautiously to him on hands and knees. Druse neither turned his head nor looked at him, but lay without motion or sign of recognition.

"Did you fire?" the sergeant whispered.

"Yes."

"At what?"

"A horse. It was standing on yonder rock—pretty far out. You see it is no longer there. It went over the cliff."

The man's face was white, but he showed no other sign of emotion. Having answered, he turned away his eyes and said no more. The sergeant did not understand.

"See here, Druse," he said, after a moment's silence, "it's no use making a mystery. I order you to report. Was there anybody on the horse?"

"Yes."

"Well?"

"My father."

The sergeant rose to his feet and walked away. "Good God!" he said.

An Occurrence at
Owl Creek Bridge

I

A man stood upon a railroad bridge in northern Alabama,³ looking down into the swift water twenty feet below. The man's hands were behind his back, the wrists bound with a cord. A rope closely encircled his neck. It was attached to a stout cross-timber above his head and the slack fell to the level of his knees. Some loose boards laid upon the sleepers⁴ supporting the metals of the railway supplied a footing for him and his executioners—two private soldiers of the Federal army, directed by a sergeant who in civil life may have been a deputy sheriff. At a short remove upon the same temporary platform was an officer in the uniform of his rank, armed. He was a captain. A sentinel at each end of the bridge stood with his rifle in the position known as "support," that is to say, vertical in front of the left shoulder, the hammer resting on the forearm thrown straight across the chest—a formal and unnatural position, enforcing an erect carriage of the body. It did not appear to be the duty of these two men to know what was occurring at the centre of the bridge; they merely blockaded the two ends of the foot planking that traversed it.

Beyond one of the sentinels nobody was in sight; the railroad ran straight away into a forest for a hundred yards, then, curving, was lost to view. Doubtless there was an outpost farther along. The other bank of the stream was open ground—a gentle acclivity topped with a stockade of vertical tree trunks, loopholed for rifles, with a single embrasure through which protruded the muzzle of a brass cannon commanding the bridge. Midway of the slope between bridge and fort were the spectators—a single company of infantry in line, at "parade rest," the butts of the rifles on the ground, the barrels inclining slightly backward against the right shoulder, the hands crossed upon the stock. A lieutenant stood at the right of the line, the point of his sword upon the ground, his left hand resting upon his right. Excepting the group of four at the centre of the bridge, not a man moved. The company faced the bridge, staring stonily, motionless. The sentinels, facing the banks of the stream, might have been statues to adorn the bridge. The captain stood with folded arms, silent, observing the work of his subordinates, but making no sign. Death is a dignitary who when he comes announced is to be received with formal manifestations of respect, even by those most familiar with him. In the code of military etiquette silence and fixity are forms of deference.

The man who was engaged in being hanged was apparently about thirty-five years of age. He was a civilian, if one might judge from his habit, which was that of a planter. His features were good—a straight nose, firm mouth, broad forehead, from which his long, dark hair was combed straight back, falling behind his ears to the collar of his well-fitting frock-coat. He wore a mustache and pointed beard, but no whiskers; his eyes were large and dark gray, and had a kindly expression which one would hardly have expected in one whose neck was in the hemp. Evidently this was no vulgar assassin. The liberal military code makes provision for hanging many kinds of persons, and gentlemen are not excluded.

The preparations being complete, the two private soldiers stepped aside and each drew away the plank upon which he had been standing. The sergeant turned to the captain, saluted and placed himself immediately behind that officer, who in turn moved apart one pace. These movements left the condemned man and the sergeant standing on the two ends of the same plank, which spanned three of the cross-ties of the bridge. The end upon which the civilian stood almost, but not quite, reached a fourth. This plank had been held in place by the weight of the captain; it was now held by that of the sergeant. At a signal from the former the latter would step aside, the plank would tilt and the condemned man go down between two ties. The arrangement commended itself to his judgment as simple and effective. His face had not been covered nor his eyes bandaged. He looked a moment at his "unsteadfast footing," then let his gaze wander to the swirling water of the stream racing madly beneath his feet. A piece of dancing driftwood caught his attention and his eyes followed it down the current. How slowly it appeared to move! What a sluggish stream!

He closed his eyes in order to fix his last thoughts upon his wife and children. The water, touched to gold by the early sun, the brooding mists under the banks at some distance down the stream, the fort, the soldiers, the piece of drift—all had distracted him. And now he became conscious of a new disturbance. Striking through the thought of his dear ones was a sound which he could neither ignore nor understand, a sharp, distinct, metallic percussion like the stroke of a blacksmith's hammer upon the anvil; it had the same ringing quality. He wondered what it was, and whether immeasurably distant or near by—it seemed both. Its recurrence was regular, but as slow as the tolling of a death knell. He awaited each stroke with impatience and—he knew not why—apprehension. The intervals of silence grew progressively longer; the delays became maddening. With their greater infrequency the sounds increased in strength and sharpness. They hurt his ear like the thrust of a knife; he feared he would shriek. What he heard was the ticking of his watch.

He unclosed his eyes and saw again the water below him. "If I could free my hands," he thought, "I might throw off the noose and spring into the stream. By diving I could evade the bullets and, swimming vigorously, reach the bank, take to the woods and get away home. My home, thank God, is as yet outside their lines; my wife and little ones are still beyond the invader's farthest advance."

As these thoughts, which have here to be set down in words, were flashed into the doomed man's brain rather than evolved from it the captain nodded to the sergeant. The sergeant stepped aside.

II

Peyton Farquhar was a well-to-do planter, of an old and highly respected Alabama family. Being a slave owner and like other slave owners a politician he was naturally an original secessionist and ardently devoted to the Southern cause. Circumstances of an imperious nature, which it is unnecessary to relate here, had prevented him from taking service with the gallant army that had fought the disastrous campaigns ending with the fall of Corinth, and he chafed under the inglorious restraint, longing for the release of his energies, the larger life of the soldier, the opportunity for distinction. That opportunity, he felt, would come, as it comes to all in war time. Meanwhile he did what he could. No service was too humble for him to perform in aid of the South, no adventure too perilous for him to undertake if consistent with the character of a civilian who was at heart a soldier, and who in good faith and without too much qualification assented to at least a part of the frankly villainous dictum that all is fair in love and war.

One evening while Farquhar and his wife were sitting on a rustic bench near the entrance to his grounds, a gray-clad soldier rode up to the gate and asked for a drink of water. Mrs. Farquhar was only too happy to serve him with her own white hands. While she was fetching the water her husband approached the dusty horseman and inquired eagerly for news from the front.

"The Yanks are repairing the railroads," said the man, "and are getting ready for another advance. They have reached the Owl Creek bridge, put it in order and built a stockade on the north bank. The commandant has issued an order, which is posted everywhere, declaring that any civilian caught interfering with the railroad, its bridges, tunnels or trains will be summarily hanged. I saw the order."

"How far is it to the Owl Creek bridge?" Farquhar asked.

"About thirty miles."

"Is there no force on this side the creek?"

"Only a picket post half a mile out, on the railroad, and a single sentinel at this end of the bridge."

"Suppose a man—a civilian and student of hanging—should elude the picket post and perhaps get the better of the sentinel," said Farquhar, smiling, "what could he accomplish?"

The soldier reflected. "I was there a month ago," he replied. "I observed that the flood of last winter had lodged a great quantity of driftwood against the wooden pier at this end of the bridge. It is now dry and would burn like tow."

The lady had now brought the water, which the soldier drank. He thanked her ceremoniously, bowed to her husband and rode away. An hour later, after nightfall, he repassed the plantation, going northward in the direction from which he had come. He was a Federal scout.

III

As Peyton Farquhar fell straight downward through the bridge he lost consciousness and was as one already dead. From this state he was awakened—ages later, it seemed to him—by the pain of a sharp pressure upon his throat, followed by a sense of suffocation. Keen, poignant agonies seemed to shoot from his neck downward through every fibre of his body and limbs. These pains appeared to flash along well-defined lines of ramification and to beat with an inconceivably rapid periodicity. They seemed like streams of pulsating fire heating him to an intolerable temperature. As to his head, he was conscious of nothing but a feeling of fulness—of congestion. These sensations were unaccompanied by thought. The intellectual part of his nature was already effaced; he had power only to feel, and feeling was torment. He was conscious of motion. Encompassed in a luminous cloud, of which he was now merely the fiery heart, without material substance, he swung through unthinkable arcs of oscillation, like a vast pendulum. Then all at once, with terrible suddenness, the light about him shot upward with the noise of a loud plash; a frightful roaring was in his ears, and all was cold and dark. The power of thought was restored; he knew that the rope had broken and he had fallen into the stream. There was no additional strangulation; the noose about his neck was already suffocating him and kept the water from his lungs. To die of hanging at the bottom of a river!—the idea seemed to him ludicrous. He opened his eyes in the darkness and saw above him a gleam of light, but how distant, how inaccessible! He was still sinking, for the light became fainter and fainter until it was a mere glimmer. Then it began to grow and brighten, and he knew that he was rising toward the surface—knew it with reluctance, for he was now very comfortable. "To be hanged and drowned," he thought, "that is not so bad; but I do not wish to be shot. No; I will not be shot; that is not fair."

He was not conscious of an effort, but a sharp pain in his wrist apprised him that he was trying to free his hands. He gave the struggle his attention, as an idler might observe the feat of a juggler, without interest in the outcome. What splendid effort!—what magnificent, what superhuman strength! Ah, that was a fine endeavor! Bravo! The cord fell away; his arms parted and floated upward, the hands dimly seen on each side in the growing light. He watched them with a new interest as first one and then the other pounced upon the noose at his neck. They tore it away and thrust it fiercely aside, its undulations resembling those of a water-snake. "Put it back, put it back!" He thought he shouted these words to his hands, for the undoing of the noose had been succeeded by the direst pang that he had yet experienced. His neck ached horribly; his brain was on fire; his heart, which had been fluttering faintly, gave a great leap, trying to force itself out at his mouth. His whole body was racked and wrenched with an insupportable anguish! But his disobedient hands gave no heed to the command. They beat the water vigorously with quick, downward strokes, forcing him to the surface. He felt his head emerge; his eyes were blinded by the sunlight; his chest expanded convulsively, and with a supreme and crowning agony his lungs engulfed a great draught of air, which instantly he expelled in a shriek!

He was now in full possession of his physical senses. They were, indeed, preternaturally keen and alert. Something in the awful disturbance of his organic system had so exalted and refined them that they made record of things never before perceived. He felt the ripples upon his face and heard their separate sounds as they struck. He looked at the forest on the bank of the stream, saw the individual trees, the leaves and the veining of each leaf—saw the very insects upon them: the locusts, the brilliant-bodied flies, the gray spiders stretching their webs from twig to twig. He noted the prismatic colors in all the dewdrops upon a million blades of grass. The humming of the gnats that danced above the eddies of the stream, the beating of the dragon-flies' wings, the strokes of the water-spiders' legs, like oars which had lifted their boat—all these made audible music. A fish slid along beneath his eyes and he heard the rush of its body parting the water.

He had come to the surface facing down the stream; in a moment the visible world seemed to wheel slowly round, himself the pivotal point, and he saw the bridge, the fort, the soldiers upon the bridge, the captain, the sergeant, the two privates, his executioners. They were in silhouette against the blue sky. They shouted and gesticulated, pointing at him. The captain had drawn his pistol, but did not fire; the others were unarmed. Their movements were grotesque and horrible, their forms gigantic.

Suddenly he heard a sharp report and something struck the water smartly within a few inches of his head, spattering his face with spray. He heard a second report, and saw one of the sentinels with his rifle at his shoulder, a light cloud of blue smoke rising from the muzzle. The man in the water saw the eye of the man on the bridge gazing into his own through the sights of the rifle. He observed that it was a gray eye and remembered having read that gray eyes were keenest, and that all famous markmen had them. Nevertheless, this one had missed.

A counter-swirl had caught Farquhar and turned him half round; he was again looking into the forest on the bank opposite the fort.

The sound of a clear, high voice in a monotonous singsong now rang out behind him and came across the water with a distinctness that pierced and subdued all other sounds, even the beating of the ripples in his ears. Although no soldier, he had frequented camps enough to know the dread significance of that deliberate, drawling, aspirated chant; the lieutenant on shore was taking a part in the morning's work. How coldly and pitilessly—with what an even, calm intonation, presaging, and enforcing tranquility in the men—with what accurately measured intervals fell those cruel words:

"Attention company! . . . Shoulder arms! . . . Ready! . . . Aim! . . . Fire!"

Farquhar dived—dived as deeply as he could. The water roared in his ears like the voice of Niagara, yet he heard the dulled thunder of the volley and, rising again toward the surface, met shining bits of metal, singularly flattened, oscillating slowly downward. Some of them touched him on the face and hands, then fell away, continuing their descent. One lodged between his collar and neck; it was uncomfortably warm and he snatched it out.

As he rose to the surface, gasping for breath, he saw that he had been a long time under water; he was perceptibly farther down stream—nearer to safety. The soldiers had almost finished reloading; the metal ramrods flashed all at once in the sunshine as they were drawn from the barrels, turned in the air, and thrust into their sockets. The two sentinels fired again, independently and ineffectually.

The hunted man saw all this over his shoulder; he was now swimming vigorously with the current. His brain was as energetic as his arms and legs; he thought with the rapidity of lightning.

"The officer," he reasoned, "will not make that martinet's error a second time. It is as easy to dodge a volley as a single shot. He has probably already given the command to fire at will. God help me, I cannot dodge them all!"

An appalling plash within two yards of him was followed by a loud, rushing sound, *diminuendo*,[5] which seemed to travel back through the air to the fort and died in an explosion which stirred the very river to its deeps! A rising sheet of water curved over him, fell down upon him, blinded him, strangled him! The cannon had taken a hand in the game. As he shook his head free from the commotion of the smitten water he heard the deflected shot humming through the air ahead, and in an instant it was cracking and smashing the branches in the forest beyond.

"They will not do that again," he thought; "the next time they will use a charge of grape. I must keep my eye upon the gun; the smoke will apprise me—the report arrives too late; it lags behind the missile. That is a good gun."

Suddenly he felt himself whirled round and round—spinning like a top. The water, the banks, the forests, the now distant bridge, fort and men—all were commingled and blurred. Objects were represented by their colors only; circular horizontal streaks of color—that was all he saw. He had been caught in a vortex and was being whirled on with a velocity of advance and gyration that made him giddy and sick. In a few moments he was flung upon the gravel at the foot of the left bank of the stream—the southern bank—and behind a projecting point which concealed him from his enemies. The sudden arrest of his motion, the abrasion of one of his hands on the gravel, restored him, and he wept with delight. He dug his fingers into the sand, threw it over himself in handfuls and audibly blessed it. It looked like diamonds, rubies, emeralds; he could think of nothing beautiful which it did not resemble. The trees upon the bank were giant garden plants; he noted a definite order in their arrangement, inhaled the fragrance of their blooms. A strange, roseate light shone through the spaces among their trunks and the wind made in their branches the music of æolian harps.[6] He had no wish to perfect his escape—was content to remain in that enchanting spot until retaken.

A whiz and rattle of grapeshot among the branches high above his head roused him from his dream. The baffled cannoneer had fired him a random farewell. He sprang to his feet, rushed up the sloping bank, and plunged into the forest.

All that day he traveled, laying his course by the rounding sun. The forest seemed interminable; nowhere did he discover a break in it, not even a woodman's road. He had not known that he lived in so wild a region. There was something uncanny in the revelation.

By nightfall he was fatigued, footsore, famishing. The thought of his wife and children urged him on. At last he found a road which led him in what he knew to be the right direction. It was as wide and straight as a city street, yet it seemed untraveled. No fields bordered it, no dwelling anywhere. Not so much as the barking of a dog suggested human habitation. The black bodies of the trees formed a straight wall on both sides, terminating on the horizon in a point, like a diagram in a lesson in perspective. Overhead, as he looked up through this rift in the wood, shone great golden stars looking unfamiliar and grouped in strange constellations. He was sure they were arranged in some order which had a secret and malign significance. The wood on either side was full of singular noises, among which—once, twice, and again—he distinctly heard whispers in an unknown tongue.

His neck was in pain and lifting his hand to it he found it horribly swollen. He knew that it had a circle of black where the rope had bruised it. His eyes felt congested; he could no longer close them. His tongue was swollen with thirst; he relieved its fever by thrusting it forward from between his teeth into the cold air. How softly the turf had carpeted the untraveled avenue—he could no longer feel the roadway beneath his feet!

Doubtless, despite his suffering, he had fallen asleep while walking, for now he sees another scene—perhaps he has merely recovered from a delirium. He stands at the gate of his own home. All is as he left it, and all bright and beautiful in the morning sunshine. He must have traveled the entire night. As he pushes open the gate and passes up the wide white walk, he sees a flutter of female garments; his wife, looking fresh and cool and sweet, steps down from the veranda to meet him. At the bottom of the steps she stands waiting, with a smile of ineffable joy, an attitude of matchless grace and dignity. Ah, how beautiful she is! He springs forward with extended arms. As he is about to clasp her he feels a stunning blow upon the back of the neck; a blinding white light blazes all about him with a sound like the shock of a cannon—then all is darkness and silence!

Peyton Farquhar was dead; his body, with a broken neck, swung gently from side to side beneath the timbers of the Owl Creek bridge.

Chickamauga

One sunny autumn afternoon a child strayed away from its rude home in a small field and entered a forest unobserved. It was happy in a new sense of freedom from control, happy in the opportunity of exploration and adventure; for this child's spirit, in bodies of its ancestors, had for thousands of years been trained to memorable feats of discovery and conquest—victories in battles whose critical moments were centuries, whose victors' camps were cities of hewn stone. From the cradle of its race it had conquered its way through two continents and passing a great sea had penetrated a third, there to be born to war and dominion as a heritage.

The child was a boy aged about six years, the son of a poor planter. In his younger manhood the father had been a soldier, had fought against naked savages[7] and followed the flag of his country into the capital of a civilized race to the far South.[8] In the peaceful life of a planter the warrior-fire survived; once kindled, it is never extinguished. The man loved military books and pictures and the boy had understood enough to make himself a wooden sword, though even the eye of his father would hardly have known it for what it was. This weapon he now bore bravely, as became the son of an heroic race, and pausing now and again in the sunny space of the forest assumed, with some exaggeration, the postures of aggression and defense that he had been taught by the engraver's art. Made reckless by the ease with which he overcame invisible foes attempting to stay his advance, he committed the common enough military error of pushing the pursuit to a dangerous extreme, until he found himself upon the margin of a wide but shallow brook, whose rapid waters barred his direct advance against the flying foe that had crossed with illogical ease. But the intrepid victor was not to be baffled; the spirit of the race which had passed the great sea burned unconquerable in that small breast and would not be denied. Finding a place where some bowlders in the bed of the stream lay but a step or a leap apart, he made his way across and fell again upon the rear-guard of his imaginary foe, putting all to the sword.

Now that the battle had been won, prudence required that he

withdraw to his base of operations. Alas; like many a mightier conqueror, and like one, the mightiest, he could not

> *curb the lust for war,*
> *Nor learn that tempted Fate will leave the loftiest star.*[9]

Advancing from the bank of the creek he suddenly found himself confronted with a new and more formidable enemy: in the path that he was following, sat, bolt upright, with ears erect and paws suspended before it, a rabbit! With a startled cry the child turned and fled, he knew not in what direction, calling with inarticulate cries for his mother, weeping, stumbling, his tender skin cruelly torn by brambles, his little heart beating hard with terror—breathless, blind with tears—lost in the forest! Then, for more than an hour, he wandered with erring feet through the tangled undergrowth, till at last, overcome by fatigue, he lay down in a narrow space between two rocks, within a few yards of the stream and still grasping his toy sword, no longer a weapon but a companion, sobbed himself to sleep. The wood birds sang merrily above his head; the squirrels, whisking their bravery of tail, ran barking from tree to tree, unconscious of the pity of it, and somewhere far away was a strange, muffled thunder, as if the partridges were drumming in celebration of nature's victory over the son of her immemorial enslavers. And back at the little plantation, where white men and black were hastily searching the fields and hedges in alarm, a mother's heart was breaking for her missing child.

Hours passed, and then the little sleeper rose to his feet. The chill of the evening was in his limbs, the fear of the gloom in his heart. But he had rested, and he no longer wept. With some blind instinct which impelled to action he struggled through the undergrowth about him and came to a more open ground—on his right the brook, to the left a gentle acclivity studded with infrequent trees; over all, the gathering gloom of twilight. A thin, ghostly mist rose along the water. It frightened and repelled him; instead of recrossing, in the direction whence he had come, he turned his back upon it, and went forward toward the dark inclosing wood. Suddenly he saw before him a strange moving object which he took to be some large animal—a dog, a pig—he could not name it; perhaps it was a bear. He had seen pictures of bears, but knew of nothing to their discredit and had vaguely wished to meet one. But something in form or

movement of this object—something in the awkwardness of its approach—told him that it was not a bear, and curiosity was stayed
by fear. He stood still and as it came slowly on gained courage
every moment, for he saw that at least it had not the long, menacing
ears of the rabbit. Possibly his impressionable mind was half conscious of something familiar in its shambling, awkward gait. Before
it had approached near enough to resolve his doubts he saw that it
was followed by another and another. To right and to left were
many more; the whole open space about him was alive with them—
all moving toward the brook.

They were men. They crept upon their hands and knees. They
used their hands only, dragging their legs. They used their knees
only, their arms hanging idle at their sides. They strove to rise to
their feet, but fell prone in the attempt. They did nothing naturally,
and nothing alike, save only to advance foot by foot in the same direction. Singly, in pairs and in little groups, they came on through
the gloom, some halting now and again while others crept slowly
past them, then resuming their movement. They came by doz-
ens and by hundreds; as far on either hand as one could see in
the deepening gloom they extended and the black wood behind
them appeared to be inexhaustible. The very ground seemed in motion toward the creek. Occasionally one who had paused did not
again go on, but lay motionless. He was dead. Some, pausing, made
strange gestures with their hands, erected their arms and lowered
them again clasped their heads; spread their palms upward, as men
are sometimes seen to do in public prayer.

Not all of this did the child note; it is what would have been
noted by an elder observer; he saw little but that these were men,
yet crept like babes. Being men, they were not terrible, though un-
familiarly clad. He moved among them freely, going from one
to another and peering into their faces with childish curiosity. All
their faces were singularly white and many were streaked and
gouted[10] with red. Something in this—something too, perhaps, in
their grotesque attitudes and movements—reminded him of the
painted clown whom he had seen last summer in the circus, and he
laughed as he watched them. But on and ever on they crept, these
maimed and bleeding men, as heedless as he of the dramatic contrast
between his laughter and their own ghastly gravity. To him it was a
merry spectacle. He had seen his father's negroes creep upon their
hands and knees for his amusement—had ridden them so, "making

believe" they were his horses. He now approached one of these crawling figures from behind and with an agile movement mounted it astride. The man sank upon his breast, recovered, flung the small boy fiercely to the ground as an unbroken colt might have done, then turned upon him a face that lacked a lower jaw—from the upper teeth to the throat was a great red gap fringed with hanging shreds of flesh and splinters of bone. The unnatural prominence of nose, the absence of chin, the fierce eyes, gave this man the appearance of a great bird of prey crimsoned in throat and breast by the blood of its quarry. The man rose to his knees, the child to his feet. The man shook his fist at the child; the child, terrified at last, ran to a tree near by, got upon the farther side of it and took a more serious view of the situation. And so the clumsy multitude dragged itself slowly and painfully along in hideous pantomime—moved forward down the slope like a swarm of great black beetles, with never a sound of going—in silence profound, absolute.

Instead of darkening, the haunted landscape began to brighten. Through the belt of trees beyond the brook shone a strange red light, the trunks and branches of the trees making a black lacework against it. It struck the creeping figures and gave them monstrous shadows, which caricatured their movements on the lit grass. It fell upon their faces, touching their whiteness with a ruddy tinge, accentuating the stains with which so many of them were freaked and maculated.[11] It sparkled on buttons and bits of metal in their clothing. Instinctively the child turned toward the growing splendor and moved down the slope with his horrible companions; in a few moments had passed the foremost of the throng—not much of a feat, considering his advantages. He placed himself in the lead, his wooden sword still in hand, and solemnly directed the march, conforming his pace to theirs and occasionally turning as if to see that his forces did not straggle. Surely such a leader never before had such a following.

Scattered about upon the ground now slowly narrowing by the encroachment of this awful march to water, were certain articles to which, in the leader's mind, were coupled no significant associations: an occasional blanket, tightly rolled lengthwise, doubled and the ends bound together with a string; a heavy knapsack here, and there a broken rifle—such things, in short, as are found in the rear of retreating troops, the "spoor"[12] of men flying from their hunters. Everywhere near the creek, which here had a margin of lowland, the earth was trodden into mud by the feet of men and horses. An observer of better experience in the use of his eyes would have noticed that these footprints pointed in both directions; the ground had been twice passed over—in advance and in retreat. A few hours before, these desperate, stricken men, with their more fortunate and now distant comrades, had penetrated the forest in thousands. Their successive battalions, breaking into swarms and re-forming in lines, had passed the child on every side—had almost trodden on him as he slept. The rustle and murmur of their march had not awakened him. Almost within a stone's throw of where he lay they had fought a battle; but all unheard by him were the roar of the musketry, the shock of the cannon, "the thunder of the captains and the shouting."[13] He had slept through it all, grasping his little wooden sword with perhaps a tighter clutch in unconscious sympathy with his martial environment, but as heedless of the grandeur of the struggle as the dead who had died to make the glory.

The fire beyond the belt of woods on the farther side of the creek, reflected to earth from the canopy of its own smoke, was now suffusing the whole landscape. It transformed the sinuous line of mist to the vapor of gold. The water gleamed with dashes of red, and red, too, were many of the stones protruding above the surface. But that was blood; the less desperately wounded had stained them in crossing. On them, too, the child now crossed with eager steps; he was going to the fire. As he stood upon the farther bank he turned about to look at the companions of his march. The advance was arriving at the creek. The stronger had already drawn themselves to the brink and plunged their faces into the flood. Three or four who lay without motion appeared to have no heads. At this the child's eyes expanded with wonder; even his hospitable understanding could not accept a phenomenon implying such vitality as that. After slaking their thirst these men had not had the strength to back away from the water, nor to keep their heads above it. They were drowned. In rear of these, the open spaces of the forest showed the leader as many formless figures of his grim command as at first; but not nearly so many were in motion. He waved his cap for their encouragement and smilingly pointed with his weapon in the direction of the guiding light—a pillar of fire[14] to this strange exodus.

Confident of the fidelity of his forces, he now entered the belt of woods, passed through it easily in the red illumination, climbed a fence, ran across a field, turning now and again to coquet with his responsive shadow, and so approached the blazing ruin of a dwelling. Desolation everywhere! In all the wide glare not a living thing was visible. He cared nothing for that; the spectacle pleased, and he danced with glee in imitation of the wavering flames. He ran about, collecting fuel, but every object that he found was too heavy for him to cast in from the distance to which the heat limited his approach. In despair he flung in his sword—a surrender to the superior forces of nature. His military career was at an end.

Shifting his position, his eyes fell upon some outbuildings which had an oddly familiar appearance, as if he had dreamed of them. He stood considering them with wonder, when suddenly the entire plantation, with its inclosing forest, seemed to turn as if upon a pivot. His little world swung half around; the points of the compass were reversed. He recognized the blazing building as his own home!

For a moment he stood stupefied by the power of the revelation, then ran with stumbling feet, making a half-circuit of the ruin. There, conspicuous in the light of the conflagration, lay the dead body of a woman—the white face turned upward, the hands thrown out and clutched full of grass, the clothing deranged, the long dark hair in tangles and full of clotted blood. The greater part of the forehead was torn away and from the jagged hole the brain protruded, overflowing the temple, a frothy mass of gray, crowned with clusters of crimson bubbles—the work of a shell.

The child moved his little hands, making wild, uncertain gestures. He uttered a series of inarticulate and indescribable cries—something between the chattering of an ape and the gobbling of a turkey—a startling, soulless, unholy sound, the language of a devil. The child was a deaf mute.

Then he stood motionless, with quivering lips, looking down upon the wreck.

A Son of the Gods

A STUDY IN THE PRESENT TENSE

A breezy day and a sunny landscape. An open country to right and left and forward; behind, a wood. In the edge of this wood, facing the open but not venturing into it, long lines of troops, halted. The wood is alive with them, and full of confused noises—the occasional rattle of wheels as a battery of artillery goes into position to cover the advance; the hum and murmur of the soldiers talking; a sound of innumerable feet in the dry leaves that strew the interspaces among the trees; hoarse commands of officers. Detached groups of horsemen are well in front—not altogether exposed—many of them intently regarding the crest of a hill a mile away in the direction of the interrupted advance. For this powerful army, moving in battle order through a forest, has met with a formidable obstacle—the open country. The crest of that gentle hill a mile away has a sinister look; it says, Beware! Along it runs a stone wall extending to left and right a great distance. Behind the wall is a hedge; behind the hedge are seen the tops of trees in rather straggling order. Among the trees—what? It is necessary to know.

Yesterday, and for many days and nights previously, we were fighting somewhere; always there was cannonading, with occasional keen rattlings of musketry, mingled with cheers, our own or the enemy's, we seldom knew, attesting some temporary advantage. This morning at daybreak the enemy was gone. We have moved forward across his earthworks, across which we have so often vainly attempted to move before, through the débris of his abandoned camps, among the graves of his fallen, into the woods beyond.

How curiously we had regarded everything! how odd it all had seemed! Nothing had appeared quite familiar; the most commonplace objects—an old saddle, a splintered wheel, a forgotten canteen—everything had related something of the mysterious personality of those strange men who had been killing us. The soldier never becomes wholly familiar with the conception of his foes as men like himself; he cannot divest himself of the feeling that they are another order of beings, differently conditioned, in an environment not altogether of the earth. The smallest vestiges of them rivet his attention and engage his interest. He thinks of them as inaccessible; and, catching an unexpected glimpse of them, they appear farther away, and therefore larger, than they really are—like objects in a fog. He is somewhat in awe of them.

From the edge of the wood leading up the acclivity are the tracks of horses and wheels—the wheels of cannon. The yellow grass is beaten down by the feet of infantry. Clearly they have passed this way in thousands; they have not withdrawn by the country roads. This is significant—it is the difference between retiring and re-treating.

That group of horsemen is our commander, his staff and escort. He is facing the distant crest, holding his field-glass against his eyes with both hands, his elbows needlessly elevated. It is a fashion; it seems to dignify the act; we are all addicted to it. Suddenly he low-ers the glass and says a few words to those about him. Two or three aides detach themselves from the group and canter away into the woods, along the lines in each direction. We did not hear his words, but we know them: "Tell General X. to send forward the skirmish line." Those of us who have been out of place resume our positions; the men resting at ease straighten themselves and the ranks are re-formed without a command. Some of us staff officers dismount and look at our saddle girths; those already on the ground remount.

Galloping rapidly along in the edge of the open ground comes a young officer on a snow-white horse. His saddle blanket is scarlet. What a fool! No one who has ever been in action but remembers how naturally every rifle turns toward the man on a white horse; no one but has observed how a bit of red enrages the bull of battle. That such colors are fashionable in military life must be accepted as the most astonishing of all the phenomena of human vanity. They would seem to have been devised to increase the death-rate.

This young officer is in full uniform, as if on parade. He is all agleam with bullion—a blue-and-gold edition of the Poetry of War. A wave of derisive laughter runs abreast of him all along the line. But how handsome he is!—with what careless grace he sits his horse!

He reins up within a respectful distance of the corps commander and salutes. The old soldier nods familiarly; he evidently knows him. A brief colloquy between them is going on; the young man seems to be preferring some request which the elder one is

indisposed to grant. Let us ride a little nearer. Ah! too late—it is
ended. The young officer salutes again, wheels his horse, and rides
straight toward the crest of the hill!

A thin line of skirmishers, the men deployed at six paces or so
apart, now pushes from the wood into the open. The commander
speaks to his bugler, who claps his instrument to his lips. *Tra-la-la!*
Tra-la-la! The skirmishers halt in their tracks.

Meantime the young horseman has advanced a hundred yards.
He is riding at a walk, straight up the long slope, with never a turn
of the head. How glorious! Gods! what would we not give to be in
his place—with his soul! He does not draw his sabre; his right hand
hangs easily at his side. The breeze catches the plume in his hat and
flutters it smartly. The sunshine rests upon his shoulder-straps, lov-
ingly, like a visible benediction. Straight on he rides. Ten thousand
pairs of eyes are fixed upon him with an intensity that he can hardly
fail to feel; ten thousand hearts keep quick time to the inaudible
hoof-beats of his snowy steed. He is not alone—he draws all souls
after him. But we remember that we laughed! On and on, straight
for the hedge-lined wall, he rides. Not a look backward. O, if he
would but turn—if he could but see the love, the adoration, the
atonement!

Not a word is spoken; the populous depths of the forest still
murmur with their unseen and unseeing swarm, but all along the
fringe is silence. The burly commander is an equestrian statue of
himself. The mounted staff officers, their field-glasses up, are motionless all. The line of battle in the edge of the wood stands at a
new kind of "attention," each man in the attitude in which he was
caught by the consciousness of what is going on. All these hardened
and impenitent man-killers, to whom death in its awfulest forms is
a fact familiar to their every-day observation; who sleep on hills
trembling with the thunder of great guns, dine in the midst of
streaming missiles, and play at cards among the dead faces of their
dearest friends—all are watching with suspended breath and beating
hearts the outcome of an act involving the life of one man. Such is
the magnetism of courage and devotion.

If now you should turn your head you would see a simultaneous
movement among the spectators—a start, as if they had received
an electric shock—and looking forward again to the now distant
horseman you would see that he has in that instant altered his direction and is riding at an angle to his former course. The spectators

suppose the sudden deflection to be caused by a shot, perhaps a wound; but take this field-glass and you will observe that he is riding toward a break in the wall and hedge. He means, if not killed, to ride through and overlook the country beyond.

You are not to forget the nature of this man's act; it is not permitted to you to think of it as an instance of bravado, nor, on the other hand, a needless sacrifice of self. If the enemy has not retreated he is in force on that ridge. The investigator will encounter nothing less than a line-of-battle; there is no need of pickets, videttes, skirmishers, to give warning of our approach; our attacking lines will be visible, conspicuous, exposed to an artillery fire that will shave the ground the moment they break from cover, and for half the distance to a sheet of rifle bullets in which nothing can live. In short, if the enemy is there, it would be madness to attack him in front; he must be manœuvred out by the immemorial plan of threatening his line of communication, as necessary to his existence as to the diver at the bottom of the sea his air tube. But how ascertain if the enemy is there? There is but one way,—somebody must go and see. The natural and customary thing to do is to send forward a line of skirmishers. But in this case they will answer in the affirmative with all their lives; the enemy, crouching in double ranks behind the stone wall and in cover of the hedge, will wait until it is possible to count each assailant's teeth. At the first volley a half of the questioning line will fall, the other half before it can accomplish the predestined retreat. What a price to pay for gratified curiosity! At what a dear rate an army must sometimes purchase knowledge! "Let me pay all," says this gallant man—this military Christ!

There is no hope except the hope against hope that the crest is clear. True, he might prefer capture to death. So long as he advances, the line will not fire—why should it? He can safely ride into the hostile ranks and become a prisoner of war. But this would defeat his object. It would not answer our question; it is necessary either that he return unharmed or be shot to death before our eyes. Only so shall we know how to act. If captured—why, that might have been done by a half-dozen stragglers.

Now begins an extraordinary contest of intellect between a man and an army. Our horseman, now within a quarter of a mile of the crest, suddenly wheels to the left and gallops in a direction parallel to it. He has caught sight of his antagonist; he knows all. Some

slight advantage of ground has enabled him to overlook a part of
the line. If he were here he could tell us in words. But that is now
hopeless; he must make the best use of the few minutes of life remaining to him, by compelling the enemy himself to tell us as much
and as plainly as possible—which, naturally, that discreet power is
reluctant to do. Not a rifleman in those crouching ranks, not a cannoneer at those masked and shotted guns, but knows the needs of
the situation, the imperative duty of forbearance. Besides, there has
been time enough to forbid them all to fire. True, a single rifle-
shot might drop him and be no great disclosure. But firing is
infectious—and see how rapidly he moves, with never a pause except as he whirls his horse about to take a new direction, never directly backward toward us, never directly forward toward his
executioners. All this is visible through the glass; it seems occurring
within pistol-shot; we see all but the enemy, whose presence, whose
thoughts, whose motives we infer. To the unaided eye there is nothing but a black figure on a white horse, tracing slow zigzags against
the slope of a distant hill—so slowly they seem almost to creep.

Now—the glass again—he has tired of his failure, or sees his error, or has gone mad; he is dashing directly forward at the wall, as if
to take it at a leap, hedge and all! One moment only and he wheels
right about and is speeding like the wind straight down the slope—
toward his friends, toward his death! Instantly the wall is topped
with a fierce roll of smoke for a distance of hundreds of yards to
right and left. This is as instantly dissipated by the wind, and before
the rattle of the rifles reaches us he is down. No, he recovers his
seat; he has but pulled his horse upon its haunches. They are up and
away! A tremendous cheer bursts from our ranks, relieving the insupportable tension of our feelings. And the horse and its rider?
Yes, they are up and away. Away, indeed—they are making directly
to our left, parallel to the now steadily blazing and smoking wall.
The rattle of the musketry is continuous, and every bullet's target is
that courageous heart.

Suddenly a great bank of white smoke pushes upward from
behind the wall. Another and another—a dozen roll up before the
thunder of the explosions and the humming of the missiles reach
our ears and the missiles themselves come bounding through clouds
of dust into our covert, knocking over here and there a man and
causing a temporary distraction, a passing thought of self.

The dust drifts away. Incredible!—that enchanted horse and rider have passed a ravine and are climbing another slope to unveil another conspiracy of silence, to thwart the will of another armed host. Another moment and that crest too is in eruption. The horse rears and strikes the air with its forefeet. They are down at last. But look again—the man has detached himself from the dead animal. He stands erect, motionless, holding his sabre in his right hand straight above his head. His face is toward us. Now he lowers his hand to a level with his face and moves it outward, the blade of the sabre describing a downward curve. It is a sign to us, to the world, to posterity. It is a hero's salute to death and history.

Again the spell is broken; our men attempt to cheer; they are choking with emotion; they utter hoarse, discordant cries; they clutch their weapons and press tumultuously forward into the open. The skirmishers, without orders, against orders, are going forward at a keen run, like hounds unleashed. Our cannon speak and the enemy's now open in full chorus; to right and left as far as we can see, the distant crest, seeming now so near, erects its towers of cloud and the great shot pitch roaring down among our moving masses. Flag after flag of ours emerges from the wood, line after line sweeps forth, catching the sunlight on its burnished arms. The rear battalions alone are in obedience; they preserve their proper distance from the insurgent front.

The commander has not moved. He now removes his field-glass from his eyes and glances to the right and left. He sees the human current flowing on either side of him and his huddled escort, like tide waves parted by a rock. Not a sign of feeling in his face; he is thinking. Again he directs his eyes forward; they slowly traverse that malign and awful crest. He addresses a calm word to his bugler. *Tra-la-la! Tra-la-la!* The injunction has an imperiousness which enforces it. It is repeated by all the bugles of all the subordinate commanders; the sharp metallic notes assert themselves above the hum of the advance and penetrate the sound of the cannon. To halt is to withdraw. The colors move slowly back; the lines face about and sullenly follow, bearing their wounded; the skirmishers return, gathering up the dead.

Ah, those many, many needless dead! That great soul whose beautiful body is lying over yonder, so conspicuous against the sere hillside—could it not have been spared the bitter consciousness of a vain devotion? Would one exception have marred too much the pitiless perfection of the divine, eternal plan?

One of the Missing

Jerome Searing, a private soldier of General Sherman's army, then confronting the enemy at and about Kennesaw Mountain, Georgia, turned his back upon a small group of officers with whom he had been talking in low tones, stepped across a light line of earthworks, and disappeared in a forest. None of the men in line behind the works had said a word to him, nor had he so much as nodded to them in passing, but all who saw understood that this brave man had been intrusted with some perilous duty. Jerome Searing, though a private, did not serve in the ranks; he was detailed for service at division headquarters, being borne upon the rolls as an orderly. "Orderly" is a word covering a multitude of duties. An orderly may be a messenger, a clerk, an officer's servant—anything. He may perform services for which no provision is made in orders and army regulations. Their nature may depend upon his aptitude, upon favor, upon accident. Private Searing, an incomparable marksman, young, hardy, intelligent and insensible to fear, was a scout. The general commanding his division was not content to obey orders blindly without knowing what was in his front, even when his command was not on detached service, but formed a fraction of the line of the army; nor was he satisfied to receive his knowledge of his *vis-à-vis*[15] through the customary channels; he wanted to know more than he was apprised of by the corps commander and the collisions of pickets and skirmishers. Hence Jerome Searing, with his extraordinary daring, his woodcraft, his sharp eyes, and truthful tongue. On this occasion his instructions were simple: to get as near the enemy's lines as possible and learn all that he could.

In a few moments he had arrived at the picket-line, the men on duty there lying in groups of two and four behind little banks of earth scooped out of the slight depression in which they lay, their rifles protruding from the green boughs with which they had masked their small defenses. The forest extended without a break toward the front, so solemn and silent that only by an effort of the imagination could it be conceived as populous with armed men, alert and vigilant—a forest formidable with possibilities of battle. Pausing a moment in one of these rifle-pits to apprise the men of his intention Searing crept stealthily forward on his hands and knees and was soon lost to view in a dense thicket of underbrush.

"That is the last of him," said one of the men; "I wish I had his rifle; those fellows will hurt some of us with it."

Searing crept on, taking advantage of every accident of ground and growth to give himself better cover. His eyes penetrated everywhere, his ears took note of every sound. He stilled his breathing, and at the cracking of a twig beneath his knee stopped his progress and hugged the earth. It was slow work, but not tedious; the danger made it exciting, but by no physical signs was the excitement manifest. His pulse was as regular, his nerves were as steady as if he were trying to trap a sparrow.

"It seems a long time," he thought, "but I cannot have come very far; I am still alive."

He smiled at his own method of estimating distance, and crept forward. A moment later he suddenly flattened himself upon the earth and lay motionless, minute after minute. Through a narrow opening in the bushes he had caught sight of a small mound of yellow clay—one of the enemy's rifle-pits. After some little time he cautiously raised his head, inch by inch, then his body upon his hands, spread out on each side of him, all the while intently regarding the hillock of clay. In another moment he was upon his feet, rifle in hand, striding rapidly forward with little attempt at concealment. He had rightly interpreted the signs, whatever they were; the enemy was gone.

To assure himself beyond a doubt before going back to report upon so important a matter, Searing pushed forward across the line of abandoned pits, running from cover to cover in the more open forest, his eyes vigilant to discover possible stragglers. He came to the edge of a plantation—one of those forlorn, deserted homesteads of the last years of the war, upgrown with brambles, ugly with broken fences and desolate with vacant buildings having blank apertures in place of doors and windows. After a keen reconnaissance from the safe seclusion of a clump of young pines Searing ran lightly across a field and through an orchard to a small structure which stood apart from the other farm buildings, on a slight elevation. This he thought would enable him to overlook a large scope of country in the direction that he supposed the enemy to have taken in withdrawing. This building, which had originally consisted of a single room elevated upon four posts about ten feet high, was now

little more than a roof; the floor had fallen away, the joists and
planks loosely piled on the ground below or resting on end at various angles, not wholly torn from their fastenings above. The supporting posts were themselves no longer vertical. It looked as if the
whole edifice would go down at the touch of a finger.

Concealing himself in the débris of joists and flooring Searing
looked across the open ground between his point of view and a spur
of Kennesaw Mountain, a half-mile away. A road leading up and
across this spur was crowded with troops—the rear-guard of the retiring enemy, their gun-barrels gleaming in the morning sunlight.

Searing had now learned all that he could hope to know. It was
his duty to return to his own command with all possible speed and
report his discovery. But the gray column of Confederates toiling
up the mountain road was singularly tempting. His rifle—an ordinary "Springfield,"[16] but fitted with a globe sight and hair-trigger—
would easily send its ounce and a quarter of lead hissing into their
midst. That would probably not affect the duration and result of
the war, but it is the business of a soldier to kill. It is also his habit
if he is a good soldier. Searing cocked his rifle and "set" the trigger.

But it was decreed from the beginning of time that Private Searing was not to murder anybody that bright summer morning, nor
was the Confederate retreat to be announced by him. For countless
ages events had been so matching themselves together in that won-
drous mosaic to some parts of which, dimly discernible, we give the
name of history, that the acts which he had in will would have
marred the harmony of the pattern. Some twenty-five years previously the Power charged with the execution of the work according
to the design had provided against that mischance by causing the
birth of a certain male child in a little village at the foot of the
Carpathian Mountains,[17] had carefully reared it, supervised its education, directed its desires into a military channel, and in due time
made it an officer of artillery. By the concurrence of an infinite
number of favoring influences and their preponderance over an infinite number of opposing ones, this officer of artillery had been
made to commit a breach of discipline and flee from his native
country to avoid punishment. He had been directed to New Orleans (instead of New York), where a recruiting officer awaited him
on the wharf. He was enlisted and promoted, and things were so ordered that he now commanded a Confederate battery some two
miles along the line from where Jerome Searing, the Federal scout,

stood cocking his rifle. Nothing had been neglected—at every step in the progress of both these men's lives, and in the lives of their contemporaries and ancestors, and in the lives of the contemporaries of their ancestors, the right thing had been done to bring about the desired result. Had anything in all this vast concatenation been overlooked Private Searing might have fired on the retreating Confederates that morning, and would perhaps have missed. As it fell out, a Confederate captain of artillery, having nothing better to do while awaiting his turn to pull out and be off, amused himself by sighting a field-piece obliquely to his right at what he mistook for some Federal officers on the crest of a hill, and discharged it. The shot flew high of its mark.

As Jerome Searing drew back the hammer of his rifle and with his eyes upon the distant Confederates considered where he could plant his shot with the best hope of making a widow or an orphan or a childless mother,—perhaps all three, for Private Searing, although he had repeatedly refused promotion was not without a certain kind of ambition,—he heard a rushing sound in the air, like that made by the wings of a great bird swooping down upon its prey. More quickly than he could apprehend the gradation, it increased to a hoarse and horrible roar, as the missile that made it sprang at him out of the sky, striking with a deafening impact one of the posts supporting the confusion of timbers above him, smashing it into matchwood, and bringing down the crazy edifice with a loud clatter, in clouds of blinding dust!

When Jerome Searing recovered consciousness he did not at once understand what had occurred. It was, indeed, some time before he opened his eyes. For a while he believed that he had died and been buried, and he tried to recall some portions of the burial service. He thought that his wife was kneeling upon his grave, adding her weight to that of the earth upon his breast. The two of them, widow and earth, had crushed his coffin. Unless the children should persuade her to go home he would not much longer be able to breathe. He felt a sense of wrong. "I cannot speak to her," he thought; "the dead have no voice; and if I open my eyes I shall get them full of earth."

He opened his eyes. A great expanse of blue sky, rising from a fringe of the tops of trees. In the foreground, shutting out some of the trees, a high, dun[18] mound, angular in outline and crossed by an intricate, patternless system of straight lines; the whole an

immeasurable distance away—a distance so inconceivably great that
it fatigued him, and he closed his eyes. The moment that he did so
he was conscious of an insufferable light. A sound was in his ears
like the low, rhythmic thunder of a distant sea breaking in successive waves upon the beach, and out of this noise, seeming a part of
it, or possibly coming from beyond it, and intermingled with its
ceaseless undertone, came the articulate words: "Jerome Searing,
you are caught like a rat in a trap—in a trap, trap, trap."

Suddenly there fell a great silence, a black darkness, an infinite
tranquillity, and Jerome Searing, perfectly conscious of his rathood,
and well assured of the trap that he was in, remembering all and no-
wise alarmed, again opened his eyes to reconnoitre, to note the
strength of his enemy, to plan his defense.

He was caught in a reclining posture, his back firmly supported
by a solid beam. Another lay across his breast, but he had been able
to shrink a little away from it so that it no longer oppressed him,
though it was immovable. A brace joining it at an angle had wedged
him against a pile of boards on his left, fastening the arm on that
side. His legs, slightly parted and straight along the ground, were
covered upward to the knees with a mass of débris which towered
above his narrow horizon. His head was as rigidly fixed as in a vise;
he could move his eyes, his chin—no more. Only his right arm was
partly free. "You must help us out of this," he said to it. But he
could not get it from under the heavy timber athwart his chest, nor
move it outward more than six inches at the elbow.

Searing was not seriously injured, nor did he suffer pain. A smart
rap on the head from a flying fragment of the splintered post, incurred simultaneously with the frightfully sudden shock to the
nervous system, had momentarily dazed him. His term of unconsciousness, including the period of recovery, during which he had
had the strange fancies, had probably not exceeded a few seconds,
for the dust of the wreck had not wholly cleared away as he began
an intelligent survey of the situation.

With his partly free right hand he now tried to get hold of the
beam that lay across, but not quite against, his breast. In no way
could he do so. He was unable to depress the shoulder so as to push
the elbow beyond that edge of the timber which was nearest his
knees; failing in that, he could not raise the forearm and hand to
grasp the beam. The brace that made an angle with it downward
and backward prevented him from doing anything in that direction,

and between it and his body the space was not half so wide as the length of his forearm. Obviously he could not get his hand under the beam nor over it; the hand could not, in fact, touch it at all. Having demonstrated his inability, he desisted, and began to think whether he could reach any of the débris piled upon his legs.

In surveying the mass with a view to determining that point, his attention was arrested by what seemed to be a ring of shining metal immediately in front of his eyes. It appeared to him at first to surround some perfectly black substance, and it was somewhat more than a half-inch in diameter. It suddenly occurred to his mind that the blackness was simply shadow and that the ring was in fact the muzzle of his rifle protruding from the pile of débris. He was not long in satisfying himself that this was so—if it was a satisfaction. By closing either eye he could look a little way along the barrel—to the point where it was hidden by the rubbish that held it. He could see the one side, with the corresponding eye, at apparently the same angle as the other side with the other eye. Looking with the right eye, the weapon seemed to be directed at a point to the left of his head, and *vice versa.* He was unable to see the upper surface of the barrel, but could see the under surface of the stock at a slight angle. The piece was, in fact, aimed at the exact centre of his forehead.

In the perception of this circumstance, in the recollection that just previously to the mischance of which this uncomfortable situation was the result he had cocked the rifle and set the trigger so that a touch would discharge it, Private Searing was affected with a feeling of uneasiness. But that was as far as possible from fear; he was a brave man, somewhat familiar with the aspect of rifles from that point of view, and of cannon too. And now he recalled, with something like amusement, an incident of his experience at the storming of Missionary Ridge, where, walking up to one of the enemy's embrasures from which he had seen a heavy gun throw charge after charge of grape among the assailants he had thought for a moment that the piece had been withdrawn; he could see nothing in the opening but a brazen circle. What that was he had understood just in time to step aside as it pitched another peck of iron down that swarming slope. To face firearms is one of the commonest incidents in a soldier's life—firearms, too, with malevolent eyes blazing behind them. That is what a soldier is for. Still, Private Searing did not altogether relish the situation, and turned away his eyes.

After groping, aimless, with his right hand for a time he made an ineffectual attempt to release his left. Then he tried to disengage his head, the fixity of which was the more annoying from his ignorance of what held it. Next he tried to free his feet, but while exerting the powerful muscles of his legs for that purpose it occurred to him that a disturbance of the rubbish which held them might discharge the rifle; how it could have endured what had already befallen it he could not understand, although memory assisted him with several instances in point. One in particular he recalled, in which in a moment of mental abstraction he had clubbed his rifle and beaten out another gentleman's brains, observing afterward that the weapon which he had been diligently swinging by the muzzle was loaded, capped, and at full cock—knowledge of which circumstance would doubtless have cheered his antagonist to longer endurance. He had always smiled in recalling that blunder of his "green and salad days" as a soldier, but now he did not smile. He turned his eyes again to the muzzle of the rifle and for a moment fancied that it had moved; it seemed somewhat nearer.

Again he looked away. The tops of the distant trees beyond the bounds of the plantation interested him: he had not before observed how light and feathery they were, nor how darkly blue the sky was, even among their branches, where they somewhat paled it with their green; above him it appeared almost black. "It will be uncomfortably hot here," he thought, "as the day advances. I wonder which way I am looking."

Judging by such shadows as he could see, he decided that his face was due north; he would at least not have the sun in his eyes, and north—well, that was toward his wife and children.

"Bah!" he exclaimed aloud, "what have they to do with it?"

He closed his eyes. "As I can't get out I may as well go to sleep. The rebels are gone and some of our fellows are sure to stray out here foraging. They'll find me."

But he did not sleep. Gradually he became sensible of a pain in his forehead—a dull ache, hardly perceptible at first, but growing more and more uncomfortable. He opened his eyes and it was gone—closed them and it returned. "The devil!" he said, irrelevantly, and stared again at the sky. He heard the singing of birds, the strange metallic note of the meadow lark, suggesting the clash of vibrant blades. He fell into pleasant memories of his childhood, played again with his brother and sister, raced across the fields, shouting to alarm the sedentary larks, entered the sombre forest beyond and with timid steps followed the faint path to Ghost Rock, standing at last with audible heart-throbs before the Dead Man's Cave and seeking to penetrate its awful mystery. For the first time he observed that the opening of the haunted cavern was encircled by a ring of metal. Then all else vanished and left him gazing into the barrel of his rifle as before. But whereas before it had seemed nearer, it now seemed an inconceivable distance away, and all the more sinister for that. He cried out and, startled by something in his own voice—the note of fear—lied to himself in denial: "If I don't sing out I may stay here till I die."

He now made no further attempt to evade the menacing stare of the gun barrel. If he turned away his eyes an instant it was to look for assistance (although he could not see the ground on either side the ruin), and he permitted them to return, obedient to the imperative fascination. If he closed them it was from weariness, and instantly the poignant pain in his forehead—the prophecy and menace of the bullet—forced him to reopen them.

The tension of nerve and brain was too severe; nature came to his relief with intervals of unconsciousness. Reviving from one of these he became sensible of a sharp, smarting pain in his right hand, and when he worked his fingers together, or rubbed his palm with them, he could feel that they were wet and slippery. He could not see the hand, but he knew the sensation; it was running blood. In his delirium he had beaten it against the jagged fragments of the wreck, had clutched it full of splinters. He resolved that he would meet his fate more manly. He was a plain, common soldier, had no religion and not much philosophy; he could not die like a hero, with great and wise last words, even if there had been some one to hear them, but he could die "game," and he would. But if he could only knew when to expect the shot!

Some rats which had probably inhabited the shed came sneaking and scampering about. One of them mounted the pile of débris that held the rifle; another followed and another. Searing regarded them at first with indifference, then with friendly interest; then, as the thought flashed into his bewildered mind that they might touch the trigger of his rifle, he cursed them and ordered them to go away. "It is no business of yours," he cried.

The creatures went away; they would return later, attack his face, gnaw away his nose, cut his throat—he knew that, but he hoped by that time to be dead.

Nothing could now unfix his gaze from the little ring of metal with its black interior. The pain in his forehead was fierce and incessant. He felt it gradually penetrating the brain more and more deeply, until at last its progress was arrested by the wood at the back of his head. It grew momentarily more insufferable: he began wantonly beating his lacerated hand against the splinters again to counteract that horrible ache. It seemed to throb with a slow, regular recurrence, each pulsation sharper than the preceding, and sometimes he cried out, thinking he felt the fatal bullet. No thoughts of home, of wife and children, of country, of glory. The whole record of memory was effaced. The world had passed away—not a vestige remained. Here in this confusion of timbers and boards is the sole universe. Here is immortality in time—each pain an everlasting life. The throbs tick off eternities.

Jerome Searing, the man of courage, the formidable enemy, the strong, resolute warrior, was as pale as a ghost. His jaw was fallen; his eyes protruded; he trembled in every fibre; a cold sweat bathed his entire body; he screamed with fear. He was not insane—he was terrified.

In groping about with his torn and bleeding hand he seized at last a strip of board, and, pulling, felt it give way. It lay parallel with his body, and by bending his elbow as much as the contracted space would permit, he could draw it a few inches at a time. Finally it was altogether loosened from the wreckage covering his legs; he could lift it clear of the ground its whole length. A great hope came into his mind: perhaps he could work it upward, that is to say backward, far enough to lift the end and push aside the rifle; or, if that were too tightly wedged, so place the strip of board as to deflect the bullet. With this object he passed it backward inch by inch, hardly daring to breathe lest that act somehow defeat his intent, and more than ever unable to remove his eyes from the rifle, which might perhaps now hasten to improve its waning opportunity. Something at least had been gained: in the occupation of his mind in this attempt at self-defense he was less sensible of the pain in his head and had ceased to wince. But he was still dreadfully frightened and his teeth rattled like castanets.

The strip of board ceased to move to the suasion of his hand. He tugged at it with all his strength, changed the direction of its length all he could, but it had met some extended obstruction behind him and the end in front was still too far away to clear the pile of débris and reach the muzzle of the gun. It extended, indeed, nearly as far as the trigger guard, which, uncovered by the rubbish, he could imperfectly see with his right eye. He tried to break the strip with his hand, but had no leverage. In his defeat, all his terror returned, augmented tenfold. The black aperture of the rifle appeared to threaten a sharper and more imminent death in punishment of his rebellion. The track of the bullet through his head ached with an intenser anguish. He began to tremble again.

Suddenly he became composed. His tremor subsided. He clenched his teeth and drew down his eyebrows. He had not exhausted his means of defense; a new design had shaped itself in his mind—another plan of battle. Raising the front end of the strip of board, he carefully pushed it forward through the wreckage at the side of the rifle until it pressed against the trigger guard. Then he moved the end slowly outward until he could feel that it had cleared it, then, closing his eyes, thrust it against the trigger with all his strength! There was no explosion; the rifle had been discharged as it dropped from his hand when the building fell. But it did its work.

Lieutenant Adrian Searing, in command of the picket-guard on that part of the line through which his brother Jerome had passed on his mission, sat with attentive ears in his breastwork behind the line. Not the faintest sound escaped him; the cry of a bird, the barking of a squirrel, the noise of the wind among the pines—all were anxiously noted by his overstrained sense. Suddenly, directly in front of his line, he heard a faint, confused rumble, like the clatter of a falling building translated by distance. The lieutenant mechanically looked at his watch. Six o'clock and eighteen minutes. At the same moment an officer approached him on foot from the rear and saluted.

"Lieutenant," said the officer, "the colonel directs you to move forward your line and feel the enemy if you find him. If not, continue the advance until directed to halt. There is reason to think that the enemy has retreated."

The lieutenant nodded and said nothing; the other officer retired. In a moment the men, apprised of their duty by the non-commissioned officers in low tones, had deployed from their rifle-pits and were moving forward in skirmishing order, with set teeth and beating hearts.

This line of skirmishers sweeps across the plantation toward the mountain. They pass on both sides of the wrecked building, observing nothing. At a short distance in their rear their commander comes. He casts his eyes curiously upon the ruin and sees a dead body half buried in boards and timbers. It is so covered with dust that its clothing is Confederate gray. Its face is yellowish white; the cheeks are fallen in, the temples sunken, too, with sharp ridges about them, making the forehead forbiddingly narrow; the upper lip, slightly lifted, shows the white teeth, rigidly, clenched. The hair is heavy with moisture, the face as wet as the dewy grass all about. From his point of view the officer does not observe the rifle; the man was apparently killed by the fall of the building.

"Dead a week," said the officer curtly, moving on and absently pulling out his watch as if to verify his estimate of time. Six o'clock and forty minutes.

Killed at Resaca

The best soldier of our staff was Lieutenant Herman Brayle, one of the two aides-de-camp. I don't remember where the general picked him up; from some Ohio regiment, I think; none of us had previously known him, and it would have been strange if we had, for no two of us came from the same State, nor even from adjoining States. The general seemed to think that a position on his staff was a distinction that should be so judiciously conferred as not to beget any sectional jealousies and imperil the integrity of that part of the country which was still an integer. He would not even choose officers from his own command, but by some jugglery at department headquarters obtained them from other brigades. Under such circumstances, a man's services had to be very distinguished indeed to be heard of by his family and the friends of his youth; and "the speaking trump of fame" was a trifle hoarse from loquacity, anyhow.

Lieutenant Brayle was more than six feet in height and of splendid proportions, with the light hair and gray-blue eyes which men so gifted usually find associated with a high order of courage. As he was commonly in full uniform, especially in action, when most officers are content to be less flamboyantly attired, he was a very striking and conspicuous figure. As to the rest, he had a gentleman's manners, a scholar's head, and a lion's heart. His age was about thirty.

We all soon came to like Brayle as much as we admired him, and it was with sincere concern that in the engagement at Stone's River—our first action after he joined us—we observed that he had one most objectionable and unsoldierly quality: he was vain of his courage. During all the vicissitudes and mutations of that hideous encounter, whether our troops were fighting in the open cotton fields, in the cedar thickets, or behind the railway embankment, he did not once take cover, except when sternly commanded to do so by the general, who usually had other things to think of than the lives of his staff officers—or those of his men, for that matter.

In every later engagement while Brayle was with us it was the same way. He would sit his horse like an equestrian statue, in a storm of bullets and grape, in the most exposed places—wherever,

43

in fact, duty requiring him to go, permitted him to remain—when, without trouble and with distinct advantage to his reputation for common sense, he might have been in such security as is possible on a battlefield in the brief intervals of personal inaction.

On foot, from necessity or in deference to his dismounted commander or associates, his conduct was the same. He would stand like a rock in the open when officers and men alike had taken to cover; while men older in service and years, higher in rank and of unquestionable intrepidity, were loyally preserving behind the crest of a hill lives infinitely precious to their country, this fellow would stand, equally idle, on the ridge, facing in the direction of the sharpest fire.

When battles are going on in open ground it frequently occurs that the opposing lines, confronting each other within a stone's throw for hours, hug the earth as closely as if they loved it. The line officers in their proper places flatten themselves no less, and the field officers, their horses all killed or sent to the rear, crouch beneath the infernal canopy of hissing lead and screaming iron without a thought of personal dignity.

In such circumstances the life of a staff officer of a brigade is distinctly "not a happy one," mainly because of its precarious tenure and the unnerving alternations of emotion to which he is exposed. From a position of that comparative security from which a civilian would ascribe his escape to a "miracle," he may be despatched with an order to some commander of a prone regiment in the front line—a person for the moment inconspicuous and not always easy to find without a deal of search among men somewhat preoccupied, and in a din in which question and answer alike must be imparted in the sign language. It is customary in such cases to duck the head and scuttle away on a keen run, an object of lively interest to some thousands of admiring marksmen. In returning—well, it is not customary to return.

Brayle's practice was different. He would consign his horse to the care of an orderly—he loved his horse,—and walk quietly away on his perilous errand with never a stoop of the back, his splendid figure, accentuated by his uniform, holding the eye with a strange fascination. We watched him with suspended breath, our hearts in our mouths. On one occasion of this kind, indeed, one of our number, an impetuous stammerer, was so possessed by his emotion that he shouted at me:

"I'll b-b-bet you t-two d-d-dollars they d-drop him b-b-before he g-gets to that d-d-ditch!"

I did not accept the brutal wager; I thought they would.

Let me do justice to a brave man's memory; in all these needless exposures of life there was no visible bravado nor subsequent narration. In the few instances when some of us had ventured to remonstrate, Brayle had smiled pleasantly and made some light reply, which, however, had not encouraged a further pursuit of the subject. Once he said:

"Captain, if ever I come to grief by forgetting your advice, I hope my last moments will be cheered by the sound of your beloved voice breathing into my ear the blessed words, 'I told you so.' "

We laughed at the captain—just why we could probably not have explained—and that afternoon when he was shot to rags from an ambuscade Brayle remained by the body for some time, adjusting the limbs with needless care—there in the middle of a road swept by gusts of grape and canister! It is easy to condemn this kind of thing, and not very difficult to refrain from imitation, but it is impossible not to respect, and Brayle was liked none the less for the weakness which had so heroic an expression. We wished he were not a fool, but he went on that way to the end, sometimes hard hit, but always returning to duty about as good as new.

Of course, it came at last; he who ignores the law of probabilities challenges an adversary that is seldom beaten. It was at Resaca, in Georgia, during the movement that resulted in the taking of Atlanta. In front of our brigade the enemy's line of earthworks ran through open fields along a slight crest. At each end of this open ground we were close up to him in the woods, but the clear ground we could not hope to occupy until night, when darkness would enable us to burrow like moles and throw up earth. At this point our line was a quarter-mile away in the edge of a wood. Roughly, we formed a semicircle, the enemy's fortified line being the chord of the arc.

"Lieutenant, go tell Colonel Ward to work up as close as he can get cover, and not to waste much ammunition in unnecessary firing. You may leave your horse."

When the general gave this direction we were in the fringe of the forest, near the right extremity of the arc. Colonel Ward was at the left. The suggestion to leave the horse obviously enough meant that Brayle was to take the longer line, through the woods and among the men. Indeed, the suggestion was needless; to go by the short route meant absolutely certain failure to deliver the message. Before anybody could interpose, Brayle had cantered lightly into the field and the enemy's works were in crackling conflagration.

"Stop that damned fool!" shouted the general.

A private of the escort, with more ambition than brains, spurred forward to obey, and within ten yards left himself and his horse dead on the field of honor.

Brayle was beyond recall, galloping easily along, parallel to the enemy and less than two hundred yards distant. He was a picture to see! His hat had been blown or shot from his head, and his long, blond hair rose and fell with the motion of his horse. He sat erect in the saddle, holding the reins lightly in his left hand, his right hanging carelessly at his side. An occasional glimpse of his handsome profile as he turned his head one way or the other proved that the interest which he took in what was going on was natural and without affectation.

The picture was intensely dramatic, but in no degree theatrical. Successive scores of rifles spat at him viciously as he came within range, and our own line in the edge of the timber broke out in visible and audible defense. No longer regardful of themselves or their orders, our fellows sprang to their feet, and swarming into the open sent broad sheets of bullets against the blazing crest of the offending works, which poured an answering fire into their unprotected groups with deadly effect. The artillery on both sides joined the battle, punctuating the rattle and roar with deep, earth-shaking explosions and tearing the air with storms of screaming grape, which from the enemy's side splintered the trees and spattered them with blood, and from ours defiled the smoke of his arms with banks and clouds of dust from his parapet.

My attention had been for a moment drawn to the general combat, but now, glancing down the unobscured avenue between these two thunderclouds, I saw Brayle, the cause of the carnage. Invisible now from either side, and equally doomed by friend and foe, he stood in the shot-swept space, motionless, his face toward the enemy. At some little distance lay his horse. I instantly saw what had stopped him.

As topographical engineer I had, early in the day, made a hasty examination of the ground, and now remembered that at that point was a deep and sinuous gully, crossing half the field from the enemy's line, its general course at right angles to it. From where we now were it was invisible, and Brayle had evidently not known about it. Clearly, it was impassable. Its salient angles would have afforded him absolute security if he had chosen to be satisfied with the miracle already wrought in his favor and leapt into it. He could not go forward, he would not turn back; he stood awaiting death. It did not keep him long waiting.

By some mysterious coincidence, almost instantaneously as he fell, the firing ceased, a few desultory shots at long intervals serving rather to accentuate than break the silence. It was as if both sides had suddenly repented of their profitless crime. Four stretcher-bearers of ours, following a sergeant with a white flag, soon afterward moved unmolested into the field, and made straight for Brayle's body. Several Confederate officers and men came out to meet them, and with uncovered heads assisted them to take up their sacred burden. As it was borne toward us we heard beyond the hostile works fifes and a muffled drum—a dirge. A generous enemy honored the fallen brave.

Amongst the dead man's effects was a soiled Russia-leather pocketbook. In the distribution of mementoes of our friend, which the general, as administrator, decreed, this fell to me.

A year after the close of the war, on my way to California, I opened and idly inspected it. Out of an overlooked compartment fell a letter without envelope or address. It was in a woman's handwriting, and began with words of endearment, but no name.

It had the following date line: "San Francisco, Cal., July 9, 1862." The signature was "Darling," in marks of quotation. Incidentally, in the body of the text, the writer's full name was given—Marian Mendenhall.

The letter showed evidence of cultivation and good breeding, but it was an ordinary love letter, if a love letter can be ordinary. There was not much in it, but there was something. It was this:

"Mr. Winters, whom I shall always hate for it, has been telling that at some battle in Virginia, where he got his hurt, you were seen crouching behind a tree. I think he wants to injure you in my regard, which he knows the story would do if I believed it. I could bear to hear of my soldier lover's death, but not of his cowardice."

These were the words which on that sunny afternoon, in a distant region, had slain a hundred men. Is woman weak?

One evening I called on Miss Mendenhall to return the letter to her. I intended, also, to tell her what she had done—but not that she did it. I found her in a handsome dwelling on Rincon Hill.[19] She was beautiful, well bred—in a word, charming.

"You knew Lieutenant Herman Brayle," I said, rather abruptly. "You know, doubtless, that he fell in battle. Among his effects was found this letter from you. My errand here is to place it in your hands."

She mechanically took the letter, glanced through it with deepening color, and then, looking at me with a smile, said:

"It is very good of you, though I am sure it was hardly worth while." She started suddenly and changed color. "This stain," she said, "is it—surely it is not——"

"Madam," I said, "pardon me, but that is the blood of the truest and bravest heart that ever beat."

She hastily flung the letter on the blazing coals. "Uh! I cannot bear the sight of blood!" she said. "How did he die?"

I had involuntarily risen to rescue that scrap of paper, sacred even to me, and now stood partly behind her. As she asked the question she turned her face about and slightly upward. The light of the burning letter was reflected in her eyes and touched her cheek with a tinge of crimson like the stain upon its page. I had never seen anything so beautiful as this detestable creature.

"He was bitten by a snake," I replied.

The Affair at Coulter's Notch

"Do you think, Colonel, that your brave Coulter would like to put one of his guns in here?" the general asked.

He was apparently not altogether serious; it certainly did not seem a place where any artillerist, however brave, would like to put a gun. The colonel thought that possibly his division commander meant good-humoredly to intimate that in a recent conversation between them Captain Coulter's courage had been too highly extolled.

"General," he replied warmly, "Coulter would like to put a gun anywhere within reach of those people," with a motion of his hand in the direction of the enemy.

"It is the only place," said the general. He was serious, then.

The place was a depression, a "notch," in the sharp crest of a hill. It was a pass, and through it ran a turnpike, which reaching this highest point in its course by a sinuous ascent through a thin forest made a similar, though less steep, descent toward the enemy. For a mile to the left and a mile to the right, the ridge, though occupied by Federal infantry lying close behind the sharp crest and appearing as if held in place by atmospheric pressure, was inaccessible to artillery. There was no place but the bottom of the notch, and that was barely wide enough for the roadbed. From the Confederate side this point was commanded by two batteries posted on a slightly lower elevation beyond a creek, and a half-mile away. All the guns but one were masked by the trees of an orchard; that one—it seemed a bit of impudence—was on an open lawn directly in front of a rather grandiose building, the planter's dwelling. The gun was safe enough in its exposure—but only because the Federal infantry had been forbidden to fire. Coulter's Notch—it came to be called so—was not, that pleasant summer afternoon, a place where one would "like to put a gun."

Three or four dead horses lay there sprawling in the road, three or four dead men in a trim row at one side of it, and a little back, down the hill. All but one were cavalrymen belonging to the Federal advance. One was a quartermaster. The general commanding the division and the colonel commanding the brigade, with their staffs and escorts, had ridden into the notch to have a look at the enemy's guns—which had straightway obscured themselves in towering clouds of smoke. It was hardly profitable to be curious about guns which had the trick of the cuttlefish,[20] and the season of observation had been brief. At its conclusion—a short remove backward from where it began—occurred the conversation already partly reported. "It is the only place," the general repeated thoughtfully, "to get at them."

The colonel looked at him gravely. "There is room for only one gun, General—one against twelve."

"That is true—for only one at a time," said the commander with something like, yet not altogether like, a smile. "But then, your brave Coulter—a whole battery in himself."

The tone of irony was now unmistakable. It angered the colonel, but he did not know what to say. The spirit of military subordination is not favorable to retort, nor even to deprecation.

At this moment a young officer of artillery came riding slowly up the road attended by his bugler. It was Captain Coulter. He could not have been more than twenty-three years of age. He was of medium height, but very slender and lithe, and sat his horse with something of the air of a civilian. In face he was of a type singularly unlike the men about him; thin, high-nosed, gray-eyed, with a slight blond mustache, and long, rather straggling hair of the same color. There was an apparent negligence in his attire. His cap was worn with the visor a trifle askew; his coat was buttoned only at the sword-belt, showing a considerable expanse of white shirt, tolerably clean for that stage of the campaign. But the negligence was all in his dress and bearing; in his face was a look of intense interest in his surroundings. His gray eyes, which seemed occasionally to strike right and left across the landscape, like search-lights, were for the most part fixed upon the sky beyond the Notch; until he should arrive at the summit of the road there was nothing else in that direction to see. As he came opposite his division and brigade commanders at the roadside he saluted mechanically and was about to pass on. The colonel signed to him to halt.

"Captain Coulter," he said, "the enemy has twelve pieces over there on the next ridge. If I rightly understand the general, he directs that you bring up a gun and engage them."

There was a blank silence; the general looked stolidly at a distant regiment swarming slowly up the hill through rough undergrowth,

like a torn and draggled cloud of blue smoke; the captain appeared
not to have observed him. Presently the captain spoke, slowly and
with apparent effort:

"On the next ridge, did you say, sir? Are the guns near the
house?"

"Ah, you have been over this road before. Directly at the house."

"And it is—necessary—to engage them? The order is imperative?"

His voice was husky and broken. He was visibly paler. The colonel
was astonished and mortified. He stole a glance at the commander.
In that set, immobile face was no sign; it was as hard as bronze. A
moment later the general rode away, followed by his staff and escort. The colonel, humiliated and indignant, was about to order
Captain Coulter in arrest, when the latter spoke a few words in a
low tone to his bugler, saluted, and rode straight forward into the
Notch, where, presently, at the summit of the road, his field-glass at
his eyes, he showed against the sky, he and his horse, sharply defined and statuesque. The bugler had dashed down the speed and
disappeared behind a wood. Presently his bugle was heard singing
in the cedars, and in an incredibly short time a single gun with its
caisson, each drawn by six horses and manned by its full comple-
ment of gunners, came bounding and banging up the grade in a
storm of dust, unlimbered under cover, and was run forward by
hand to the fatal crest among the dead horses. A gesture of the captain's arm, some strangely agile movements of the men in loading,
and almost before the troops along the way had ceased to hear the
rattle of the wheels, a great white cloud sprang forward down the
slope, and with a deafening report the affair at Coulter's Notch had
begun.

It is not intended to relate in detail the progress and incidents
of that ghastly contest—a contest without vicissitudes, its alternations only different degrees of despair. Almost at the instant when
Captain Coulter's gun blew its challenging cloud twelve answering
clouds rolled upward from among the trees about the plantation
house, a deep multiple report roared back like a broken echo and
thenceforth to the end the Federal cannoneers fought their hopeless
battle in an atmosphere of living iron whose thoughts were light-
nings and whose deeds were death.

Unwilling to see the efforts which he could not aid and the
slaughter which he could not stay, the colonel ascended the ridge at

a point a quarter of a mile to the left, whence the Notch, itself invisible, but pushing up successive masses of smoke, seemed the crater of a volcano in thundering eruption. With his glass he watched the enemy's guns, noting as he could the effects of Coulter's fire—if Coulter still lived to direct it. He saw that the Federal gunners, ignoring those of the enemy's pieces whose positions could be determined by their smoke only, gave their whole attention to the one that maintained its place in the open—the lawn in front of the house. Over and about that hardy piece the shells exploded at intervals of a few seconds. Some exploded in the house, as could be seen by thin ascensions of smoke from the breached roof. Figures of prostrate men and horses were plainly visible.

"If our fellows are doing so good work with a single gun," said the colonel to an aide who happened to be nearest, "they must be suffering like the devil from twelve. Go down and present the commander of that piece with my congratulations on the accuracy of his fire."

Turning to his adjutant-general he said, "Did you observe Coulter's damned reluctance to obey orders?"

"Yes, sir, I did."

"Well, say nothing about it, please. I don't think the general will care to make any accusations. He will probably have enough to do in explaining his own connection with this uncommon way of amusing the rear-guard of a retreating enemy."

A young officer approached from below, climbing breathless up the acclivity. Almost before he had saluted, he gasped out:

"Colonel, I am directed by Colonel Harmon to say that the enemy's guns are within easy reach of our rifles, and most of them visible from several points along the ridge."

The brigade commander looked at him without a trace of interest in his expression. "I know it," he said quietly.

The young adjutant was visibly embarrassed. "Colonel Harmon would like to have permission to silence those guns," he stammered.

"So should I," the colonel said in the same tone. "Present my compliments to Colonel Harmon and say to him that the general's orders for the infantry not to fire are still in force."

The adjutant saluted and retired. The colonel ground his heel into the earth and turned to look again at the enemy's guns.

"Colonel," said the adjutant-general, "I don't know that I ought to say anything, but there is something wrong in all this. Do you happen to know that Captain Coulter is from the South?"

"No; *was* he, indeed?"

"I heard that last summer the division which the general then commanded was in the vicinity of Coulter's home—camped there for weeks, and——"

"Listen!" said the colonel, interrupting with an upward gesture. "Do you hear *that*?"

"That" was the silence of the Federal gun. The staff, the orderlies, the lines of infantry behind the crest—all had "heard," and were looking curiously in the direction of the crater, whence no smoke now ascended except desultory cloudlets from the enemy's shells. Then came the blare of a bugle, a faint rattle of wheels; a minute later the sharp reports recommenced with double activity. The demolished gun had been replaced with a sound one.

"Yes," said the adjutant-general, resuming his narrative, "the general made the acquaintance of Coulter's family. There was trouble—I don't know the exact nature of it—something about Coulter's wife. She is a red-hot Secessionist, as they all are, except Coulter himself, but she is a good wife and high-bred lady. There was a complaint to army headquarters. The general was transferred to this division. It is odd that Coulter's battery should afterward have been assigned to it."

The colonel had risen from the rock upon which they had been sitting. His eyes were blazing with a generous indignation.

"See here, Morrison," said he, looking his gossiping staff officer straight in the face, "did you get that story from a gentleman or a liar?"

"I don't want to say how I got it, Colonel, unless it is necessary"—he was blushing a trifle—"but I'll stake my life upon its truth in the main."

The colonel turned toward a small knot of officers some distance away. "Lieutenant Williams!" he shouted.

One of the officers detached himself from the group and coming forward saluted, saying: "Pardon me, Colonel, I thought you had been informed. Williams is dead down there by the gun. What can I do, sir?"

Lieutenant Williams was the aide who had had the pleasure of conveying to the officer in charge of the gun his brigade commander's congratulations.

"Go," said the colonel, "and direct the withdrawal of that gun instantly. No—I'll go myself."

He strode down the declivity toward the rear of the Notch at a break-neck pace, over rocks and through brambles, followed by his little retinue in tumultuous disorder. At the foot of the declivity they mounted their waiting animals and took to the road at a lively trot, round a bend and into the Notch. The spectacle which they encountered there was appalling!

Within that defile, barely broad enough for a single gun, were piled the wrecks of no fewer than four. They had noted the silencing of only the last one disabled—there had been a lack of men to replace it quickly with another. The débris lay on both sides of the road; the men had managed to keep an open way between, through which the fifth piece was now firing. The men?—they looked like demons of the pit! All were hatless, all stripped to the waist, their reeking skins black with blotches of powder and spattered with gouts of blood. They worked like madmen, with rammer and cartridge, lever and lanyard. They set their swollen shoulders and bleeding hands against the wheels at each recoil and heaved the heavy gun back to its place. There were no commands; in that awful environment of whooping shot, exploding shells, shrieking fragments of iron, and flying splinters of wood, none could have been heard. Officers, if officers there were, were indistinguishable; all worked together—each while he lasted—governed by the eye. When the gun was sponged, it was loaded; when loaded, aimed and fired. The colonel observed something new to his military experience—something horrible and unnatural: the gun was bleeding at the mouth! In temporary default of water, the man sponging had dipped his sponge into a pool of comrade's blood. In all this work there was no clashing; the duty of the instant was obvious. When one fell, another, looking a trifle cleaner, seemed to rise from the earth in the dead man's tracks, to fall in his turn.

With the ruined guns lay the ruined men—alongside the wreckage, under it and atop of it; and back down the road—a ghastly procession!—crept on hands and knees such of the wounded as were able to move. The colonel—he had compassionately sent his cavalcade to the right about—had to ride over those who were entirely dead in order not to crush those who were partly alive. Into that hell he tranquilly held his way, rode up alongside the gun, and, in the obscurity of the last discharge, tapped upon the cheek the man holding the rammer—who straightway fell, thinking himself killed. A fiend seven times damned sprang out of the smoke to take his place, but paused and gazed up at the mounted officer with an unearthly regard, his teeth flashing between his black lips, his eyes, fierce and expanded, burning like coals beneath his bloody brow. The colonel made an authoritative gesture and pointed to the rear. The fiend bowed in token of obedience. It was Captain Coulter.

Simultaneously with the colonel's arresting sign, silence fell upon the whole field of action. The procession of missiles no longer streamed into that defile of death, for the enemy also had ceased firing. His army had been gone for hours, and the commander of his rear-guard, who had held his position perilously long in hope to silence the Federal fire, at that strange moment had silenced his own. "I was not aware of the breadth of my authority," said the colonel to anybody, riding forward to the crest to see what had really happened.

An hour later his brigade was in bivouac on the enemy's ground, and its idlers were examining, with something of awe, as the faithful inspect a saint's relics, a score of straddling dead horses and three disabled guns, all spiked. The fallen men had been carried away; their torn and broken bodies would have given too great satisfaction.

Naturally, the colonel established himself and his military family in the plantation house. It was somewhat shattered, but it was better than the open air. The furniture was greatly deranged and broken. Walls and ceilings were knocked away here and there, and a lingering odor of powder smoke was everywhere. The beds, the closets of women's clothing, the cupboards were not greatly damaged. The new tenants for a night made themselves comfortable, and the virtual effacement of Coulter's battery supplied them with an interesting topic.

During supper an, orderly of the escort showed himself into the dining-room and asked permission to speak to the colonel.

"What is it, Barbour?" said that officer pleasantly, having overheard the request.

"Colonel, there is something wrong in the cellar; I don't know what—somebody there. I was down there rummaging about."

"I will go down and see," said a staff officer, rising.

"So will I," the colonel said; "let the others remain. Lead on, orderly."

They took a candle from the table and descended the cellar stairs, the orderly in visible trepidation. The candle made but a feeble light, but presently, as they advanced, its narrow circle of illumination revealed a human figure seated on the ground against the black stone wall which they were skirting, its knees elevated, its head bowed sharply forward. The face, which should have been seen in profile, was invisible, for the man was bent so far forward that his long hair concealed it; and, strange to relate, the beard, of a much darker hue, fell in a great tangled mass and lay along the ground at his side. They involuntarily paused; then the colonel, taking the candle from the orderly's shaking hand, approached the man and attentively considered him. The long dark beard was the hair of a woman— dead. The dead woman clasped in her arms a dead babe. Both were clasped in the arms of the man, pressed against his breast, against his lips. There was blood in the hair of the woman; there was blood in the hair of the man. A yard away, near an irregular depression in the beaten earth which formed the cellar's floor—a fresh excavation with a convex bit of iron, having jagged edges, visible in one of the sides—lay an infant's foot. The colonel held the light as high as he could. The floor of the room above was broken through, the splinters pointing at all angles downward. "This casemate is not bomb-proof," said the colonel gravely. It did not occur to him that his summing up of the matter had any levity in it.

They stood about the group awhile in silence; the staff officer was thinking of his unfinished supper, the orderly of what might possibly be in one of the casks on the other side of the cellar. Suddenly the man whom they had thought dead raised his head and gazed tranquilly into their faces. His complexion was coal black; the cheeks were apparently tattooed in irregular sinuous lines from the eyes downward. The lips, too, were white, like those of a stage negro. There was blood upon his forehead.

The staff officer drew back a pace, the orderly two paces.

"What are you doing here, my man?" said the colonel, unmoved.

"This house belongs to me, sir," was the reply, civilly delivered.

"To you? Ah, I see! And these?"

"My wife and child. I am Captain Coulter."

The Coup De Grâce[21]

The fighting had been hard and continuous; that was attested by all the senses. The very taste of battle was in the air. All was now over; it remained only to succor the wounded and bury the dead—to "tidy up a bit," as the humorist of a burial squad put it. A good deal of "tidying up" was required. As far as one could see through the forests, among the splintered trees, lay wrecks of men and horses. Among them moved the stretcher-bearers, gathering and carrying away the few who showed signs of life. Most of the wounded had died of neglect while the right to minister to their wants was in dispute. It is an army regulation that the wounded must wait; the best way to care for them is to win the battle. It must be confessed that victory is a distinct advantage to a man requiring attention, but many do not live to avail themselves of it.

The dead were collected in groups of a dozen or a score and laid side by side in rows while the trenches were dug to receive them. Some, found at too great a distance from these rallying points, were buried where they lay. There was little attempt at identification, though in most cases, the burial parties being detailed to glean the same ground which they had assisted to reap, the names of the victorious dead were known and listed. The enemy's fallen had to be content with counting. But of that they got enough: many of them were counted several times, and the total, as given afterward in the official report of the victorious commander, denoted rather a hope than a result.

At some little distance from the spot where one of the burial parties had established its "bivouac of the dead," a man in the uniform of a Federal officer stood leaning against a tree. From his feet upward to his neck his attitude was that of weariness reposing; but he turned his head uneasily from side to side; his mind was apparently not at rest. He was perhaps uncertain in which direction to go; he was not likely to remain long where he was, for already the level rays of the setting sun straggled redly through the open spaces of the wood and the weary soldiers were quitting their task for the day. He would hardly make a night of it alone there among the dead. Nine men in ten whom you meet after a battle inquire the way to some fraction of the army—as if any one could know. Doubtless this officer was lost. After resting himself a moment he would presumably follow one of the retiring burial squads.

When all were gone he walked straight away into the forest toward the red west, its light staining his face like blood. The air of confidence with which he now strode along showed that he was on familiar ground; he had recovered his bearings. The dead on his right and on his left were unregarded as he passed. An occasional low moan from some sorely-stricken wretch whom the relief-parties had not reached, and who would have to pass a comfortless night beneath the stars with his thirst to keep him company, was equally unheeded. What, indeed, could the officer have done, being no surgeon and having no water?

At the head of a shallow ravine, a mere depression of the ground, lay a small group of bodies. He saw, and swerving suddenly from his course walked rapidly toward them. Scanning each one sharply as he passed, he stopped at last above one which lay at a slight remove from the others, near a clump of small trees. He looked at it narrowly. It seemed to stir. He stooped, and laid his hand upon its face. It screamed.

The officer was Captain Downing Madwell, of a Massachusetts regiment of infantry, a daring and intelligent soldier, an honorable man.

In the regiment were two brothers named Halcrow—Caffal and Creede Halcrow. Caffal Halcrow was a sergeant in Captain Madwell's company, and these two men, the sergeant and the captain, were devoted friends. In so far as disparity of rank, difference in duties and considerations of military discipline would permit they were commonly together. They had, indeed, grown up together from childhood. A habit of the heart is not easily broken off. Caffal Halcrow had nothing military in his taste nor disposition, but the thought of separation from his friend was disagreeable; he enlisted in the company in which Madwell was second-lieutenant. Each had taken two steps upward in rank, but between the highest non-commissioned and the lowest commissioned officer the gulf is deep and wide and the old relation was maintained with difficulty and a difference.

Creede Halcrow, the brother of Caffal, was the major of the regiment—a cynical, saturnine man, between whom and Captain

Madwell there was a natural antipathy which circumstances had nourished and strengthened to an active animosity. But for the restraining influence of their mutual relation to Caffal these two patriots would doubtless have endeavored to deprive their country of each other's services.

At the opening of the battle that morning the regiment was performing outpost duty a mile away from the main army. It was attacked and nearly surrounded in the forest, but stubbornly held its ground. During a lull in the fighting, Major Halcrow came to Captain Madwell. The two exchanged formal salutes, and the major said: "Captain, the colonel directs that you push your company to the head of this ravine and hold your place there until recalled. I need hardly apprise you of the dangerous character of the movement, but if you wish, you can, I suppose, turn over the command to your first-lieutenant. I was not, however, directed to authorize the substitution; it is merely a suggestion of my own, unofficially made."

To this deadly insult Captain Madwell coolly replied:

"Sir, I invite you to accompany the movement. A mounted officer would be a conspicuous mark, and I have long held the opinion that it would be better if you were dead."

The art of repartee was cultivated in military circles as early as 1862.

A half-hour later Captain Madwell's company was driven from its position at the head of the ravine, with a loss of one-third its number. Among the fallen was Sergeant Halcrow. The regiment was soon afterward forced back to the main line, and at the close of the battle was miles away. The captain was now standing at the side of his subordinate and friend.

Sergeant Halcrow was mortally hurt. His clothing was deranged; it seemed to have been violently torn apart, exposing the abdomen. Some of the buttons of his jacket had been pulled off and lay on the ground beside him and fragments of his other garments were strewn about. His leather belt was parted and had apparently been dragged from beneath him as he lay. There had been no great effusion of blood. The only visible wound was a wide, ragged opening in the abdomen. It was defiled with earth and dead leaves. Protruding from it was a loop of small intestine. In all his experience Captain Madwell had not seen a wound like this. He could neither conjecture how it was made nor explain the attendant circumstances—the strangely torn clothing, the parted belt, the besmirching of the white skin. He knelt and made a closer examination. When he rose to his feet, he turned his eyes in different directions as if looking for an enemy. Fifty yards away, on the crest of a low, thinly wooded hill, he saw several dark objects moving about among the fallen men—a herd of swine. One stood with its back to him, its shoulders sharply elevated. Its forefeet were upon a human body, its head was depressed and invisible. The bristly ridge of its chine[22] showed black against the red west. Captain Madwell drew away his eyes and fixed them again upon the thing which had been his friend.

The man who had suffered these monstrous mutilations was alive. At intervals he moved his limbs; he moaned at every breath. He stared blankly into the face of his friend and if touched screamed. In his giant agony he had torn up the ground on which he lay; his clenched hands were full of leaves and twigs and earth. Articulate speech was beyond his power; it was impossible to know if he were sensible to anything but pain. The expression of his face was an appeal; his eyes were full of prayer. For what?

There was no misreading that look; the captain had too frequently seen it in eyes of those whose lips had still the power to formulate it by an entreaty for death. Consciously or unconsciously, this writhing fragment of humanity, this type and example of acute sensation, this handiwork of man and beast, this humble, unheroic Prometheus,[23] was imploring everything, all, the whole non-ego, for the boon of oblivion. To the earth and the sky alike, to the trees, to the man, to whatever took form in sense or consciousness, this incarnate suffering addressed that silent plea.

For what, indeed? For that which we accord to even the meanest creature without sense to demand it, denying it only to the wretched of our own race: for the blessed release, the rite of uttermost compassion, the *coup de grâce.*

Captain Madwell spoke the name of his friend. He repeated it over and over without effect until emotion choked his utterance. His tears plashed upon the livid face beneath his own and blinded himself. He saw nothing but a blurred and moving object, but the moans were more distinct than ever, interrupted at briefer intervals by sharper shrieks. He turned away, struck his hand upon his forehead, and strode from the spot. The swine, catching sight of him, threw up their crimson muzzles, regarding him suspiciously a second, and then with a gruff, concerted grunt, raced away out of sight. A horse, its foreleg splintered by a cannon-shot, lifted its head sidewise from the ground and neighed piteously. Madwell stepped forward, drew his revolver and shot the poor beast between the eyes, narrowly observing its death-struggle, which, contrary to his expectation, was violent and long; but at last it lay still. The tense muscles of its lips, which had uncovered the teeth in a horrible grin, relaxed; the sharp, clean-cut profile took on a look of profound peace and rest.

Along the distant, thinly wooded crest to westward the fringe of sunset fire had now nearly burned itself out. The light upon the trunks of the trees had faded to a tender gray; shadows were in their tops, like great dark birds aperch. Night was coming and there were miles of haunted forest between Captain Madwell and camp. Yet he stood there at the side of the dead animal, apparently lost to all sense of his surroundings. His eyes were bent upon the earth at his feet; his left hand hung loosely at his side, his right still held the pistol. Presently he lifted his face, turned it toward his dying friend and walked rapidly back to his side. He knelt upon one knee, cocked the weapon, placed the muzzle against the man's forehead, and turning away his eyes pulled the trigger. There was no report. He had used his last cartridge for the horse.

The sufferer moaned and his lips moved convulsively. The froth that ran from them had a tinge of blood.

Captain Madwell rose to his feet and drew his sword from the scabbard. He passed the fingers of his left hand along the edge from hilt to point. He held it out straight before him, as if to test his nerves. There was no visible tremor of the blade; the ray of bleak skylight that it reflected was steady and true. He stooped and with his left hand tore away the dying man's shirt, rose and placed the point of the sword just over the heart. This time he did not withdraw his eyes. Grasping the hilt with both hands, he thrust downward with all his strength and weight. The blade sank into the man's body—through his body into the earth; Captain Madwell came near falling forward upon his work. The dying man drew up his knees and at the same time threw his right arm across his breast and grasped the steel so tightly that the knuckles of the hand visibly whitened. By a violent but vain effort to withdraw the blade the wound was enlarged; a rill of blood escaped, running sinuously down into the deranged clothing. At that moment three men stepped silently forward from behind the clump of young trees which had concealed their approach. Two were hospital attendants and carried a stretcher.

The third was Major Creede Halcrow.

Parker Adderson, Philosopher

"Prisoner, what is your name?"

"As I am to lose it at daylight to-morrow morning it is hardly worth while concealing it. Parker Adderson."

"Your rank?"

"A somewhat humble one; commissioned officers are too precious to be risked in the perilous business of a spy. I am a sergeant."

"Of what regiment?"

"You must excuse me; my answer might, for anything I know, give you an idea of whose forces are in your front. Such knowledge as that is what I came into your lines to obtain, not to impart."

"You are not without wit."

"If you have the patience to wait you will find me dull enough to-morrow."

"How do you know that you are to die to-morrow morning?"

"Among spies captured by night that is the custom. It is one of the nice observances of the profession."

The general so far laid aside the dignity appropriate to a Confederate officer of high rank and wide renown as to smile. But no one in his power and out of his favor would have drawn any happy augury from that outward and visible sign of approval. It was neither genial nor infectious; it did not communicate itself to the other persons exposed to it—the caught spy who had provoked it and the armed guard who had brought him into the tent and now stood a little apart, watching his prisoner in the yellow candle-light. It was no part of that warrior's duty to smile; he had been detailed for another purpose. The conversation was resumed; it was in character a trial for a capital offense.

"You admit, then, that you are a spy—that you came into my camp, disguised as you are in the uniform of a Confederate soldier, to obtain information secretly regarding the numbers and disposition of my troops."

"Regarding, particularly, their numbers. Their disposition I already knew. It is morose."

The general brightened again; the guard, with a severer sense of his responsibility, accentuated the austerity of his expression and stood a trifle more erect than before. Twirling his gray slouch hat round and round upon his forefinger, the spy took a leisurely survey of his surroundings. They were simple enough. The tent was a common "wall tent," about eight feet by ten in dimensions, lighted by a single tallow candle stuck into the haft[24] of a bayonet, which was itself stuck into a pine table at which the general sat, now busily writing and apparently forgetful of his unwilling guest. An old rag carpet covered the earthen floor; an older leather trunk, a second chair and a roll of blankets were about all else that the tent contained; in General Clavering's command Confederate simplicity and penury of "pomp and circumstance" had attained their highest development. On a large nail driven into the tent pole at the entrance was suspended a sword-belt supporting a long sabre, a pistol in its holster and, absurdly enough, a bowie-knife. Of that most unmilitary weapon it was the general's habit to explain that it was a souvenir of the peaceful days when he was a civilian.

It was a stormy night. The rain cascaded upon the canvas in torrents, with the dull, drum-like sound familiar to dwellers in tents. As the whooping blasts charged upon it the frail structure shook and swayed and strained at its confining stakes and ropes.

The general finished writing, folded the half-sheet of paper and spoke to the soldier guarding Adderson: "Here, Tassman, take that to the adjutant-general; then return."

"And the prisoner, General?" said the soldier, saluting, with an inquiring glance in the direction of that unfortunate.

"Do as I said," replied the officer, curtly.

The soldier took the note and ducked himself out of the tent. General Clavering turned his handsome face toward the Federal spy, looked him in the eyes, not unkindly, and said: "It is a bad night, my man."

"For me, yes."

"Do you guess what I have written?"

"Something worth reading, I dare say. And—perhaps it is my vanity—I venture to suppose that I am mentioned in it."

"Yes; it is a memorandum for an order to be read to the troops at *reveille* concerning your execution. Also some notes for the guidance of the provost-marshal in arranging the details of that event."

"I hope, General, the spectacle will be intelligently arranged, for I shall attend it myself."

"Have you any arrangements of your own that you wish to make? Do you wish to see a chaplain, for example?"

"I could hardly secure a longer rest for myself by depriving him of some of his."

"Good God, man! do you mean to go to your death with nothing but jokes upon your lips? Do you know that this is a serious matter?"

"How can I know that? I have never been dead in all my life. I have heard that death is a serious matter, but never from any of those who have experienced it."

The general was silent for a moment; the man interested, perhaps amused him—a type not previously encountered.

"Death," he said, "is at least a loss—a loss of such happiness as we have, and of opportunities for more."

"A loss of which we shall never be conscious can be borne with composure and therefore expected without apprehension. You must have observed, General, that of all the dead men with whom it is your soldierly pleasure to strew your path none shows signs of regret."

"If the being dead is not a regrettable condition, yet the becoming so—the act of dying—appears to be distinctly disagreeable to one who has not lost the power to feel."

"Pain is disagreeable, no doubt. I never suffer it without more or less discomfort. But he who lives longest is most exposed to it. What you call dying is simply the last pain—there is really no such thing as dying. Suppose, for illustration, that I attempt to escape. You lift the revolver that you are courteously concealing in your lap, and——"

The general blushed like a girl, then laughed softly, disclosing his brilliant teeth, made a slight inclination of his handsome head and said nothing. The spy continued: "You fire, and I have in my stomach what I did not swallow. I fall, but am not dead. After a half-hour of agony I am dead. But at any given instant of that half-hour I was either alive or dead. There is no transition period.

"When I am hanged to-morrow morning it will be quite the same; while conscious I shall be living; when dead, unconscious. Nature appears to have ordered the matter quite in my interest— the way that I should have ordered it myself. It is so simple," he added with a smile, "that it seems hardly worth while to be hanged at all."

At the finish of his remarks there was a long silence. The general sat impassive, looking into the man's face, but apparently not attentive to what had been said. It was as if his eyes had mounted guard over the prisoner while his mind concerned itself with other matters. Presently he drew a long, deep breath, shuddered, as one awakened from a dreadful dream, and exclaimed almost inaudibly: "Death is horrible!"—this man of death.

"It was horrible to our savage ancestors," said the spy, gravely, "because they had not enough intelligence to dissociate the idea of consciousness from the idea of the physical forms in which it is manifested—as an even lower order of intelligence, that of the monkey, for example, may be unable to imagine a house without inhabitants, and seeing a ruined hut fancies a suffering occupant. To us it is horrible because we have inherited the tendency to think it so, accounting for the notion by wild and fanciful theories of another world—as names of places give rise to legends explaining them and reasonless conduct to philosophies in justification. You can hang me, General, but there your power of evil ends; you cannot condemn me to heaven."

The general appeared not to have heard; the spy's talk had merely turned his thoughts into an unfamiliar channel, but there they pursued their will independently to conclusions of their own. The storm had ceased, and something of the solemn spirit of the night had imparted itself to his reflections, giving them the sombre tinge of a supernatural dread. Perhaps there was an element of prescience in it. "I should not like to die," he said—"not to-night."

He was interrupted—if, indeed, he had intended to speak further—by the entrance of an officer of his staff, Captain Hasterlick, the provost-marshal. This recalled him to himself; the absent look passed away from his face.

"Captain," he said, acknowledging the officer's salute, "this man is a Yankee spy captured inside our lines with incriminating papers on him. He has confessed. How is the weather?"

"The storm is over, sir, and the moon shining."

"Good; take a file of men, conduct him at once to the parade ground, and shoot him."

A sharp cry broke from the spy's lips. He threw himself forward, thrust out his neck, expanded his eyes, clenched his hands.

"Good God!" he cried hoarsely, almost inarticulately; "you do not mean that! You forget—I am not to die until morning."

"I have said nothing of morning," replied the general, coldly; "that was an assumption of your own. You die now."

"But, General, I beg—I implore you to remember; I am to hang! It will take some time to erect the gallows—two hours—an hour. Spies are hanged; I have rights under military law. For Heaven's sake, General, consider how short——"

"Captain, observe my directions."

The officer drew his sword and fixing his eyes upon the prisoner pointed silently to the opening of the tent. The prisoner hesitated; the officer grasped him by the collar and pushed him gently forward. As he approached the tent pole the frantic man sprang to it and with cat-like agility seized the handle of the bowie-knife, plucked the weapon from the scabbard and thrusting the captain aside leaped upon the general with the fury of a madman, hurling him to the ground and falling headlong upon him as he lay. The table was overturned, the candle extinguished and they fought blindly in the darkness. The provost-marshal sprang to the assistance of his superior officer and was himself prostrated upon the struggling forms. Curses and inarticulate cries of rage and pain came from the welter of limbs and bodies; the tent came down upon them and beneath its hampering and enveloping folds the struggle went on. Private Tassman, returning from his errand and dimly conjecturing the situation, threw down his rifle and laying hold of the flouncing canvas at random vainly tried to drag it off the men under it; and the sentinel who paced up and down in front, not daring to leave his beat though the skies should fall, discharged his rifle. The report alarmed the camp; drums beat the long roll and bugles sounded the assembly, bringing swarms of half-clad men into the moonlight, dressing as they ran, and falling into line at the sharp commands of their officers. This was well; being in line the men were under control; they stood at arms while the general's staff and the men of his escort brought order out of confusion by lifting off the fallen tent and pulling apart the breathless and bleeding actors in that strange contention.

Breathless, indeed, was one: the captain was dead; the handle of the bowie-knife, protruding from his throat, was pressed back beneath his chin until the end had caught in the angle of the jaw and the hand that delivered the blow had been unable to remove the weapon. In the dead man's hand was his sword, clenched with a grip that defied the strength of the living. Its blade was streaked with red to the hilt.

Lifted to his feet, the general sank back to the earth with a moan and fainted. Besides his bruises he had two sword-thrusts—one through the thigh, the other through the shoulder.

The spy had suffered the least damage. Apart from a broken right arm, his wounds were such only as might have been incurred in an ordinary combat with nature's weapons. But he was dazed and seemed hardly to know what had occurred. He shrank away from those attending him, cowered upon the ground and uttered unintelligible remonstrances. His face, swollen by blows and stained with gouts of blood, nevertheless showed white beneath his disheveled hair—as white as that of a corpse.

"The man is not insane," said the surgeon, preparing bandages and replying to a question; "he is suffering from fright. Who and what is he?"

Private Tassman began to explain. It was the opportunity of his life; he omitted nothing that could in any way accentuate the importance of his own relation to the night's events. When he had finished his story and was ready to begin it again nobody gave him any attention.

The general had now recovered consciousness. He raised himself upon his elbow, looked about him, and, seeing the spy crouching by a camp-fire, guarded, said simply:

"Take that man to the parade ground and shoot him."

"The general's mind wanders," said an officer standing near.

"His mind does *not* wander," the adjutant-general said. "I have a memorandum from him about this business; he had given that same order to Hasterlick"—with a motion of the hand toward the dead provost-marshal—"and, by God! it shall be executed."

Ten minutes later Sergeant Parker Adderson, of the Federal army, philosopher and wit, kneeling in the moonlight and begging incoherently for his life, was shot to death by twenty men. As the volley rang out upon the keen air of the midnight, General Clavering, lying white and still in the red glow of the camp-fire, opened his big blue eyes, looked pleasantly upon those about him and said: "How silent it all is!"

The surgeon looked at the adjutant-general, gravely and significantly. The patient's eyes slowly closed, and thus he lay for a few moments; then, his face suffused with a smile of ineffable sweetness, he said, faintly: "I suppose this must be death," and so passed away.

An Affair of Outposts

I

Two men sat in conversation. One was the Governor of the State. The year was 1861; the war was on and the Governor already famous for the intelligence and zeal with which he directed all the powers and resources of his State to the service of the Union.

"What! *you*?" the Governor was saying in evident surprise— "you too want a military commission? Really, the fifing and drumming must have effected a profound alteration in your convictions. In my character of recruiting sergeant I suppose I ought not to be fastidious, but"—there was a touch of irony in his manner—"well, have you forgotten that an oath of allegiance is required?"

"I have altered neither my convictions nor my sympathies," said the other, tranquilly. "While my sympathies are with the South, as you do me the honor to recollect, I have never doubted that the North was in the right. I am a Southerner in fact and in feeling, but it is my habit in matters of importance to act as I think, not as I feel."

The Governor was absently tapping his desk with a pencil; he did not immediately reply. After a while he said: "I have heard that there are all kinds of men in the world, so I suppose there are some like that, and doubtless you think yourself one. I've known you a long time and—pardon me—I don't think so."

"Then I am to understand that my application is denied?"

"Unless you can remove my belief that your Southern sympathies are in some degree a disqualification, yes. I do not doubt your good faith, and I know you to be abundantly fitted by intelligence and special training for the duties of an officer. Your convictions, you say, favor the Union cause, but I prefer a man with his heart in it. The heart is what men fight with."

"Look here, Governor," said the younger man, with a smile that had more light than warmth: "I have something up my sleeve—a qualification which I had hoped it would not be necessary to mention. A great military authority has given a simple recipe for being a good soldier: 'Try always to get yourself killed.' It is with that purpose that I wish to enter the service. I am not, perhaps, much of a patriot, but I wish to be dead."

The Governor looked at him rather sharply, then a little coldly. "There is a simpler and franker way," he said.

"In my family, sir," was the reply, "we do not do that—no Armisted has ever done that."

A long silence ensued and neither man looked at the other. Presently the Governor lifted his eyes from the pencil, which had resumed its tapping, and said:

"Who is she?"

"My wife."

The Governor tossed the pencil into the desk, rose and walked two or three times across the room. Then he turned to Armisted, who also had risen, looked at him more coldly than before and said: "But the man—would it not be better that he—could not the country spare him better than it can spare you? Or are the Armisteds opposed to 'the unwritten law'?"

The Armisteds, apparently, could feel an insult: the face of the younger man flushed, then paled, but he subdued himself to the service of his purpose.

"The man's identity is unknown to me," he said, calmly enough.

"Pardon me," said the Governor, with even less of visible contrition than commonly underlies those words. After a moment's reflection he added: "I shall send you to-morrow a captain's commission in the Tenth Infantry, now at Nashville, Tennessee. Good night."

"Good night, sir. I thank you."

Left alone, the Governor remained for a time motionless, leaning against his desk. Presently he shrugged his shoulders as if throwing off a burden. "This is a bad business," he said.

Seating himself at a reading-table before the fire, he took up the book nearest his hand, absently opening it. His eyes fell upon this sentence:

"When God made it necessary for an unfaithful wife to lie about her husband in justification of her own sins He had the tenderness to endow men with the folly to believe her."

He looked at the title of the book; it was, *His Excellency the Fool.*[25]

He flung the volume into the fire.

II

HOW TO SAY WHAT IS WORTH HEARING

The enemy, defeated in two days of battle at Pittsburg Landing, had sullenly retired to Corinth, whence he had come. For manifest incompetence Grant, whose beaten army had been saved from destruction and capture by Buell's soldierly activity and skill, had been relieved of his command, which nevertheless had not been given to Buell, but to Halleck, a man of unproved powers, a theorist, sluggish, irresolute. Foot by foot his troops, always deployed in line-of-battle to resist the enemy's bickering skirmishers, always entrenching against the columns that never came, advanced across the thirty miles of forest and swamp toward an antagonist prepared to vanish at contact, like a ghost at cock-crow. It was a campaign of "excursions and alarums," of reconnaissances and countermarches, of cross-purposes and countermanded orders. For weeks the solemn farce held attention, luring distinguished civilians from fields of political ambition to see what they safely could of the horrors of war. Among these was our friend the Governor. At the headquarters of the army and in the camps of the troops from his State he was a familiar figure, attended by the several members of his personal staff, showily horsed, faultlessly betailored and bravely silk-hatted. Things of charm they were, rich in suggestions of peaceful lands beyond a sea of strife. The bedraggled soldier looked up from his trench as they passed, leaned upon his spade and audibly damned them to signify his sense of their ornamental irrelevance to the austerities of his trade.

"I think, Governor," said General Masterson one day, going into informal session atop of his horse and throwing one leg across the pommel of his saddle, his favorite posture—"I think I would not ride any farther in that direction if I were you. We've nothing out there but a line of skirmishers. That, I presume, is why I was directed to put these siege guns here: if the skirmishers are driven in the enemy will die of dejection at being unable to haul them away—they're a trifle heavy."

There is reason to fear that the unstrained quality of this military humor dropped not as the gentle rain from heaven upon the place beneath the civilian's silk hat. Anyhow he abated none of his dignity in recognition.

"I understand," he said, gravely, "that some of my men are out there—a company of the Tenth, commanded by Captain Armisted. I should like to meet him if you do not mind."

"He is worth meeting. But there's a bad bit of jungle out there, and I should advise that you leave your horse and"—with a look at the Governor's retinue—"your other impedimenta."[26]

The Governor went forward alone and on foot. In a half-hour he had pushed through a tangled undergrowth covering a boggy soil and entered upon firm and more open ground. Here he found a half-company of infantry lounging behind a line of stacked rifles. The men wore their accoutrements—their belts, cartridge-boxes, haversacks and canteens. Some lying at full length on the dry leaves were fast asleep: others in small groups gossiped idly of this and that; a few played at cards; none was far from the line of stacked arms. To the civilian's eye the scene was one of carelessness, confusion, indifference; a soldier would have observed expectancy and readiness.

At a little distance apart an officer in fatigue uniform, armed, sat on a fallen tree noting the approach of the visitor, to whom a sergeant, rising from one of the groups, now came forward.

"I wish to see Captain Armisted," said the Governor.

The sergeant eyed him narrowly, saying nothing, pointed to the officer, and taking a rifle from one of the stacks, accompanied him.

"This man wants to see you, sir," said the sergeant, saluting. The officer rose.

It would have been a sharp eye that would have recognized him. His hair, which but a few months before had been brown, was streaked with gray. His face, tanned by exposure, was seamed as with age. A long livid scar across the forehead marked the stroke of a sabre; one cheek was drawn and puckered by the work of a bullet. Only a woman of the loyal North would have thought the man handsome.

"Armisted—Captain," said the Governor, extending his hand, "do you not know me?"

"I know you, sir, and I salute you—as the Governor of my State."

Lifting his right hand to the level of his eyes he threw it outward and downward. In the code of military etiquette there is no provision for shaking hands. That of the civilian was withdrawn. If he felt either surprise or chagrin his face did not betray it.

"It is the hand that signed your commission," he said.

"And it is the hand——"

The sentence remains unfinished. The sharp report of a rifle came from the front, followed by another and another. A bullet hissed through the forest and struck a tree near by. The men sprang from the ground and even before the captain's high, clear voice was done intoning the command "At-ten-tion!" had fallen into line in rear of the stacked arms. Again—and now through the din of a crackling fusillade—sounded the strong, deliberate sing-song of authority: "Take . . . arms!" followed by the rattle of unlocking bayonets.

Bullets from the unseen enemy were now flying thick and fast, though mostly well spent and emitting the humming sound which signified interference by twigs and rotation in the plane of flight. Two or three of the men in the line were already struck and down. A few wounded men came limping awkwardly out of the undergrowth from the skirmish line in front; most of them did not pause, but held their way with white faces and set teeth to the rear.

Suddenly there was a deep, jarring report in front, followed by the startling rush of a shell, which passing overhead exploded in the edge of a thicket, setting afire the fallen leaves. Penetrating the din—seeming to float above it like the melody of a soaring bird— rang the slow, aspirated monotones of the captain's several commands, without emphasis, without accent, musical and restful as an evensong under the harvest moon. Familiar with this tranquilizing chant in moments of imminent peril, these raw soldiers of less than a year's training yielded themselves to the spell, executing its mandates with the composure and precision of veterans. Even the distinguished civilian behind his tree, hesitating between pride and terror, was accessible to its charm and suasion. He was conscious of a fortified resolution and ran away only when the skirmishers, under orders to rally on the reserve, came out of the woods like hunted hares and formed on the left of the stiff little line, breathing hard and thankful for the boon of breath.

III

THE FIGHTING OF ONE
WHOSE HEART WAS NOT IN THE QUARREL

Guided in his retreat by that of the fugitive wounded, the Governor struggled bravely to the rear through the "bad bit of jungle." He was well winded and a trifle confused. Excepting a single rifle-shot now and again, there was no sound of strife behind him; the enemy was pulling himself together for a new onset against an antagonist of whose numbers and tactical disposition he was in doubt. The fugitive felt that he would probably be spared to his country, and only commended the arrangements of Providence to that end, but in leaping a small brook in more open ground one of the arrangements incurred the mischance of a disabling sprain at the ankle. He was unable to continue his flight, for he was too fat to hop, and after several vain attempts, causing intolerable pain, seated himself on the earth to nurse his ignoble disability and deprecate the military situation.

A brisk renewal of the firing broke out and stray bullets came flitting and droning by. Then came the crash of two clean, definite volleys, followed by a continuous rattle, through which he heard the yells and cheers of the combatants, punctuated by thunderclaps of cannon. All this told him that Armisted's little command was bitterly beset and fighting at close quarters. The wounded men whom he had distanced began to straggle by on either hand, their numbers visibly augmented by new levies from the line.[27] Singly and by twos and threes, some supporting comrades more desperately hurt than themselves, but all deaf to his appeals for assistance, they sifted through the underbrush and disappeared. The firing was increasingly louder and more distinct, and presently the ailing fugitives were succeeded by men who strode with a firmer tread, occasionally facing about and discharging their pieces, then doggedly resuming their retreat, reloading as they walked. Two or three fell as he looked, and lay motionless. One had enough of life left in him to make a pitiful attempt to drag himself to cover. A passing comrade paused beside him long enough to fire, appraised the poor devil's disability with a look and moved sullenly on, inserting a cartridge in his weapon.

In all this was none of the pomp of war—no hint of glory. Even in his distress and peril the helpless civilian could not forbear to contrast it with the gorgeous parades and reviews held in honor of himself—with the brilliant uniforms, the music, the banners, and the marching. It was an ugly and sickening business: to all that was artistic in his nature, revolting, brutal, in bad taste.

"Ugh!" he grunted, shuddering—"this is beastly! Where is the charm of it all? Where are the elevated sentiments, the devotion, the heroism, the——"

From a point somewhere near, in the direction of the pursuing enemy, rose the clear, deliberate sing-song of Captain Armisted.

"Stead-y, men—stead-y. Halt! Commence fir-ing."

The rattle of fewer than a score of rifles could be distinguished through the general uproar, and again that penetrating falsetto:

"Cease fir-ing. In re-treat . . . maaarch!"

In a few moments this remnant had drifted slowly past the Governor, all to the right of him as they faced in retiring, the men deployed at intervals of a half-dozen paces. At the extreme left and a few yards behind came the captain. The civilian called out his name, but he did not hear. A swarm of men in gray now broke out of cover in pursuit, making directly for the spot where the Governor lay—some accident of the ground had caused them to converge upon that point: their line had become a crowd. In a last struggle for life and liberty the Governor attempted to rise, and looking back the captain saw him. Promptly, but with the same slow precision as before, he sang his commands:

"Skirm-ish-ers, halt!" The men stopped and according to rule turned to face the enemy.

"Ral-ly on the right!"—and they came in at a run, fixing bayonets and forming loosely on the man at that end of the line.

"Forward . . . to save the Gov-ern-or of your State . . . doub-le quick . . . maaarch!"

Only one man disobeyed this astonishing command! He was dead. With a cheer they sprang forward over the twenty or thirty paces between them and their task. The captain having a shorter distance to go arrived first—simultaneously with the enemy. A half-dozen hasty shots were fired at him, and the foremost man—a fellow of heroic stature, hatless and bare-breasted—made a vicious sweep at his head with a clubbed rifle. The officer parried the blow at the cost of a broken arm and drove his sword to the hilt into the giant's breast. As the body fell the weapon was wrenched from his hand and before he could pluck his revolver from the scabbard at his belt another man leaped upon him like a tiger, fastening both hands upon his throat and bearing him backward upon the prostrate Governor, still struggling to rise. This man was promptly spitted upon the bayonet of a Federal sergeant and his death-gripe on the captain's throat loosened by a kick upon each wrist. When the captain had risen he was at the rear of his men, who had all passed over and around him and were thrusting fiercely at their more numerous but

less coherent antagonists. Nearly all the rifles on both sides were
empty and in the crush there was neither time nor room to reload.
The Confederates were at a disadvantage in that most of them
lacked bayonets; they fought by bludgeoning—and a clubbed rifle
is a formidable arm. The sound of the conflict was a clatter like that
of the interlocking horns of battling bulls—now and then the pash[28]
of a crushed skull, an oath, or a grunt caused by the impact of
a rifle's muzzle against the abdomen transfixed by its bayonet.
Through an opening made by the fall of one of his men Captain
Armisted sprang, with his dangling left arm; in his right hand a full-
charged revolver, which he fired with rapidity and terrible effect
into the thick of the gray crowd: but across the bodies of the slain the
survivors in the front were pushed forward by their comrades in the
rear till again they breasted the tireless bayonets. There were fewer
bayonets now to breast—a beggarly half-dozen, all told. A few minutes more of this rough work—a little fighting back to back—and all
would be over.

Suddenly a lively firing was heard on the right and the left: a
fresh line of Federal skirmishers came forward at a run, driving before them those parts of the Confederate line that had been separated by staying the advance of the centre. And behind these new
and noisy combatants, at a distance of two or three hundred yards,
could be seen, indistinct among the trees a line-of-battle!

Instinctively before retiring, the crowd in gray made a tremendous rush upon its handful of antagonists, overwhelming them by
mere momentum and, unable to use weapons in the crush, trampled
them, stamped savagely on their limbs, their bodies, their necks,
their faces; then retiring with bloody feet across its own dead it
joined the general rout and the incident was at an end.

IV

THE GREAT HONOR THE GREAT

The Governor, who had been unconscious, opened his eyes and
stared about him, slowly recalling the day's events. A man in the
uniform of a major was kneeling beside him; he was a surgeon.
Grouped about were the civilian members of the Governor's staff,
their faces expressing a natural solicitude regarding their offices. A
little apart stood General Masterson addressing another officer and

gesticulating with a cigar. He was saying: "It was the beautifulest fight ever made—by God, sir, it was great!"

The beauty and greatness were attested by a row of dead, trimly disposed, and another of wounded, less formally placed, restless, half-naked, but bravely bebandaged.

"How do you feel, sir?" said the surgeon. "I find no wound."

"I think I am all right," the patient replied, sitting up. "It is that ankle."

The surgeon transferred his attention to the ankle, cutting away the boot. All eyes followed the knife.

In moving the leg a folded paper was uncovered. The patient picked it up and carelessly opened it. It was a letter three months old, signed "Julia." Catching sight of his name in it he read it. It was nothing very remarkable—merely a weak woman's confession of unprofitable sin—the penitence of a faithless wife deserted by her betrayer. The letter had fallen from the pocket of Captain Armisted; the reader quietly transferred it to his own.

An aide-de-camp rode up and dismounted. Advancing to the Governor he saluted.

"Sir," he said, "I am sorry to find you wounded—the Commanding General has not been informed. He presents his compliments and I am directed to say that he has ordered for to-morrow a grand review of the reserve corps in your honor. I venture to add that the General's carriage is at your service if you are able to attend."

"Be pleased to say to the Commanding General that I am deeply touched by his kindness. If you have the patience to wait a few moments you shall convey a more definite reply."

He smiled brightly and glancing at the surgeon and his assistants added: "At present—if you will permit an allusion to the horrors of peace—I am 'in the hands of my friends.'"

The humor of the great is infectious; all laughed who heard.

"Where is Captain Armisted?" the Governor asked, not altogether carelessly.

The surgeon looked up from his work, pointing silently to the nearest body in the row of dead, the features discreetly covered with a handkerchief. It was so near that the great man could have laid his hand upon it, but he did not. He may have feared that it would bleed.

The Story of a Conscience

I

Captain Parrol Hartroy stood at the advanced post of his picket-guard, talking in low tones with the sentinel. This post was on a turnpike which bisected the captain's camp, a half-mile in rear, though the camp was not in sight from that point. The officer was apparently giving the soldier certain instructions—was perhaps merely inquiring if all were quiet in front. As the two stood talking a man approached them from the direction of the camp, carelessly whistling, and was promptly halted by the soldier. He was evidently a civilian—a tall person, coarsely clad in the home-made stuff of yellow gray, called "butternut," which was men's only wear in the latter days of the Confederacy. On his head was a slouch felt hat, once white, from beneath which hung masses of uneven hair, seemingly unacquainted with either scissors or comb. The man's face was rather striking; a broad forehead, high nose, and thin cheeks, the mouth invisible in the full dark beard, which seemed as neglected as the hair. The eyes were large and had that steadiness and fixity of attention which so frequently mark a considering intelligence and a will not easily turned from its purpose—so say those physiognomists who have that kind of eyes. On the whole, this was a man whom one would be likely to observe and be observed by. He carried a walking-stick freshly cut from the forest and his ailing cowskin boots were white with dust.

"Show your pass," said the Federal soldier, a trifle more imperiously perhaps than he would have thought necessary if he had not been under the eye of his commander, who with folded arms looked on from the roadside.

" 'Lowed you'd rec'lect me, Gineral," said the wayfarer tranquilly, while producing the paper from the pocket of his coat. There was something in his tone—perhaps a faint suggestion of irony—which made his elevation of his obstructor to exalted rank less agreeable to that worthy warrior than promotion is commonly found to be. "You-all have to be purty pertickler, I reckon," he added, in a more conciliatory tone, as if in half-apology for being halted.

Having read the pass, with his rifle resting on the ground, the

78

soldier handed the document back without a word, shouldered his weapon, and returned to his commander. The civilian passed on in the middle of the road, and when he had penetrated the circumjacent Confederacy a few yards resumed his whistling and was soon out of sight beyond an angle in the road, which at that point entered a thin forest. Suddenly the officer undid his arms from his breast, drew a revolver from his belt and sprang forward at a run in the same direction, leaving his sentinel in gaping astonishment at his post. After making to the various visible forms of nature a solemn promise to be damned, that gentleman resumed the air of stolidity which is supposed to be appropriate to a state of alert military attention.

II

Captain Hartroy held an independent command. His force consisted of a company of infantry, a squadron of cavalry, and a section of artillery, detached from the army to which they belonged, to defend an important defile in the Cumberland Mountains[29] in Tennessee. It was a field officer's command held by a line officer promoted from the ranks, where he had quietly served until "discovered." His post was one of exceptional peril; its defense entailed a heavy responsibility and he had wisely been given corresponding discretionary powers, all the more necessary because of his distance from the main army, the precarious nature of his communications and the lawless character of the enemy's irregular troops infesting that region. He had strongly fortified his little camp, which embraced a village of a half-dozen dwellings and a country store, and had collected a considerable quantity of supplies. To a few resident civilians of known loyalty, with whom it was desirable to trade, and of whose services in various ways he sometimes availed himself, he had given written passes admitting them within his lines. It is easy to understand that an abuse of this privilege in the interest of the enemy might entail serious consequences. Captain Hartroy had made an order to the effect that any one so abusing it would be summarily shot.

While the sentinel had been examining the civilian's pass the captain had eyed the latter narrowly. He thought his appearance familiar and had at first no doubt of having given him the pass which had satisfied the sentinel. It was not until the man had got

out of sight and hearing that his identity was disclosed by a revealing light from memory. With soldierly promptness of decision the
officer had acted on the revelation.

III

To any but a singularly self-possessed man the apparition of an officer of the military forces, formidably clad, bearing in one hand a
sheathed sword and in the other a cocked revolver, and rushing in
furious pursuit, is no doubt disquieting to a high degree; upon the
man to whom the pursuit was in this instance directed it appeared to
have no other effect than somewhat to intensify his tranquillity. He
might easily enough have escaped into the forest to the right or the
left, but chose another course of action—turned and quietly faced
the captain, saying as he came up: "I reckon ye must have something
to say to me, which ye disremembered. What mout it be, neighbor?"

But the "neighbor" did not answer, being engaged in the un-
neighborly act of covering him with a cocked pistol.

"Surrender," said the captain as calmly as a slight breathlessness
from exertion would permit, "or you die."

There was no menace in the manner of this demand; that was all
in the matter and in the means of enforcing it. There was, too, something not altogether reassuring in the cold gray eyes that glanced
along the barrel of the weapon. For a moment the two men stood
looking at each other in silence; then the civilian, with no appearance of fear—with as great apparent unconcern as when complying
with the less austere demand of the sentinel—slowly pulled from
his pocket the paper which had satisfied that humble functionary
and held it out, saying:

"I reckon this 'ere parss from Mister Hartroy is——"

"The pass is a forgery," the officer said, interrupting. "I am Captain Hartroy—and you are Dramer Brune."

It would have required a sharp eye to observe the slight pallor of
the civilian's face at these words, and the only other manifestation
attesting their significance was a voluntary relaxation of the thumb
and fingers holding the dishonored paper, which, falling to the
road, unheeded, was rolled by a gentle wind and then lay still, with
a coating of dust, as in humiliation for the lie that it bore. A moment later the civilian, still looking unmoved into the barrel of the
pistol, said:

"Yes, I am Dramer Brune, a Confederate spy, and your prisoner.
I have on my person, as you will soon discover, a plan of your fort
and its armament, a statement of the distribution of your men and
their number, a map of the approaches, showing the positions of all
your outposts. My life is fairly yours, but if you wish it taken in a
more formal way than by your own hand, and if you are willing to
spare me the indignity of marching into camp at the muzzle of your
pistol, I promise you that I will neither resist, escape, nor remonstrate, but will submit to whatever penalty may be imposed."

The officer lowered his pistol, uncocked it, and thrust it into its
place in his belt. Brune advanced a step, extending his right hand.

"It is the hand of a traitor and a spy," said the officer coldly, and
did not take it. The other bowed.

"Come," said the captain, "let us go to camp; you shall not die
until to-morrow morning."

He turned his back upon his prisoner, and these two enigmatical
men retraced their steps and soon passed the sentinel, who expressed
his general sense of things by a needless and exaggerated salute to
his commander.

IV

Early on the morning after these events the two men, captor and
captive, sat in the tent of the former. A table was between them
on which lay, among a number of letters, official and private, which
the captain had written during the night, the incriminating papers
found upon the spy. That gentleman had slept through the night in
an adjoining tent, unguarded. Both, having breakfasted, were now
smoking.

"Mr. Brune," said Captain Hartroy, "you probably do not understand why I recognized you in your disguise, nor how I was
aware of your name."

"I have not sought to learn, Captain," the prisoner said with
quiet dignity.

"Nevertheless I should like you to know—if the story will not
offend. You will perceive that my knowledge of you goes back to
the autumn of 1861. At that time you were a private in an Ohio regiment—a brave and trusted soldier. To the surprise and grief of your
officers and comrades you deserted and went over to the enemy.
Soon afterward you were captured in a skirmish, recognized, tried

by court-martial and sentenced to be shot. Awaiting the execution of the sentence you were confined, unfettered, in a freight car standing on a side track of a railway."

"At Grafton, Virginia," said Brune, pushing the ashes from his cigar with the little finger of the hand holding it, and without looking up.

"At Grafton, Virginia," the captain repeated. "One dark and stormy night a soldier who had just returned from a long, fatiguing march was put on guard over you. He sat on a cracker box inside the car, near the door, his rifle loaded and the bayonet fixed. You sat in a corner and his orders were to kill you if you attempted to rise."

"But if I *asked* to rise he might call the corporal of the guard."

"Yes. As the long silent hours wore away the soldier yielded to the demands of nature: he himself incurred the death penalty by sleeping at his post of duty."

"You did."

"What! you recognize me? you have known me all along?"

The captain had risen and was walking the floor of his tent, visibly excited. His face was flushed, the gray eyes had lost the cold, pitiless look which they had shown when Brune had seen them over the pistol barrel; they had softened wonderfully.

"I knew you," said the spy, with his customary tranquillity, "the moment you faced me, demanding my surrender. In the circumstances it would have been hardly becoming in me to recall these matters. I am perhaps a traitor, certainly a spy; but I should not wish to seem a suppliant."

The captain had paused in his walk and was facing his prisoner. There was a singular huskiness in his voice as he spoke again.

"Mr. Brune, whatever your conscience may permit you to be, you saved my life at what you must have believed the cost of your own. Until I saw you yesterday when halted by my sentinel I believed you dead—thought that you had suffered the fate which through my own crime you might easily have escaped. You had only to step from the car and leave me to take your place before the firing-squad. You had a divine compassion. You pitied my fatigue. You let me sleep, watched over me, and as the time drew near for the relief-guard to come and detect me in my crime, you gently waked me. Ah, Brune, Brune, that was well done—that was great—that——"

The captain's voice failed him; the tears were running down his face and sparkled upon his beard and his breast. Resuming his seat at the table, he buried his face in his arms and sobbed. All else was silence.

Suddenly the clear warble of a bugle was heard sounding the "assembly." The captain started and raised his wet face from his arms; it had turned ghastly pale. Outside, in the sunlight, were heard the stir of the men falling into line; the voices of the sergeants calling the roll; the tapping of the drummers as they braced their drums. The captain spoke again:

"I ought to have confessed my fault in order to relate the story of your magnanimity; it might have procured you a pardon. A hundred times I resolved to do so, but shame prevented. Besides, your sentence was just and righteous. Well, Heaven forgive me! I said nothing, and my regiment was soon afterward ordered to Tennessee and I never heard about you."

"It was all right, sir," said Brune, without visible emotion; "I escaped and returned to my colors—the Confederate colors. I should like to add that before deserting from the Federal service I had earnestly asked a discharge, on the ground of altered convictions. I was answered by punishment."

"Ah, but if I had suffered the penalty of my crime—if you had not generously given me the life that I accepted without gratitude you would not be again in the shadow and imminence of death."

The prisoner started slightly and a look of anxiety came into his face. One would have said, too, that he was surprised. At that moment a lieutenant, the adjutant, appeared at the opening of the tent and saluted. "Captain," he said, "the battalion is formed."

Captain Hartroy had recovered his composure. He turned to the officer and said: "Lieutenant, go to Captain Graham and say that I direct him to assume command of the battalion and parade it outside the parapet. This gentleman is a deserter and a spy; he is to be shot to death in the presence of the troops. He will accompany you, unbound and unguarded."

While the adjutant waited at the door the two men inside the tent rose and exchanged ceremonious bows, Brune immediately retiring.

Half an hour later an old negro cook, the only person left in camp except the commander, was so startled by the sound of a volley of musketry that he dropped the kettle that he was lifting from a fire. But for his consternation and the hissing which the contents of the kettle made among the embers, he might also have heard, nearer at hand, the single pistol shot with which Captain Hartroy renounced the life which in conscience he could no longer keep.

In compliance with the terms of a note that he left for the officer who succeeded him in command, he was buried, like the deserter and spy, without military honors; and in the solemn shadow of the mountain which knows no more of war the two sleep well in long-forgotten graves.

One Kind of Officer

I

OF THE USES OF CIVILITY

"Captain Ransome, it is not permitted to you to know *anything*. It is sufficient that you obey my order—which permit me to repeat. If you perceive any movement of troops in your front you are to open fire, and if attacked hold this position as long as you can. Do I make myself understood, sir?"

"Nothing could be plainer. Lieutenant Price,"—this to an officer of his own battery, who had ridden up in time to hear the order—"the general's meaning is clear, is it not?"

"Perfectly."

The lieutenant passed on to his post. For a moment General Cameron and the commander of the battery sat in their saddles, looking at each other in silence. There was no more to say; apparently too much had already been said. Then the superior officer nodded coldly and turned his horse to ride away. The artillerist saluted slowly, gravely, and with extreme formality. One acquainted with the niceties of military etiquette would have said that by his manner he attested a sense of the rebuke that he had incurred. It is one of the important uses of civility to signify resentment.

When the general had joined his staff and escort, awaiting him at a little distance, the whole cavalcade moved off toward the right of the guns and vanished in the fog. Captain Ransome was alone, silent, motionless as an equestrian statue. The gray fog, thickening every moment, closed in about him like a visible doom.

II

UNDER WHAT CIRCUMSTANCES
MEN DO NOT WISH TO BE SHOT

The fighting of the day before had been desultory and indecisive. At the points of collision the smoke of battle had hung in blue sheets among the branches of the trees till beaten into nothing by the falling rain. In the softened earth the wheels of cannon and

ammunition wagons cut deep, ragged furrows, and movements of
infantry seemed impeded by the mud that clung to the soldiers' feet
as, with soaken garments and rifles imperfectly protected by capes
of overcoats they went dragging in sinuous lines hither and thither
through dripping forest and flooded field. Mounted officers, their
heads protruding from rubber ponchos that glittered like black armor, picked their way, singly and in loose groups, among the men,
coming and going with apparent aimlessness and commanding attention from nobody but one another. Here and there a dead man,
his clothing defiled with earth, his face covered with a blanket or
showing yellow and claylike in the rain, added his dispiriting influence to that of the other dismal features of the scene and augmented
the general discomfort with a particular dejection. Very repulsive
these wrecks looked—not at all heroic, and nobody was accessible
to the infection of their patriotic example. Dead upon the field of
honor, yes; but the field of honor was so very wet! It makes a difference.

The general engagement that all expected did not occur, none of
the small advantages accruing, now to this side and now to that, in
isolated and accidental collisions being followed up. Half-hearted
attacks provoked a sullen resistance which was satisfied with mere
repulse. Orders were obeyed with mechanical fidelity; no one did
any more than his duty.

"The army is cowardly to-day," said General Cameron, the
commander of a Federal brigade, to his adjutant-general.

"The army is cold," replied the officer addressed, "and—yes, it
doesn't wish to be like that."

He pointed to one of the dead bodies, lying in a thin pool of yellow water, its face and clothing bespattered with mud from hoof
and wheel.

The army's weapons seemed to share its military delinquency.
The rattle of rifles sounded flat and contemptible. It had no meaning and scarcely roused to attention and expectancy the unengaged
parts of the line-of-battle and the waiting reserves. Heard at a little
distance, the reports of cannon were feeble in volume and *timbre*:
they lacked sting and resonance. The guns seemed to be fired with
light charges, unshotted. And so the futile day wore on to its dreary
close, and then to a night of discomfort succeeded a day of apprehension.

An army has a personality. Beneath the individual thoughts and emotions of its component parts it thinks and feels as a unit. And in this large, inclusive sense of things lies a wiser wisdom than the mere sum of all that it knows. On that dismal morning this great brute force, groping at the bottom of a white ocean of fog among trees that seemed as sea weeds, had a dumb consciousness that all was not well; that a day's manœuvring had resulted in a faulty disposition of its parts, a blind diffusion of its strength. The men felt insecure and talked among themselves of such tactical errors as with their meager military vocabulary they were able to name. Field and line officers gathered in groups and spoke more learnedly of what they apprehended with no greater clearness. Commanders of brigades and divisions looked anxiously to their connections on the right and on the left, sent staff officers on errands of inquiry and pushed skirmish lines silently and cautiously forward into the dubious region between the known and the unknown. At some points on the line the troops, apparently of their own volition, constructed such defenses as they could without the silent spade and the noisy ax.

One of these points was held by Captain Ransome's battery of six guns. Provided always with intrenching tools, his men had labored with diligence during the night, and now his guns thrust their black muzzles through the embrasures of a really formidable earthwork. It crowned a slight acclivity devoid of undergrowth and providing an unobstructed fire that would sweep the ground for an unknown distance in front. The position could hardly have been better chosen. It had this peculiarity, which Captain Ransome, who was greatly addicted to the use of the compass, had not failed to observe: it faced northward, whereas he knew that the general line of the army must face eastward. In fact, that part of the line was "refused"—that is to say, bent backward, away from the enemy. This implied that Captain Ransome's battery was somewhere near the left flank of the army; for an army in line of battle retires its flanks if the nature of the ground will permit, they being its vulnerable points. Actually, Captain Ransome appeared to hold the extreme left of the line, no troops being visible in that direction beyond his own. Immediately in rear of his guns occurred that conversation between him and his brigade commander, the concluding and more picturesque part of which is reported above.

III

HOW TO PLAY THE CANNON WITHOUT NOTES

Captain Ransome sat motionless and silent on horseback. A few yards away his men were standing at their guns. Somewhere—everywhere within a few miles—were a hundred thousand men, friends and enemies. Yet he was alone. The mist had isolated him as completely as if he had been in the heart of a desert. His world was a few square yards of wet and trampled earth about the feet of his horse. His comrades in that ghostly domain were invisible and inaudible. These were conditions favorable to thought, and he was thinking. Of the nature of his thoughts his clear-cut handsome features yielded no attesting sign. His face was as inscrutable as that of the sphinx. Why should it have made a record which there was none to observe? At the sound of a footstep he merely turned his eyes in the direction whence it came; one of his sergeants, looking a giant in stature in the false perspective of the fog, approached, and when clearly defined and reduced to his true dimensions by propinquity, saluted and stood at attention.

"Well, Morris," said the officer, returning his subordinate's salute.

"Lieutenant Price directed me to tell you, sir, that most of the infantry has been withdrawn. We have not sufficient support."

"Yes, I know."

"I am to say that some of our men have been out over the works a hundred yards and report that our front is not picketed."

"Yes."

"They were so far forward that they heard the enemy."

"Yes."

"They heard the rattle of the wheels of artillery and the commands of officers."

"Yes."

"The enemy is moving toward our works."

Captain Ransome, who had been facing to the rear of his line—toward the point where the brigade commander and his cavalcade had been swallowed up by the fog—reined his horse about and faced the other way. Then he sat motionless as before.

"Who are the men who made that statement?" he inquired, without looking at the sergeant; his eyes were directed straight into the fog over the head of his horse.

"Corporal Hassman and Gunner Manning."

Captain Ransome was a moment silent. A slight pallor came into his face, a slight compression affected the lines of his lips, but it would have required a closer observer than Sergeant Morris to note the change. There was none in the voice.

"Sergeant, present my compliments to Lieutenant Price and direct him to open fire with all the guns. Grape."

The sergeant saluted and vanished in the fog.

IV

TO INTRODUCE GENERAL MASTERSON

Searching for his division commander, General Cameron and his escort had followed the line of battle for nearly a mile to the right of Ransome's battery, and there learned that the division commander had gone in search of the corps commander. It seemed that everybody was looking for his immediate superior—an ominous circumstance. It meant that nobody was quite at ease. So General Cameron rode on for another half-mile, where by good luck he met General Masterson, the division commander, returning.

"Ah, Cameron," said the higher officer, reining up, and throwing his right leg across the pommel of his saddle in a most unmilitary way—"anything up? Found a good position for your battery, I hope—if one place is better than another in a fog."

"Yes, general," said the other, with the greater dignity appropriate to his less exalted rank, "my battery is very well placed. I wish I could say that it is as well commanded."

"Eh, what's that? Ransome? I think him a fine fellow. In the army we should be proud of him."

It was customary for officers of the regular army to speak of it as "the army." As the greatest cities are most provincial, so the self-complacency of aristocracies is most frankly plebeian.

"He is too fond of his opinion. By the way, in order to occupy the hill that he holds I had to extend my line dangerously. The hill is on my left—that is to say the left flank of the army."

"Oh, no, Hart's brigade is beyond. It was ordered up from Drytown during the night and directed to hook on to you. Better go and——"

The sentence was unfinished: a lively cannonade had broken out on the left, and both officers, followed by their retinues of aides and orderlies making a great jingle and clank, rode rapidly toward the spot. But they were soon impeded, for they were compelled by the fog to keep within sight of the line-of-battle, behind which were swarms of men, all in motion across their way. Everywhere the line was assuming a sharper and harder definition, as the men sprang to arms and the officers, with drawn swords, "dressed" the ranks. Color-bearers unfurled the flags, buglers blew the "assembly," hospital attendants appeared with stretchers. Field officers mounted and sent their impedimenta to the rear in care of negro servants. Back in the ghostly spaces of the forest could be heard the rustle and murmur of the reserves, pulling themselves together.

Nor was all this preparation vain, for scarcely five minutes had passed since Captain Ransome's guns had broken the truce of doubt before the whole region was aroar: the enemy had attacked nearly everywhere.

V

HOW SOUNDS CAN FIGHT SHADOWS

Captain Ransome walked up and down behind his guns, which were firing rapidly but with steadiness. The gunners worked alertly, but without haste or apparent excitement. There was really no reason for excitement; it is not much to point a cannon into a fog and fire it. Anybody can do as much as that.

The men smiled at their noisy work, performing it with a lessening alacrity. They cast curious regards upon their captain, who had now mounted the banquette of the fortification and was looking across the parapet as if observing the effect of his fire. But the only visible effect was the substitution of wide, low-lying sheets of smoke for their bulk of fog. Suddenly out of the obscurity burst a great sound of cheering, which filled the intervals between the reports of the guns with startling distinctness! To the few with leisure and opportunity to observe, the sound was inexpressibly strange—so loud, so near, so menacing, yet nothing seen! The men who had smiled at their work smiled no more, but performed it with a serious and feverish activity.

From his station at the parapet Captain Ransome now saw a great multitude of dim gray figures taking shape in the mist below him and swarming up the slope. But the work of the guns was now fast and furious. They swept the populous declivity with gusts of grape and canister, the whirring of which could be heard through the thunder of the explosions. In this awful tempest of iron the assailants struggled forward foot by foot across their dead, firing into the embrasures, reloading, firing again, and at last falling in their turn, a little in advance of those who had fallen before. Soon the smoke was dense enough to cover all. It settled down upon the attack and, drifting back, involved the defense. The gunners could hardly see to serve their pieces, and when occasional figures of the enemy appeared upon the parapet—having had the good luck to get near enough to it, between two embrasures, to be protected from the guns—they looked so unsubstantial that it seemed hardly worth while for the few infantrymen to go to work upon them with the bayonet and tumble them back into the ditch.

As the commander of a battery in action can find something better to do than cracking individual skulls, Captain Ransome had retired from the parapet to his proper post in rear of his guns, where he stood with folded arms, his bugler beside him. Here, during the hottest of the fight, he was approached by Lieutenant Price, who had just sabred a daring assailant inside the work. A spirited colloquy ensued between the two officers—spirited, at least, on the part of the lieutenant, who gesticulated with energy and shouted again and again into his commander's ear in the attempt to make himself heard above the infernal din of the guns. His gestures, if coolly noted by an actor, would have been pronounced to be those of protestation: one would have said that he was opposed to the proceedings. Did he wish to surrender?

Captain Ransome listened without a change of countenance or attitude, and when the other man had finished his harangue, looked him coldly in the eyes and during a seasonable abatement of the uproar said:

"Lieutenant Price, it is not permitted to you to know *anything*. It is sufficient that you obey my orders."

The lieutenant went to his post, and the parapet being now apparently clear Captain Ransome returned to it to have a look over. As he mounted the banquette a man sprang upon the crest, waving a great brilliant flag. The captain drew a pistol from his belt and shot him dead. The body, pitching forward, hung over the inner edge of the embankment, the arms straight downward, both hands still grasping the flag. The man's few followers turned and fled down the slope. Looking over the parapet, the captain saw no living thing. He observed also that no bullets were coming into the work.

He made a sign to the bugler, who sounded the command to cease firing. At all other points the action had already ended with a repulse of the Confederate attack; with the cessation of this cannonade the silence was absolute.

VI

WHY, BEING AFFRONTED BY A, IT IS NOT BEST TO AFFRONT B

General Masterson rode into the redoubt. The men, gathered in groups, were talking loudly and gesticulating. They pointed at the dead, running from one body to another. They neglected their foul and heated guns and forgot to resume their outer clothing. They ran to the parapet and looked over, some of them leaping down into the ditch. A score were gathered about a flag rigidly held by a dead man.

"Well, my men," said the general cheerily, "you have had a pretty fight of it."

They stared; nobody replied; the presence of the great man seemed to embarrass and alarm.

Getting no response to his pleasant condescension, the easy-mannered officer whistled a bar or two of a popular air, and riding forward to the parapet, looked over at the dead. In an instant he had whirled his horse about and was spurring along in rear of the guns, his eyes everywhere at once. An officer sat on the trail of one of the guns, smoking a cigar. As the general dashed up he rose and tranquilly saluted.

"Captain Ransome!"—the words fell sharp and harsh, like the clash of steel blades—"you have been fighting our own men—our own men, sir; do you hear? Hart's brigade!"

"General, I know that."

"You know it—you know that, and you sit here smoking? Oh, damn it, Hamilton, I'm losing my temper,"—this to his provost-marshal. "Sir—Captain Ransome, be good enough to say—to say why you fought our own men."

"That I am unable to say. In my orders that information was withheld."

Apparently the general did not comprehend.

"Who was the aggressor in this affair, you or General Hart?" he asked.

"I was."

"And could you not have known—could you not see, sir, that you were attacking our own men?"

The reply was astounding!

"I knew that, general. It appeared to be none of my business."

Then, breaking the dead silence that followed his answer, he said: "I must refer you to General Cameron."

"General Cameron is dead, sir—as dead as he can be—as dead as any man in this army. He lies back yonder under a tree. Do you mean to say that he had anything to do with this horrible business?"

Captain Ransome did not reply. Observing the altercation his men had gathered about to watch the outcome. They were greatly excited. The fog, which had been partly dissipated by the firing, had again closed in so darkly about them that they drew more closely together till the judge on horseback and the accused standing calmly before him had but a narrow space free from intrusion. It was the most informal of courts-martial, but all felt that the formal one to follow would but affirm its judgment. It had no jurisdiction, but it had the significance of prophecy.

"Captain Ransome," the general cried impetuously, but with something in his voice that was almost entreaty, "if you can say anything to put a better light upon your incomprehensible conduct I beg you will do so."

Having recovered his temper this generous soldier sought for something to justify his naturally sympathetic attitude toward a brave man in the imminence of a dishonorable death.

"Where is Lieutenant Price?" the captain said.

That officer stood forward, his dark saturnine face looking somewhat forbidding under a bloody handkerchief bound about his brow. He understood the summons and needed no invitation to speak. He did not look at the captain, but addressed the general:

"During the engagement I discovered the state of affairs, and apprised the commander of the battery. I ventured to urge that the firing cease. I was insulted and ordered to my post."

"Do you know anything of the orders under which I was acting?" asked the captain.

"Of any orders under which the commander of the battery was acting," the lieutenant continued, still addressing the general, "I know nothing."

Captain Ransome felt his world sink away from his feet. In those cruel words he heard the murmur of the centuries breaking upon the shore of eternity. He heard the voice of doom; it said, in cold, mechanical, and measured tones: "Ready, aim, fire!" and he felt the bullets tear his heart to shreds. He heard the sound of the earth upon his coffin and (if the good God was so merciful) the song of a bird above his forgotten grave. Quietly detaching his sabre from its supports, he handed it up to the provost-marshal.

The Mocking-Bird

The time, a pleasant Sunday afternoon in the early autumn of 1861. The place, a forest's heart in the mountain region of southwestern Virginia. Private Grayrock of the Federal Army is discovered seated comfortably at the root of a great pine tree, against which he leans, his legs extended straight along the ground, his rifle lying across his thighs, his hands (clasped in order that they may not fall away to his sides) resting upon the barrel of the weapon. The contact of the back of his head with the tree has pushed his cap downward over his eyes, almost concealing them; one seeing him would say that he slept.

Private Grayrock did not sleep; to have done so would have imperiled the interests of the United States, for he was a long way outside the lines and subject to capture or death at the hands of the enemy. Moreover, he was in a frame of mind unfavorable to repose. The cause of his perturbation of spirit was this: during the previous night he had served on the picket-guard, and had been posted as a sentinel in this very forest. The night was clear, though moonless, but in the gloom of the wood the darkness was deep. Grayrock's post was at a considerable distance from those to right and left, for the pickets had been thrown out a needless distance from the camp, making the line too long for the force detailed to occupy it. The war was young, and military camps entertained the error that while sleeping they were better protected by thin lines a long way out toward the enemy than by thicker ones close in. And surely they needed as long notice as possible of an enemy's approach, for they were at that time addicted to the practice of undressing—than which nothing could be more unsoldierly. On the morning of the memorable 6th of April, at Shiloh, many of Grant's men when spitted on Confederate bayonets were as naked as civilians; but it should be allowed that this was not because of any defect in their picket line. Their error was of another sort: they had no pickets. This is perhaps a vain digression. I should not care to undertake to interest the reader in the fate of an army; what we have here to consider is that of Private Grayrock.

For two hours after he had been left at his lonely post that Saturday night he stood stock-still, leaning against the trunk of a large tree, staring into the darkness in his front and trying to recognize known objects; for he had been posted at the same spot during the day. But all was now different; he saw nothing in detail, but only groups of things, whose shapes, not observed when there was something more of them to observe, were now unfamiliar. They seemed not to have been there before. A landscape that is all trees and undergrowth, moreover, lacks definition, is confused and without accentuated points upon which attention can gain a foothold. Add the gloom of a moonless night, and something more than great natural intelligence and a city education is required to preserve one's knowledge of direction. And that is how it occurred that Private Grayrock, after vigilantly watching the spaces in his front and then imprudently executing a circumspection of his whole dimly visible environment (silently walking around his tree to accomplish it) lost his bearings and seriously impaired his usefulness as a sentinel. Lost at his post—unable to say in which direction to look for an enemy's approach, and in which lay the sleeping camp for whose security he was accountable with his life—conscious, too, of many another awkward feature of the situation and of considerations affecting his own safety, Private Grayrock was profoundly disquieted. Nor was he given time to recover his tranquillity, for almost at the moment that he realized his awkward predicament he heard a stir of leaves and a snap of fallen twigs, and turning with a stilled heart in the direction whence it came, saw in the gloom the indistinct outlines of a human figure.

"Halt!" shouted Private Grayrock, peremptorily as in duty bound, backing up the command with the sharp metallic snap of his cocking rifle—"who goes there?"

There was no answer; at least there was an instant's hesitation, and the answer, if it came, was lost in the report of the sentinel's rifle. In the silence of the night and the forest the sound was deafening, and hardly had it died away when it was repeated by the pieces of the pickets to right and left, a sympathetic fusillade. For two hours every unconverted civilian of them had been evolving enemies from his imagination, and peopling the woods in his front with them, and Grayrock's shot had started the whole encroaching host into visible existence. Having fired, all retreated, breathless, to the reserves—all but Grayrock, who did not know in what direction to retreat. When, no enemy appearing, the roused camp two miles away had undressed and got itself into bed again, and the picket line was cautiously re-established, he was discovered bravely holding his ground, and was complimented by the officer of the guard as the one soldier of that devoted band who could rightly be considered the moral equivalent of that uncommon unit of value, "a whoop in hell."

In the mean time, however, Grayrock had made a close but unavailing search for the mortal part of the intruder at whom he had fired, and whom he had a marksman's intuitive sense of having hit; for he was one of those born experts who shoot without aim by an instinctive sense of direction, and are nearly as dangerous by night as by day. During a full half of his twenty-four years he had been a terror to the targets of all the shooting-galleries in three cities. Unable now to produce his dead game he had the discretion to hold his tongue, and was glad to observe in his officer and comrades the natural assumption that not having run away he had seen nothing hostile. His "honorable mention" had been earned by not running away anyhow.

Nevertheless, Private Grayrock was far from satisfied with the night's adventure, and when the next day he made some fair enough pretext to apply for a pass to go outside the lines, and the general commanding promptly granted it in recognition of his bravery the night before, he passed out at the point where that had been displayed. Telling the sentinel then on duty there that he had lost something,—which was true enough—he renewed the search for the person whom he supposed himself to have shot, and whom if only wounded he hoped to trail by the blood. He was no more successful by daylight than he had been in the darkness, and after covering a wide area and boldly penetrating a long distance into "the Confederacy" he gave up the search, somewhat fatigued, seated himself at the root of the great pine tree, where we have seen him, and indulged his disappointment.

It is not to be inferred that Grayrock's was the chagrin of a cruel nature balked of its bloody deed. In the clear large eyes, finely wrought lips, and broad forehead of that young man one could read quite another story, and in point of fact his character was a singularly felicitous compound of boldness and sensibility, courage and conscience.

"I find myself disappointed," he said to himself, sitting there at the bottom of the golden haze submerging the forest like a subtler

sea—"disappointed in failing to discover a fellow-man dead by my
hand! Do I then really wish that I had taken life in the performance
of a duty as well performed without? What more could I wish? If
any danger threatened, my shot averted it; that is what I was there
to do. No, I am glad indeed if no human life was needlessly extinguished by me. But I am in a false position. I have suffered myself
to be complimented by my officers and envied by my comrades.
The camp is ringing with praise of my courage. That is not just; I
know myself courageous, but this praise is for specific acts which I
did not perform, or performed—otherwise. It is believed that I remained at my post bravely, without firing, whereas it was I who began the fusillade, and I did not retreat in the general alarm because
bewildered. What, then, shall I do? Explain that I saw an enemy and
fired? They have all said that of themselves, yet none believes it.
Shall I tell a truth which, discrediting my courage, will have the effect of a lie? Ugh! it is an ugly business altogether. I wish to God I
could find my man!"

And so wishing, Private Grayrock, overcome at last by the languor of the afternoon and lulled by the stilly sounds of insects
droning and prosing in certain fragrant shrubs, so far forgot the interests of the United States as to fall asleep and expose himself to
capture. And sleeping he dreamed.

He thought himself a boy, living in a far, fair land by the border
of a great river upon which the tall steamboats moved grandly
up and down beneath their towering evolutions of black smoke,
which announced them long before they had rounded the bends
and marked their movements when miles out of sight. With him always, at his side as he watched them, was one to whom he gave his
heart and soul in love—a twin brother. Together they strolled along
the banks of the stream; together explored the fields lying farther
away from it, and gathered pungent mints and sticks of fragrant sas-
safras in the hills overlooking all—beyond which lay the Realm of
Conjecture, and from which, looking southward across the great
river, they caught glimpses of the Enchanted Land. Hand in hand
and heart in heart they two, the only children of a widowed mother,
walked in paths of light through valleys of peace, seeing new things
under a new sun. And through all the golden days floated one unceasing sound—the rich, thrilling melody of a mocking-bird in a
cage by the cottage door. It pervaded and possessed all the spiritual
intervals of the dream, like a musical benediction. The joyous bird

was always in song; its infinitely various notes seemed to flow from its throat, effortless, in bubbles and rills at each heart-beat, like the waters of a pulsing spring. That fresh, clear melody seemed, indeed, the spirit of the scene, the meaning and interpretation to sense of the mysteries of life and love.

But there came a time when the days of the dream grew dark with sorrow in a rain of tears. The good mother was dead, the meadowside home by the great river was broken up, and the brothers were parted between two of their kinsmen. William (the dreamer) went to live in a populous city in the Realm of Conjecture, and John, crossing the river into the Enchanted Land, was taken to a distant region whose people in their lives and ways were said to be strange and wicked. To him, in the distribution of the dead mother's estate, had fallen all that they deemed of value—the mocking-bird. They could be divided, but it could not, so it was carried away into the strange country, and the world of William knew it no more forever. Yet still through the aftertime of his loneliness its song filled all the dream, and seemed always sounding in his ear and in his heart.

The kinsmen who had adopted the boys were enemies, holding no communication. For a time letters full of boyish bravado and boastful narratives of the new and larger experience—grotesque descriptions of their widening lives and the new worlds they had conquered—passed between them; but these gradually became less frequent, and with William's removal to another and greater city ceased altogether. But ever through it all ran the song of the mocking-bird, and when the dreamer opened his eyes and stared through the vistas of the pine forest the cessation of its music first apprised him that he was awake.

The sun was low and red in the west; the level rays projected from the trunk of each giant pine a wall of shadow traversing the golden haze to eastward until light and shade were blended in undistinguishable blue.

Private Grayrock rose to his feet, looked cautiously about him, shouldered his rifle and set off toward camp. He had gone perhaps a half-mile, and was passing a thicket of laurel, when a bird rose from the midst of it and perching on the branch of a tree above, poured from its joyous breast so inexhaustible floods of song as but one of all God's creatures can utter in His praise. There was little in that—it was only to open the bill and breathe; yet the man stopped as if struck—stopped and let fall his rifle, looked upward at the bird, covered his eyes with his hands and wept like a child! For the moment he was, indeed, a child, in spirit and in memory, dwelling again by the great river, over-against the Enchanted Land! Then with an effort of the will he pulled himself together, picked up his weapon and audibly damning himself for an idiot strode on. Passing an opening that reached into the heart of the little thicket he looked in, and there, supine upon the earth, its arms all abroad, its gray uniform stained with a single spot of blood upon the breast, its white face turned sharply upward and backward, lay the image of himself!—the body of John Grayrock, dead of a gunshot wound, and still warm! He had found his man.

As the unfortunate soldier knelt beside that masterwork of civil war the shrilling bird upon the bough overhead stilled her song and, flushed with sunset's crimson glory, glided silently away through the solemn spaces of the wood. At roll-call that evening in the Federal camp the name William Grayrock brought no response, nor ever again thereafter.

CIVILIANS

The Man Out of the Nose

At the intersection of two certain streets in that part of San Francisco known by the rather loosely applied name of North Beach,[30] is a vacant lot, which is rather more nearly level than is usually the case with lots, vacant or otherwise, in that region. Immediately at the back of it, to the south, however, the ground slopes steeply upward, the acclivity broken by three terraces cut into the soft rock. It is a place for goats and poor persons, several families of each class having occupied it jointly and amicably "from the foundation of the city." One of the humble habitations of the lowest terrace is noticeable for its rude resemblance to the human face, or rather to such a simulacrum of it as a boy might cut out of a hollowed pumpkin, meaning no offense to his race. The eyes are two circular windows, the nose is a door, the mouth an aperture caused by removal of a board below. There are no doorsteps. As a face, this house is too large; as a dwelling, too small. The blank, unmeaning stare of its lidless and browless eyes is uncanny.

Sometimes a man steps out of the nose, turns, passes the place where the right ear should be and making his way through the throng of children and goats obstructing the narrow walk between his neighbors' doors and the edge of the terrace gains the street by descending a flight of rickety stairs. Here he pauses to consult his watch and the stranger who happens to pass wonders why such a man as that can care what is the hour. Longer observations would show that the time of day is an important element in the man's movements, for it is at precisely two o'clock in the afternoon that he comes forth 365 times in every year.

Having satisfied himself that he has made no mistake in the hour he replaces the watch and walks rapidly southward up the street two squares, turns to the right and as he approaches the next corner fixes his eyes on an upper window in a three-story building across the way. This is a somewhat dingy structure, originally of red brick and now gray. It shows the touch of age and dust. Built for a dwelling, it is now a factory. I do not know what is made there; the things that are commonly made in a factory, I suppose. I only know that at two o'clock in the afternoon of every day but Sunday it is full of activity and clatter; pulsations of some great engine shake it and there are recurrent screams of wood tormented by the saw. At the window on which the man fixes an intensely expectant gaze nothing ever appears; the glass, in truth, has such a coating of dust that it has long ceased to be transparent. The man looks at it without stopping; he merely keeps turning his head more and more backward as he leaves the building behind. Passing along to the next corner, he turns to the left, goes round the block, and comes back till he reaches the point diagonally across the street from the factory—a point on his former course, which he then retraces, looking frequently backward over his right shoulder at the window while it is in sight. For many years he has not been known to vary his route nor to introduce a single innovation into his action. In a quarter of an hour he is again at the mouth of his dwelling, and a woman, who has for some time been standing in the nose, assists him to enter. He is seen no more until two o'clock the next day.

The woman is his wife. She supports herself and him by washing for the poor people among whom they live, at rates which destroy Chinese and domestic competition.

This man is about fifty-seven years of age, though he looks greatly older. His hair is dead white. He wears no beard, and is always newly shaven. His hands are clean, his nails well kept. In the matter of dress he is distinctly superior to his position, as indicated by his surroundings and the business of his wife. He is, indeed, very neatly, if not quite fashionably, clad. His silk hat has a date no earlier than the year before the last, and his boots, scrupulously polished, are innocent of patches. I am told that the suit which he wears during his daily excursions of fifteen minutes is not the one that he wears at home. Like everything else that he has, this is provided and kept in repair by the wife, and is renewed as frequently as her scanty means permit.

Thirty years ago John Hardshaw and his wife lived on Rincon Hill[31] in one of the finest residences of that once aristocratic quarter. He had once been a physician, but having inherited a considerable estate from his father concerned himself no more about the ailments of his fellow-creatures and found as much work as he cared for in managing his own affairs. Both he and his wife were highly cultivated persons, and their house was frequented by a small set of such men and women as persons of their tastes would think worth knowing. So far as these knew, Mr. and Mrs. Hard-shaw lived happily together; certainly the wife was devoted to her handsome and accomplished husband and exceedingly proud of him.

Among their acquaintances were the Barwells—man, wife and two young children—of Sacramento. Mr. Barwell was a civil and mining engineer, whose duties took him much from home and frequently to San Francisco. On these occasions his wife commonly accompanied him and passed much of her time at the house of her friend, Mrs. Hardshaw, always with her two children, of whom Mrs. Hardshaw, childless herself, grew fond. Unluckily, her husband grew equally fond of their mother—a good deal fonder. Still more unluckily, that attractive lady was less wise than weak.

At about three o'clock one autumn morning Officer No. 13 of the Sacramento police saw a man stealthily leaving the rear entrance of a gentleman's residence and promptly arrested him. The man—who wore a slouch hat and shaggy overcoat—offered the policeman one hundred, then five hundred, then one thousand dollars to be released. As he had less than the first mentioned sum on his person the officer treated his proposal with virtuous contempt. Before reaching the station the prisoner agreed to give him a check for ten thousand dollars and remain ironed in the willows along the river bank until it should be paid. As this only provoked new derision he would say no more, merely giving an obviously fictitious name. When he was searched at the station nothing of value was found on him but a miniature portrait of Mrs. Barwell—the lady of the house at which he was caught. The case was set with costly diamonds; and something in the quality of the man's linen sent a pang of unavailing regret through the severely incorruptible bosom of Officer No. 13. There was nothing about the prisoner's clothing nor person to identify him and he was booked for burglary under the name that he had given, the honorable name of John K. Smith. The K. was an inspiration upon which, doubtless, he greatly prided himself.

In the mean time the mysterious disappearance of John Hardshaw was agitating the gossips of Rincon Hill in San Francisco, and was even mentioned in one of the newspapers. It did not occur to the lady whom that journal considerately described as his "widow," to look for him in the city prison at Sacramento—a town which he was not known ever to have visited. As John K. Smith he was arraigned and, waiving examination, committed for trial.

About two weeks before the trial, Mrs. Hardshaw, accidentally learning that her husband was held in Sacramento under an assumed name on a charge of burglary, hastened to that city without daring to mention the matter to any one and presented herself at the prison, asking for an interview with her husband, John K. Smith. Haggard and ill with anxiety, wearing a plain traveling wrap which covered her from neck to foot, and in which she had passed the night on the steamboat, too anxious to sleep, she hardly showed for what she was, but her manner pleaded for her more strongly than anything that she chose to say in evidence of her right to admittance. She was permitted to see him alone.

What occurred during that distressing interview has never transpired; but later events prove that Hardshaw had found means to subdue her will to his own. She left the prison, a broken-hearted woman, refusing to answer a single question, and returning to her desolate home renewed, in a half-hearted way, her inquiries for her missing husband. A week later she was herself missing: she had "gone back to the States"—nobody knew any more than that.

On his trial the prisoner pleaded guilty—"by advice of his counsel," so his counsel said. Nevertheless, the judge, in whose mind several unusual circumstances had created a doubt, insisted on the district attorney placing Officer No. 13 on the stand, and the deposition of Mrs. Barwell, who was too ill to attend, was read to the jury. It was very brief: she knew nothing of the matter except that the likeness of herself was her property, and had, she thought, been left on the parlor table when she had retired on the night of the arrest. She had intended it as a present to her husband, then and still absent in Europe on business for a mining company.

This witness's manner when making the deposition at her residence was afterward described by the district attorney as most extraordinary. Twice she had refused to testify, and once, when the deposition lacked nothing but her signature, she had caught it from the clerk's hands and torn it in pieces. She had called her children to the bedside and embraced them with streaming eyes, then suddenly sending them from the room, she verified her statement by oath and signature, and fainted—"slick away," said the district attorney. It was at that time that her physician, arriving upon the scene, took in the situation at a glance and grasping the representative of the law by the collar chucked him into the street and kicked his assistant after him. The insulted majesty of the law was not vindicated; the victim of the indignity did not even mention anything of all this in court. He was ambitious to win his case, and the circumstances of the taking of that deposition were not such as would give it weight if related; and after all, the man on trial had committed an offense against the law's majesty only less heinous than that of the irascible physician.

By suggestion of the judge the jury rendered a verdict of guilty; there was nothing else to do, and the prisoner was sentenced to the penitentiary for three years. His counsel, who had objected to nothing and had made no plea for lenity—had, in fact, hardly said a word—wrung his client's hand and left the room. It was obvious to the whole bar that he had been engaged only to prevent the court from appointing counsel who might possibly insist on making a defense.

John Hardshaw served out his term at San Quentin, and when discharged was met at the prison gates by his wife, who had returned from "the States" to receive him. It is thought they went straight to Europe; anyhow, a general power-of-attorney to a lawyer still living among us—from whom I have many of the facts of this simple history—was executed in Paris. This lawyer in a short time sold everything that Hardshaw owned in California, and for years nothing was heard of the unfortunate couple; though many to whose ears had come vague and inaccurate intimations of their strange story, and who had known them, recalled their personality with tenderness and their misfortunes with compassion.

Some years later they returned, both broken in fortune and spirits and he in health. The purpose of their return I have not been able to ascertain. For some time they lived, under the name of Johnson, in a respectable enough quarter south of Market Street, pretty well out, and were never seen away from the vicinity of their dwelling. They must have had a little money left, for it is not known that the man had any occupation, the state of his health probably not permitting. The woman's devotion to her invalid husband was matter of remark among their neighbors; she seemed never absent from his side and always supporting and cheering him. They would sit for hours on one of the benches in a little public park, she reading to him, his hand in hers, her light touch occasionally visiting his pale brow, her still beautiful eyes frequently lifted from the book to look into his as she made some comment on the text, or closed the volume to beguile his mood with talk of—what? Nobody ever

overheard a conversation between these two. The reader who has
had the patience to follow their history to this point may possibly
find a pleasure in conjecture: there was probably something to be
avoided. The bearing of the man was one of profound dejection; indeed, the unsympathetic youth of the neighborhood, with that keen
sense for visible characteristics which ever distinguishes the young
male of our species, sometimes mentioned him among themselves
by the name of Spoony Glum.

It occurred one day that John Hardshaw was possessed by the
spirit of unrest. God knows what led him whither he went, but
he crossed Market Street and held his way northward over the
hills, and downward into the region known as North Beach. Turning aimlessly to the left he followed his toes along an unfamiliar
street until he was opposite what for that period was a rather grand
dwelling, and for this is a rather shabby factory. Casting his eyes casually upward he saw at an open window what it had been better
that he had not seen—the face and figure of Elvira Barwell. Their
eyes met. With a sharp exclamation, like the cry of a startled bird,
the lady sprang to her feet and thrust her body half out of the window, clutching the casing on each side. Arrested by the cry, the
people in the street below looked up. Hardshaw stood motionless,
speechless, his eyes two flames. "Take care!" shouted some one in
the crowd, as the woman strained further and further forward, de-
fying the silent, implacable law of gravitation, as once she had
defied that other law which God thundered from Sinai.[32] The suddenness of her movements had tumbled a torrent of dark hair down
her shoulders, and now it was blown about her cheeks, almost concealing her face. A moment so, and then—! A fearful cry rang
through the street, as, losing her balance, she pitched headlong from
the window, a confused and whirling mass of skirts, limbs, hair, and
white face, and struck the pavement with a horrible sound and a
force of impact that was felt a hundred feet away. For a moment all
eyes refused their office and turned from the sickening spectacle on
the sidewalk. Drawn again to that horror, they saw it strangely augmented. A man, hatless, seated flat upon the paving stones, held the
broken, bleeding body against his breast, kissing the mangled
cheeks and streaming mouth through tangles of wet hair, his own
features indistinguishably crimson with the blood that half-
strangled him and ran in rills from his soaken beard.

The reporter's task is nearly finished. The Barwells had that very morning returned from a two years' absence in Peru. A week later the widower, now doubly desolate, since there could be no missing the significance of Hardshaw's horrible demonstration, had sailed for I know not what distant port; he has never come back to stay. Hardshaw—as Johnson no longer—passed a year in the Stockton asylum for the insane, where also, through the influence of pitying friends, his wife was admitted to care for him. When he was discharged, not cured but harmless, they returned to the city; it would seem ever to have had some dreadful fascination for them. For a time they lived near the Mission Dolores,[33] in poverty only less abject than that which is their present lot; but it was too far away from the objective point of the man's daily pilgrimage. They could not afford car fare. So that poor devil of an angel from Heaven—wife to this convict and lunatic—obtained, at a fair enough rental, the blank-faced shanty on the lower terrace of Goat Hill.[34] Thence to the structure that was a dwelling and is a factory the distance is not so great; it is, in fact, an agreeable walk, judging from the man's eager and cheerful look as he takes it. The return journey appears to be a trifle wearisome.

The Man and the Snake

*It is of veritabyll report, and attested of so many that
there be nowe of wyse and learned none to gaynsaye it, that y^e
serpente hys eye hath a magnetick propertie that whosoe
falleth into its svasion is drawn forwards in despyte of
his wille, and perisheth miserabyll by ye creature hys byte.*

Stretched at ease upon a sofa, in gown and slippers, Harker Brayton
smiled as he read the foregoing sentence in old Morryster's *Marvells of Science*.[35] "The only marvel in the matter," he said to himself, "is that the wise and learned in Morryster's day should have
believed such nonsense as is rejected by most of even the ignorant
in ours."

A train of reflection followed—for Brayton was a man of
thought—and he unconsciously lowered his book without altering
the direction of his eyes. As soon as the volume had gone below the
line of sight, something in an obscure corner of the room recalled
his attention to his surroundings. What he saw, in the shadow under his bed, was two small points of light, apparently about an inch
apart. They might have been reflections of the gas jet above him, in
metal nail heads; he gave them but little thought and resumed his
reading. A moment later something—some impulse which it did
not occur to him to analyze—impelled him to lower the book again
and seek for what he saw before. The points of light were still there.
They seemed to have become brighter than before, shining with a
greenish lustre that he had not at first observed. He thought, too,
that they might have moved a trifle—were somewhat nearer. They
were still too much in shadow, however, to reveal their nature and
origin to an indolent attention, and again he resumed his reading.
Suddenly something in the text suggested a thought that made him
start and drop the book for the third time to the side of the sofa,
whence, escaping from his hand, it fell sprawling to the floor, back
upward. Brayton, half-risen, was staring intently into the obscurity
beneath the bed, where the points of light shone with, it seemed to
him, an added fire. His attention was now fully aroused, his gaze

eager and imperative. It disclosed, almost directly under the foot-rail of the bed, the coils of a large serpent—the points of light were its eyes! Its horrible head, thrust flatly forth from the innermost coil and resting upon the outermost, was directed straight toward him, the definition of the wide, brutal jaw and the idiot-like fore-head serving to show the direction of its malevolent gaze. The eyes were no longer merely luminous points; they looked into his own with a meaning, a malign significance.

II

A snake in a bedroom of a modern city dwelling of the better sort is, happily, not so common a phenomenon as to make explanation altogether needless. Harker Brayton, a bachelor of thirty-five, a scholar, idler and something of an athlete, rich, popular and of sound health, had returned to San Francisco from all manner of re-mote and unfamiliar countries. His tastes, always a trifle luxurious, had taken on an added exuberance from long privation; and the re-sources of even the Castle Hotel being inadequate to their perfect gratification, he had gladly accepted the hospitality of his friend, Dr. Druring, the distinguished scientist. Dr. Druring's house, a large, old-fashioned one in what is now an obscure quarter of the city, had an outer and visible aspect of proud reserve. It plainly would not associate with the contiguous elements of its altered environment, and appeared to have developed some of the eccentricities which come of isolation. One of these was a "wing," conspicuously irrelevant in point of architecture, and no less rebellious in matter of purpose; for it was a combination of laboratory, menagerie and museum. It was here that the doctor indulged the scientific side of his nature in the study of such forms of animal life as engaged his interest and comforted his taste—which, it must be confessed, ran rather to the lower types. For one of the higher nimbly and sweetly to recommend itself unto his gentle senses it had at least to retain certain rudimentary characteristics allying it to such "dragons of the prime" as toads and snakes. His scientific sympathies were distinctly reptilian; he loved nature's vulgarians and described himself as the Zola[36] of zoölogy. His wife and daughters not having the advantage to share his enlightened curiosity regarding the works and ways of our ill-starred fellow-creatures, were with needless austerity excluded from what he called the

Snakery and doomed to companionship with their own kind, though to soften the rigors of their lot he had permitted them out of his great wealth to outdo the reptiles in the gorgeousness of their surroundings and to shine with a superior splendor.

Architecturally and in point of "furnishing" the Snakery had a severe simplicity befitting the humble circumstances of its occupants, many of whom, indeed, could not safely have been intrusted with the liberty that is necessary to the full enjoyment of luxury, for they had the troublesome peculiarity of being alive. In their own apartments, however, they were under as little personal restraint as was compatible with their protection from the baneful habit of swallowing one another; and, as Brayton had thoughtfully been appraised, it was more than a tradition that some of them had at divers times been found in parts of the premises where it would have embarrassed them to explain their presence. Despite the Snakery and its uncanny associations—to which, indeed, he gave little attention—Brayton found life at the Druring mansion very much to his mind.

III

Beyond a smart shock of surprise and a shudder of mere loathing Mr. Brayton was not greatly affected. His first thought was to ring the call bell and bring a servant; but although the bell cord dangled within easy reach he made no movement toward it; it had occurred to his mind that the act might subject him to the suspicion of fear, which he certainly did not feel. He was more keenly conscious of the incongruous nature of the situation than affected by its perils; it was revolting, but absurd.

The reptile was of a species with which Brayton was unfamiliar. Its length he could only conjecture; the body at the largest visible part seemed about as thick as his forearm. In what way was it dangerous, if in any way? Was it venomous? Was it a constrictor? His knowledge of nature's danger signals did not enable him to say; he had never deciphered the code.

If not dangerous the creature was at least offensive. It was *de trop*[37]—"matter out of place"—an impertinence. The gem was unworthy of the setting. Even the barbarous taste of our time and country, which had loaded the walls of the room with pictures, the floor with furniture and the furniture with bric-a-brac, had not quite fitted the place for this bit of the savage life of the jungle. Besides—insupportable thought!—the exhalations of its breath mingled with the atmosphere which he himself was breathing.

These thoughts shaped themselves with greater or less definition in Brayton's mind and begot action. The process is what we call consideration and decision. It is thus that we are wise and unwise. It is thus that the withered leaf in an autumn breeze shows greater or less intelligence than its fellows, falling upon the land or upon the lake. The secret of human action is an open one: something contracts our muscles. Does it matter if we give to the preparatory molecular changes the name of will?

Brayton rose to his feet and prepared to back softly away from the snake, without disturbing it if possible, and through the door. Men retire so from the presence of the great, for greatness is power and power is a menace. He knew that he could walk backward without error. Should the monster follow, the taste which had plastered the walls with paintings had consistently supplied a rack of murderous Oriental weapons from which he could snatch one to suit the occasion. In the mean time the snake's eyes burned with a more pitiless malevolence than before.

Brayton lifted his right foot free of the floor to step backward. That moment he felt a strong aversion to doing so.

"I am accounted brave," he thought; "is bravery, then, no more than pride? Because there are none to witness the shame shall I retreat?"

He was steadying himself with his right hand upon the back of a chair, his foot suspended.

"Nonsense!" he said aloud; "I am not so great a coward as to fear to seem to myself afraid."

He lifted the foot a little higher by slightly bending the knee and thrust it sharply to the floor—an inch in front of the other! He could not think how that occurred. A trial with the left foot had the same result; it was again in advance of the right. The hand upon the chair back was grasping it; the arm was straight, reaching somewhat backward. One might have said that he was reluctant to lose his hold. The snake's malignant head was still thrust forth from the inner coil as before, the neck level. It had not moved, but its eyes were now electric sparks, radiating an infinity of luminous needles.

The man had an ashy pallor. Again he took a step forward, and another, partly dragging the chair, which when finally released fell upon the floor with a crash. The man groaned; the snake made neither sound nor motion, but its eyes were two dazzling suns. The reptile itself was wholly concealed by them. They gave off enlarging rings of rich and vivid colors, which at their greatest expansion successively vanished like soap-bubbles; they seemed to approach his very face, and anon were an immeasurable distance away. He heard, somewhere, the continuous throbbing of a great drum, with desultory bursts of far music, inconceivably sweet, like the tones of an æolian harp.[38] He knew it for the sunrise melody of Memnon's statue,[39] and thought he stood in the Nileside reeds hearing with exalted sense that immortal anthem through the silence of the centuries.

The music ceased; rather, it became by insensible degrees the distant roll of a retreating thunder-storm. A landscape, glittering with sun and rain, stretched before him, arched with a vivid rainbow framing in its giant curve a hundred visible cities. In the middle distance a vast serpent, wearing a crown, reared its head out of its voluminous convolutions and looked at him with his dead mother's eyes. Suddenly this enchanting landscape seemed to rise swiftly upward like the drop scene at a theatre, and vanished in a blank. Something struck him a hard blow upon the face and breast. He had fallen to the floor; the blood ran from his broken nose and his bruised lips. For a time he was dazed and stunned, and lay with closed eyes, his face against the floor. In a few moments he had recovered, and then knew that this fall, by withdrawing his eyes, had broken the spell that held him. He felt that now, by keeping his gaze averted, he would be able to retreat. But the thought of the serpent within a few feet of his head, yet unseen—perhaps in the very act of springing upon him and throwing its coils about his throat—was too horrible! He lifted his head, stared again into those baleful eyes and was again in bondage.

The snake had not moved and appeared somewhat to have lost its power upon the imagination; the gorgeous illusions of a few moments before were not repeated. Beneath that flat and brainless brow its black, beady eyes simply glittered as at first with an expression unspeakably malignant. It was as if the creature, assured of its triumph, had determined to practise no more alluring wiles.

Now ensued a fearful scene. The man, prone upon the floor, within a yard of his enemy, raised the upper part of his body upon his elbows, his head thrown back, his legs extended to their full

length. His face was white between its stains of blood; his eyes were
strained open to their uttermost expansion. There was froth upon
his lips; it dropped off in flakes. Strong convulsions ran through his
body, making almost serpentile undulations. He bent himself at
the waist, shifting his legs from side to side. And every movement
left him a little nearer to the snake. He thrust his hands forward to
brace himself back, yet constantly advanced upon his elbows.

IV

Dr. Druring and his wife sat in the library. The scientist was in rare
good humor.

"I have just obtained by exchange with another collector," he
said, "a splendid specimen of the *ophiophagus.*"[40]

"And what may that be?" the lady inquired with a somewhat
languid interest.

"Why, bless my soul, what profound ignorance! My dear, a man
who ascertains after marriage that his wife does not know Greek is
entitled to a divorce. The *ophiophagus* is a snake that eats other
snakes."

"I hope it will eat all yours," she said, absently shifting the lamp.
"But how does it get the other snakes? By charming them, I
suppose."

"That is just like you, dear," said the doctor, with an affectation
of petulance. "You know how irritating to me is any allusion to that
vulgar superstition about a snake's power of fascination."

The conversation was interrupted by a mighty cry, which rang
through the silent house like the voice of a demon shouting in a
tomb! Again and yet again it sounded, with terrible distinctness.
They sprang to their feet, the man confused, the lady pale and
speechless with fright. Almost before the echoes of the last cry had
died away the doctor was out of the room, springing up the stairs
two steps at a time. In the corridor in front of Brayton's chamber he
met some servants who had come from the upper floor. Together
they rushed at the door without knocking. It was unfastened and
gave way. Brayton lay upon his stomach on the floor, dead. His
head and arms were partly concealed under the foot-rail of the bed.
They pulled the body away, turning it upon the back. The face was
daubed with blood and froth, the eyes were wide open, staring—a
dreadful sight!

"Died in a fit," said the scientist, bending his knee and placing his hand upon the heart. While in that position, he chanced to look under the bed. "Good God!" he added, "how did this thing get in here?"

He reached under the bed, pulled out the snake and flung it, still coiled, to the center of the room, whence with a harsh, shuffling sound it slid across the polished floor till stopped by the wall, where it lay without motion. It was a stuffed snake; its eyes were two shoe buttons.

The Boarded Window

In 1830, only a few miles away from what is now the great city of Cincinnati, lay an immense and almost unbroken forest. The whole region was sparsely settled by people of the frontier—restless souls who no sooner had hewn fairly habitable homes out of the wilderness and attained to that degree of prosperity which to-day we should call indigence than impelled by some mysterious impulse of their nature they abandoned all and pushed farther westward, to encounter new perils and privations in the effort to regain the meagre comforts which they had voluntarily renounced. Many of them had already forsaken that region for the remoter settlements, but among those remaining was one who had been of those first arriving. He lived alone in a house of logs surrounded on all sides by the great forest, of whose gloom and silence he seemed a part, for no one had ever known him to smile nor speak a needless word. His simple wants were supplied by the sale or barter of skins of wild animals in the river town, for not a thing did he grow upon the land which, if needful, he might have claimed by right of undisturbed possession. There were evidences of "improvement"—a few acres of ground immediately about the house had once been cleared of its trees, the decayed stumps of which were half concealed by the new growth that had been suffered to repair the ravage wrought by the ax. Apparently the man's zeal for agriculture had burned with a failing flame, expiring in penitential ashes.

The little log house, with its chimney of sticks, its roof of warping clapboards weighted with traversing poles and its "chinking" of clay, had a single door and, directly opposite, a window. The latter, however, was boarded up—nobody could remember a time when it was not. And none knew why it was so closed; certainly not because of the occupant's dislike of light and air, for on those rare occasions when a hunter had passed that lonely spot the recluse had commonly been seen sunning himself on his doorstep if heaven had provided sunshine for his need. I fancy there are few persons living to-day who ever knew the secret of that window, but I am one, as you shall see.

The man's name was said to be Murlock. He was apparently

seventy years old, actually about fifty. Something besides years had had a hand in his aging. His hair and long, full beard were white, his gray, lustreless eyes sunken, his face singularly seamed with wrinkles which appeared to belong to two intersecting systems. In figure he was tall and spare, with a stoop of the shoulders—a burden bearer. I never saw him; these particulars I learned from my grandfather, from whom also I got the man's story when I was a lad. He had known him when living near by in that early day.

One day Murlock was found in his cabin, dead. It was not a time and place for coroners and newspapers, and I suppose it was agreed that he had died from natural causes or I should have been told, and should remember. I know only that with what was probably a sense of the fitness of things the body was buried near the cabin, alongside the grave of his wife, who had preceded him by so many years that local tradition had retained hardly a hint of her existence. That closes the final chapter of this true story—excepting, indeed, the circumstance that many years afterward, in company with an equally intrepid spirit, I penetrated to the place and ventured near enough to the ruined cabin to throw a stone against it, and ran away to avoid the ghost which every well-informed boy thereabout knew haunted the spot. But there is an earlier chapter—that supplied by my grandfather.

When Murlock built his cabin and began laying sturdily about with his ax to hew out a farm—the rifle, meanwhile, his means of support—he was young, strong and full of hope. In that eastern country whence he came he had married, as was the fashion, a young woman in all ways worthy of his honest devotion, who shared the dangers and privations of his lot with a willing spirit and light heart. There is no known record of her name; of her charms of mind and person tradition is silent and the doubter is at liberty to entertain his doubt; but God forbid that I should share it! Of their affection and happiness there is abundant assurance in every added day of the man's widowed life; for what but the magnetism of a blessed memory could have chained that venturesome spirit to a lot like that?

One day Murlock returned from gunning in a distant part of the forest to find his wife prostrate with fever, and delirious. There was no physician within miles, no neighbor; nor was she in a condition to be left, to summon help. So he set about the task of nursing her back to health, but at the end of the third day she fell into unconsciousness and so passed away, apparently, with never a gleam of returning reason.

From what we know of a nature like his we may venture to sketch in some of the details of the outline picture drawn by my grandfather. When convinced that she was dead, Murlock had sense enough to remember that the dead must be prepared for burial. In performance of this sacred duty he blundered now and again, did certain things incorrectly, and others which he did correctly were done over and over. His occasional failures to accomplish some simple and ordinary act filled him with astonishment, like that of a drunken man who wonders at the suspension of familiar natural laws. He was surprised, too, that he did not weep—surprised and a little ashamed; surely it is unkind not to weep for the dead. "To-morrow," he said aloud, "I shall have to make the coffin and dig the grave; and then I shall miss her, when she is no longer in sight; but now—she is dead, of course, but it is all right—it *must* be all right, somehow. Things cannot be so bad as they seem."

He stood over the body in the fading light, adjusting the hair and putting the finishing touches to the simple toilet, doing all mechanically, with soulless care. And still through his consciousness ran an undersense of conviction that all was right—that he should have her again as before, and everything explained. He had had no experience in grief; his capacity had not been enlarged by use. His heart could not contain it all, nor his imagination rightly conceive it. He did not know he was so hard struck; *that* knowledge would come later, and never go. Grief is an artist of powers as various as the instruments upon which he plays his dirges for the dead, evoking from some the sharpest, shrillest notes, from others the low, grave chords that throb recurrent like the slow beating of a distant drum. Some natures it startles; some it stupefies. To one it comes like the stroke of an arrow, stinging all the sensibilities to a keener life; to another as the blow of a bludgeon, which in crushing benumbs. We may conceive Murlock to have been that way affected, for (and here we are upon surer ground than that of conjecture) no sooner had he finished his pious work than, sinking into a chair by the side of the table upon which the body lay, and noting how white the profile showed in the deepening gloom, he laid his arms upon the table's edge, and dropped his face into them, tearless yet and unutterably weary. At that moment came in through the open window a long, wailing sound like the cry of a lost child in the far deeps of the darkening wood! But the man did not move. Again, and nearer than before, sounded that unearthly cry upon his failing sense. Perhaps it was a wild beast; perhaps it was a dream. For Murlock was asleep.

Some hours later, as it afterward appeared, this unfaithful watcher awoke and lifting his head from his arms intently listened—he knew not why. There in the black darkness by the side of the dead, recalling all without a shock, he strained his eyes to see—he knew not what. His senses were all alert, his breath was suspended, his blood had stilled its tides as if to assist the silence. Who—what had waked him, and where was it?

Suddenly the table shook beneath his arms, and at the same moment he heard or fancied that he heard, a light, soft step—another—sounds as of bare feet upon the floor!

He was terrified beyond the power to cry out or move. Perforce he waited—waited there in the darkness through seeming centuries of such dread as one may know, yet live to tell. He tried vainly to speak the dead woman's name, vainly to stretch forth his hand across the table to learn if she were there. His throat was powerless, his arms and hands were like lead. Then occurred something most frightful. Some heavy body seemed hurled against the table with an impetus that pushed it against his breast so sharply as nearly to overthrow him, and at the same instant he heard and felt the fall of something upon the floor with so violent a thump that the whole house was shaken by the impact. A scuffling ensued, and a confusion of sounds impossible to describe. Murlock had risen to his feet. Fear had by excess forfeited control of his faculties. He flung his hands upon the table. Nothing was there!

There is a point at which terror may turn to madness; and madness incites to action. With no definite intent, from no motive but the wayward impulse of a madman, Murlock sprang to the wall, with a little groping seized his loaded rifle, and without aim discharged it. By the flash which lit up the room with a vivid illumination, he saw an enormous panther dragging the dead woman to-ward the window, its teeth fixed in her throat! Then there were darkness blacker than before, and silence; and when he returned to consciousness the sun was high and the wood vocal with songs of birds.

The body lay near the window, where the beast had left it when frightened away by the flash and report of the rifle. The clothing was deranged, the long hair in disorder, the limbs lay anyhow. From the throat, dreadfully lacerated, had issued a pool of blood not yet entirely coagulated. The ribbon with which he had bound the wrists was broken; the hands were tightly clenched. Between the teeth was a fragment of the animal's ear.

From CAN SUCH THINGS BE?[41]

CAN SUCH THINGS BE?

Moxon's Master

"Are you serious?—do you really believe that a machine thinks?"

I got no immediate reply; Moxon was apparently intent upon the coals in the grate, touching them deftly here and there with the fire-poker till they signified a sense of his attention by a brighter glow. For several weeks I had been observing in him a growing habit of delay in answering even the most trivial of commonplace questions. His air, however, was that of preoccupation rather than delibera-tion: one might have said that he had "something on his mind."

Presently he said:

"What is a 'machine'? The word has been variously defined. Here is one definition from a popular dictionary: 'Any instrument or or-ganization by which power is applied and made effective, or a de-sired effect produced.' Well, then, is not a man a machine? And you will admit that he thinks—or thinks he thinks."

"If you do not wish to answer my question," I said, rather testily, "why not say so?—all that you say is mere evasion. You know well enough that when I say 'machine' I do not mean a man, but some-thing that man has made and controls."

"When it does not control him," he said, rising abruptly and looking out of a window, whence nothing was visible in the black-ness of a stormy night. A moment later he turned about and with a smile said: "I beg your pardon; I had no thought of evasion. I con-sidered the dictionary man's unconscious testimony suggestive and worth something in the discussion. I can give your question a direct answer easily enough: I do believe that a machine thinks about the work that it is doing."

That was direct enough, certainly. It was not altogether pleasing, for it tended to confirm a sad suspicion that Moxon's devotion to study and work in his machine-shop had not been good for him. I knew, for one thing, that he suffered from insomnia, and that is no light affliction. Had it affected his mind? His reply to my question seemed to me then evidence that it had; perhaps I should think dif-ferently about it now. I was younger then, and among the blessings that are not denied to youth is ignorance. Incited by that great stimu-lant to controversy, I said:

"And what, pray, does it think with—in the absence of a brain?"

The reply, coming with less than his customary delay, took his favorite form of counter-interrogation:

"With what does a plant think—in the absence of a brain?"

"Ah, plants also belong to the philosopher class! I should be pleased to know some of their conclusions; you may omit the premises."

"Perhaps," he replied, apparently unaffected by my foolish irony, "you may be able to infer their convictions from their acts. I will spare you the familiar examples of the sensitive mimosa, the several insectivorous flowers and those whose stamens bend down and shake their pollen upon the entering bee in order that he may fertilize their distant mates. But observe this. In an open spot in my garden I planted a climbing vine. When it was barely above the surface I set a stake into the soil a yard away. The vine at once made for it, but as it was about to reach it after several days I removed it a few feet. The vine at once altered its course, making an acute angle, and again made for the stake. This manœuvre was repeated several times but finally, as if discouraged, the vine abandoned the pursuit and ignoring further attempts to divert it traveled to a small tree, further away, which it climbed.

"Roots of the eucalyptus will prolong themselves incredibly in search of moisture. A well-known horticulturist relates that one entered an old drain pipe and followed it until it came to a break, where a section of the pipe had been removed to make way for a stone wall that had been built across its course. The root left the drain and followed the wall until it found an opening where a stone had fallen out. It crept through and following the other side of the wall back to the drain, entered the unexplored part and resumed its journey."

"And all this?"

"Can you miss the significance of it? It shows the consciousness of plants. It proves that they think."

"Even if it did—what then? We were speaking, not of plants, but of machines. They may be composed partly of wood—wood that has no longer vitality—or wholly of metal. Is thought an attribute also of the mineral kingdom?"

"How else do you explain the phenomena, for example, of crystallization?"

"I do not explain them."

"Because you cannot without affirming what you wish to deny, namely, intelligent cooperation among the constituent elements of the crystals. When soldiers form lines, or hollow squares, you call it reason. When wild geese in flight take the form of a letter V you say instinct. When the homogeneous atoms of a mineral, moving freely in solution arrange themselves into shapes mathematically perfect, or particles of frozen moisture into the symmetrical and beautiful forms of snowflakes, you have nothing to say. You have not even invented a name to conceal your heroic unreason."

Moxon was speaking with unusual animation and earnestness. As he paused I heard in an adjoining room known to me as his "machine-shop," which no one but himself was permitted to enter, a singular thumping sound, as of some one pounding upon a table with an open hand. Moxon heard it at the same moment and, visibly agitated, rose and hurriedly passed into the room whence it came. I thought it odd that any one else should be in there, and my interest in my friend—with doubtless a touch of unwarrantable curiosity—led me to listen intently, though, I am happy to say, not at the key-hole. There were confused sounds, as of a struggle or scuffle; the floor shook. I distinctly heard hard breathing and a hoarse whisper which said "Damn you!" Then all was silent, and presently Moxon reappeared and said, with a rather sorry smile:

"Pardon me for leaving you so abruptly. I have a machine in there that lost its temper and cut up rough."

Fixing my eyes steadily upon his left cheek which was traversed by four parallel excoriations showing blood, I said:

"How would it do to trim its nails?"

I could have spared myself the jest; he gave it no attention, but seated himself in the chair that he had left and resumed the interrupted monologue as if nothing had occurred:

"Doubtless you do not hold with those (I need not name them to a man of your reading) who have taught that all matter is sentient, that every atom is a living, feeling, conscious being. *I* do. There is no such thing as dead, inert matter; it is all alive; all instinct with force, actual and potential; all sensitive to the same forces in its environment and susceptible to the contagion of higher and subtler ones residing in such superior organisms as it may be brought into relation with, as those of man when he is fashioning it into an instrument of his will. It absorbs something of his intelligence and purpose—more of them in proportion to the complexity of the resulting machine and that of its work.

"Do you happen to recall Herbert Spencer's definition of 'Life'?[42] I read it thirty years ago. He may have altered it afterward, for anything I know, but in all that time I have been unable to think of a single word that could profitably be changed or added or removed. It seems to me not only the best definition, but the only possible one.

" 'Life,' he says, 'is a definite combination of heterogeneous changes, both simultaneous and successive, in correspondence with external coexistences and sequences.' "

"That defines the phenomenon," I said, "but gives no hint of its cause."

"That," he replied, is all that any definition can do. As Mill[43] points out, we know nothing of cause except as an antecedent—nothing of effect except as a consequent. Of certain phenomena, one never occurs without another, which is dissimilar: the first in point of time we call cause, the second, effect. One who had many times seen a rabbit pursued by a dog, and had never seen rabbits and dogs otherwise, would think the rabbit the cause of the dog.

"But I fear," he added, laughing naturally enough, "that my rabbit is leading me a long way from the track of my legitimate quarry: I'm indulging in the pleasure of the chase for its own sake. What I want you to observe is that in Herbert Spencer's definition of 'life' the activity of a machine is included—there is nothing in the definition that is not applicable to it. According to this sharpest of observers and deepest of thinkers, if a man during his period of activity is alive, so is a machine when in operation. As an inventor and constructor of machines I know that to be true."

Moxon was silent for a long time, gazing absently into the fire. It was growing late and I thought it time to be going, but somehow I did not like the notion of leaving him in that isolated house, all alone except for the presence of some person of whose nature my conjectures could go no further than that it was unfriendly, perhaps malign. Leaning toward him and looking earnestly into his eyes while making a motion with my hand through the door of his workshop, I said:

"Moxon, whom have you in there?"

Somewhat to my surprise he laughed lightly and answered without hesitation:

"Nobody; the incident that you have in mind was caused by my
folly in leaving a machine in action with nothing to act upon, while
I undertook the interminable task of enlightening your understanding. Do you happen to know that Consciousness is the creature of
Rhythm?"

"O bother them both!" I replied, rising and laying hold of my
overcoat. "I'm going to wish you good night; and I'll add the hope
that the machine which you inadvertently left in action will have
her gloves on the next time you think it needful to stop her."

Without waiting to observe the effect of my shot I left the house.

Rain was falling, and the darkness was intense. In the sky beyond the crest of a hill toward which I groped my way along
precarious plank sidewalks and across miry, unpaved streets I could
see the faint glow of the city's lights, but behind me nothing
was visible but a single window of Moxon's house. It glowed with
what seemed to me a mysterious and fateful meaning. I knew it
was an uncurtained aperture in my friend's "machine-shop," and
I had little doubt that he had resumed the studies interrupted by
his duties as my instructor in mechanical consciousness and the
fatherhood of Rhythm. Odd, and in some degree humorous, as
his convictions seemed to me at that time, I could not wholly divest
myself of the feeling that they had some tragic relation to his
life and character—perhaps to his destiny—although I no longer
entertained the notion that they were the vagaries of a disordered
mind. Whatever might be thought of his views, his exposition of
them was too logical for that. Over and over, his last words came
back to me: "Consciousness is the creature of Rhythm." Bald and
terse as the statement was, I now found it infinitely alluring. At
each recurrence it broadened in meaning and deepened in suggestion. Why, here, (I thought) is something upon which to found
a philosophy. If consciousness is the product of rhythm all things
are conscious, for all have motion, and all motion is rhythmic. I
wondered if Moxon knew the significance and breadth of his
thought—the scope of this momentous generalization, or had he arrived at his philosophic faith by the tortuous and uncertain road of
observation?

That faith was then new to me, and all Moxon's expounding had failed to make me a convert; but now it seemed as if a great light shone about me, like that which fell upon Saul of Tarsus;[44] and out there in the storm and darkness and solitude I experienced what Lewes[45] calls "The endless variety and excitement of philosophic thought." I exulted in a new sense of knowledge, a new pride of reason. My feet seemed hardly to touch the earth; it was as if I were uplifted and borne through the air by invisible wings.

Yielding to an impulse to seek further light from him whom I now recognized as my master and guide, I had unconsciously turned about, and almost before I was aware of having done so found myself again at Moxon's door. I was drenched with rain, but felt no discomfort. Unable in my excitement to find the doorbell I instinctively tried the knob. It turned and, entering, I mounted the stairs to the room that I had so recently left. All was dark and silent; Moxon, as I had supposed, was in the adjoining room—the "machine-shop." Groping along the wall until I found the communicating door I knocked loudly several times, but got no response, which I attributed to the uproar outside, for the wind was blowing a gale and dashing the rain against the thin walls in sheets. The drumming upon the shingle roof spanning the unceiled room was loud and incessant.

I had never been invited into the machine-shop—had, indeed, been denied admittance, as had all others, with one exception, a skilled metal worker, of whom no one knew anything except that his name was Haley and his habit silence. But in my spiritual exaltation, discretion and civility were alike forgotten and I opened the door. What I saw took all philosophical speculation out of me in short order.

Moxon sat facing me at the farther side of a small table upon which a single candle made all the light that was in the room. Opposite him, his back toward me, sat another person. On the table between the two was a chess-board; the men were playing. I knew little of chess, but as only a few pieces were on the board it was obvious that the game was near its close. Moxon was intensely interested—not so much, it seemed to me, in the game as in his antagonist, upon whom he had fixed so intent a look that, standing though I did directly in the line of his vision, I was altogether unobserved. His face was ghastly white, and his eyes glittered like diamonds. Of his antagonist I had only a back view, but that was sufficient; I should not have cared to see his face.

He was apparently not more than five feet in height, with proportions suggesting those of a gorilla—a tremendous breadth of
shoulders, thick, short neck and broad, squat head, which had a
tangled growth of black hair and was topped with a crimson fez. A
tunic of the same color, belted tightly to the waist, reached the
seat—apparently a box—upon which he sat; his legs and feet were
not seen. His left forearm appeared to rest in his lap; he moved his
pieces with his right hand, which seemed disproportionately long.

I had shrunk back and now stood a little to one side of the door-
way and in shadow. If Moxon had looked farther than the face of
his opponent he could have observed nothing now, except that the
door was open. Something forbade me either to enter or to retire, a
feeling—I know not how it came—that I was in the presence of an
imminent tragedy and might serve my friend by remaining. With a
scarcely conscious rebellion against the indelicacy of the act I remained.

The play was rapid. Moxon hardly glanced at the board before
making his moves, and to my unskilled eye seemed to move the
piece most convenient to his hand, his motions in doing so being
quick, nervous and lacking in precision. The response of his antagonist, while equally prompt in the inception, was made with a slow,
uniform, mechanical and, I thought, somewhat theatrical movement
of the arm, that was a sore trial to my patience. There was something unearthly about it all, and I caught myself shuddering. But I
was wet and cold.

Two or three times after moving a piece the stranger slightly in-
clined his head, and each time I observed that Moxon shifted his
king. All at once the thought came to me that the man was dumb.
And then that he was a machine—an automaton chess-player! Then
I remembered that Moxon had once spoken to me of having invented such a piece of mechanism, though I did not understand that
it had actually been constructed. Was all his talk about the consciousness and intelligence of machines merely a prelude to eventual
exhibition of this device—only a trick to intensify the effect of its
mechanical action upon me in my ignorance of its secret?

A fine end, this, of all my intellectual transports—my "endless
variety and excitement of philosophic thought!" I was about to retire in disgust when something occurred to hold my curiosity. I observed a shrug of the thing's great shoulders, as if it were irritated:
and so natural was this—so entirely human—that in my new view

of the matter it startled me. Nor was that all, for a moment later it struck the table sharply with its clenched hand. At that gesture Moxon seemed even more startled than I: he pushed his chair a little backward, as in alarm.

Presently Moxon, whose play it was, raised his hand high above the board, pounced upon one of his pieces like a sparrow-hawk and with the exclamation "checkmate!" rose quickly to his feet and stepped behind his chair. The automaton sat motionless.

The wind had now gone down, but I heard, at lessening intervals and progressively louder, the rumble and roll of thunder. In the pauses between I now became conscious of a low humming or buzzing which, like the thunder, grew momentarily louder and more distinct. It seemed to come from the body of the automaton, and was unmistakably a whirring of wheels. It gave me the impression of a disordered mechanism which had escaped the repressive and regulating action of some controlling part—an effect such as might be expected if a pawl[46] should be jostled from the teeth of a ratchet-wheel. But before I had time for much conjecture as to its nature my attention was taken by the strange motions of the automaton itself. A slight but continuous convulsion appeared to have possession of it. In body and head it shook like a man with palsy or an ague chill, and the motion augmented every moment until the entire figure was in violent agitation. Suddenly it sprang to its feet and with a movement almost too quick for the eye to follow shot forward across table and chair, with both arms thrust forth to their full length—the posture and lunge of a diver. Moxon tried to throw himself backward out of reach, but he was too late: I saw the horrible thing's hands close upon his throat, his own clutch its wrists. Then the table was overturned, the candle thrown to the floor and extinguished, and all was black dark. But the noise of the struggle was dreadfully distinct, and most terrible of all were the raucous, squawking sounds made by the strangled man's efforts to breathe. Guided by the infernal hubbub, I sprang to the rescue of my friend, but had hardly taken a stride in the darkness when the whole room blazed with a blinding white light that burned into my brain and heart and memory a vivid picture of the combatants on the floor, Moxon underneath, his throat still in the clutch of those iron hands, his head forced backward, his eyes protruding, his mouth wide open and his tongue thrust out; and—horrible contrast!—upon the painted face of his assassin an expression of tranquil and profound thought, as in the solution of a problem in chess! This I observed, then all was blackness and silence.

Three days later I recovered consciousness in a hospital. As the memory of that tragic night slowly evolved in my ailing brain I recognized in my attendant Moxon's confidential workman, Haley. Responding to a look he approached, smiling.

"Tell me about it," I managed to say, faintly—"all about it."

"Certainly," he said; "you were carried unconscious from a burning house—Moxon's. Nobody knows how you came to be there. You may have to do a little explaining. The origin of the fire is a bit mysterious, too. My own notion is that the house was struck by lightning."

"And Moxon?"

"Buried yesterday—what was left of him."

Apparently this reticent person could unfold himself on occasion. When imparting shocking intelligence to the sick he was affable enough. After some moments of the keenest mental suffering I ventured to ask another question:

"Who rescued me?"

"Well, if that interests you—I did."

"Thank you, Mr. Haley, and may God bless you for it. Did you rescue, also, that charming product of your skill, the automaton chess-player that murdered its inventor?"

The man was silent a long time, looking away from me. Presently he turned and gravely said:

"Do you know that?"

"I do," I replied; "I saw it done."

That was many years ago. If asked to-day I should answer less confidently.

A Tough Tussle

One night in the autumn of 1861 a man sat alone in the heart of a forest in western Virginia. The region was one of the wildest on the continent—the Cheat Mountain country. There was no lack of people close at hand, however; within a mile of where the man sat was the now silent camp of a whole Federal brigade. Somewhere about—it might be still nearer—was a force of the enemy, the numbers unknown. It was this uncertainty as to its numbers and position that accounted for the man's presence in that lonely spot; he was a young officer of a Federal infantry regiment and his business there was to guard his sleeping comrades in the camp against a surprise. He was in command of a detachment of men constituting a picket-guard. These men he had stationed just at nightfall in an irregular line, determined by the nature of the ground, several hundred yards in front of where he now sat. The line ran through the forest, among the rocks and laurel thickets, the men fifteen or twenty paces apart, all in concealment and under injunction of strict silence and unremitting vigilance. In four hours, if nothing occurred, they would be relieved by a fresh detachment from the reserve now resting in care of its captain some distance away to the left and rear. Before stationing his men the young officer of whom we are writing had pointed out to his two sergeants the spot at which he would be found if it should be necessary to consult him, or if his presence at the front line should be required.

It was a quiet enough spot—the fork of an old wood-road, on the two branches of which, prolonging themselves deviously forward in the dim moonlight, the sergeants were themselves stationed, a few paces in rear of the line. If driven sharply back by a sudden onset of the enemy—and pickets are not expected to make a stand after firing—the men would come into the converging roads and naturally following them to their point of intersection could be rallied and "formed." In his small way the author of these dispositions was something of a strategist; if Napoleon had planned as intelligently at Waterloo he would have won that memorable battle and been overthrown later.

Second-Lieutenant Brainerd Byring was a brave and efficient officer, young and comparatively inexperienced as he was in the business of killing his fellow-men. He had enlisted in the very first days of the war as a private, with no military knowledge whatever, had been made first-sergeant of his company on account of his education and engaging manner, and had been lucky enough to lose his captain by a Confederate bullet; in the resulting promotions he had gained a commission. He had been in several engagements, such as they were—at Philippi, Rich Mountain, Carrick's Ford and Greenbrier—and had borne himself with such gallantry as not to attract the attention of his superior officers. The exhilaration of battle was agreeable to him, but the sight of the dead, with their clay faces, blank eyes and stiff bodies, which when not unnaturally shrunken were unnaturally swollen, had always intolerably affected him. He felt toward them a kind of reasonless antipathy that was something more than the physical and spiritual repugnance common to us all. Doubtless this feeling was due to his unusually acute sensibilities—his keen sense of the beautiful, which these hideous things outraged. Whatever may have been the cause, he could not look upon a dead body without a loathing which had in it an element of resentment. What others have respected as the dignity of death had to him no existence—was altogether unthinkable. Death was a thing to be hated. It was not picturesque, it had no tender and solemn side—a dismal thing, hideous in all its manifestations and suggestions. Lieutenant Byring was a braver man than anybody knew, for nobody knew his horror of that which he was ever ready to incur.

Having posted his men, instructed his sergeants and retired to his station, he seated himself on a log, and with senses all alert began his vigil. For greater ease he loosened his sword-belt and taking his heavy revolver from his holster laid it on the log beside him. He felt very comfortable, though he hardly gave the fact a thought, so intently did he listen for any sound from the front which might have a menacing significance—a shout, a shot, or the footfall of one of his sergeants coming to apprise him of something worth knowing. From the vast, invisible ocean of moonlight overhead fell, here and there, a slender, broken stream that seemed to plash against the intercepting branches and trickle to earth, forming small white pools among the clumps of laurel. But these leaks were few and served only to accentuate the blackness of his environment, which his imagination found it easy to people with all manner of unfamiliar shapes, menacing, uncanny, or merely grotesque.

He to whom the portentous conspiracy of night and solitude and silence in the heart of a great forest is not an unknown experience needs not to be told what another world it all is—how even the most commonplace and familiar objects take on another character. The trees group themselves differently; they draw closer together, as if in fear. The very silence has another quality than the silence of the day. And it is full of half-heard whispers—whispers that startle—ghosts of sounds long dead. There are living sounds, too, such as are never heard under other conditions: notes of strange night-birds, the cries of small animals in sudden encounters with stealthy foes or in their dreams, a rustling in the dead leaves—it may be the leap of a wood-rat, it may be the footfall of a panther. What caused the breaking of that twig?—what the low, alarmed twittering in that bushful of birds? There are sounds without a name, forms without substance, translations in space of objects which have not been seen to move, movements wherein nothing is observed to change its place. Ah, children of the sunlight and the gaslight, how little you know of the world in which you live!

Surrounded at a little distance by armed and watchful friends, Byring felt utterly alone. Yielding himself to the solemn and mysterious spirit of the time and place, he had forgotten the nature of his connection with the visible and audible aspects and phases of the night. The forest was boundless; men and the habitations of men did not exist. The universe was one primeval mystery of darkness, without form and void, himself the sole, dumb questioner of its eternal secret. Absorbed in thoughts born of this mood, he suffered the time to slip away unnoted. Meantime the infrequent patches of white light lying amongst the tree-trunks had undergone changes of size, form and place. In one of them near by, just at the roadside, his eye fell upon an object that he had not previously observed. It was almost before his face as he sat; he could have sworn that it had not before been there. It was partly covered in shadow, but he could see that it was a human figure. Instinctively he adjusted the clasp of his sword-belt and laid hold of his pistol—again he was in a world of war, by occupation an assassin.

The figure did not move. Rising, pistol in hand, he approached. The figure lay upon its back, its upper part in shadow, but standing above it and looking down upon the face, he saw that it was a dead body. He shuddered and turned from it with a feeling of sickness and disgust, resumed his seat upon the log, and forgetting military prudence struck a match and lit a cigar. In the sudden blackness that followed the extinction of the flame he felt a sense of relief; he could no longer see the object of his aversion. Nevertheless, he kept his eyes set in that direction until it appeared again with growing distinctness. It seemed to have moved a trifle nearer.

"Damn the thing!" he muttered. "What does it want?"

It did not appear to be in need of anything but a soul.

Byring turned away his eyes and began humming a tune, but he broke off in the middle of a bar and looked at the dead body. Its presence annoyed him, though he could hardly have had a quieter neighbor. He was conscious, too, of a vague, indefinable feeling that was new to him. It was not fear, but rather a sense of the supernatural—in which he did not at all believe.

"I have inherited it," he said to himself. "I suppose it will require a thousand ages—perhaps ten thousand—for humanity to outgrow this feeling. Where and when did it originate? Away back, probably, in what is called the cradle of the human race—the plains of Central Asia. What we inherit as a superstition our barbarous ancestors must have held as a reasonable conviction. Doubtless they believed themselves justified by facts whose nature we cannot even conjecture in thinking a dead body a malign thing endowed with some strange power of mischief, with perhaps a will and a purpose to exert it. Possibly they had some awful form of religion of which that was one of the chief doctrines, sedulously taught by their priesthood, as ours teach the immortality of the soul. As the Aryans moved slowly on, to and through the Caucasus passes, and spread over Europe, new conditions of life must have resulted in the formulation of new religions. The old belief in the malevolence of the dead body was lost from the creeds and even perished from tradition, but it left its heritage of terror, which is transmitted from generation to generation—is as much a part of us as are our blood and bones."

In following out his thought he had forgotten that which suggested it; but now his eye fell again upon the corpse. The shadow had now altogether uncovered it. He saw the sharp profile, the chin in the air, the whole face, ghastly white in the moonlight. The clothing was gray, the uniform of a Confederate soldier. The coat and waistcoat, unbuttoned, had fallen away on each side, exposing the white shirt. The chest seemed unnaturally prominent, but the abdomen had sunk in, leaving a sharp projection at the line of the lower ribs. The arms were extended, the left knee was thrust upward. The whole posture impressed Byring as having been studied with a view to the horrible.

"Bah!" he exclaimed; "he was an actor—he knows how to be dead."

He drew away his eyes, directing them resolutely along one of the roads leading to the front, and resumed his philosophizing where he had left off.

"It may be that our Central Asian ancestors had not the custom of burial. In that case it is easy to understand their fear of the dead, who really were a menace and an evil. They bred pestilences. Children were taught to avoid the places where they lay, and to run away if by inadvertence they came near a corpse. I think, indeed, I'd better go away from this chap."

He half rose to do so, then remembered that he had told his men in front and the officer in the rear who was to relieve him that he could at any time be found at that spot. It was a matter of pride, too. If he abandoned his post he feared they would think he feared the corpse. He was no coward and he was unwilling to incur anybody's ridicule. So he again seated himself, and to prove his courage looked boldly at the body. The right arm—the one farthest from him—was now in shadow. He could barely see the hand which, he had before observed, lay at the root of a clump of laurel. There had been no change, a fact which gave him a certain comfort, he could not have said why. He did not at once remove his eyes; that which we do not wish to see has a strange fascination, sometimes irresistible. Of the woman who covers her eyes with her hands and looks between the fingers let it be said that the wits have dealt with her not altogether justly.

Byring suddenly became conscious of a pain in his right hand. He withdrew his eyes from his enemy and looked at it. He was grasping the hilt of his drawn sword so tightly that it hurt him. He observed, too, that he was leaning forward in a strained attitude—crouching like a gladiator ready to spring at the throat of an antagonist. His teeth were clenched and he was breathing hard. This matter was soon set right, and as his muscles relaxed and he drew a long breath he felt keenly enough the ludicrousness of the incident. It affected him to laughter. Heavens! what sound was that? what mindless devil was uttering an unholy glee in mockery of human merriment? He sprang to his feet and looked about him, not recognizing his own laugh.

He could no longer conceal from himself the horrible fact of his cowardice; he was thoroughly frightened! He would have run from the spot, but his legs refused their office; they gave way beneath him and he sat again upon the log, violently trembling. His face was wet, his whole body bathed in a chill perspiration. He could not even cry out. Distinctly he heard behind him a stealthy tread, as of some wild animal, and dared not look over his shoulder. Had the soulless living joined forces with the soulless dead?—was it an animal? Ah, if he could but be assured of that! But by no effort of will could he now unfix his gaze from the face of the dead man.

I repeat that Lieutenant Byring was a brave and intelligent man. But what would you have? Shall a man cope, single-handed, with so monstrous an alliance as that of night and solitude and silence and the dead,—while an incalculable host of his own ancestors shriek into the ear of his spirit their coward counsel, sing their doleful death-songs in his heart, and disarm his very blood of all its iron? The odds are too great—courage was not made for so rough use as that.

One sole conviction now had the man in possession: that the body had moved. It lay nearer to the edge of its plot of light—there could be no doubt of it. It had also moved its arms, for, look, they are both in the shadow! A breath of cold air struck Byring full in the face; the boughs of trees above him stirred and moaned. A strongly defined shadow passed across the face of the dead, left it luminous, passed back upon it and left it half obscured. The horrible thing was visibly moving! At that moment a single shot rang out upon the picket-line—a lonelier and louder, though more distant, shot than ever had been heard by mortal ear! It broke the spell of that enchanted man; it slew the silence and the solitude, dispersed the hindering host from Central Asia and released his modern manhood. With a cry like that of some great bird pouncing upon its prey he sprang forward, hot-hearted for action!

Shot after shot now came from the front. There were shoutings and confusion, hoof-beats and desultory cheers. Away to the rear, in the sleeping camp, were a singing of bugles and grumble of drums. Pushing through the thickets on either side the roads came the Federal pickets, in full retreat, firing backward at random as they ran. A straggling group that had followed back one of the roads, as instructed, suddenly sprang away into the bushes as half a hundred horsemen thundered by them, striking wildly with their sabres as they passed. At headlong speed these mounted madmen shot past the spot where Byring had sat, and vanished round an angle of the road, shouting and firing their pistols. A moment later there was a roar of musketry followed by dropping shots—they had encountered the reserve-guard in line; and back they came in dire confusion, with here and there an empty saddle and many a maddened horse, bullet-stung, snorting and plunging with pain. It was all over—"an affair of out-posts."

The line was reëstablished with fresh men, the roll called, the stragglers were re-formed. The Federal commander with a part of his staff, imperfectly clad, appeared upon the scene, asked a few questions, looked exceedingly wise and retired. After standing at arms for an hour the brigade in camp "swore a prayer or two" and went to bed.

Early the next morning a fatigue-party, commanded by a captain and accompanied by a surgeon, searched the ground for dead and wounded. At the fork of the road, a little to one side, they found two bodies lying close together—that of a Federal officer and that of a Confederate private. The officer had died of a sword-thrust through the heart, but not, apparently, until he had inflicted upon his enemy no fewer than five dreadful wounds. The dead officer lay on his face in a pool of blood, the weapon still in his breast. They turned him on his back and the surgeon removed it.

"Gad!" said the captain—"It is Byring!"—adding, with a glance at the other, "They had a tough tussle."

The surgeon was examining the sword. It was that of a line officer of Federal infantry—exactly like the one worn by the captain. It was, in fact, Byring's own. The only other weapon discovered was an undischarged revolver in the dead officer's belt.

The surgeon laid down the sword and approached the other body. It was frightfully gashed and stabbed, but there was no blood. He took hold of the left foot and tried to straighten the leg. In the effort the body was displaced. The dead do not wish to be moved—it protested with a faint, sickening odor. Where it had lain were a few maggots, manifesting an imbecile activity.

The surgeon looked at the captain. The captain looked at the surgeon.

A Resumed Identity

THE REVIEW AS A FORM OF WELCOME

One summer night a man stood on a low hill overlooking a wide expanse of forest and field. By the full moon hanging low in the west he knew what he might not have known otherwise: that it was near the hour of dawn. A light mist lay along the earth, partly veiling the lower features of the landscape, but above it the taller trees showed in well-defined masses against a clear sky. Two or three farmhouses were visible through the haze, but in none of them, naturally, was a light. Nowhere, indeed, was any sign or suggestion of life except the barking of a distant dog, which, repeated with mechanical iteration, served rather to accentuate than dispel the loneliness of the scene.

The man looked curiously about him on all sides, as one who among familiar surroundings is unable to determine his exact place and part in the scheme of things. It is so, perhaps, that we shall act when, risen from the dead, we await the call to judgment.

A hundred yards away was a straight road, showing white in the moonlight. Endeavoring to orient himself, as a surveyor or navigator might say, the man moved his eyes slowly along its visible length and at a distance of a quarter-mile to the south of his station saw, dim and gray in the haze, a group of horsemen riding to the north. Behind them were men afoot, marching in column, with dimly gleaming rifles aslant above their shoulders. They moved slowly and in silence. Another group of horsemen, another regiment of infantry, another and another—all in unceasing motion toward the man's point of view, past it, and beyond. A battery of artillery followed, the cannoneers riding with folded arms on limber and caisson. And still the interminable procession came out of the obscurity to south and passed into the obscurity to north, with never a sound of voice, nor hoof, nor wheel.

The man could not rightly understand: he thought himself deaf; said so, and heard his own voice, although it had an unfamiliar quality that almost alarmed him; it disappointed his ear's expectancy in the matter of *timbre* and resonance. But he was not deaf, and that for the moment sufficed.

Then he remembered that there are natural phenomena to which some one has given the name "acoustic shadows."[47] If you stand in an acoustic shadow there is one direction from which you will hear nothing. At the battle of Gaines's Mill, one of the fiercest conflicts of the Civil War, with a hundred guns in play, spectators a mile and a half away on the opposite side of the Chickahominy valley heard nothing of what they clearly saw. The bombardment of Port Royal, heard and felt at St. Augustine, a hundred and fifty miles to the south, was inaudible two miles to the north in a still atmosphere. A few days before the surrender at Appomattox a thunderous engagement between the commands of Sheridan and Pickett was unknown to the latter commander, a mile in the rear of his own line.

These instances were not known to the man of whom we write, but less striking ones of the same character had not escaped his observation. He was profoundly disquieted, but for another reason than the uncanny silence of that moonlight march.

"Good Lord!" he said to himself—and again it was as if another had spoken his thought—"if those people are what I take them to be we have lost the battle and they are moving on Nashville!"

Then came a thought of self—an apprehension—a strong sense of personal peril, such as in another we call fear. He stepped quickly into the shadow of a tree. And still the silent battalions moved slowly forward in the haze.

The chill of a sudden breeze upon the back of his neck drew his attention to the quarter whence it came, and turning to the east he saw a faint gray light along the horizon—the first sign of returning day. This increased his apprehension.

"I must get away from here," he thought, "or I shall be discovered and taken."

He moved out of the shadow, walking rapidly toward the graying east. From the safer seclusion of a clump of cedars he looked back. The entire column had passed out of sight: the straight white road lay bare and desolate in the moonlight!

Puzzled before, he was now inexpressibly astonished. So swift a passing of so slow an army!—he could not comprehend it. Minute after minute passed unnoted; he had lost his sense of time. He sought with a terrible earnestness a solution of the mystery, but sought in vain. When at last he roused himself from his abstraction the sun's rim was visible above the hills, but in the new conditions he found no other light than that of day; his understanding was involved as darkly in doubt as before.

On every side lay cultivated fields showing no sign of war and war's ravages. From the chimneys of the farmhouses thin ascensions of blue smoke signaled preparations for a day's peaceful toil. Having stilled its immemorial allocution[48] to the moon, the watchdog was assisting a negro who, prefixing a team of mules to the plow, was flatting and sharping contentedly at his task. The hero of this tale stared stupidly at the pastoral picture as if he had never seen such a thing in all his life; then he put his hand to his head, passed it through his hair and, withdrawing it, attentively considered the palm—a singular thing to do. Apparently reassured by the act, he walked confidently toward the road.

II

WHEN YOU HAVE
LOST YOUR LIFE CONSULT A PHYSICIAN

Dr. Stilling Malson, of Murfreesboro, having visited a patient six or seven miles away, on the Nashville road, had remained with him all night. At daybreak he set out for home on horseback, as was the custom of doctors of the time and region. He had passed into the neighborhood of Stone's River battlefield when a man approached him from the roadside and saluted in the military fashion, with a movement of the right hand to the hatbrim. But the hat was not a military hat, the man was not in uniform and had not a martial bearing. The doctor nodded civilly, half thinking that the stranger's uncommon greeting was perhaps in deference to the historic surroundings. As the stranger evidently desired speech with him he courteously reined in his horse and waited.

"Sir," said the stranger, "although a civilian, you are perhaps an enemy."

"I am a physician," was the non-committal reply.

"Thank you," said the other. "I am a lieutenant, of the staff of General Hazen." He paused a moment and looked sharply at the person whom he was addressing, then added, "Of the Federal army."

The physician merely nodded.

"Kindly tell me," continued the other, "what has happened here. Where are the armies? Which has won the battle?"

The physician regarded his questioner curiously with half-shut eyes. After a professional scrutiny, prolonged to the limit of politeness, "Pardon me," he said; "one asking information should be willing to impart it. Are you wounded?" he added, smiling.

"Not seriously—it seems."

The man removed the unmilitary hat, put his hand to his head, passed it through his hair and, withdrawing it, attentively considered the palm.

"I was struck by a bullet and have been unconscious. It must have been a light, glancing blow: I find no blood and feel no pain. I will not trouble you for treatment, but will you kindly direct me to my command—to any part of the Federal army—if you know?"

Again the doctor did not immediately reply: he was recalling much that is recorded in the books of his profession—something about lost identity and the effect of familiar scenes in restoring it. At length he looked the man in the face, smiled, and said:

"Lieutenant, you are not wearing the uniform of your rank and service."

At this the man glanced down at his civilian attire, lifted his eyes, and said with hesitation:

"That is true. I—I don't quite understand."

Still regarding him sharply but not unsympathetically the man of science bluntly inquired:

"How old are you?"

"Twenty-three—if that has anything to do with it."

"You don't look it; I should hardly have guessed you to be just that."

The man was growing impatient. "We need not discuss that," he said; "I want to know about the army. Not two hours ago I saw a column of troops moving northward on this road. You must have met them. Be good enough to tell me the color of their clothing, which I was unable to make out, and I'll trouble you no more."

"You are quite sure that you saw them?"

"Sure? My God, sir, I could have counted them!"

"Why, really," said the physician, with an amusing consciousness of his own resemblance to the loquacious barber of the Arabian Nights,[49] "this is very interesting. I met no troops."

The man looked at him coldly, as if he had himself observed the likeness to the barber. "It is plain," he said, "that you do not care to assist me. Sir, you may go to the devil!"

He turned and strode away, very much at random, across the dewy fields, his half-penitent tormentor quietly watching him from his point of vantage in the saddle till he disappeared beyond an array of trees.

III

THE DANGER OF
LOOKING INTO A POOL OF WATER

After leaving the road the man slackened his pace, and now went forward, rather deviously, with a distinct feeling of fatigue. He could not account for this, though truly the interminable loquacity of that country doctor offered itself in explanation. Seating himself upon a rock, he laid one hand upon his knee, back upward, and casually looked at it. It was lean and withered. He lifted both hands to his face. It was seamed and furrowed; he could trace the lines with the tips of his fingers. How strange!—a mere bullet-stroke and a brief unconsciousness should not make one a physical wreck.

"I must have been a long time in hospital," he said aloud. "Why, what a fool I am! The battle was in December, and it is now summer!" He laughed. "No wonder that fellow thought me an escaped lunatic. He was wrong: I am only an escaped patient."

At a little distance a small plot of ground enclosed by a stone wall caught his attention. With no very definite intent he rose and went to it. In the center was a square, solid monument of hewn stone. It was brown with age, weather-worn at the angles, spotted with moss and lichen. Between the massive blocks were strips of grass the leverage of whose roots had pushed them apart. In answer to the challenge of this ambitious structure Time had laid his destroying hand upon it, and it would soon be "one with Nineveh[50] and Tyre."[51] In an inscription on one side his eye caught a familiar name. Shaking with excitement, he craned his body across the wall and read:

HAZEN'S BRIGADE
to
The Memory of Its Soldiers
who fell at
Stone River, Dec. 31, 1862.

The man fell back from the wall, faint and sick. Almost within an arm's length was a little depression in the earth; it had been filled by a recent rain—a pool of clear water. He crept to it to revive himself, lifted the upper part of his body on his trembling arms, thrust forward his head and saw the reflection of his face, as in a mirror. He uttered a terrible cry. His arms gave way; he fell, face downward, into the pool and yielded up the life that had spanned another life.

The Night-Doings at "Deadman's"

A STORY THAT IS UNTRUE

It was a singularly sharp night, and clear as the heart of a diamond. Clear nights have a trick of being keen. In darkness you may be cold and not know it; when you see, you suffer. This night was bright enough to bite like a serpent. The moon was moving mysteriously along behind the giant pines crowning the South Mountain, striking a cold sparkle from the crusted snow, and bringing out against the black west the ghostly outlines of the Coast Range, beyond which lay the invisible Pacific. The snow had piled itself, in the open spaces along the bottom of the gulch, into long ridges that seemed to heave, and into hills that appeared to toss and scatter spray. The spray was sunlight, twice reflected: dashed once from the moon, once from the snow.

In this snow many of the shanties of the abandoned mining camp were obliterated, (a sailor might have said they had gone down) and at irregular intervals it had overtopped the tall trestles which had once supported a river called a flume; for, of course, "flume" is *flumen*.[52] Among the advantages of which the mountains cannot deprive the gold-hunter is the privilege of speaking Latin. He says of his dead neighbor, "He has gone up the flume." This is not a bad way to say, "His life has returned to the Fountain of Life."

While putting on its armor against the assaults of the wind, this snow had neglected no coign of vantage. Snow pursued by the wind is not wholly unlike a retreating army. In the open field it ranges itself in ranks and battalions; where it can get a foothold it makes a stand; where it can take cover it does so. You may see whole platoons of snow cowering behind a bit of broken wall. The devious old road, hewn out of the mountain side, was full of it. Squadron upon squadron had struggled to escape by this line, when suddenly pursuit had ceased. A more desolate and dreary spot than Deadman's Gulch in a winter midnight it is impossible to imagine. Yet Mr. Hiram Beeson elected to live there, the sole inhabitant.

Away up the side of the North Mountain his little pine-log shanty projected from its single pane of glass a long, thin beam of light, and looked not altogether unlike a black beetle fastened to the hillside with a bright new pin. Within it sat Mr. Beeson himself, before a roaring fire, staring into its hot heart as if he had never before seen such a thing in all his life. He was not a comely man. He was gray; he was ragged and slovenly in his attire; his face was wan and haggard; his eyes were too bright. As to his age, if one had attempted to guess it, one might have said forty-seven, then corrected himself and said seventy-four. He was really twenty-eight. Emaciated he was; as much, perhaps, as he dared be, with a needy undertaker at Bentley's Flat and a new and enterprising coroner at Sonora. Poverty and zeal are an upper and a nether millstone. It is dangerous to make a third in that kind of sandwich.

As Mr. Beeson sat there, with his ragged elbows on his ragged knees, his lean jaws buried in his lean hands, and with no apparent intention of going to bed, he looked as if the slightest movement would tumble him to pieces. Yet during the last hour he had winked no fewer than three times.

There was a sharp rapping at the door. A rap at that time of night and in that weather might have surprised an ordinary mortal who had dwelt two years in the gulch without seeing a human face, and could not fail to know that the country was impassable; but Mr. Beeson did not so much as pull his eyes out of the coals. And even when the door was pushed open he only shrugged a little more closely into himself, as one does who is expecting something that he would rather not see. You may observe this movement in women when, in a mortuary chapel, the coffin is borne up the aisle behind them.

But when a long old man in a blanket overcoat, his head tied up in a handkerchief and nearly his entire face in a muffler, wearing green goggles and with a complexion of glittering whiteness where it could be seen, strode silently into the room, laying a hard, gloved hand on Mr. Beeson's shoulder, the latter so far forgot himself as to look up with an appearance of no small astonishment; whomever he may have been expecting, he had evidently not counted on meeting anyone like this. Nevertheless, the sight of this unexpected guest produced in Mr. Beeson the following sequence: a feeling of astonishment; a sense of gratification; a sentiment of profound good will. Rising from his seat, he took the knotty hand from his shoulder, and shook it up and down with a fervor quite unaccountable; for in

the old man's aspect was nothing to attract, much to repel. However, attraction is too general a property for repulsion to be without
it. The most attractive object in the world is the face we instinctively cover with a cloth. When it becomes still more attractive—
fascinating—we put seven feet of earth above it.

"Sir," said Mr. Beeson, releasing the old man's hand, which fell
passively against his thigh with a quiet clack, "it is an extremely disagreeable night. Pray be seated; I am very glad to see you."

Mr. Beeson spoke with an easy good breeding that one would
hardly have expected, considering all things. Indeed, the contrast
between his appearance and his manner was sufficiently surprising
to be one of the commonest of social phenomena in the mines. The
old man advanced a step toward the fire, glowing cavernously in the
green goggles. Mr. Beeson resumed:

"You bet your life I am!"

Mr. Beeson's elegance was not too refined; it had made reasonable concessions to local taste. He paused a moment, letting his eyes
drop from the muffled head of his guest, down along the row of
moldy buttons confining the blanket overcoat, to the greenish cow-
hide boots powdered with snow, which had begun to melt and run
along the floor in little rills. He took an inventory of his guest, and
appeared satisfied. Who would not have been? Then he continued:

"The cheer I can offer you is, unfortunately, in keeping with my
surroundings; but I shall esteem myself highly favored if it is your
pleasure to partake of it, rather than seek better at Bentley's Flat."

With a singular refinement of hospitable humility Mr. Beeson
spoke as if a sojourn in his warm cabin on such a night, as compared
with walking fourteen miles up to the throat in snow with a cutting
crust, would be an intolerable hardship. By way of reply, his guest
unbuttoned the blanket overcoat. The host laid fresh fuel on the
fire, swept the hearth with the tail of a wolf, and added:

"But *I* think you'd better skedaddle."

The old man took a seat by the fire, spreading his broad soles to
the heat without removing his hat. In the mines the hat is seldom
removed except when the boots are. Without further remark Mr.
Beeson also seated himself in a chair which had been a barrel, and
which, retaining much of its original character, seemed to have been
designed with a view to preserving his dust if it should please him
to crumble. For a moment there was silence; then, from somewhere
among the pines, came the snarling yelp of a coyote; and simultane-

ously the door rattled in its frame. There was no other connection
between the two incidents than that the coyote has an aversion to
storms, and the wind was rising; yet there seemed somehow a kind
of supernatural conspiracy between the two, and Mr. Beeson shuddered with a vague sense of terror. He recovered himself in a moment and again addressed his guest.

"There are strange doings here. I will tell you everything, and
then if you decide to go I shall hope to accompany you over the
worst of the way; as far as where Baldy Peterson shot Ben Hike—I
dare say you know the place."

The old man nodded emphatically, as intimating not merely that
he did, but that he did indeed.

"Two years ago," began Mr. Beeson, "I, with two companions,
occupied this house; but when the rush to the Flat occurred we left,
along with the rest. In ten hours the Gulch was deserted. That
evening, however, I discovered I had left behind me a valuable pistol (that is it) and returned for it, passing the night here alone, as I
have passed every night since. I must explain that a few days before
we left, our Chinese domestic had the misfortune to die while the
ground was frozen so hard that it was impossible to dig a grave in
the usual way. So, on the day of our hasty departure, we cut through
the floor there, and gave him such burial as we could. But before
putting him down I had the extremely bad taste to cut off his pigtail
and spike it to that beam above his grave, where you may see it at
this moment, or, preferably, when warmth has given you leisure for
observation.

"I stated, did I not, that the Chinaman came to his death from
natural causes? I had, of course, nothing to do with that, and returned through no irresistible attraction, or morbid fascination, but
only because I had forgotten a pistol. This is clear to you, is it
not, sir?"

The visitor nodded gravely. He appeared to be a man of few
words, if any. Mr. Beeson continued:

"According to the Chinese faith, a man is like a kite: he cannot
go to heaven without a tail. Well, to shorten this tedious story—
which, however, I thought it my duty to relate—on that night,
while I was here alone and thinking of anything but him, that Chinaman came back for his pigtail.

"He did not get it."

At this point Mr. Beeson relapsed into blank silence. Perhaps he was fatigued by the unwonted exercise of speaking; perhaps he had conjured up a memory that demanded his undivided attention. The wind was now fairly abroad, and the pines along the mountain-side sang with singular distinctness. The narrator continued:

"You say you do not see much in that, and I must confess I do not myself.

"But he keeps coming!"

There was another long silence, during which both stared into the fire without the movement of a limb. Then Mr. Beeson broke out, almost fiercely, fixing his eyes on what he could see of the impassive face of his auditor:

"Give it him? Sir, in this matter I have no intention of troubling anyone for advice. You will pardon me, I am sure"—here he became singularly persuasive—"but I have ventured to nail that pigtail fast, and have assumed the somewhat onerous obligation of guarding it. So it is quite impossible to act on your considerate suggestion.

"Do you play me for a Modoc?"

Nothing could exceed the sudden ferocity with which he thrust this indignant remonstrance into the ear of his guest. It was as if he had struck him on the side of the head with a steel gauntlet. It was a protest, but it was a challenge. To be mistaken for a coward—to be played for a Modoc: these two expressions are one. Sometimes it is a Chinaman. Do you play me for a Chinaman? is a question frequently addressed to the ear of the suddenly dead.

Mr. Beeson's buffet produced no effect, and after a moment's pause, during which the wind thundered in the chimney like the sound of clods upon a coffin, he resumed:

"But, as you say, it is wearing me out. I feel that the life of the last two years has been a mistake—a mistake that corrects itself; you see how. The grave! No; there is no one to dig it. The ground is frozen, too. But you are very welcome. You may stay at Bentley's—but that is not important. It was very tough to cut: they braid silk into their pigtails. Kwaagh."

Mr. Beeson was speaking with his eyes shut, and he wandered. His last word was a snore. A moment later he drew a long breath, opened his eyes with an effort, made a single remark, and fell into a deep sleep. What he said was this:

"They are swiping my dust!"

Then the aged stranger, who had not uttered one word since his

arrival, arose from his seat and deliberately laid off his outer clothing, looking as angular in his flannels as the late Signorina Fes-
torazzi, an Irish woman, six feet in height, and weighing fifty-six
pounds, who used to exhibit herself in her chemise to the people of
San Francisco. He then crept into one of the "bunks," having first
placed a revolver in easy reach, according to the custom of the
country. This revolver he took from a shelf, and it was the one
which Mr. Beeson had mentioned as that for which he had returned
to the Gulch two years before.

In a few moments Mr. Beeson awoke, and seeing that his guest
had retired he did likewise. But before doing so he approached the
long, plaited wisp of pagan hair and gave it a powerful tug, to assure
himself that it was fast and firm. The two beds—mere shelves covered with blankets not overclean—faced each other from opposite
sides of the room, the little square trapdoor that had given access to
the Chinaman's grave being midway between. This, by the way,
was crossed by a double row of spike-heads. In his resistance to the
supernatural, Mr. Beeson had not disdained the use of material pre-
cautions.

The fire was now low, the flames burning bluely and petulantly,
with occasional flashes projecting spectral shadows on the walls—
shadows that moved mysteriously about, now dividing, now unit-
ing. The shadow of the pendent queue, however, kept moodily apart,
near the roof at the further end of the room, looking like a note of
admiration. The song of the pines outside had now risen to the dignity of a triumphal hymn. In the pauses the silence was dreadful.

It was during one of these intervals that the trap in the floor began to lift. Slowly and steadily it rose, and slowly and steadily rose
the swaddled head of the old man in the bunk to observe it. Then,
with a clap that shook the house to its foundation, it was thrown
clean back, where it lay with its unsightly spikes pointing threaten-
ingly upward. Mr. Beeson awoke, and without rising, pressed his
fingers into his eyes. He shuddered; his teeth chattered. His guest
was now reclining on one elbow, watching the proceedings with the
goggles that glowed like lamps.

Suddenly a howling gust of wind swooped down the chimney,
scattering ashes and smoke in all directions, for a moment obscur-
ing everything. When the firelight again illuminated the room there
was seen, sitting gingerly on the edge of a stool by the hearthside, a
swarthy little man of prepossessing appearance and dressed with

faultless taste, nodding to the old man with a friendly and engaging smile. "From San Francisco, evidently," thought Mr. Beeson, who having somewhat recovered from his fright was groping his way to a solution of the evening's events.

But now another actor appeared upon the scene. Out of the square black hole in the middle of the floor protruded the head of the departed Chinaman, his glassy eyes turned upward in their angular slits and fastened on the dangling queue above with a look of yearning unspeakable. Mr. Beeson groaned, and again spread his hands upon his face. A mild odor of opium pervaded the place. The phantom, clad only in a short blue tunic quilted and silken but covered with grave-mold, rose slowly, as if pushed by a weak spiral spring. Its knees were at the level of the floor, when with a quick upward impulse like the silent leaping of a flame it grasped the queue with both hands, drew up its body and took the tip in its horrible yellow teeth. To this it clung in a seeming frenzy, grimacing ghastly, surging and plunging from side to side in its efforts to disengage its property from the beam, but uttering no sound. It was like a corpse artificially convulsed by means of a galvanic battery. The contrast between its superhuman activity and its silence was no less than hideous!

Mr. Beeson cowered in his bed. The swarthy little gentleman uncrossed his legs, beat an impatient tattoo with the toe of his boot and consulted a heavy gold watch. The old man sat erect and quietly laid hold of the revolver.

Bang!

Like a body cut from the gallows the Chinaman plumped into the black hole below, carrying his tail in his teeth. The trapdoor turned over, shutting down with a snap. The swarthy little gentleman from San Francisco sprang nimbly from his perch, caught something in the air with his hat, as a boy catches a butterfly, and vanished into the chimney as if drawn up by suction.

From away somewhere in the outer darkness floated in through the open door a faint, far cry—a long, sobbing wail, as of a child death-strangled in the desert, or a lost soul borne away by the Adversary.[53] It may have been the coyote.

In the early days of the following spring a party of miners on their way to new diggings passed along the Gulch, and straying through the deserted shanties found in one of them the body of Hiram Beeson, stretched upon a bunk, with a bullet hole through the heart. The ball had evidently been fired from the opposite side of the room, for in one of the oaken beams overhead was a shallow blue dint, where it had struck a knot and been deflected downward to the breast of its victim. Strongly attached to the same beam was what appeared to be an end of a rope of braided horsehair, which had been cut by the bullet in its passage to the knot. Nothing else of interest was noted, excepting a suit of moldy and incongruous clothing, several articles of which were afterward identified by respectable witnesses as those in which certain deceased citizens of Deadman's had been buried years before. But it is not easy to understand how that could be, unless, indeed, the garments had been worn as a disguise by Death himself—which is hardly credible.

The Realm of the Unreal

I

For a part of the distance between Auburn and Newcastle the road—first on one side of a creek and then on the other—occupies the whole bottom of the ravine, being partly cut out of the steep hillside, and partly built up with bowlders removed from the creek-bed by the miners. The hills are wooded, the course of the ravine is sinuous. In a dark night careful driving is required in order not to go off into the water. The night that I have in memory was dark, the creek a torrent, swollen by a recent storm. I had driven up from Newcastle and was within about a mile of Auburn in the darkest and narrowest part of the ravine, looking intently ahead of my horse for the roadway. Suddenly I saw a man almost under the animal's nose, and reined in with a jerk that came near setting the creature up on its haunches.

"I beg your pardon," I said; "I did not see you, sir."

"You could hardly be expected to see me," the man replied, civilly, approaching the side of the vehicle; "and the noise of the creek prevented my hearing you."

I at once recognized the voice, although five years had passed since I had heard it. I was not particularly well pleased to hear it now.

"You are Dr. Dorrimore, I think," said I.

"Yes; and you are my good friend Mr. Manrich. I am more than glad to see you—the excess," he added, with a light laugh, "being due to the fact that I am going your way, and naturally expect an invitation to ride with you."

"Which I extend with all my heart."

That was not altogether true.

Dr. Dorrimore thanked me as he seated himself beside me, and I drove cautiously forward, as before. Doubtless it is fancy, but it seems to me now that the remaining distance was made in a chill fog; that I was uncomfortably cold; that the way was longer than ever before, and the town, when we reached it, cheerless, forbidding, and desolate. It must have been early in the evening, yet I do not recollect a light in any of the houses nor a living thing in the streets. Dorrimore explained at some length how he happened to be there, and where he had been during the years that had elapsed since I had seen him. I recall the fact of the narrative, but none of the facts narrated. He had been in foreign countries and had returned—this is all that my memory retains, and this I already knew. As to myself I cannot remember that I spoke a word, though doubtless I did. Of one thing I am distinctly conscious: the man's presence at my side was strangely distasteful and disquieting—so much so that when I at last pulled up under the lights of the Putnam House I experienced a sense of having escaped some spiritual peril of a nature peculiarly forbidding. This sense of relief was somewhat modified by the discovery that Dr. Dorrimore was living at the same hotel.

II

In partial explanation of my feelings regarding Dr. Dorrimore I will relate briefly the circumstances under which I had met him some years before. One evening a half-dozen men of whom I was one were sitting in the library of the Bohemian Club in San Francisco. The conversation had turned to the subject of sleight-of-hand and the feats of the *prestidigitateurs*,[54] one of whom was then exhibiting at a local theatre.

"These fellows are pretenders in a double sense," said one of the party; "they can do nothing which it is worth one's while to be made a dupe by. The humblest wayside juggler in India could mystify them to the verge of lunacy."

"For example, how?" asked another, lighting a cigar.

"For example, by all their common and familiar performances—throwing large objects into the air which never come down; causing plants to sprout, grow visibly and blossom, in bare ground chosen by spectators; putting a man into a wicker basket, piercing him through and through with a sword while he shrieks and bleeds, and then—the basket being opened nothing is there; tossing the free end of a silken ladder into the air, mounting it and disappearing."

"Nonsense!" I said, rather uncivilly, I fear. "You surely do not believe such things?"

"Certainly not: I have seen them too often."

"But I do," said a journalist of considerable local fame as a picturesque reporter. "I have so frequently related them that nothing but observation could shake my conviction. Why, gentlemen, I have my own word for it."

Nobody laughed—all were looking at something behind me. Turning in my seat I saw a man in evening dress who had just entered the room. He was exceedingly dark, almost swarthy, with a thin face, black-bearded to the lips, an abundance of coarse black hair in some disorder, a high nose and eyes that glittered with as soulless an expression as those of a cobra. One of the group rose and introduced him as Dr. Dorrimore, of Calcutta. As each of us was presented in turn he acknowledged the fact with a profound bow in the Oriental manner, but with nothing of Oriental gravity. His smile impressed me as cynical and a trifle contemptuous. His whole demeanor I can describe only as disagreeably engaging.

His presence led the conversation into other channels. He said little—I do not recall anything of what he did say. I thought his voice singularly rich and melodious, but it affected me in the same way as his eyes and smile. In a few minutes I rose to go. He also rose and put on his overcoat.

"Mr. Manrich," he said, "I am going your way."

"The devil you are!" I thought. "How do you know which way I am going?" Then I said, "I shall be pleased to have your company."

We left the building together. No cabs were in sight, the street cars had gone to bed, there was a full moon and the cool night air was delightful; we walked up the California street hill. I took that direction thinking he would naturally wish to take another, toward one of the hotels.

"You do not believe what is told of the Hindu jugglers," he said abruptly.

"How do you know that?" I asked.

Without replying he laid his hand lightly upon my arm and with the other pointed to the stone sidewalk directly in front. There, almost at our feet, lay the dead body of a man, the face upturned and white in the moonlight! A sword whose hilt sparkled with gems stood fixed and upright in the breast; a pool of blood had collected on the stones of the sidewalk.

I was startled and terrified—not only by what I saw, but by the circumstances under which I saw it. Repeatedly during our ascent of the hill my eyes, I thought, had traversed the whole reach of that sidewalk, from street to street. How could they have been insen-

sible to this dreadful object now so conspicuous in the white moonlight?

As my dazed faculties cleared I observed that the body was in
evening dress; the overcoat thrown wide open revealed the dress-
coat, the white tie, the broad expanse of shirt front pierced by the
sword. And—horrible revelation!—the face, except for its pallor,
was that of my companion! It was to the minutest detail of dress
and feature Dr. Dorrimore himself. Bewildered and horrified, I turned
to look for the living man. He was nowhere visible, and with an
added terror I retired from the place, down the hill in the direction
whence I had come. I had taken but a few strides when a strong
grasp upon my shoulder arrested me. I came near crying out with
terror: the dead man, the sword still fixed in his breast, stood beside
me! Pulling out the sword with his disengaged hand, he flung it
from him, the moonlight glinting upon the jewels of its hilt and the
unsullied steel of its blade. It fell with a clang upon the sidewalk
ahead and—vanished! The man, swarthy as before, relaxed his grasp
upon my shoulder and looked at me with the same cynical regard
that I had observed on first meeting him. The dead have not that
look—it partly restored me, and turning my head backward, I saw
the smooth white expanse of sidewalk, unbroken from street to
street.

"What is all this nonsense, you devil?" I demanded, fiercely
enough, though weak and trembling in every limb.

"It is what some are pleased to call jugglery," he answered, with
a light, hard laugh.

He turned down Dupont street and I saw him no more until we
met in the Auburn ravine.

III

On the day after my second meeting with Dr. Dorrimore I did not
see him; the clerk in the Putnam House explained that a slight ill-
ness confined him to his rooms. That afternoon at the railway station I was surprised and made happy by the unexpected arrival of
Miss Margaret Corray and her mother, from Oakland.

This is not a love story. I am no storyteller, and love as it is cannot be portrayed in a literature dominated and enthralled by the de-
basing tyranny which "sentences letters" in the name of the Young
Girl. Under the Young Girl's blighting reign—or rather under the

rule of those false Ministers of the Censure who have appointed
themselves to the custody of her welfare—love

veils her sacred fires,
And, unaware, Morality expires,[55]

famished upon the sifted meal and distilled water of a prudish pur-
veyance.

Let it suffice that Miss Corray and I were engaged in marriage. She and her mother went to the hotel at which I lived, and for
two weeks I saw her daily. That I was happy needs hardly be said;
the only bar to my perfect enjoyment of those golden days was the
presence of Dr. Dorrimore, whom I had felt compelled to introduce
to the ladies.

By them he was evidently held in favor. What could I say? I
knew absolutely nothing to his discredit. His manners were those
of a cultivated and considerate gentleman; and to women a man's
manner is the man. On one or two occasions when I saw Miss Corray walking with him I was furious, and once had the indiscretion
to protest. Asked for reasons, I had none to give and fancied I saw
in her expression a shade of contempt for the vagaries of a jealous
mind. In time I grew morose and consciously disagreeable, and resolved in my madness to return to San Francisco the next day. Of
this, however, I said nothing.

IV

There was at Auburn an old, abandoned cemetery. It was nearly in
the heart of the town, yet by night it was as gruesome a place as the
most dismal of human moods could crave. The railings about
the plats were prostrate, decayed, or altogether gone. Many of the
graves were sunken, from others grew sturdy pines, whose roots
had committed unspeakable sin. The headstones were fallen and broken across; brambles overran the ground; the fence was mostly gone,
and cows and pigs wandered there at will; the place was a dishonor to
the living, a calumny on the dead, a blasphemy against God.

The evening of the day on which I had taken my madman's resolution to depart in anger from all that was dear to me found me in
that congenial spot. The light of the half moon fell ghostly through
the foliage of trees in spots and patches, revealing much that was

unsightly, and the black shadows seemed conspiracies withholding to the proper time revelations of darker import. Passing along what had been a gravel path, I saw emerging from shadow the figure of Dr. Dorrimore. I was myself in shadow, and stood still with clenched hands and set teeth, trying to control the impulse to leap upon and strangle him. A moment later a second figure joined him and clung to his arm. It was Margaret Corray!

I cannot rightly relate what occurred. I know that I sprang forward, bent upon murder; I know that I was found in the gray of the morning, bruised and bloody, with finger marks upon my throat. I was taken to the Putnam House, where for days I lay in a delirium. All this I know, for I have been told. And of my own knowledge I know that when consciousness returned with convalescence I sent for the clerk of the hotel.

"Are Mrs. Corray and her daughter still here?" I asked.

"What name did you say?"

"Corray."

"Nobody of that name has been here."

"I beg you will not trifle with me," I said petulantly. "You see that I am all right now; tell me the truth."

"I give you my word," he replied with evident sincerity, "we have had no guests of that name."

His words stupefied me. I lay for a few moments in silence; then I asked: "Where is Dr. Dorrimore?"

"He left on the morning of your fight and has not been heard of since. It was a rough deal he gave you."

V

Such are the facts of this case. Margaret Corray is now my wife. She has never seen Auburn, and during the weeks whose history as it shaped itself in my brain I have endeavored to relate, was living at her home in Oakland, wondering where her lover was and why he did not write. The other day I saw in the Baltimore *Sun* the following paragraph:

"Professor Valentine Dorrimore, the hypnotist, had a large audience last night. The lecturer, who has lived most of his life in India, gave some marvelous exhibitions of his power, hypnotizing anyone who chose to submit himself to the experiment, by merely looking at him. In fact, he twice hypnotized the entire audience (reporters

alone exempted), making all entertain the most extraordinary illusions. The most valuable feature of the lecture was the disclosure of
the methods of the Hindu jugglers in their famous performances,
familiar in the mouths of travelers. The professor declares that these
thaumaturgists[56] have acquired such skill in the art which he learned
at their feet that they perform their miracles by simply throwing the
'spectators' into a state of hypnosis and telling them what to see and
hear. His assertion that a peculiarly susceptible subject may be kept
in the realm of the unreal for weeks, months, and even years, dominated by whatever delusions and hallucinations the operator may
from time to time suggest, is a trifle disquieting."

The Damned Thing

I

ONE DOES NOT ALWAYS EAT
WHAT IS ON THE TABLE

By the light of a tallow candle which had been placed on one end of
a rough table a man was reading something written in a book. It
was an old account book, greatly worn; and the writing was not,
apparently, very legible, for the man sometimes held the page close
to the flame of the candle to get a stronger light on it. The shadow
of the book would then throw into obscurity a half of the room,
darkening a number of faces and figures; for besides the reader, eight
other men were present. Seven of them sat against the rough log
walls, silent, motionless, and the room being small, not very far
from the table. By extending an arm any one of them could have
touched the eighth man, who lay on the table, face upward, partly
covered by a sheet, his arms at his sides. He was dead.

The man with the book was not reading aloud, and no one spoke;
all seemed to be waiting for something to occur; the dead man only
was without expectation. From the blank darkness outside came in,
through the aperture that served for a window, all the ever unfamiliar noises of night in the wilderness—the long nameless note of a
distant coyote; the stilly pulsing thrill of tireless insects in trees;
strange cries of night birds, so different from those of the birds of
day; the drone of great blundering beetles, and all that mysterious
chorus of small sounds that seem always to have been but half heard
when they have suddenly ceased, as if conscious of an indiscretion.
But nothing of all this was noted in that company; its members
were not overmuch addicted to idle interest in matters of no practical importance; that was obvious in every line of their rugged
faces—obvious even in the dim light of the single candle. They were
evidently men of the vicinity—farmers and woodsmen.

The person reading was a trifle different; one would have said of
him that he was of the world, worldly, albeit there was that in
his attire which attested a certain fellowship with the organisms of
his environment. His coat would hardly have passed muster in San

Francisco; his foot-gear was not of urban origin, and the hat that lay
by him on the floor (he was the only one uncovered) was such that
if one had considered it as an article of mere personal adornment he
would have missed its meaning. In countenance the man was rather
prepossessing, with just a hint of sternness; though that he may have
assumed or cultivated, as appropriate to one in authority. For he
was a coroner. It was by virtue of his office that he had possession
of the book in which he was reading; it had been found among the
dead man's effects—in his cabin, where the inquest was now taking
place.

When the coroner had finished reading he put the book into his
breast pocket. At that moment the door was pushed open and a
young man entered. He, clearly, was not of mountain birth and
breeding: he was clad as those who dwell in cities. His clothing was
dusty, however, as from travel. He had, in fact, been riding hard to
attend the inquest.

The coroner nodded; no one else greeted him.

"We have waited for you," said the coroner. "It is necessary to
have done with this business to-night."

The young man smiled. "I am sorry to have kept you," he said.
"I went away, not to evade your summons, but to post to my newspaper an account of what I suppose I am called back to relate."

The coroner smiled.

"The account that you posted to your newspaper," he said, "differs, probably, from that which you will give here under oath."

"That," replied the other, rather hotly and with a visible flush,
"is as you please. I used manifold paper and have a copy of what I
sent. It was not written as news, for it is incredible, but as fiction. It
may go as a part of my testimony under oath."

"But you say it is incredible."

"That is nothing to you, sir, if I also swear that it is true."

The coroner was silent for a time, his eyes upon the floor. The
men about the sides of the cabin talked in whispers, but seldom
withdrew their gaze from the face of the corpse. Presently the coroner lifted his eyes and said: "We will resume the inquest."

The men removed their hats. The witness was sworn.

"What is your name?" the coroner asked.

"William Harker."

"Age?"

"Twenty-seven."

"You knew the deceased, Hugh Morgan?"

"Yes."

"You were with him when he died?"

"Near him."

"How did that happen—your presence, I mean?"

"I was visiting him at this place to shoot and fish. A part of my purpose, however, was to study him and his odd, solitary way of life. He seemed a good model for a character in fiction. I sometimes write stories."

"I sometimes read them."

"Thank you."

"Stories in general—not yours."

Some of the jurors laughed. Against a sombre background humor shows high lights. Soldiers in the intervals of battle laugh easily, and a jest in the death chamber conquers by surprise.

"Relate the circumstances of this man's death," said the coroner. "You may use any notes or memoranda that you please."

The witness understood. Pulling a manuscript from his breast pocket he held it near the candle and turning the leaves until he found the passage that he wanted began to read.

II

WHAT MAY HAPPEN IN A FIELD OF WILD OATS

". . . The sun had hardly risen when we left the house. We were looking for quail, each with a shotgun, but we had only one dog. Morgan said that our best ground was beyond a certain ridge that he pointed out, and we crossed it by a trail through the *chaparral*.[57] On the other side was comparatively level ground, thickly covered with wild oats. As we emerged from the *chaparral* Morgan was but a few yards in advance. Suddenly we heard, at a little distance to our right and partly in front, a noise as of some animal thrashing about in the bushes, which we could see were violently agitated.

" 'We've started a deer,' I said. 'I wish we had brought a rifle.'

"Morgan, who had stopped and was intently watching the agitated *chaparral*, said nothing, but had cocked both barrels of his gun and was holding it in readiness to aim. I thought him a trifle excited, which surprised me, for he had a reputation for exceptional coolness, even in moments of sudden and imminent peril.

" 'O, come,' I said. 'You are not going to fill up a deer with quail-shot, are you?'

"Still he did not reply; but catching a sight of his face as he turned it slightly toward me I was struck by the intensity of his look. Then I understood that we had serious business in hand and my first conjecture was that we had 'jumped' a grizzly. I advanced to Morgan's side, cocking my piece as I moved.

"The bushes were now quiet and the sounds had ceased, but Morgan was as attentive to the place as before.

" 'What is it? What the devil is it?' I asked.

" 'That Damned Thing!' he replied, without turning his head. His voice was husky and unnatural. He trembled visibly.

"I was about to speak further, when I observed the wild oats near the place of the disturbance moving in the most inexplicable way. I can hardly describe it. It seemed as if stirred by a streak of wind, which not only bent it, but pressed it down—crushed it so that it did not rise; and this movement was slowly prolonging itself directly toward us.

"Nothing that I had ever seen had affected me so strangely as this unfamiliar and unaccountable phenomenon, yet I am unable to recall any sense of fear. I remember—and tell it here because, singularly enough, I recollected it then—that once in looking carelessly out of an open window I momentarily mistook a small tree close at hand for one of a group of larger trees at a little distance away. It looked the same size as the others, but being more distinctly and sharply defined in mass and detail seemed out of harmony with them. It was a mere falsification of the law of aërial perspective, but it startled, almost terrified me. We so rely upon the orderly operation of familiar natural laws that any seeming suspension of them is noted as a menace to our safety, a warning of unthinkable calamity. So now the apparently causeless movement of the herbage and the slow, undeviating approach of the line of disturbance were distinctly disquieting. My companion appeared actually frightened, and I could hardly credit my senses when I saw him suddenly throw his gun to his shoulder and fire both barrels at the agitated grain! Before the smoke of the discharge had cleared away I heard a loud savage cry—a scream like that of a wild animal—and flinging his gun upon the ground Morgan sprang away and ran swiftly from the spot. At the same instant I was thrown violently to the ground by the impact of something unseen in the smoke—some soft, heavy substance that seemed thrown against me with great force.

"Before I could get upon my feet and recover my gun, which seemed to have been struck from my hands, I heard Morgan crying out as if in mortal agony, and mingling with his cries were such hoarse, savage sounds as one hears from fighting dogs. Inexpressibly terrified, I struggled to my feet and looked in the direction of Morgan's retreat; and may Heaven in mercy spare me from another sight like that! At a distance of less than thirty yards was my friend, down upon one knee, his head thrown back at a frightful angle, hatless, his long hair in disorder and his whole body in violent movement from side to side, backward and forward. His right arm was lifted and seemed to lack the hand—at least, I could see none. The other arm was invisible. At times, as my memory now reports this extraordinary scene, I could discern but a part of his body; it was as if he had been partly blotted out—I cannot otherwise express it— then a shifting of his position would bring it all into view again.

"All this must have occurred within a few seconds, yet in that time Morgan assumed all the postures of a determined wrestler vanquished by superior weight and strength. I saw nothing but him, and him not always distinctly. During the entire incident his shouts and curses were heard, as if through an enveloping uproar of such sounds of rage and fury as I had never heard from the throat of man or brute!

"For a moment only I stood irresolute, then throwing down my gun I ran forward to my friend's assistance. I had a vague belief that he was suffering from a fit, or some form of convulsion. Before I could reach his side he was down and quiet. All sounds had ceased, but with a feeling of such terror as even these awful events had not inspired I now saw again the mysterious movement of the wild oats, prolonging itself from the trampled area about the prostrate man toward the edge of a wood. It was only when it had reached the wood that I was able to withdraw my eyes and look at my companion. He was dead."

III

A MAN THOUGH NAKED MAY BE IN RAGS

The coroner rose from his seat and stood beside the dead man. Lifting an edge of the sheet he pulled it away, exposing the entire body, altogether naked and showing in the candle-light a claylike yellow. It had, however, broad maculations[58] of bluish black, obviously caused by extravasated blood[59] from contusions. The chest and sides looked as if they had been beaten with a bludgeon. There were dreadful lacerations; the skin was torn in strips and shreds.

The coroner moved round to the end of the table and undid a silk handkerchief which had been passed under the chin and knotted on the top of the head. When the handkerchief was drawn away it exposed what had been the throat. Some of the jurors who had risen to get a better view repented their curiosity and turned away their faces. Witness Harker went to the open window and leaned out across the sill, faint and sick. Dropping the handkerchief upon the dead man's neck the coroner stepped to an angle of the room and from a pile of clothing produced one garment after another, each of which he held up a moment for inspection. All were torn, and stiff with blood. The jurors did not make a closer inspection. They seemed rather uninterested. They had, in truth, seen all this before; the only thing that was new to them being Harker's testimony.

"Gentlemen," the coroner said, "we have no more evidence, I think. Your duty has been already explained to you; if there is nothing you wish to ask you may go outside and consider your verdict."

The foreman rose—a tall, bearded man of sixty, coarsely clad.

"I should like to ask one question, Mr. Coroner," he said. "What asylum did this yer last witness escape from?"

"Mr. Harker," said the coroner, gravely and tranquilly, "from what asylum did you last escape?"

Harker flushed crimson again, but said nothing, and the seven jurors rose and solemnly filed out of the cabin.

"If you have done insulting me, sir," said Harker, as soon as he and the officer were left alone with the dead man, "I suppose I am at liberty to go?"

"Yes."

Harker started to leave, but paused, with his hand on the door latch. The habit of his profession was strong in him—stronger than his sense of personal dignity. He turned about and said:

"The book that you have there—I recognize it as Morgan's diary. You seemed greatly interested in it; you read in it while I was testifying. May I see it? The public would like——"

"The book will cut no figure in this matter," replied the official, slipping it into his coat pocket; "all the entries in it were made before the writer's death."

As Harker passed out of the house the jury reëntered and stood about the table, on which the now covered corpse showed under the sheet with sharp definition. The foreman seated himself near the candle, produced from his breast pocket a pencil and scrap of paper and wrote rather laboriously the following verdict, which with various degrees of effort all signed:

"We, the jury, do find that the remains come to their death at the hands of a mountain lion, but some of us thinks, all the same, they had fits."

IV

AN EXPLANATION FROM THE TOMB

In the diary of the late Hugh Morgan are certain interesting entries having, possibly, a scientific value as suggestions. At the inquest upon his body the book was not put in evidence; possibly the coroner thought it not worth while to confuse the jury. The date of the first of the entries mentioned cannot be ascertained; the upper part of the leaf is torn away; the part of the entry remaining follows:

" . . . would run in a half-circle, keeping his head turned always toward the centre, and again he would stand still, barking furiously. At last he ran away into the brush as fast as he could go. I thought at first that he had gone mad, but on returning to the house found no other alteration in his manner than what was obviously due to fear of punishment.

"Can a dog see with his nose? Do odors impress some cerebral centre with images of the thing that emitted them? . . .

"Sept. 2.—Looking at the stars last night as they rose above the crest of the ridge east of the house, I observed them successively disappear—from left to right. Each was eclipsed but an instant, and only a few at the same time, but along the entire length of the ridge all that were within a degree or two of the crest were blotted out. It was as if something had passed along between me and them; but I could not see it, and the stars were not thick enough to define its outline. Ugh! I don't like this." . . .

Several weeks' entries are missing, three leaves being torn from the book.

"Sept. 27.—It has been about here again—I find evidences of its presence every day. I watched again all last night in the same cover, gun in hand, double-charged with buckshot. In the morning the fresh footprints were there, as before. Yet I would have sworn that I did not sleep—indeed, I hardly sleep at all. It is terrible, insupportable! If these amazing experiences are real I shall go mad; if they are fanciful I am mad already.

"Oct. 3.—I shall not go—it shall not drive me away. No, this is *my* house, *my* land. God hates a coward. . . .

"Oct. 5.—I can stand it no longer; I have invited Harker to pass a few weeks with me—he has a level head. I can judge from his manner if he thinks me mad.

"Oct. 7.—I have the solution of the mystery; it came to me last night—suddenly, as by revelation. How simple—how terribly simple!

"There are sounds that we cannot hear. At either end of the scale are notes that stir no chord of that imperfect instrument, the human ear. They are too high or too grave. I have observed a flock of blackbirds occupying an entire tree-top—the tops of several trees—and all in full song. Suddenly—in a moment—at absolutely the same instant—all spring into the air and fly away. How? They could not all see one another—whole tree-tops intervened. At no point could a leader have been visible to all. There must have been a signal of warning or command, high and shrill above the din, but by me unheard. I have observed, too, the same simultaneous flight when all were silent, among not only blackbirds, but other birds—quail, for example, widely separated by bushes—even on opposite sides of a hill.

"It is known to seamen that a school of whales basking or sporting on the surface of the ocean, miles apart, with the convexity of the earth between, will sometimes dive at the same instant—all gone out of sight in a moment. The signal has been sounded—too grave for the ear of the sailor at the masthead and his comrades on the deck—who nevertheless feel its vibrations in the ship as the stones of a cathedral are stirred by the bass of the organ.

"As with sounds, so with colors. At each end of the solar spectrum the chemist can detect the presence of what are known as 'actinic' rays.[60] They represent colors—integral colors in the composition of light—which we are unable to discern. The human eye is an imperfect instrument; its range is but a few octaves of the real 'chromatic scale.' I am not mad; there are colors that we cannot see.

"And, God help me! the Damned Thing is of such a color!"

Haïta the Shepherd

In the heart of Haïta the illusions of youth had not been supplanted by those of age and experience. His thoughts were pure and pleasant, for his life was simple and his soul devoid of ambition. He rose with the sun and went forth to pray at the shrine of Hastur, the god of shepherds, who heard and was pleased. After performance of this pious rite Haïta unbarred the gate of the fold and with a cheerful mind drove his flock afield, eating his morning meal of curds and oat cake as he went, occasionally pausing to add a few berries, cold with dew, or to drink of the waters that came away from the hills to join the stream in the middle of the valley and be borne along with it, he knew not whither.

During the long summer day, as his sheep cropped the good grass which the gods had made to grow for them, or lay with their forelegs doubled under their breasts and chewed the cud, Haïta, reclining in the shadow of a tree, or sitting upon a rock, played so sweet music upon his reed pipe that sometimes from the corner of his eye he got accidental glimpses of the minor sylvan deities, leaning forward out of the copse to hear; but if he looked at them directly they vanished. From this—for he must be thinking if he would not turn into one of his own sheep—he drew the solemn inference that happiness may come if not sought, but if looked for will never be seen; for next to the favor of Hastur, who never disclosed himself, Haïta most valued the friendly interest of his neighbors, the shy immortals of the wood and stream. At nightfall he drove his flock back to the fold, saw that the gate was secure and retired to his cave for refreshment and for dreams.

So passed his life, one day like another, save when the storms uttered the wrath of an offended god. Then Haïta cowered in his cave, his face hidden in his hands, and prayed that he alone might be punished for his sins and the world saved from destruction. Sometimes when there was a great rain, and the stream came out of its banks, compelling him to urge his terrified flock to the uplands, he interceded for the people in the cities which he had been told lay in the plain beyond the two blue hills forming the gateway of his valley.

"It is kind of three, O Hastur," so he prayed, "to give me mountains so near to my dwelling and my fold that I and my sheep can escape the angry torrents; but the rest of the world thou must thyself deliver in some way that I know not of, or I will no longer worship thee."

And Hastur, knowing that Haïta was a youth who kept his word, spared the cities and turned the waters into the sea.

So he had lived since he could remember. He could not rightly conceive any other mode of existence. The holy hermit who dwelt at the head of the valley, a full hour's journey away, from whom he had heard the tale of the great cities where dwelt people—poor souls!—who had no sheep, gave him no knowledge of that early time, when, so he reasoned, he must have been small and helpless like a lamb.

It was through thinking on these mysteries and marvels, and on that horrible change to silence and decay which he felt sure must some time come to him, as he had seen it come to so many of his flock—as it came to all living things except the birds—that Haïta first became conscious how miserable and hopeless was his lot.

"It is necessary," he said, "that I know whence and how I came; for how can one perform his duties unless able to judge what they are by the way in which he was intrusted with them? And what contentment can I have when I know not how long it is going to last? Perhaps before another sun I may be changed, and then what will become of the sheep? What, indeed, will have become of me?"

Pondering these things Haïta became melancholy and morose. He no longer spoke cheerfully to his flock, nor ran with alacrity to the shrine of Hastur. In every breeze he heard whispers of malign deities whose existence he now first observed. Every cloud was a portent signifying disaster, and the darkness was full of terrors. His reed pipe when applied to his lips gave out no melody, but a dismal wail; the sylvan and riparian intelligences no longer thronged the thicket-side to listen, but fled from the sound, as he knew by the stirred leaves and bent flowers. He relaxed his vigilance and many of his sheep strayed away into the hills and were lost. Those that remained became lean and ill for lack of good pasturage, for he would not seek it for them, but conducted them day after day to the same spot, through mere abstraction, while puzzling about life and death—of immortality he knew not.

One day while indulging in the gloomiest reflections he suddenly sprang from the rock upon which he sat, and with a determined gesture of the right hand exclaimed: "I will no longer be a suppliant for knowledge which the gods withhold. Let them look to it that they do me no wrong. I will do my duty as best I can and if I err upon their own heads be it!"

Suddenly, as he spoke, a great brightness fell about him, causing him to look upward, thinking the sun had burst through a rift in the clouds; but there were no clouds. No more than an arm's length away stood a beautiful maiden. So beautiful she was that the flowers about her feet folded their petals in despair and bent their heads in token of submission; so sweet her look that the humming birds thronged her eyes, thrusting their thirsty bills almost into them, and the wild bees were about her lips. And such was her brightness that the shadows of all objects lay divergent from her feet, turning as she moved.

Haïta was entranced. Rising, he knelt before her in adoration, and she laid her hand upon his head.

"Come," she said in a voice that had the music of all the bells of his flock—"come, thou art not to worship me, who am no goddess, but if thou art truthful and dutiful I will abide with thee."

Haïta seized her hand, and stammering his joy and gratitude arose, and hand in hand they stood and smiled into each other's eyes. He gazed on her with reverence and rapture. He said: "I pray thee, lovely maid, tell me thy name and whence and why thou comest."

At this she laid a warning finger on her lip and began to withdraw. Her beauty underwent a visible alteration that made him shudder, he knew not why, for still she was beautiful. The landscape was darkened by a giant shadow sweeping across the valley with the speed of a vulture. In the obscurity the maiden's figure grew dim and indistinct and her voice seemed to come from a distance, as she said, in a tone of sorrowful reproach: "Presumptuous and ungrateful youth! must I then so soon leave thee? Would nothing do but thou must at once break the eternal compact?"

Inexpressibly grieved, Haïta fell upon his knees and implored her to remain—rose and sought her in the deepening darkness—ran in circles, calling to her aloud, but all in vain. She was no longer visible, but out of the gloom he heard her voice saying: "Nay, thou shalt not have me by seeking. Go to thy duty, faithless shepherd, or we shall never meet again."

Night had fallen; the wolves were howling in the hills and the terrified sheep crowding about Haïta's feet. In the demands of the hour he forgot his disappointment, drove his sheep to the fold and repairing to the place of worship poured out his heart in gratitude to Hastur for permitting him to save his flock, then retired to his cave and slept.

When Haïta awoke the sun was high and shone in at the cave, illuminating it with a great glory. And there, beside him, sat the maiden. She smiled upon him with a smile that seemed the visible music of his pipe of reeds. He dared not speak, fearing to offend her as before, for he knew not what he could venture to say.

"Because," she said, "thou didst thy duty by the flock, and didst not forget to thank Hastur for staying the wolves of the night, I am come to thee again. Wilt thou have me for a companion?"

"Who would not have thee forever?" replied Haïta. "Oh! never again leave me until—until I—change and become silent and motionless."

Haïta had no word for death.

"I wish, indeed," he continued, "that thou wert of my own sex, that we might wrestle and run races and so never tire of being together."

At these words the maiden arose and passed out of the cave, and Haïta, springing from his couch of fragrant boughs to overtake and detain her, observed to his astonishment that the rain was falling and the stream in the middle of the valley had come out of its banks. The sheep were bleating in terror, for the rising waters had invaded their fold. And there was danger for the unknown cities of the distant plain.

It was many days before Haïta saw the maiden again. One day he was returning from the head of the valley, where he had gone with ewe's milk and oat cake and berries for the holy hermit, who was too old and feeble to provide himself with food.

"Poor old man!" he said aloud, as he trudged along homeward. "I will return tomorrow and bear him on my back to my own dwelling, where I can care for him. Doubtless it is for this that Hastur has reared me all these many years, and gives me health and strength."

As he spoke, the maiden, clad in glittering garments, met him in the path with a smile that took away his breath.

"I am come again," she said, "to dwell with thee if thou wilt now have me, for none else will. Thou mayest have learned wisdom, and art willing to take me as I am, nor care to know."

Haïta threw himself at her feet. "Beautiful being," he cried, "if thou wilt but deign to accept all the devotion of my heart and soul—after Hastur be served—it is thine forever. But, alas! thou art capricious and wayward. Before to-morrow's sun I may lose thee again. Promise, I beseech thee, that however in my ignorance I may offend, thou wilt forgive and remain always with me."

Scarcely had he finished speaking when a troop of bears came out of the hills, racing toward him with crimson mouths and fiery eyes. The maiden again vanished, and he turned and fled for his life. Nor did he stop until he was in the cot of the holy hermit, whence he had set out. Hastily barring the door against the bears he cast himself upon the ground and wept.

"My son," said the hermit from his couch of straw, freshly gathered that morning by Haïta's hands, "it is not like thee to weep for bears—tell me what sorrow hath befallen thee, that age may minister to the hurts of youth with such balms as it hath of its wisdom."

Haïta told him all: how thrice he had met the radiant maid, and thrice she had left him forlorn. He related minutely all that had passed between them, omitting no word of what had been said.

When he had ended, the holy hermit was a moment silent, then said: "My son, I have attended to thy story, and I know the maiden. I have myself seen her, as have many. Know, then, that her name, which she would not even permit thee to inquire, is Happiness. Thou saidst the truth to her, that she is capricious for she imposeth conditions that man can not fulfill, and delinquency is punished by desertion. She cometh only when unsought, and will not be questioned. One manifestation of curiosity, one sign of doubt, one expression of misgiving, and she is away! How long didst thou have her at any time before she fled?"

"Only a single instant," answered Haïta, blushing with shame at the confession. "Each time I drove her away in one moment."

"Unfortunate youth!" said the holy hermit, "but for thine indiscretion thou mightst have had her for two."

THE WAYS OF GHOSTS

Present at a Hanging

An old man named Daniel Baker, living near Lebanon, Iowa, was suspected by his neighbors of having murdered a peddler who had obtained permission to pass the night at his house. This was in 1853, when peddling was more common in the Western country than it is now, and was attended with considerable danger. The peddler with his pack traversed the country by all manner of lonely roads, and was compelled to rely upon the country people for hospitality. This brought him into relation with queer characters, some of whom were not altogether scrupulous in their methods of making a living, murder being an acceptable means to that end. It occasionally occurred that a peddler with diminished pack and swollen purse would be traced to the lonely dwelling of some rough character and never could be traced beyond. This was so in the case of "old man Baker," as he was always called. (Such names are given in the western "settlements" only to elderly persons who are not esteemed; to the general disrepute of social unworth is affixed the special reproach of age.) A peddler came to his house and none went away—that is all that anybody knew.

Seven years later the Rev. Mr. Cummings, a Baptist minister well known in that part of the country, was driving by Baker's farm one night. It was not very dark: there was a bit of moon somewhere above the light veil of mist that lay along the earth. Mr. Cummings, who was at all times a cheerful person, was whistling a tune, which he would occasionally interrupt to speak a word of friendly encouragement to his horse. As he came to a little bridge across a dry ravine he saw the figure of a man standing upon it, clearly outlined against the gray background of a misty forest. The man had something strapped on his back and carried a heavy stick—obviously an itinerant peddler. His attitude had in it a suggestion of abstraction, like that of a sleepwalker. Mr. Cummings reined in his horse when he arrived in front of him, gave him a pleasant salutation and invited him to a seat in the vehicle—"if you are going my way," he added. The man raised his head, looked him full in the face, but neither answered nor made any further movement. The minister with good-natured persistence, repeated his invitation. At this the man threw

his right hand forward from his side and pointed downward as he
stood on the extreme edge of the bridge. Mr. Cummings looked
past him, over into the ravine, saw nothing unusual and withdrew
his eyes to address the man again. He had disappeared. The horse,
which all this time had been uncommonly restless, gave at the same
moment a snort of terror and started to run away. Before he had re-
gained control of the animal the minister was at the crest of the hill
a hundred yards along. He looked back and saw the figure again,
at the same place and in the same attitude as when he had first
observed it. Then for the first time he was conscious of a sense of
the supernatural and drove home as rapidly as his willing horse
would go.

On arriving at home he related his adventure to his family, and
early the next morning, accompanied by two neighbors, John White
Corwell and Abner Raiser, returned to the spot. They found the
body of old man Baker hanging by the neck from one of the beams
of the bridge, immediately beneath the spot where the apparition
had stood. A thick coating of dust, slightly dampened by the mist,
covered the floor of the bridge, but the only footprints were those
of Mr. Cummings' horse.

In taking down the body the men disturbed the loose, friable
earth of the slope below it, disclosing human bones already nearly
uncovered by the action of water and frost. They were identified as
those of the lost peddler. At the double inquest the coroner's jury
found that Daniel Baker died by his own hand while suffering from
temporary insanity, and that Samuel Morritz was murdered by some
person or persons to the jury unknown.

A Wireless Message

In the summer of 1896 Mr. William Holt, a wealthy manufacturer of Chicago, was living temporarily in a little town of central New York, the name of which the writer's memory has not retained. Mr. Holt had had "trouble with his wife," from whom he had parted a year before. Whether the trouble was anything more serious than "incompatibility of temper," he is probably the only living person that knows: he is not addicted to the vice of confidences. Yet he has related the incident herein set down to at least one person without exacting a pledge of secrecy. He is now living in Europe.

One evening he had left the house of a brother whom he was visiting, for a stroll in the country. It may be assumed—whatever the value of the assumption in connection with what is said to have occurred—that his mind was occupied with reflections on his domestic infelicities and the distressing changes that they had wrought in his life. Whatever may have been his thoughts, they so possessed him that he observed neither the lapse of time nor whither his feet were carrying him; he knew only that he had passed far beyond the town limits and was traversing a lonely region by a road that bore no resemblance to the one by which he had left the village. In brief, he was "lost."

Realizing his mischance, he smiled; central New York is not a region of perils, nor does one long remain lost in it. He turned about and went back the way that he had come. Before he had gone far he observed that the landscape was growing more distinct—was brightening. Everything was suffused with a soft, red glow in which he saw his shadow projected in the road before him. "The moon is rising," he said to himself. Then he remembered that it was about the time of the new moon, and if that tricksy orb was in one of its stages of visibility it had set long before. He stopped and faced about, seeking the source of the rapidly broadening light. As he did so, his shadow turned and lay along the road in front of him as before. The light still came from behind him. That was surprising; he could not understand. Again he turned, and again, facing successively to every point of the horizon. Always the shadow was before—always the light behind, "a still and awful red."

Holt was astonished—"dumfounded" is the word that he used in telling it—yet seems to have retained a certain intelligent curiosity. To test the intensity of the light whose nature and cause he could not determine, he took out his watch to see if he could make out the figures on the dial. They were plainly visible, and the hands indicated the hour of eleven o'clock and twenty-five minutes. At that moment the mysterious illumination suddenly flared to an intense, an almost blinding splendor, flushing the entire sky, extinguishing the stars and throwing the monstrous shadow of himself athwart the landscape. In that unearthly illumination he saw near him, but apparently in the air at a considerable elevation, the figure of his wife, clad in her night-clothing and holding to her breast the figure of his child. Her eyes were fixed upon his with an expression which he afterward professed himself unable to name or describe, further than that it was "not of this life."

The flare was momentary, followed by black darkness, in which, however, the apparition still showed white and motionless; then by insensible degrees it faded and vanished, like a bright image on the retina after the closing of the eyes. A peculiarity of the apparition, hardly noted at the time, but afterward recalled, was that it showed only the upper half of the woman's figure: nothing was seen below the waist.

The sudden darkness was comparative, not absolute, for gradually all objects of his environment became again visible.

In the dawn of the morning Holt found himself entering the village at a point opposite to that at which he had left it. He soon arrived at the house of his brother, who hardly knew him. He was wild-eyed, haggard, and gray as a rat. Almost incoherently, he related his night's experience.

"Go to bed, my poor fellow," said his brother, "and—wait. We shall hear more of this."

An hour later came the predestined telegram. Holt's dwelling in one of the suburbs of Chicago had been destroyed by fire. Her escape cut off by the flames, his wife had appeared at an upper window, her child in her arms. There she had stood, motionless, apparently dazed. Just as the firemen had arrived with a ladder, the floor had given way, and she was seen no more.

The moment of this culminating horror was eleven o'clock and twenty-five minutes, standard time.

SOLDIER FOLK

Three and One Are One

In the year 1861 Barr Lassiter, a young man of twenty-two, lived with his parents and an elder sister near Carthage, Tennessee. The family were in somewhat humble circumstances, subsisting by cultivation of a small and not very fertile plantation. Owning no slaves, they were not rated among "the best people" of their neighborhood; but they were honest persons of good education, fairly well mannered and as respectable as any family could be if uncredentialed by personal dominion over the sons and daughters of Ham.[61] The elder Lassiter had that severity of manner that so frequently affirms an uncompromising devotion to duty and conceals a warm and affectionate disposition. He was of the iron of which martyrs are made, but in the heart of the matrix had lurked a nobler metal, fusible at a milder heat, yet never coloring nor softening the hard exterior. By both heredity and environment something of the man's inflexible character had touched the other members of the family; the Lassiter home, though not devoid of domestic affection, was a veritable citadel of duty, and duty—ah, duty is as cruel as death!

When the war came on it found in the family, as in so many others in that State, a divided sentiment; the young man was loyal to the Union, the others savagely hostile. This unhappy division begot an insupportable domestic bitterness, and when the offending son and brother left home with the avowed purpose of joining the Federal army not a hand was laid in his, not a word of farewell was spoken, not a good wish followed him out into the world whither he went to meet with such spirit as he might whatever fate awaited him.

Making his way to Nashville, already occupied by the Army of General Buell, he enlisted in the first organization that he found, a Kentucky regiment of cavalry, and in due time passed through all the stages of military evolution from raw recruit to experienced trooper. A right good trooper he was, too, although in his oral narrative from which this tale is made there was no mention of that; the fact was learned from his surviving comrades. For Barr Lassiter has answered "Here" to the sergeant whose name is Death.

Two years after he had joined it his regiment passed through the

region whence he had come. The country thereabout had suffered
severely from the ravages of war having been occupied alternately
(and simultaneously) by the belligerent forces, and a sanguinary
struggle had occurred in the immediate vicinity of the Lassiter home-
stead. But of this the young trooper was not aware.

Finding himself in camp near his home, he felt a natural longing
to see his parents and sister, hoping that in them, as in him, the unnatural animosities of the period had been softened by time and
separation. Obtaining a leave of absence, he set foot in the late summer afternoon, and soon after the rising of the full moon was walking up the gravel path leading to the dwelling in which he had been
born.

Soldiers in war age rapidly, and in youth two years are a long
time. Barr Lassiter felt himself an old man, and had almost expected
to find the place a ruin and a desolation. Nothing, apparently, was
changed. At the sight of each dear and familiar object he was profoundly affected. His heart beat audibly, his emotion nearly suffo-
cated him; an ache was in his throat. Unconsciously he quickened
his pace until he almost ran, his long shadow making grotesque efforts to keep its place beside him.

The house was unlighted, the door open. As he approached and
paused to recover control of himself his father came out and stood
bare-headed in the moonlight.

"Father!" cried the young man, springing forward with out-
stretched hand—"Father!"

The elder man looked him sternly in the face, stood a moment
motionless and without a word withdrew into the house. Bitterly
disappointed, humiliated, inexpressibly hurt and altogether unnerved,
the soldier dropped upon a rustic seat in deep dejection, supporting
his head upon his trembling hand. But he would not have it so; he
was too good a soldier to accept repulse as defeat. He rose and entered the house, passing directly to the "sitting-room."

It was dimly lighted by an uncurtained east window. On a low
stool by the hearthside, the only article of furniture in the place, sat
his mother, staring into a fireplace strewn with blackened embers
and cold ashes. He spoke to her—tenderly, interrogatively, and with
hesitation, but she neither answered, nor moved, nor seemed in any
way surprised. True, there had been time for her husband to apprise
her of their guilty son's return. He moved nearer and was about to
lay his hand upon her arm, when his sister entered from an adjoin-

ing room, looked him full in the face, passed him without a sign of recognition and left the room by a door that was partly behind him. He had turned his head to watch her, but when she was gone his eyes again sought his mother. She too had left the place.

Barr Lassiter strode to the door by which he had entered. The moonlight on the lawn was tremulous, as if the sward were a rippling sea. The trees and their black shadows shook as in a breeze. Blended with its borders, the gravel walk seemed unsteady and insecure to step on. This young soldier knew the optical illusions produced by tears. He felt them on his cheek, and saw them sparkle on the breast of his trooper's jacket. He left the house and made his way back to camp.

The next day, with no very definite intention, with no dominant feeling that he could rightly have named, he again sought the spot. Within a half-mile of it he met Bushrod Albro, a former playfellow and schoolmate, who greeted him warmly.

"I am going to visit my home," said the soldier.

The other looked at him rather sharply, but said nothing.

"I know," continued Lassiter, "that my folks have not changed, but——"

"There have been changes," Albro interrupted—"everything changes. I'll go with you if you don't mind. We can talk as we go."

But Albro did not talk.

Instead of a house they found only fire-blackened foundations of stone, enclosing an area of compact ashes pitted by rains.

Lassiter's astonishment was extreme.

"I could not find the right way to tell you," said Albro. "In the fight a year ago your house was burned by a Federal shell."

"And my family—where are they?"

"In Heaven, I hope. All were killed by the shell."

From NEGLIGIBLE TALES

NEGLIGIBLE TALES

A Bottomless Grave

My name is John Brenwalter. My father, a drunkard, had a patent for an invention for making coffee-berries out of clay; but he was an honest man and would not himself engage in the manufacture. He was, therefore, only moderately wealthy, his royalties from his really valuable invention bringing him hardly enough to pay his expenses of litigation with rogues guilty of infringement. So I lacked many advantages enjoyed by the children of unscrupulous and dishonorable parents, and had it not been for a noble and devoted mother, who neglected all my brothers and sisters and personally supervised my education, should have grown up in ignorance and been compelled to teach school. To be the favorite child of a good woman is better than gold.

When I was nineteen years of age my father had the misfortune to die. He had always had perfect health, and his death, which occurred at the dinner table without a moment's warning, surprised no one more than himself. He had that very morning been notified that a patent had been granted him for a device to burst open safes by hydraulic pressure, without noise. The Commissioner of Patents had pronounced it the most ingenious, effective and generally meritorious invention that had ever been submitted to him, and my father had naturally looked forward to an old age of prosperity and honor. His sudden death was, therefore, a deep disappointment to him; but my mother, whose piety and resignation to the will of Heaven were conspicuous virtues of her character, was apparently less affected. At the close of the meal, when my poor father's body had been removed from the floor, she called us all into an adjoining room and addressed us as follows:

"My children, the uncommon occurrence that you have just witnessed is one of the most disagreeable incidents in a good man's life, and one in which I take little pleasure, I assure you. I beg you to believe that I had no hand in bringing it about. Of course," she added, after a pause, during which her eyes were cast down in deep thought, "of course it is better that he is dead."

She uttered this with so evident a sense of its obviousness as a self-evident truth that none of us had the courage to brave her surprise by asking an explanation. My mother's air of surprise when any of us went wrong in any way was very terrible to us. One day, when in a fit of peevish temper, I had taken the liberty to cut off the baby's ear, her simple words, "John, you surprise me!" appeared to me so sharp a reproof that after a sleepless night I went to her in tears, and throwing myself at her feet, exclaimed: "Mother, forgive me for surprising you." So now we all—including the one-eared baby—felt that it would keep matters smoother to accept without question the statement that it was better, somehow, for our dear father to be dead. My mother continued:

"I must tell you, my children, that in a case of sudden and mysterious death the law requires the Coroner to come and cut the body into pieces and submit them to a number of men who, having inspected them, pronounce the person dead. For this the Coroner gets a large sum of money. I wish to avoid that painful formality in this instance; it is one which never had the approval of—of the remains. John"—here my mother turned her angel face to me—"you are an educated lad, and very discreet. You have now an opportunity to show your gratitude for all the sacrifices that your education has entailed upon the rest of us. John, go and remove the Coroner."

Inexpressibly delighted by this proof of my mother's confidence, and by the chance to distinguish myself by an act that squared with my natural disposition, I knelt before her, carried her hand to my lips and bathed it with tears of sensibility. Before five o'clock that afternoon I had removed the Coroner.

I was immediately arrested and thrown into jail, where I passed a most uncomfortable night, being unable to sleep because of the profanity of my fellow-prisoners, two clergymen, whose theological training had given them a fertility of impious ideas and a command of blasphemous language altogether unparalleled. But along toward morning the jailer, who, sleeping in an adjoining room, had been equally disturbed, entered the cell and with a fearful oath warned the reverend gentlemen that if he heard any more swearing their sacred calling would not prevent him from turning them into the street. After that they moderated their objectionable conversation, substituting an accordion, and I slept the peaceful and refreshing sleep of youth and innocence.

The next morning I was taken before the Superior Judge, sitting as a committing magistrate, and put upon my preliminary examination. I pleaded not guilty, adding that the man whom I had murdered was a notorious Democrat. (My good mother was a Republican, and from early childhood I had been carefully instructed by her in the principles of honest government and the necessity of suppressing factional opposition.) The Judge, elected by a Republican ballot-box with a sliding bottom,[62] was visibly impressed by the cogency of my plea and offered me a cigarette.

"May it please your Honor," began the District Attorney, "I do not deem it necessary to submit any evidence in this case. Under the law of the land you sit here as a committing magistrate. It is therefore your duty to commit. Testimony and argument alike would imply a doubt that your Honor means to perform your sworn duty. That is my case."

My counsel, a brother of the deceased Coroner, rose and said: "May it please the Court, my learned friend on the other side has so well and eloquently stated the law governing in this case that it only remains for me to inquire to what extent it has been already complied with. It is true, your Honor is a committing magistrate, and as such it is your duty to commit—what? That is a matter which the law has wisely and justly left to your own discretion, and wisely you have discharged already every obligation that the law imposes. Since I have known your Honor you have done nothing but commit. You have committed embracery,[63] theft, arson, perjury, adultery, murder—every crime in the calendar and every excess known to the sensual and depraved, including my learned friend, the District Attorney. You have done your whole duty as a committing magistrate, and as there is no evidence against this worthy young man, my client, I move that he be discharged."

An impressive silence ensued. The Judge arose, put on the black cap and in a voice trembling with emotion sentenced me to life and liberty. Then turning to my counsel he said, coldly but significantly:

"I will see you later."

The next morning the lawyer who had so conscientiously defended me against a charge of murdering his own brother—with whom he had a quarrel about some land—had disappeared and his fate is to this day unknown.

In the meantime my poor father's body had been secretly buried at midnight in the back yard of his late residence, with his late boots on and the contents of his late stomach unanalyzed. "He was opposed to display," said my dear mother, as she finished tamping down the earth above him and assisted the children to litter the place with straw; "his instincts were all domestic and he loved a quiet life."

My mother's application for letters of administration stated that she had good reason to believe that the deceased was dead, for he had not come home to his meals for several days; but the Judge of the Crowbait Court—as she ever afterward contemptuously called it—decided that the proof of death was insufficient, and put the estate into the hands of the Public Administrator, who was his son-in-law. It was found that the liabilities were exactly balanced by the assets; there was left only the patent for the device for bursting open safes without noise, by hydraulic pressure and this had passed into the ownership of the Probate Judge and the Public Adminis-traitor—as my dear mother preferred to spell it. Thus, within a few brief months a worthy and respectable family was reduced from prosperity to crime; necessity compelled us to go to work.

In the selection of occupations we were governed by a variety of considerations, such as personal fitness, inclination, and so forth. My mother opened a select private school for instruction in the art of changing the spots upon leopard-skin rugs; my eldest brother, George Henry, who had a turn for music, became a bugler in a neighboring asylum for deaf mutes; my sister, Mary Maria, took orders for Professor Pumpernickel's Essence of Latchkeys for flavoring mineral springs, and I set up as an adjuster and gilder of crossbeams for gibbets.[64] The other children, too young for labor, continued to steal small articles exposed in front of shops, as they had been taught.

In our intervals of leisure we decoyed travelers into our house and buried the bodies in a cellar.

In one part of this cellar we kept wines, liquors and provisions. From the rapidity of their disappearance we acquired the supersti-tious belief that the spirits of the persons buried there came at dead of night and held a festival. It was at least certain that frequently of a morning we would discover fragments of pickled meats, canned goods and such débris, littering the place, although it had been se-curely locked and barred against human intrusion. It was proposed to remove the provisions and store them elsewhere, but our dear mother, always generous and hospitable, said it was better to en-dure the loss than risk exposure: if the ghosts were denied this trifling gratification they might set on foot an investigation, which would overthrow our scheme of the division of labor, by diverting the energies of the whole family into the single industry pursued by me—we might all decorate the crossbeams of gibbets. We accepted her decision with filial submission, due to our reverence for her wordly wisdom and the purity of her character.

One night while we were all in the cellar—none dared to enter it alone—engaged in bestowing upon the Mayor of an adjoining town the solemn offices of Christian burial, my mother and the younger children, holding a candle each, while George Henry and I labored with a spade and pick, my sister Mary Maria uttered a shriek and covered her eyes with her hands. We were all dreadfully startled and the Mayor's obsequies were instantly suspended, while with pale faces and in trembling tones we begged her to say what had alarmed her. The younger children were so agitated that they held their candles unsteadily, and the waving shadows of our figures danced with uncouth and grotesque movements on the walls and flung themselves into the most uncanny attitudes. The face of the dead man, now gleaming ghastly in the light, and now extinguished by some floating shadow, appeared at each emergence to have taken on a new and more forbidding expression, a maligner menace. Frightened even more than ourselves by the girl's scream, rats raced in multitudes about the place, squeaking shrilly, or starred the black opacity of some distant corner with steadfast eyes, mere points of green light, matching the faint phosphorescence of decay that filled the half-dug grave and seemed the visible manifestation of that faint odor of mortality which tainted the unwholesome air. The children now sobbed and clung about the limbs of their elders, dropping their candles, and we were near being left in total darkness, except for that sinister light, which slowly welled upward from the disturbed earth and overflowed the edges of the grave like a fountain.

Meanwhile my sister, crouching in the earth that had been thrown out of the excavation, had removed her hands from her face and was staring with expanded eyes into an obscure space between two wine-casks.

"There it is!—there it is!" she shrieked, pointing; "God in heaven! can't you see it?"

And there indeed it was!—a human figure, dimly discernible in the gloom—a figure that wavered from side to side as if about to fall, clutching at the wine-casks for support, had stepped unsteadily forward and for one moment stood revealed in the light of our remaining candles; then it surged heavily and fell prone upon the earth. In that moment we had all recognized the figure, the face and bearing of our father—dead these ten months and buried by our own hands!—our father indubitably risen and ghastly drunk!

On the incidents of our precipitate flight from the horrible place—on the extinction of all human sentiment in that tumultuous, mad scramble up the damp and mouldy stairs—slipping, falling, pulling one another down and clambering over one another's back—the lights extinguished, babes trampled beneath the feet of their strong brothers and hurled backward to death by a mother's arm!—on all this I do not dare to dwell. My mother, my eldest brother and sister and I escaped; the others remained below, to perish of their wounds, or of their terror—some, perhaps, by flame. For within an hour we four, hastily gathering together what money and jewels we had and what clothing we could carry, fired the dwelling and fled by its light into the hills. We did not even pause to collect the insurance, and my dear mother said on her death-bed, years afterward in a distant land, that this was the only sin of omission that lay upon her conscience. Her confessor, a holy man, assured her that under the circumstances Heaven would pardon the neglect.

About ten years after our removal from the scenes of my childhood I, then a prosperous forger, returned in disguise to the spot with a view to obtaining, if possible, some treasure belonging to us, which had been buried in the cellar. I may say that I was unsuccessful: the discovery of many human bones in the ruins had set the authorities digging for more. They had found the treasure and had kept it for their honesty. The house had not been rebuilt; the whole suburb was, in fact, a desolation. So many unearthly sights and sounds had been reported thereabout that nobody would live there. As there was none to question nor molest, I resolved to gratify my filial piety by gazing once more upon the face of my beloved father, if indeed our eyes had deceived us and he was still in his grave. I remembered, too, that he had always worn an enormous diamond ring, and never having seen it nor heard of it since his death, I had reason to think he might have been buried in it. Procuring a spade, I soon located the grave in what had been the back yard and began digging. When I had got down about four feet the whole bottom fell out of the grave and I was precipitated into a large drain, falling through a long hole in its crumbling arch. There was no body, nor any vestige of one.

Unable to get out of the excavation, I crept through the drain, and having with some difficulty removed a mass of charred rubbish and blackened masonry that choked it, emerged into what had been that fateful cellar.

All was clear. My father, whatever had caused him to be "taken bad" at his meal (and I think my sainted mother could have thrown some light upon that matter) had indubitably been buried alive. The grave having been accidentally dug above the forgotten drain, and down almost to the crown of its arch, and no coffin having been used, his struggles on reviving had broken the rotten masonry and he had fallen through, escaping finally into the cellar. Feeling that he was not welcome in his own house, yet having no other, he had lived in subterranean seclusion, a witness to our thrift and a pensioner on our providence. It was he who had eaten our food; it was he who had drunk our wine—he was no better than a thief! In a moment of intoxication, and feeling, no doubt, that need of companionship which is the one sympathetic link between a drunken man and his race, he had left his place of concealment at a strangely inopportune time, entailing the most deplorable consequences upon those nearest and dearest to him—a blunder that had almost the dignity of crime.

Jupiter Doke,
Brigadier-General

From the Secretary of War to the Hon. Jupiter Doke,
  Hardpan Crossroads, Posey County, Illinois.

> *Washington,*
> *November 3, 1861.*

Having faith in your patriotism and ability, the President has been pleased to appoint you a brigadier-general of volunteers. Do you accept?

From the Hon. Jupiter Doke to the Secretary of War.

> *Hardpan, Illinois,*
> *November 9, 1861.*

It is the proudest moment of my life. The office is one which should be neither sought nor declined. In times that try men's souls the patriot knows no North, no South, no East, no West. His motto should be: "My country, my whole country and nothing but my country." I accept the great trust confided in me by a free and intelligent people, and with a firm reliance on the principles of constitutional liberty, and invoking the guidance of an all-wise Providence, Ruler of Nations, shall labor so to discharge it as to leave no blot upon my political escutcheon.[65] Say to his Excellency, the successor of the immortal Washington in the Seat of Power, that the patronage of my office will be bestowed with an eye single to securing the greatest good to the greatest number, the stability of republican institutions and the triumph of the party in all elections; and to this I pledge my life, my fortune and my sacred honor. I shall at once prepare an appropriate response to the speech of the chairman of the committee deputed to inform me of my appointment, and I trust the sentiments therein expressed will strike a sympathetic chord in the public heart, as well as command the Executive approval.

From the Secretary of War to Major-General Blount
  Wardorg, Commanding the Military Department
  of Eastern Kentucky.

Washington,
November 14, 1861.

I have assigned to your department Brigadier-General Jupiter Doke, who will soon proceed to Distilleryville, on the Little Buttermilk River, and take command of the Illinois Brigade at that point, reporting to you by letter for orders. Is the route from Covington by way of Bluegrass, Opossum Corners and Horsecave still infested with bushwackers,[66] as reported in your last dispatch? I have a plan for cleaning them out.

From Major-General Blount Wardorg to
  the Secretary of War.

Louisville, Kentucky,
November 20, 1861.

The name and services of Brigadier-General Doke are unfamiliar to me, but I shall be pleased to have the advantage of his skill. The route from Covington to Distilleryville *via* Opossum Corners and Horsecave I have been compelled to abandon to the enemy, whose guerilla warfare made it possible to keep it open without detaching too many troops from the front. The brigade at Distilleryville is supplied by steamboats up the Little Buttermilk.

From the Secretary of War to Brigadier-General
  Jupiter Doke, Hardpan, Illinois.

Washington,
November 26, 1861.

I deeply regret that your commission had been forwarded by mail before the receipt of your letter of acceptance; so we must dispense with the formality of official notification to you by a committee. The President is highly gratified by the noble and patriotic sentiments of your letter, and directs that you proceed at once to your command at Distilleryville, Kentucky, and there report by letter to Major-General Wardorg at Louisville, for orders. It is important that the strictest secrecy be observed regarding your movements until you have passed Covington, as it is desired to hold the enemy in front of Distilleryville until you are within three days of him. Then if your approach is known it will operate as a demonstration against his right and cause him to strengthen it with his left now at Memphis, Tennessee, which it is desirable to capture first. Go by way of Bluegrass, Opossum Corners and Horsecave. All officers are expected to be in full uniform when *en route* to the front.

*From Brigadier-General Jupiter Doke to
   the Secretary of War.*

*Covington, Kentucky,
December 7, 1861.*

I arrived yesterday at this point, and have given my proxy[67] to Joel Briller, Esq., my wife's cousin, and a staunch Republican, who will worthily represent Posey County in field and forum. He points with pride to a stainless record in the halls of legislation, which have often echoed to his soul-stirring eloquence on questions which lie at the very foundation of popular government. He has been called the Patrick Henry of Hardpan, where he has done yeoman's service in the cause of civil and religious liberty. Mr. Briller left for Distilleryville last evening, and the standard bearer of the Democratic host confronting that stronghold of freedom will find him a lion in his path. I have been asked to remain here and deliver some addresses to the people in a local contest involving issues of paramount importance. That duty being performed, I shall in person enter the arena of armed debate and move in the direction of the heaviest firing, burning my ships behind me. I forward by this mail to his Excellency the President a request for the appointment of my son, Jabez Leonidas Doke, as postmaster at Hardpan. I would take it, sir, as a great favor if you would give the application a strong oral indorsement, as the appointment is in the line of reform. Be kind enough to inform me what are the emoluments of the office I hold in the military arm, and if they are by salary or fees. Are there any perquisites? My mileage account will be transmitted monthly.

*From Brigadier-General Jupiter Doke to
   Major General Blount Wardorg.*

*Distilleryville, Kentucky,
January 12, 1862.*

I arrived on the tented field yesterday by steamboat, the recent storms having inundated the landscape, covering, I understand, the greater part of a congressional district. I am pained to find that Joel Briller, Esq., a prominent citizen of Posey County, Illinois, and a far-seeing statesman who held my proxy, and who a month ago should have been thundering at the gates of Disunion, has not been heard from, and has doubtless been sacrificed upon the altar of his country.

In him the American people lose a bulwark of freedom. I would respectfully move that you designate a committee to draw up resolutions of respect to his memory, and that the office holders and men under your command wear the usual badge of mourning for thirty days. I shall at once place myself at the head of affairs here, and am now ready to entertain any suggestions which you may make, looking to the better enforcement of the laws in this commonwealth. The militant Democrats on the other side of the river appear to be contemplating extreme measures. They have two large cannons facing this way, and yesterday morning, I am told, some of them came down to the water's edge and remained in session for some time, making infamous allegations.

*From the Diary of Brigadier-General Jupiter Doke,
    at Distilleryville, Kentucky.*

January 12, 1862—On my arrival yesterday at the Henry Clay[68] Hotel (named in honor of the late far-seeing statesman) I was waited on by a delegation consisting of the three colonels intrusted with the command of the regiments of my brigade. It was an occasion that will be memorable in the political annals of America. Forwarded copies of the speeches to the Posey *Maverick*, to be spread upon the record of the ages. The gentlemen composing the delegation unanimously reaffirmed their devotion to the principles of national unity and the Republican party. Was gratified to recognize in them men of political prominence and untarnished escutcheons. At the subsequent banquet, sentiments of lofty patriotism were expressed. Wrote to Mr. Wardorg at Louisville for instructions.

January 13, 1862.—Leased a prominent residence (the former incumbent being absent in arms against his country) for the term of one year, and wrote at once for Mrs. Brigadier-General Doke and the vital issues—excepting Jabez Leonidas. In the camp of treason opposite here there are supposed to be three thousand misguided men laying the ax at the root of the tree of liberty. They have a clear majority, many of our men having returned without leave to their constituents. We could probably not poll more than two thousand votes. Have advised my heads of regiments to make a canvass of those remaining, all bolters[69] to be read out of the phalanx.

January 14, 1862.—Wrote to the President, asking for the contract to supply this command with firearms and regalia through my brother-in-law, prominently identified with the manufacturing interests of the country. Club of cannon soldiers arrived at Jayhawk, three miles back from here, on their way to join us in battle array. Marched my whole brigade to Jayhawk to escort them into town but their chairman, mistaking us for the opposing party, opened fire on

the head of the procession and by the extraordinary noise of the cannon balls (I had no conception of it!) so frightened my horse that I
was unseated without a contest. The meeting adjourned in disorder
and returning to camp I found that a deputation of the enemy had
crossed the river in our absence and made a division of the loaves and
fishes. Wrote to the President, applying for the Gubernatorial Chair
of the Territory of Idaho.

From Editorial Article in the Posey, Illinois,
"Maverick," January 20, 1862.

Brigadier-General Doke's thrilling account, in another column, of
the Battle of Distilleryville will make the heart of every loyal Illinois-
ian leap with exultation. The brilliant exploit marks an era in military
history, and as General Doke says, "lays broad and deep the foundations of American prowess in arms." As none of the troops engaged,
except the gallant author-chieftain (a host in himself) hails from
Posey County, he justly considered that a list of the fallen would
only occupy our valuable space to the exclusion of more important
matter, but his account of the strategic ruse by which he apparently
abandoned his camp and so inveigled a perfidious enemy into it for
the purpose of murdering the sick, the unfortunate *countertempus*[70]
at Jayhawk, the subsequent dash upon a trapped enemy flushed with
a supposed success, driving their terrified legions across an impassable river which precluded pursuit—all these "moving accidents by
flood and field" are related with a pen of fire and have all the terrible
interest of romance.

Verily, truth is stranger than fiction and the pen is mightier than
the sword. When by the graphic power of the art preservative of all
arts we are brought face to face with such glorious events as these,
the *Maverick's* enterprise in securing for its thousands of readers the
services of so distinguished a contributor as the Great Captain who
made the history as well as wrote it seems a matter of almost sec-
ondary importance. For President in 1864 (subject to the decision of
the Republican National Convention) Brigadier-General Jupiter Doke,
of Illinois!

From Major-General Blount Wardorg to
Brigadier-General Jupiter Doke

Louisville,
January 22, 1862.

Your letter apprising me of your arrival at Distilleryville was delayed
in transmission, having only just been received (open) through the

courtesy of the Confederate department commander under a flag of truce. He begs me to assure you that he would consider it an act of cruelty to trouble you, and I think it would be. Maintain, however, a threatening attitude, but at the least pressure retire. Your position is simply an outpost which it is not intended to hold.

From Major-General Blount Wardorg to
the Secretary of War.

> *Louisville,*
> *January 23, 1862.*

I have certain information that the enemy has concentrated twenty thousand troops of all arms on the Little Buttermilk. According to your assignment, General Doke is in command of the small brigade of raw troops opposing them. It is no part of my plan to contest the enemy's advance at that point, but I cannot hold myself responsible for any reverses to the brigade mentioned, under its present commander. I think him a fool.

From the Secretary of War to
Major-General Blount Wardorg.

> *Washington,*
> *February 1, 1862.*

The President has great faith in General Doke. If your estimate of him is correct, however, he would seem to be singularly well placed where he now is, as your plans appear to contemplate a considerable sacrifice for whatever advantages you expect to gain.

From Brigadier-General Jupiter Doke to
Major-General Blount Wardorg.

> *Distilleryville,*
> *February 1, 1862.*

To-morrow I shall remove my headquarters to Jayhawk in order to point the way whenever my brigade retires from Distilleryville, as foreshadowed by your letter of the 22d ult.[71] I have appointed a Committee on Retreat, the minutes of whose first meeting I transmit to you. You will perceive that the committee having been duly organized by the election of a chairman and secretary, a resolution (prepared by myself) was adopted, to the effect that in case treason again raises her hideous head on this side of the river every man of the brigade is to mount a mule, the procession to move promptly in the direction of Louisville and the loyal North. In preparation for such an emergency I have for some time been collecting mules from the resident Democracy, and have on hand 2300 in a field at Jayhawk. Eternal vigilance is the price of liberty!

*From Major-General Gibeon J. Buxter, C. S. A., to
    the Confederate Secretary of War.*

*Bung Station, Kentucky,
February 4, 1862.*

On the night of the 2d inst.,[72] our entire force, consisting of 25,000 men and thirty-two field pieces, under command of Major-General Simmons B. Flood, crossed by a ford to the north side of Little But-termilk River at a point three miles above Distilleryville and moved obliquely down and away from the stream, to strike the Covington turnpike at Jayhawk; the object being, as you know, to capture Covington, destroy Cincinnati and occupy the Ohio Valley. For some months there had been in our front only a small brigade of undisci-plined troops, apparently without a commander, who were useful to us, for by not disturbing them we could create an impression of our weakness. But the movement on Jayhawk having isolated them, I was about to detach an Alabama regiment to bring them in, my divi-sion being the leading one, when an earth-shaking rumble was felt and heard, and suddenly the head-of-column was struck by one of the terrible tornadoes for which this region is famous, and utterly an-nihilated. The tornado, I believe, passed along the entire length of the road back to the ford, dispersing or destroying our entire army; but of this I cannot be sure, for I was lifted from the earth insensible and blown back to the south side of the river. Continuous firing all night on the north side and the reports of such of our men as have re-crossed at the ford convince me that the Yankee brigade has extermi-nated the disabled survivors. Our loss has been uncommonly heavy. Of my own division of 15,000 infantry, the casualties—killed, wounded, captured, and missing—are 14,994. Of General Dolliver Billow's di-vision, 11,200 strong, I can find but two officers and a nigger cook. Of the artillery, 800 men, none has reported on this side of the river. General Flood is dead. I have assumed command of the expedi-tionary force, but owing to the heavy losses have deemed it advisable to contract my line of supplies as rapidly as possible. I shall push southward to-morrow morning early. The purposes of the campaign have been as yet but partly accomplished.

*From Major-General Dolliver Billows, C. S. A., to
    the Confederate Secretary of War.*

> Buhac, Kentucky,
> February 5, 1862.

. . . But during the 2d they had, unknown to us, been reinforced by
fifty thousand cavalry, and being apprised of our movement by a
spy, this vast body was drawn up in the darkness at Jayhawk, and as
the head of our column reached that point at about 11 P.M. fell upon
it with astonishing fury, destroying the division of General Buxter in
an instant. General Baumschank's brigade of artillery, which was
in the rear, may have escaped—I did not wait to see, but withdrew
my division to the river at a point several miles above the ford, and
at daylight ferried it across on two fence rails lashed together with
a suspender. Its losses, from an effective strength of 11,200, are
11,199. General Buxter is dead. I am changing my base to Mobile,
Alabama.

*From Brigadier-General Schneddeker Baumschank,
    C. S. A., to the Confederate Secretary of War.*

> Iodine, Kentucky,
> February 6, 1862.

. . . Yoost den somdings occur, I know nod vot it vos—somdings
mackneefcent, but it vas nod vor—und I finds meinselluf, afder leedle
viles, in dis blace, midout a hors und mit no men und goons. Sheneral
Peelows is deadt. You will blease be so goot as to resign me—I vights
no more in a dam gontry vere I gets vipped und knows nod how it
vos done.

Resolutions of Congress, February 15, 1862.

Resolved, That the thanks of Congress are due, and hereby tendered,
to Brigadier-General Jupiter Doke and the gallant men under his
command for their unparalleled feat of attacking—themselves only
2000 strong—an army of 25,000 men and utterly overthrowing it,
killing 5327, making prisoners of 19,003, of whom more than half
were wounded, taking 32 guns, 20,000 stand of small arms and, in
short, the enemy's entire equipment.

Resolved, That for this unexampled victory the President be requested to designate a day of thanksgiving and public celebration of
religious rites in the various churches.

Resolved, That he be requested, in further commemoration of the
great event, and in reward of the gallant spirits whose deeds have

added such imperishable lustre to the American arms, to appoint, with the advice and consent of the Senate, the following officer:

One major-general.

*Statement of Mr. Hannibal Alcazar Peyton, of
Jayhawk, Kentucky.*

Dat wus a almighty dark night, sho', and dese yere ole eyes aint wuf shuks, but I's got a year like a sque'l, an' w'en I cotch de mummer o' v'ices I knowed dat gang b'long on de far side o' de ribber. So I jes' runs in de house an' wakes Marse Doke an' tells him: "Skin outer dis fo' yo' life!" An' de Lo'd bress my soul! ef dat man didn' go right fru de winder in his shir' tail an' break for to cross de mule patch! An' dem twenty-free hunerd mules dey jes' t'nk it is de debble hese'f wid de brandin' iron, an' dey bu'st outen dat patch like a yarthquake, an' pile inter de upper ford road, an' flash down it five deep, an' it full o' Confed'rates from en' to en'! . . .

The City of the Gone Away

I was born of poor because honest parents, and until I was twenty-three years old never knew the possibilities of happiness latent in another person's coin. At that time Providence threw me into a deep sleep and revealed to me in a dream the folly of labor. "Behold," said a vision of a holy hermit, "the poverty and squalor of your lot and listen to the teachings of nature. You rise in the morning from your pallet of straw and go forth to your daily labor in the fields. The flowers nod their heads in friendly salutation as you pass. The lark greets you with a burst of song. The early sun sheds his temperate beams upon you, and from the dewy grass you inhale an atmosphere cool and grateful to your lungs. All nature seems to salute you with the joy of a generous servant welcoming a faithful master. You are in harmony with her gentlest mood and your soul sings within you. You begin your daily task at the plow, hopeful that the noonday will fulfill the promise of the morn, maturing the charms of the landscape and confirming its benediction upon your spirit. You follow the plow until fatigue invokes repose, and seating yourself upon the earth at the end of your furrow you expect to enjoy in fulness the delights of which you did but taste.

"Alas! the sun has climbed into a brazen sky and his beams are become a torrent. The flowers have closed their petals, confining their perfume and denying their colors to the eye. Coolness no longer exhales from the grass: the dew has vanished and the dry surface of the fields repeats the fierce heat of the sky. No longer the birds of heaven salute you with melody, but the jay harshly upbraids you from the edge of the copse. Unhappy man! all the gentle and healing ministrations of nature are denied you in punishment of your sin. You have broken the First Commandment of the Natural Decalogue: you have labored!"

Awakening from my dream, I collected my few belongings, bade adieu to my erring parents and departed out of that land, pausing at the grave of my grandfather, who had been a priest, to take an oath that never again, Heaven helping me, would I earn an honest penny.

How long I traveled I know not, but I came at last to a great city by the sea, where I set up as a physician. The name of that place I do not now remember, for such were my activity and renown in my new profession that the Aldermen, moved by pressure of public opinion, altered it, and thenceforth the place was known as the City of the Gone Away. It is needless to say that I had no knowledge of medicine, but by securing the service of an eminent forger I obtained a diploma purporting to have been granted by the Royal Quackery of Charlatanic Empiricism at Hoodos, which, framed in immortelles[73] and suspended by a bit of *crêpe*[74] to a willow in front of my office, attracted the ailing in great numbers. In connection with my dispensary I conducted one of the largest undertaking establishments ever known, and as soon as my means permitted, purchased a wide tract of land and made it into a cemetery. I owned also some very profitable marble works on one side of the gateway to the cemetery, and on the other an extensive flower garden. My Mourner's Emporium was patronized by the beauty, fashion and sorrow of the city. In short, I was in a very prosperous way of business, and within a year was able to send for my parents and establish my old father very comfortably as a receiver of stolen goods—an act which I confess was saved from the reproach of filial gratitude only by my exaction of all the profits.

But the vicissitudes of fortune are avoidable only by practice of the sternest indigence: human foresight cannot provide against the envy of the gods and the tireless machinations of Fate. The widening circle of prosperity grows weaker as it spreads until the antagonistic forces which it has pushed back are made powerful by compression to resist and finally overwhelm. So great grew the renown of my skill in medicine that patients were brought to me from all the four quarters of the globe. Burdensome invalids whose tardiness in dying was a perpetual grief to their friends; wealthy testators whose legatees were desirous to come by their own; superfluous children of penitent parents and dependent parents of frugal children; wives of husbands ambitious to remarry and husbands of wives without standing in the courts of divorce—these and all conceivable classes of the surplus population were conducted to my dispensary in the City of the Gone Away. They came in incalculable multitudes.

Government agents brought me caravans of orphans, paupers, lunatics and all who had become a public charge. My skill in curing orphanism and pauperism was particularly acknowledged by a grateful parliament.

Naturally, all this promoted the public prosperity, for although I got the greater part of the money that strangers expended in the city, the rest went into the channels of trade, and I was myself a liberal investor, purchaser and employer, and a patron of the arts and sciences. The City of the Gone Away grew so rapidly that in a few years it had inclosed my cemetery, despite its own constant growth. In that fact lay the lion that rent me.

The Aldermen declared my cemetery a public evil and decided to take it from me, remove the bodies to another place and make a park of it. I was to be paid for it and could easily bribe the appraisers to fix a high price, but for a reason which will appear the decision gave me little joy. It was in vain that I protested against the sacrilege of disturbing the holy dead, although this was a powerful appeal, for in that land the dead are held in religious veneration. Temples are built in their honor and a separate priesthood maintained at the public expense, whose only duty is performance of memorial services of the most solemn and touching kind. On four days in the year there is a Festival of the Good, as it is called, when all the people lay by their work or business and, headed by the priests, march in procession through the cemeteries, adorning the graves and praying in the temples. However bad a man's life may be, it is believed that when dead he enters into a state of eternal and inexpressible happiness. To signify a doubt of this is an offense punishable by death. To deny burial to the dead, or to exhume a buried body, except under sanction of law by special dispensation and with solemn ceremony, is a crime having no stated penalty because no one has ever had the hardihood to commit it.

All these considerations were in my favor, yet so well assured were the people and their civic officers that my cemetery was injurious to the public health that it was condemned and appraised, and with terror in my heart I received three times its value and began to settle up my affairs with all speed.

A week later was the day appointed for the formal inauguration of the ceremony of removing the bodies. The day was fine and the entire population of the city and surrounding country was present at the imposing religious rites. These were directed by the mortuary priesthood in full canonicals.[75] There was propitiatory sacrifice in the Temples of the Once, followed by a processional pageant of great splendor, ending at the cemetery. The Great Mayor in his robe of state led the procession. He was armed with a golden spade and followed by one hundred male and female singers, clad all in white and chanting the Hymn to the Gone Away. Behind these came the minor priesthood of the temples, all the civic authorities, habited in their official apparel, each carrying a living pig as an offering to the gods of the dead. Of the many divisions of the line, the last was formed by the populace, with uncovered heads, sifting dust into their hair in token of humility. In front of the mortuary chapel in the midst of the necropolis,[76] the Supreme Priest stood in gorgeous vestments, supported on each hand by a line of bishops and other high dignitaries of his prelacy, all frowning with the utmost austerity. As the Great Mayor paused in the Presence, the minor clergy, the civic authorities, the choir and populace closed in and encompassed the spot. The Great Mayor, laying his golden spade at the feet of the Supreme Priest, knelt in silence.

"Why comest thou here, presumptuous mortal?" said the Supreme Priest in clear, deliberate tones. "Is it thy unhallowed purpose with this implement to uncover the mysteries of death and break the repose of the Good?"

The Great Mayor, still kneeling, drew from his robe a document with portentous seals: "Behold, O ineffable, thy servant, having warrant of his people, entreateth at thy holy hands the custody of the Good, to the end and purpose that they lie in fitter earth, by consecration duly prepared against their coming."

With that he placed in the sacerdotal[77] hands the order of the Council of Aldermen decreeing the removal. Merely touching the parchment, the Supreme Priest passed it to the Head Necropolitan at his side, and raising his hands relaxed the severity of his countenance and exclaimed: "The gods comply."

Down the line of prelates on either side, his gesture, look and words were successively repeated. The Great Mayor rose to his feet, the choir began a solemn chant and, opportunely, a funeral car drawn by ten white horses with black plumes rolled in at the gate and made its way through the parting crowd to the grave selected for the occasion—that of a high official whom I had treated for chronic incumbency. The Great Mayor touched the grave with his golden spade (which he then presented to the Supreme Priest) and two stalwart diggers with iron ones set vigorously to work.

At that moment I was observed to leave the cemetery and the

country; for a report of the rest of the proceedings I am indebted to my sainted father, who related it in a letter to me, written in jail the night before he had the irreparable misfortune to take the kink out of a rope.[78]

As the workmen proceeded with their excavation, four bishops stationed themselves at the corners of the grave and in the profound silence of the multitude, broken otherwise only by the harsh grinding sound of spades, repeated continuously, one after another, the solemn invocations and responses from the Ritual of the Disturbed, imploring the blessed brother to forgive. But the blessed brother was not there. Full fathom two they mined for him in vain, then gave it up. The priests were visibly disconcerted, the populace was aghast, for that grave was indubitably vacant.

After a brief consultation with the Supreme Priest, the Great Mayor ordered the workmen to open another grave. The ritual was omitted this time until the coffin should be uncovered. There was no coffin, no body.

The cemetery was now a scene of the wildest confusion and dismay. The people shouted and ran hither and thither, gesticulating, clamoring, all talking at once, none listening. Some ran for spades, fire-shovels, hoes, sticks, anything. Some brought carpenters' adzes, even chisels from the marble works, and with these inadequate aids set to work upon the first graves they came to. Others fell upon the mounds with their bare hands, scraping away the earth as eagerly as dogs digging for marmots. Before nightfall the surface of the greater part of the cemetery had been upturned; every grave had been explored to the bottom and thousands of men were tearing away at the interspaces with as furious a frenzy as exhaustion would permit. As night came on torches were lighted, and in the sinister glare these frantic mortals, looking like a legion of fiends performing some unholy rite, pursued their disappointing work until they had devastated the entire area. But not a body did they find—not even a coffin.

The explanation is exceedingly simple. As important part of my income had been derived from the sale of *cadavres*[79] to medical colleges, which never before had been so well supplied, and which, in added recognition of my services to science, had all bestowed upon me diplomas, degrees and fellowships without number. But their demand for *cadavres* was unequal to my supply: by even the most prodigal extravagances they could not consume the one-half of the products of my skill as a physician. As to the rest, I had owned and operated the most extensive and thoroughly appointed soapworks in all the country. The excellence of my "Toilet Homoline" was attested by certificates from scores of the saintliest theologians, and I had one in autograph from Badelina Fatti the most famous living soaprano.[80]

The Major's Tale

In the days of the Civil War practical joking had not, I think, fallen into that disrepute which characterizes it now. That, doubtless, was owing to our extreme youth—men were much younger than now, and evermore your very young man has a boisterous spirit, running easily to horse-play. You cannot think how young the men were in the early sixties! Why, the average age of the entire Federal Army was not more than twenty-five; I doubt if it was more than twenty-three, but not having the statistics on that point (if there are any) I want to be moderate: we will say twenty-five. It is true a man of twenty-five was in that heroic time a good deal more of a man than one of that age is now; you could see that by looking at him. His face had nothing of that unripeness so conspicuous in his successor. I never see a young fellow now without observing how disagreebly young he really is; but during the war we did not think of a man's age at all unless he happened to be pretty well along in life. In that case one could not help it, for the unloveliness of age assailed the human countenance then much earlier than now; the result, I suppose, of hard service—perhaps, to some extent, of hard drink, for, bless my soul! we did shed the blood of the grape and the grain abundantly during the war. I remember thinking General Grant, who could not have been more than forty, a pretty well preserved old chap, considering his habits. As to men of middle age—say from fifty to sixty—why, they all looked fit to personate the Last of the Hittites,[81] or the Madagascarene Methuselah,[82] in a museum. Depend upon it, my friends, men of that time were greatly younger than men are to-day, but looked much older. The change is quite remarkable.

I said that practical joking had not then gone out of fashion. It had not, at least, in the army; though possibly in the more serious life of the civilian it had no place except in the form of tarring and feathering an occasional "copperhead."[83] You all know, I suppose, what a "copperhead" was, so I will go directly at my story without introductory remark, as is my way.

It was a few days before the battle of Nashville. The enemy had driven us up out of northern Georgia and Alabama. At Nashville we had turned at bay and fortified, while old Pap Thomas, our commander, hurried down reinforcements and supplies from Louisville. Meantime Hood, the Confederate commander, had partly invested us and lay close enough to have tossed shells into the heart of the town. As a rule he abstained—he was afraid of killing the families of his own soldiers, I suppose, a great many of whom had lived there. I sometimes wondered what were the feelings of those fellows, gazing over our heads at their own dwellings, where their wives and children or their aged parents were perhaps suffering for the necessaries of life, and certainly (so their reasoning would run) cowering under the tyranny and power of the barbarous Yankees.

To begin, then, at the beginning, I was serving at that time on the staff of a division commander whose name I shall not disclose, for I am relating facts, and the person upon whom they bear hardest may have surviving relatives who would not care to have him traced. Our headquarters were in a large dwelling which stood just behind our line of works. This had been hastily abandoned by the civilian occupants, who had left everything pretty much as it was—had no place to store it, probably, and trusted that Heaven would preserve it from Federal cupidity and Confederate artillery. With regard to the latter we were as solicitous as they.

Rummaging about in some of the chambers and closets one evening, some of us found an abundant supply of lady-gear—gowns, shawls, bonnets, hats, petticoats and the Lord knows what; I could not at that time have named the half of it. The sight of all this pretty plunder inspired one of us with what he was pleased to call an "idea," which, when submitted to the other scamps and scapegraces of the staff, met with instant and enthusiastic approval. We proceeded at once to act upon it for the undoing of one of our comrades.

Our selected victim was an aide, Lieutenant Haberton, so to call him. He was a good soldier—as gallant a chap as ever wore spurs; but he had an intolerable weakness: he was a lady-killer, and like most of his class, even in those days, eager that all should know it. He never tired of relating his amatory exploits, and I need not say how dismal that kind of narrative is to all but the narrator. It would be dismal even if sprightly and vivacious, for all men are rivals in woman's favor, and to relate your successes to another man is to rouse in him a dumb resentment, tempered by disbelief. You will not convince him that you tell the tale for his entertainment; he will hear nothing in it but an expression of your own vanity. Moreover, as most men, whether rakes or not, are willing to be thought rakes, he is very likely to resent a stupid and unjust inference which he suspects you to have drawn from his reticence in the matter of his own adventures—namely, that he has had none. If, on the other hand, he has had no scruple in the matter and his reticence is due to lack of opportunity to talk, or of nimbleness in taking advantage of it, why, then he will be surly because you "have the floor" when he wants it himself. There are, in short, no circumstances under which a man, even from the best of motives, or no motive at all, can relate his feats of love without distinctly lowering himself in the esteem of his male auditor; and herein lies a just punishment for such as kiss and tell. In my younger days I was myself not entirely out of favor with the ladies, and have a memory stored with much concerning them which doubtless I might put into acceptable narrative had I not undertaken another tale, and if it were not my practice to relate one thing at a time, going straight away to the end, without digression.

Lieutenant Haberton was, it must be confessed, a singularly handsome man with engaging manners. He was, I suppose, judging from the imperfect view-point of my sex, what women call "fascinating." Now, the qualities which make a man attractive to ladies entail a double disadvantage. First, they are of a sort readily discerned by other men, and by none more readily than by those who lack them. Their possessor, being feared by all these, is habitually slandered by them in self-defense. To all the ladies in whose welfare they deem themselves entitled to a voice and interest they hint at the voices and general unworth of the "ladies' man" in no uncertain terms, and to their wives relate without shame the most monstrous falsehoods about him. Nor are they restrained by the consideration that he is their friend; the qualities which have engaged their own admiration make it necessary to warn away those to whom the allurement would be a peril. So the man of charming personality, while loved by all the ladies who know him well, yet not too well, must endure with such fortitude as he may the consciousness that those others who know him only "by reputation" consider him a shameless reprobate, a vicious and unworthy man—a type and example of moral depravity. To name the second disadvantage entailed by his charms: he commonly is.

In order to get forward with our busy story (and in my judg-

ment a story once begun should not suffer impedition) it is necessary to explain that a young fellow attached to our headquarters
as an orderly was notably effeminate in face and figure. He was
not more than seventeen and had a perfectly smooth face and large
lustrous eyes, which must have been the envy of many a beautiful
woman in those days. And how beautiful the women of those
days were! and how gracious! Those of the South showed in their
demeanor toward us Yankees something of *hauteur*, but, for my
part, I found it less insupportable than the studious indifference
with which one's attentions are received by the ladies of this new
generation, whom I certainly think destitute of sentiment and sensibility.

This young orderly, whose name was Arman, we persuaded—by
what arguments I am not bound to say—to clothe himself in female attire and personate a lady. When we had him arrayed to our
satisfaction—and a charming girl he looked—he was conducted to a
sofa in the office of the adjutant-general. That officer was in the secret, as indeed were all excepting Haberton and the general; within
the awful dignity hedging the latter lay possibilities of disapproval
which we were unwilling to confront.

When all was ready I went to Haberton and said: "Lieutenant,
there is a young woman in the adjutant-general's office. She is the
daughter of the insurgent gentleman who owns this house, and has,
I think, called to see about its present occupancy. We none of us
know just how to talk to her, but we think perhaps you would say
about the right thing—at least you will say things in the right way.
Would you mind coming down?"

The lieutenant would not mind; he made a hasty toilet and joined
me. As we were going along a passage toward the Presence we encountered a formidable obstacle—the general.

"I say, Broadwood," he said, addressing me in the familiar manner which meant that he was in excellent humor, "there's a lady in
Lawson's office. Looks like a devilish fine girl—came on some errand of mercy or justice, no doubt. Have the goodness to conduct
her to my quarters. I won't saddle you youngsters with *all* the business of this division," he added facetiously.

This was awkward; something had to be done.

"General," I said, "I did not think the lady's business of sufficient importance to bother you with it. She is one of the Sanitary
Commission's[84] nurses, and merely wants to see about some sup-

plies for the smallpox hospital where she is on duty. I'll send her in at once."

"You need not mind," said the general, moving on; "I dare say Lawson will attend to the matter."

Ah, the gallant general! how little I thought, as I looked after his retreating figure and laughed at the success of my ruse, that within the week he would be "dead on the field of honor!" Nor was he the only one of our little military household above whom gloomed the shadow of the death angel, and who might almost have heard "the beating of his wings." On that bleak December morning a few days later, when from an hour before dawn until ten o'clock we sat on horseback on those icy hills, waiting for General Smith to open the battle miles away to the right, there were eight of us. At the close of the fighting there were three. There is now one. Bear with him yet a little while, oh, thrifty generation; he is but one of the horrors of war strayed from his era into yours. He is only the harmless skeleton at your feast and peace-dance, responding to your laughter and your footing it featly, with rattling fingers and bobbing skull—albeit upon suitable occasion, with a partner of his choosing, he might do his little dance with the best of you.

As we entered the adjutant-general's office we observed that the entire staff was there. The adjutant-general himself was exceedingly busy at his desk. The commissary of subsistence played cards with the surgeon in a bay window. The rest were in several parts of the room, reading or conversing in low tones. On a sofa in a half lighted nook of the room, at some distance from any of the groups, sat the "lady," closely veiled, her eyes modestly fixed upon her toes.

"Madam," I said, advancing with Haberton, "this officer will be pleased to serve you if it is in his power. I trust that it is."

With a bow I retired to the farther corner of the room and took part in a conversation going on there, though I had not the faintest notion what it was about, and my remarks had no relevancy to anything under the heavens. A close observer would have noticed that we were all intently watching Haberton and only "making believe" to do anything else.

He was worth watching, too; the fellow was simply an *édition de luxe* of "Turveydrop[85] on Deportment." As the "lady" slowly unfolded her tale of grievances against our lawless soldiery and mentioned certain instances of wanton disregard of property

rights—among them, as to the imminent peril of bursting our sides
we partly overheard, the looting of her own wardrobe—the look of
sympathetic agony in Haberton's handsome face was the very
flower and fruit of histrionic art. His deferential and assenting nods
at her several statements were so exquisitely performed that one
could not help regretting their unsubstantial nature and the impos-
sibility of preserving them under glass for instruction and delight of
posterity. And all the time the wretch was drawing his chair nearer
and nearer. Once or twice he looked about to see if we were
observing, but we were in appearance blankly oblivious to all but
one another and our several diversions. The low hum of our conversation, the gentle tap-tap of the cards as they fell in play and the
furious scratching of the adjutant-general's pen as he turned off
countless pages of words without sense were the only sounds heard.
No—there was another: at long intervals the distant boom of a
heavy gun, followed by the approaching rush of the shot. The enemy was amusing himself.

On these occasions the lady was perhaps not the only member of
that company who was startled, but she was startled more than the
others, sometimes rising from the sofa and standing with clasped
hands, the authentic portrait of terror and irresolution. It was
no more than natural that Haberton should at these times reseat
her with infinite tenderness, assuring her of her safety and regretting her peril in the same breath. It was perhaps right that he should
finally possess himself of her gloved hand and a seat beside her on
the sofa; but it certainly was highly improper for him to be in
the very act of possessing himself of *both* hands when—boom,
whiz, BANG!

We all sprang to our feet. A shell had crashed into the house and
exploded in the room above us. Bushels of plaster fell among us.
That modest and murmurous young lady sprang erect.

"Jumping Jee-rusalem!" she cried.

Haberton, who had also risen, stood as one petrified—as a statue
of himself erected on the site of his assassination. He neither spoke,
nor moved, nor once took his eyes off the face of Orderly Arman,
who was now flinging his girl-gear right and left, exposing his
charms in the most shameless way; while out upon the night and
away over the lighted camps into the black spaces between the hostile lines rolled the billows of our inexhaustible laughter! Ah, what

a merry life it was in the old heroic days when men had not forgotten how to laugh!

Haberton slowly came to himself. He looked about the room less blankly; then by degrees fashioned his visage into the sickliest grin that ever libeled all smiling. He shook his head and looked knowing.

"You can't fool *me*!" he said.

Curried Cow

My Aunt Patience, who tilled a small farm in the state of Michigan, had a favorite cow. This creature was not a good cow, nor a profitable one, for instead of devoting a part of her leisure to secretion of milk and production of veal she concentrated all her faculties on the study of kicking. She would kick all day and get up in the middle of the night to kick. She would kick at anything—hens, pigs, posts, loose stones, birds in the air and fish leaping out of the water; to this impartial and catholic-minded beef, all were equal—all similarly undeserving. Like old Timotheus, who "raised a mortal to the skies,"[86] was my Aunt Patience's cow; though, in the words of a later poet than Dryden, she did it "more harder and more frequently." It was pleasing to see her open a passage for herself through a populous barnyard. She would flash out, right and left, first with one hind-leg and then with the other, and would sometimes, under favoring conditions, have a considerable number of domestic animals in the air at once.

Her kicks, too, were as admirable in quality as inexhaustible in quantity. They were incomparably superior to those of the untutored kine that had not made the art a life study—mere amateurs that kicked "by ear," as they say in music. I saw her once standing in the road, professedly fast asleep, and mechanically munching her cud with a sort of Sunday morning lassitude, as one munches one's cud in a dream. Snouting about at her side, blissfully unconscious of impending danger and wrapped up in thoughts of his sweetheart, was a gigantic black hog—a hog of about the size and general appearance of a yearling rhinoceros. Suddenly, while I looked—without a visible movement on the part of the cow—with never a perceptible tremor of her frame, nor a lapse in the placid regularity of her chewing—that hog had gone away from there—had utterly taken his leave. But away toward the pale horizon a minute black speck was traversing the empyrean with the speed of a meteor, and in a moment had disappeared, without audible report, beyond the distant hills. It may have been that hog.

Currying cows is not, I think, a common practice, even in Michigan; but as this one had never needed milking, of course she had to be subjected to some equivalent form of persecution; and irritating her skin with a curry-comb was thought as disagreeable an attention as a thoughtful affection could devise. At least she thought it so; though I suspect her mistress really meant it for the good creature's temporal advantage. Anyhow my aunt always made it a condition to the employment of a farm-servant that he should curry the cow every morning; but after just enough trials to convince himself that it was not a sudden spasm, nor a mere local disturbance, the man would always give notice of an intention to quit, by pounding the beast half-dead with some foreign body and then limping home to his couch. I don't know how many men the creature removed from my aunt's employ in this way, but judging from the number of lame persons in that part of the country, I should say a good many; though some of the lameness may have been taken at second-hand from the original sufferers by their descendants, and some may have come by contagion.

I think my aunt's was a faulty system of agriculture. It is true her farm labor cost her nothing, for the laborers all left her service before any salary had accrued; but as the cow's fame spread abroad through the several States and Territories, it became increasingly difficult to obtain hands; and, after all, the favorite was imperfectly curried. It was currently remarked that the cow had kicked the farm to pieces—a rude metaphor, implying that the land was not properly cultivated, nor the buildings and fences kept in adequate repair.

It was useless to remonstrate with my aunt: she would concede everything, amending nothing. Her late husband had attempted to reform the abuse in this manner, and had had the argument all his own way until he had remonstrated himself into an early grave; and the funeral was delayed all day, until a fresh undertaker could be procured, the one originally engaged having confidingly undertaken to curry the cow at the request of the widow.

Since that time my Aunt Patience had not been in the matrimonial market; the love of that cow had usurped in her heart the place of a more natural and profitable affection. But when she saw her seeds unsown, her harvests ungarnered, her fences overtopped with rank brambles and her meadows gorgeous with the towering Canada thistle she thought it best to take a partner.

When it transpired that my Aunt Patience intended wedlock there was intense popular excitement. Every adult single male became at once a marrying man. The criminal statistics of Badger county show that in that single year more marriages occurred than in any decade before or since. But none of them was my aunt's. Men married their cooks, their laundresses, their deceased wives' mothers, their enemies' sisters—married whomsoever would wed; and any man who, by fair means or courtship, could not obtain a wife went before a justice of the peace and made an affidavit that he had some wives in Indiana. Such was the fear of being married alive by my Aunt Patience.

Now, where my aunt's affection was concerned she was, as the reader will have already surmised, a rather determined woman; and the extraordinary marrying epidemic having left but one eligible male in all that county, she had set her heart upon that one eligible male; then she went and carted him to her home. He turned out to be a long Methodist parson, named Huggins.

Aside from his unconscionable length, the Rev. Berosus Huggins was not so bad a fellow, and was nobody's fool. He was, I suppose, the most ill-favored mortal, however, in the whole northern half of America—thin, angular, cadaverous of visage and solemn out of all reason. He commonly wore a low-crowned black hat, set so far down upon his head as partly to eclipse his eyes and wholly obscure the ample glory of his ears. The only other visible article of his attire (except a brace of wrinkled cowskin boots, by which the word "polish" would have been considered the meaningless fragment of a lost language) was a tight-fitting black frock-coat, preternaturally long in the waist, the skirts of which fell about his heels, sopping up the dew. This he always wore snugly buttoned from the throat downward. In this attire he cut a tolerably spectral figure. His aspect was so conspicuously unnatural and inhuman that whenever he went into a cornfield, the predatory crows would temporarily forsake their business to settle upon him in swarms, fighting for the best seats upon his person, by way of testifying their contempt for the weak inventions of the husbandman.

The day after the wedding my Aunt Patience summoned the Rev. Berosus to the council chamber, and uttered her mind to the following intent:

"Now, Huggy, dear, I'll tell you what there is to do about the place. First, you must repair all the fences, clearing out the weeds and repressing the brambles with a strong hand. Then you will have to exterminate the Canadian thistles, mend the wagon, rig up a plow or two, and get things into ship-shape generally. This will

keep you out of mischief for the better part of two years; of course
you will have to give up preaching, for the present. As soon as you
have—O! I forgot poor Phœbe. She"——

"Mrs. Huggins," interrupted her solemn spouse, "I shall hope to
be the means, under Providence, of effecting all needful reforms in
the husbandry of this farm. But the sister you mention (I trust she is
not of the world's people)—have I the pleasure of knowing her?
The name, indeed, sounds familiar, but"——

"Not know Phœbe!" cried my aunt, with unfeigned astonishment; "I thought everybody in Badger knew Phœbe. Why, you will
have to scratch her legs, every blessed morning of your natural
life!"

"I assure you, madam," rejoined the Rev. Berosus, with dignity,
"it would yield me a hallowed pleasure to minister to the spiritual
needs of sister Phœbe, to the extent of my feeble and unworthy
ability; but, really, I fear the merely secular ministration of which
you speak must be entrusted to abler and, I would respectfully suggest, female hands."

"Whyyy, youuu ooold, foooool!" replied my aunt, spreading her
eyes with unbounded amazement, "Phœbe is a *cow*!"

"In that case," said the husband, with unruffled composure, "it
will, of course, devolve upon me to see that her carnal welfare is
properly attended to; and I shall be happy to bestow upon her legs
such time as I may, without sin, snatch from my strife with Satan
and the Canadian thistles."

With that the Rev. Mr. Huggins crowded his hat upon his shoulders, pronounced a brief benediction upon his bride, and betook
himself to the barnyard.

Now, it is necessary to explain that he had known from the first
who Phœbe was, and was familiar, from hearsay, with all her sinful
traits. Moreover, he had already done himself the honor of making
her a visit, remaining in the vicinity of her person, just out of range,
for more than an hour and permitting her to survey him at her
leisure from every point of the compass. In short, he and Phœbe
had mutually reconnoitered and prepared for action.

Amongst the articles of comfort and luxury which went to make
up the good parson's *dot*,[87] and which his wife had already caused
to be conveyed to his new home, was a patent cast-iron pump,
about seven feet high. This had been deposited near the barnyard,
preparatory to being set up on the planks above the barnyard well.

Mr. Huggins now sought out this invention and conveying it to its destination put it into position, screwing it firmly to the planks. He next divested himself of his long gaberdine and his hat, buttoning the former loosely about the pump, which it almost concealed, and hanging the latter upon the summit of the structure. The handle of the pump, when depressed, curved outwardly between the coat-skirts, singularly like a tail, but with this inconspicuous exception, any unprejudiced observer would have pronounced the thing Mr. Huggins, looking uncommonly well.

The preliminaries completed, the good man carefully closed the gate of the barnyard, knowing that as soon as Phœbe, who was campaigning in the kitchen garden, should note the precaution she would come and jump in to frustrate it, which eventually she did. Her master, meanwhile, had laid himself, coatless and hatless, along the outside of the close board fence, where he put in the time pleas-antly, catching his death of cold and peering through a knot-hole.

At first, and for some time, the animal pretended not to see the figure on the platform. Indeed she had turned her back upon it di-rectly she arrived, affecting a light sleep. Finding that this stratagem did not achieve the success that she had expected, she abandoned it and stood for several minutes irresolute, munching her cud in a half-hearted way, but obviously thinking very hard. Then she be-gan nosing along the ground as if wholly absorbed in a search for something that she had lost, tacking about hither and thither, but all the time drawing nearer to the object of her wicked intention. Ar-rived within speaking distance, she stood for a little while con-fronting the fraudful figure, then put out her nose toward it, as if to be caressed, trying to create the impression that fondling and dal-liance were more to her than wealth, power and the plaudits of the populace—that she had been accustomed to them all her sweet young life and could not get on without them. Then she approached a little nearer, as if to shake hands, all the while maintaining the most amiable expression of countenance and executing all manner of seductive nods and winks and smiles. Suddenly she wheeled about and with the rapidity of lightning dealt out a terrible kick—a kick of inconceivable force and fury, comparable to nothing in na-ture but a stroke of paralysis out of a clear sky!

The effect was magical! Cows kick, not backward but sidewise. The impact which was intended to project the counterfeit theolo-gian into the middle of the succeeding conference week reacted upon the animal herself, and it and the pain together set her spinning like a top. Such was the velocity of her revolution that she looked like a dim, circular cow, surrounded by a continuous ring like that of the planet Saturn—the white tuft at the extremity of her sweeping tail! Presently, as the sustaining centrifugal force lessened and failed, she began to sway and wabble from side to side, and finally, toppling over on her side, rolled convulsively on her back and lay motionless with all her feet in the air, honestly believing that the world had somehow got atop of her and she was supporting it at a great sacrifice of personal comfort. Then she fainted.

How long she lay unconscious she knew not, but at last she unclosed her eyes, and catching sight of the open door of her stall, "more sweet than all the landscape smiling near," she struggled up, stood wavering upon three legs, rubbed her eyes, and was visibly bewildered as to the points of the compass. Observing the iron clergyman standing fast by its faith, she threw it a look of grieved reproach and hobbled heart-broken into her humble habitation, a subjugated cow.

For several weeks Phœbe's right hind leg was swollen to a monstrous growth, but by a season of judicious nursing she was "brought round all right," as her sympathetic and puzzled mistress phrased it, or "made whole," as the reticent man of God preferred to say. She was now as tractable and inoffensive "in her daily walk and conversation" (Huggins) as a little child. Her new master used to take her ailing leg trustfully into his lap, and for that matter, might have taken in into his mouth if he had so desired. Her entire character appeared to be radically changed—so altered that one day my Aunt Patience, who, fondly as she loved her, had never before so much as ventured to touch the hem of her garment, as it were, went confidently up to her to soothe her with a pan of turnips. Gad! how thinly she spread out that good old lady upon the face of an adjacent stone wall! You could not have done it so evenly with a trowel.

A Revolt of the Gods

My father was a deodorizer of dead dogs, my mother kept the only shop for the sale of cats'-meat in my native city. They did not live happily; the difference in social rank was a chasm which could not be bridged by the vows of marriage. It was indeed an ill-assorted and most unlucky alliance; and as might have been foreseen it ended in disaster. One morning after the customary squabbles at breakfast, my father rose from the table, quivering and pale with wrath, and proceeding to the parsonage thrashed the clergyman who had performed the marriage ceremony. The act was generally condemned and public feeling ran so high against the offender that people would permit dead dogs to lie on their property until the fragrance was deafening rather than employ him; and the municipal authorities suffered one bloated old mastiff to utter itself from a public square in so clamorous an exhalation that passing strangers supposed themselves to be in the vicinity of a saw-mill. My father was indeed unpopular. During these dark days the family's sole dependence was on my mother's emporium for cats'-meat.

The business was profitable. In that city, which was the oldest in the world, the cat was an object of veneration. Its worship was the religion of the country. The multiplication and addition of cats were a perpetual instruction in arithmetic. Naturally, any inattention to the wants of a cat was punished with great severity in this world and the next; so my good mother numbered her patrons by the hundred. Still, with an unproductive husband and seventeen children she had some difficulty in making both ends cats'-meat; and at last the necessity of increasing the discrepancy between the cost price and the selling price of her carnal wares drove her to an expedient which proved eminently disastrous: she conceived the unlucky notion of retaliating by refusing to sell cats'-meat until the boycott was taken off her husband.

On the day when she put this resolution into practice the shop was thronged with excited customers, and others extended in turbulent and restless masses up four streets, out of sight. Inside there was nothing but cursing, crowding, shouting and menace. Intimidation was freely resorted to—several of my younger brothers and sisters being threatened with cutting up for the cats—but my mother was as firm as a rock, and the day was a black one for Sardasa,[88] the ancient and sacred city that was the scene of these events. The lock-out was vigorously maintained, and seven hundred and fifty thousand cats went to bed hungry!

The next morning the city was found to have been placarded during the night with a proclamation of the Federated Union of Old Maids. This ancient and powerful order averred through its Supreme Executive Head that the boycotting of my father and the retaliatory lock-out of my mother were seriously imperiling the interests of religion. The proclamation went on to state that if arbitration were not adopted by noon that day all the old maids of the federation would strike—and strike they did.

The next act of this unhappy drama was an insurrection of cats. These sacred animals, seeing themselves doomed to starvation, held a mass-meeting and marched in procession through the streets, swearing and spitting like fiends. This revolt of the gods produced such consternation that many pious persons died of fright and all business was suspended to bury them and pass terrifying resolutions.

Matters were now about as bad as it seemed possible for them to be. Meetings among representatives of the hostile interests were held, but no understanding was arrived at that would hold. Every agreement was broken as soon as made, and each element of the discord was frantically appealing to the people. A new horror was in store.

It will be remembered that my father was a deodorizer of dead dogs, but was unable to practice his useful and humble profession because no one would employ him. The dead dogs in consequence reeked rascally. Then they struck! From every vacant lot and public dumping ground, from every hedge and ditch and gutter and cistern, every crystal rill and the clabbered waters of all the canals and estuaries—from all the places, in short, which from time immemorial have been preëmpted by dead dogs and consecrated to the uses of them and their heirs and successors forever—they trooped innumerous, a ghastly crew! Their procession was a mile in length. Midway of the town it met the procession of cats in full song. The cats instantly exalted their backs and magnified their tails; the dead dogs uncovered their teeth as in life, and erected such of their bristles as still adhered to the skin.

The carnage that ensued was too awful for relation! The light of the sun was obscured by flying fur, and the battle was waged in the darkness, blindly and regardless. The swearing of the cats was audible miles away, while the fragrance of the dead dogs desolated seven provinces.

How the battle might have resulted it is impossible to say, but when it was at its fiercest the Federated Union of Old Maids came running down a side street and sprang into the thickest of the fray. A moment later my mother herself bore down upon the warring hosts, brandishing a cleaver, and laid about her with great freedom and impartiality. My father joined the fight, the municipal authorities engaged, and the general public, converging on the battle-field from all points of the compass, consumed itself in the center as it pressed in from the circumference. Last of all, the dead held a meeting in the cemetery and resolving on a general strike, began to destroy vaults, tombs, monuments, headstones, willows, angels and young sheep in marble—everything they could lay their hands on. By nightfall the living and the dead were alike exterminated, and where the ancient and sacred city of Sardasa had stood nothing remained but an excavation filled with dead bodies and building materials, shreds of cat and blue patches of decayed dog. The place is now a vast pool of stagnant water in the center of a desert.

The stirring events of those few days constituted my industrial education, and so well have I improved my advantages that I am now Chief of Misrule to the Dukes of Disorder, an organization numbering thirteen million American workingmen.

THE PARENTICIDE CLUB

My Favorite Murder

Having murdered my mother under circumstances of singular atrocity, I was arrested and put upon my trial, which lasted seven years. In charging the jury, the judge of the Court of Acquittal remarked that it was one of the most ghastly crimes that he had ever been called upon to explain away.

At this, my attorney rose and said:

"May it please your Honor, crimes are ghastly or agreeable only by comparison. If you were familiar with the details of my client's previous murder of his uncle you would discern in his later offense (if offense it may be called) something in the nature of tender forbearance and filial consideration for the feelings of the victim. The appalling ferocity of the former assassination was indeed inconsistent with any hypothesis but that of guilt; and had it not been for the fact that the honorable judge before whom he was tried was the president of a life insurance company that took risks on hanging, and in which my client held a policy, it is hard to see how he could decently have been acquitted. If your Honor would like to hear about it for instruction and guidance of your Honor's mind, this unfortunate man, my client, will consent to give himself the pain of relating it under oath."

The district attorney said: "Your Honor, I object. Such a statement would be in the nature of evidence, and the testimony in this case is closed. The prisoner's statement should have been introduced three years ago, in the spring of 1881."

"In a statutory sense," said the judge, "you are right, and in the Court of Objections and Technicalities you would get a ruling in your favor. But not in a Court of Acquittal. The objection is overruled."

"I except," said the district attorney.

"You cannot do that," the judge said. "I must remind you that in order to take an exception you must first get this case transferred for a time to the Court of Exceptions on a formal motion duly supported by affidavits. A motion to that effect by your predecessor in office was denied by me during the first year of this trial. Mr. Clerk, swear the prisoner."

The customary oath having been administered, I made the following statement, which impressed the judge with so strong a sense of the comparative triviality of the offense for which I was on trial that he made no further search for mitigating circumstances, but simply instructed the jury to acquit, and I left the court, without a stain upon my reputation:

"I was born in 1856 in Kalamakee, Mich., of honest and reputable parents, one of whom Heaven has mercifully spared to comfort me in my later years. In 1867 the family came to California and settled near Nigger Head, where my father opened a road agency and prospered beyond the dreams of avarice. He was a reticent, saturnine man then, though his increasing years have now somewhat relaxed the austerity of his disposition, and I believe that nothing but his memory of the sad event for which I am now on trial prevents him from manifesting a genuine hilarity.

"Four years after we had set up the road agency an itinerant preacher came along, and having no other way to pay for the night's lodging that we gave him, favored us with an exhortation of such power that, praise God, we were all converted to religion. My father at once sent for his brother, the Hon. William Ridley of Stockton, and on his arrival turned over the agency to him, charging him nothing for the franchise nor plant—the latter consisting of a Winchester rifle, a sawed-off shotgun, and an assortment of masks made out of flour sacks. The family then moved to Ghost Rock and opened a dance house. It was called 'The Saints' Rest Hurdy-Gurdy,' and the proceedings each night began with prayer. It was there that my now sainted mother, by her grace in the dance, acquired the *sobriquet*[89] of 'The Bucking Walrus.'

"In the fall of '75 I had occasion to visit Coyote, on the road to Mahala, and took the stage at Ghost Rock. There were four other passengers. About three miles beyond Nigger Head, persons whom I identified as my Uncle William and his two sons held up the stage. Finding nothing in the express box, they went through the passengers. I acted a most honorable part in the affair, placing myself in line with the others, holding up my hands and permitting myself to be deprived of forty dollars and a gold watch. From my behavior no one could have suspected that I knew the gentlemen who gave the entertainment. A few days later, when I went to Nigger Head and asked for the return of my money and watch my uncle and cousins swore they knew nothing of the matter, and they affected a belief that my father and I had done the job ourselves in dishonest violation of commercial good faith. Uncle William even threatened to retaliate by starting an opposition dance house at Ghost Rock. As 'The Saints' Rest' had become rather unpopular, I saw that this would assuredly ruin it and prove a paying enterprise, so I told my uncle that I was willing to overlook the past if he would take me into the scheme and keep the partnership a secret from my father. This fair offer he rejected, and I then perceived that it would be better and more satisfactory if he were dead.

"My plans to that end were soon perfected, and communicating them to my dear parents I had the gratification of receiving their approval. My father said he was proud of me, and my mother promised that although her religion forbade her to assist in taking human life I should have the advantage of her prayers for my success. As a preliminary measure looking to my security in case of detection I made an application for membership in that powerful order, the Knights of Murder, and in due course was received as a member of the Ghost Rock commandery. On the day that my probation ended I was for the first time permitted to inspect the records of the order and learn who belonged to it—all the rites of initiation having been conducted in masks. Fancy my delight when, in looking over the roll of membership, I found the third name to be that of my uncle, who indeed was junior vice-chancellor of the order! Here was an opportunity exceeding my wildest dreams—to murder I could add insubordination and treachery. It was what my good mother would have called 'a special Providence.'

"At about this time something occurred which caused my cup of joy, already full, to overflow on all sides, a circular cataract of bliss. Three men, strangers in that locality, were arrested for the stage robbery in which I had lost my money and watch. They were brought to trial and, despite my efforts to clear them and fasten the guilt upon three of the most respectable and worthy citizens of Ghost Rock, convicted on the clearest proof. The murder would now be as wanton and reasonless as I could wish.

"One morning I shouldered my Winchester rifle, and going over to my uncle's house, near Nigger Head, asked my Aunt Mary, his wife, if he were at home, adding that I had come to kill him. My aunt replied with her peculiar smile that so many gentleman called on that errand and were afterward carried away without having performed it that I must excuse her for doubting my good faith in the matter. She said I did not look as if I would kill anybody, so, as a proof of good faith I leveled my rifle and wounded a Chinaman who happened to be passing the house. She said she knew whole families that could do a thing of that kind, but Bill Ridley was a horse of another color. She said, however, that I would find him over on the other side of the creek in the sheep lot; and she added that she hoped the best man would win.

"My Aunt Mary was one of the most fair-minded women that I have ever met.

"I found my uncle down on his knees engaged in skinning a sheep. Seeing that he had neither gun nor pistol handy I had not the heart to shoot him, so I approached him, greeted him pleasantly and struck him a powerful blow on the head with the butt of my rifle. I have a very good delivery and Uncle William lay down on his side, then rolled over on his back, spread out his fingers and shivered. Before he could recover the use of his limbs I seized the knife that he had been using and cut his hamstrings. You know, doubtless, that when you sever the *tendo Achillis*[90] the patient has no further use of his leg; it is just the same as if he had no leg. Well, I parted them both, and when he revived he was at my service. As soon as he comprehended the situation, he said:

" 'Samuel, you have got the drop on me and can afford to be generous. I have only one thing to ask of you, and that is that you carry me to the house and finish me in the bosom of my family.'

"I told him I thought that a pretty reasonable request and I would do so if he would let me put him into a wheat sack; he would be easier to carry that way and if we were seen by the neighbors *en route* it would cause less remark. He agreed to that, and going to the barn I got a sack. This, however, did not fit him; it was too short and much wider than he; so I bent his legs, forced his knees up against his breast and got him into it that way, tying the sack above his head. He was a heavy man and I had all that I could do to get him on my back, but I staggered along for some distance until I came to a swing that some of the children had suspended to the branch of an oak. Here I laid him down and sat upon him to rest, and the sight of the rope gave me a happy inspiration. In twenty minutes my uncle, still in the sack, swung free to the sport of the wind.

"I had taken down the rope, tied one end tightly about the mouth of the bag, thrown the other across the limb and hauled him up about five feet from the ground. Fastening the other end of the rope also about the mouth of the sack, I had the satisfaction to see my uncle converted into a large, fine pendulum. I must add that he was not himself entirely aware of the nature of the change that he had undergone in his relation to the exterior world, though in justice to a good man's memory I ought to say that I do not think he would in any case have wasted much of my time in vain remonstrance.

"Uncle William had a ram that was famous in all that region as a fighter. It was in a state of chronic constitutional indignation. Some deep disappointment in early life had soured its disposition and it had declared war upon the whole world. To say that it would butt anything accessible is but faintly to express the nature and scope of its military activity: the universe was its antagonist; its methods that of a projectile. It fought like the angels and devils, in mid-air, cleaving the atmosphere like a bird, describing a parabolic curve and descending upon its victim at just the exact angle of incidence to make the most of its velocity and weight. Its momentum, calculated in foot-tons, was something incredible. It had been seen to destroy a four year old bull by a single impact upon that animal's gnarly forehead. No stone wall had ever been known to resist its downward swoop; there were no trees tough enough to stay it; it would splinter them into matchwood and defile their leafy honors in the dust. This irascible and implacable brute—this incarnate thunderbolt—this monster of the upper deep, I had seen reposing in the shade of an adjacent tree, dreaming dreams of conquest and glory. It was with a view to summoning it forth to the field of honor that I suspended its master in the manner described.

"Having completed my preparations, I imparted to the avuncular pendulum a gentle oscillation, and retiring to cover behind a contiguous rock, lifted up my voice in a long rasping cry whose diminishing final note was drowned in a noise like that of a swearing cat, which emanated from the sack. Instantly that formidable sheep was upon its feet and had taken in the military situation at a glance. In a few moments it had approached, stamping, to within fifty yards of the swinging foeman, who, now retreating and anon advancing, seemed to invite the fray. Suddenly I saw the beast's head drop earthward as if depressed by the weight of its enormous horns; then a dim, white, wavy streak of sheep prolonged itself from that spot in a generally horizontal direction to within about four yards of a

point immediately beneath the enemy. There it struck sharply upward, and before it had faded from my gaze at the place whence it
had set out I heard a horrid thump and a piercing scream, and my
poor uncle shot forward, with a slack rope higher than the limb to
which he was attached. Here the rope tautened with a jerk, arresting
his flight, and back he swung in a breathless curve to the other end
of his arc. The ram had fallen, a heap of indistinguishable legs, wool
and horns, but pulling itself together and dodging as its antagonist
swept downward it retired at random, alternately shaking its head
and stamping its fore-feet. When it had backed about the same distance as that from which it had delivered the assault it paused again,
bowed its head as if in prayer for victory and again shot forward,
dimly visible as before—a prolonging white streak with monstrous
undulations, ending with a sharp ascension. Its course this time was
at a right angle to its former one, and its impatience so great that it
struck the enemy before he had nearly reached the lowest point of
his arc. In consequence he went flying round and round in a horizontal circle whose radius was about equal to half the length of the
rope, which I forgot to say was nearly twenty feet long. His shrieks,
crescendo[91] in approach and *diminuendo*[92] in recession, made the rapidity of his revolution more obvious to the ear than to the eye. He
had evidently not yet been struck in a vital spot. His posture in the
sack and the distance from the ground at which he hung compelled
the ram to operate upon his lower extremities and the end of his
back. Like a plant that has struck its root into some poisonous mineral, my poor uncle was dying slowly upward.

"After delivering its second blow the ram had not again retired.
The fever of battle burned hot in its heart; its brain was intoxicated
with the wine of strife. Like a pugilist who in his rage forgets his
skill and fights ineffectively at half-arm's length, the angry beast
endeavored to reach its fleeting foe by awkward vertical leaps as
he passed overhead, sometimes, indeed, succeeding in striking him
feebly, but more frequently overthrown by its own misguided eager-
ness. But as the impetus was exhausted and the man's circles nar-
rowed in scope and diminished in speed, bringing him nearer to the
ground, these tactics produced better results, eliciting a superior
quality of screams, which I greatly enjoyed.

"Suddenly, as if the bugles had sung truce, the ram suspended
hostilities and walked away, thoughtfully wrinkling and smoothing
its great aquiline nose, and occasionally cropping a bunch of grass

and slowly munching it. It seemed to have tired of war's alarms and resolved to beat the sword into a plowshare and cultivate the arts of peace. Steadily it held its course away from the field of fame until it had gained a distance of nearly a quarter of a mile. There it stopped and stood with its rear to the foe, chewing its cud and apparently half asleep. I observed, however, an occasional slight turn of its head, as if its apathy were more affected than real.

"Meantime Uncle William's shrieks had abated with his motion, and nothing was heard from him but long, low moans, and at long intervals my name, uttered in pleading tones exceedingly grateful to my ear. Evidently the man had not the faintest notion of what was being done to him, and was inexpressibly terrified. When Death comes cloaked in mystery he is terrible indeed. Little by little my uncle's oscillations diminished, and finally he hung motionless. I went to him and was about to give him the *coup de grâce*,[93] when I heard and felt a succession of smart shocks which shook the ground like a series of light earthquakes, and turning in the direction of the ram, saw a long cloud of dust approaching me with inconceivable rapidity and alarming effect! At a distance of some thirty yards away it stopped short, and from the near end of it rose into the air what I at first thought a great white bird. Its ascent was so smooth and easy and regular that I could not realize its extraordinary celerity, and was lost in admiration of its grace. To this day the impression remains that it was a slow, deliberate movement, the ram—for it was that animal—being upborne by some power other than its own impetus, and supported through the successive stages of its flight with infinite tenderness and care. My eyes followed its progress through the air with unspeakable pleasure, all the greater by contrast with my former terror of its approach by land. Onward and upward the noble animal sailed, its head bent down almost between its knees, its fore-feet thrown back, its hinder legs trailing to rear like the legs of a soaring heron.

"At a height of forty or fifty feet, as fond recollection presents it to view, it attained its zenith and appeared to remain an instant stationary; then, tilting suddenly forward without altering the relative position of its parts, it shot downward on a steeper and steeper course with augmenting velocity, passed immediately above me with a noise like the rush of a cannon shot and struck my poor uncle almost squarely on the top of the head! So frightful was the impact that not only the man's neck was broken, but the rope too; and the body of the deceased, forced against the earth, was crushed to pulp beneath the awful front of that meteoric sheep! The concussion stopped all the clocks between Lone Hand and Dutch Dan's, and Professor Davidson, a distinguished authority in matters seismic, who happened to be in the vicinity, promptly explained that the vibrations were from north to southwest.

"Altogether, I cannot help thinking that in point of artistic atrocity my murder of Uncle William has seldom been excelled."

Oil of Dog

My name is Boffer Bings. I was born of honest parents in one of the humbler walks of life, my father being a manufacturer of dog-oil and my mother having a small studio in the shadow of the village church, where she disposed of unwelcome babes. In my boyhood I was trained to habits of industry; I not only assisted my father in procuring dogs for his vats, but was frequently employed by my mother to carry away the debris of her work in the studio. In performance of this duty I sometimes had need of all my natural intelligence for all the law officers of the vicinity were opposed to my mother's business. They were not elected on an opposition ticket and the matter had never been made a political issue; it just happened so. My father's business of making dog-oil was, naturally, less unpopular, though the owners of missing dogs sometimes regarded him with suspicion, which was reflected, to some extent, upon me. My father had, as silent partners, all the physicians of the town, who seldom wrote a prescription which did not contain what they were pleased to designate as *Ol. can.* It is really the most valuable medicine ever discovered. But most persons are unwilling to make personal sacrifices for the afflicted, and it was evident that many of the fattest dogs in town had been forbidden to play with me—a fact which pained my young sensibilities, and at one time came near driving me to become a pirate.

Looking back upon those days, I cannot but regret, at times, that by indirectly bringing my beloved parents to their death I was the author of misfortunes profoundly affecting my future.

One evening while passing my father's oil factory with the body of a foundling from my mother's studio I saw a constable who seemed to be closely watching my movements. Young as I was, I had learned that a constable's acts, of whatever apparent character, are prompted by the most reprehensible motives, and I avoided him by dodging into the oilery by a side door which happened to stand ajar. I locked it at once and was alone with my dead. My father had retired for the night. The only light in the place came from the furnace, which glowed a deep, rich crimson under one of the vats, casting ruddy reflections on the walls. Within the cauldron the oil still rolled in indolent ebullition, occasionally pushing to the surface a piece of dog. Seating myself to wait for the constable to go away, I held the naked body of the foundling in my lap and tenderly stroked its short, silken hair. Ah, how beautiful it was! Even at that early age I was passionately fond of children, and as I looked upon this cherub I could almost find it in my heart to wish that the small, red wound upon its breast—the work of my dear mother—had not been mortal.

It had been my custom to throw the babes into the river which nature had thoughtfully provided for the purpose, but that night I did not dare to leave the oilery for fear of the constable. "After all," I said to myself, "it cannot greatly matter if I put it into this cauldron. My father will never know the bones from those of a puppy, and the few deaths which may result from administering another kind of oil for the incomparable *Ol. can.* are not important in a population which increases so rapidly." In short, I took the first step in crime and brought myself untold sorrow by casting the babe into the cauldron.

The next day, somewhat to my surprise, my father, rubbing his hands with satisfaction, informed me and my mother that he had obtained the finest quality of oil that was ever seen; that the physicians to whom he had shown samples had so pronounced it. He added that he had no knowledge as to how the result was obtained; the dogs had been treated in all respects as usual, and were of an ordinary breed. I deemed it my duty to explain—which I did, though palsied would have been my tongue if I could have foreseen the consequences. Bewailing their previous ignorance of the advantages of combining their industries, my parents at once took measures to repair the error. My mother removed her studio to a wing of the factory building and my duties in connection with the business ceased; I was no longer required to dispose of the bodies of the small superfluous, and there was no need of alluring dogs to their doom, for my father discarded them altogether, though they still had an honorable place in the name of the oil. So suddenly thrown into idleness, I might naturally have been expected to become vicious and dissolute, but I did not. The holy influence of my dear mother was ever about me to protect me from the temptations which beset youth, and my father was a deacon in a church. Alas, that through my fault these estimable persons should have come to so bad an end!

Finding a double profit in her business, my mother now devoted herself to it with a new assiduity. She removed not only superfluous and unwelcome babes to order, but went out into the highways and byways, gathering in children of a larger growth, and even such adults as she could entice to the oilery. My father, too, enamored of the superior quality of oil produced, purveyed for his vats with diligence and zeal. The conversion of their neighbors into dog-oil became, in short, the one passion of their lives—an absorbing and overwhelming greed took possession of their souls and served them in place of a hope in Heaven—by which, also, they were inspired.

So enterprising had they now become that a public meeting was held and resolutions passed severely censuring them. It was intimated by the chairman that any further raids upon the population would be met in a spirit of hostility. My poor parents left the meeting broken-hearted, desperate and, I believe, not altogether sane. Anyhow, I deemed it prudent not to enter the oilery with them that night, but slept outside in a stable.

At about midnight some mysterious impulse caused me to rise and peer through a window into the furnace-room, where I knew my father now slept. The fires were burning as brightly as if the following day's harvest had been expected to be abundant. One of the large cauldrons was slowly "walloping"[94] with a mysterious appearance of self-restraint, as if it bided its time to put forth its full energy. My father was not in bed; he had risen in his nightclothes and was preparing a noose in a strong cord. From the looks which he cast at the door of my mother's bedroom I knew too well the purpose that he had in mind. Speechless and motionless with terror, I could do nothing in prevention or warning. Suddenly the door of my mother's apartment was opened, noiselessly, and the two confronted each other, both apparently surprised. The lady, also, was in her nightclothes, and she held in her right hand the tool of her trade, a long, narrow-bladed dagger.

She, too, had been unable to deny herself the last profit which the unfriendly action of the citizens and my absence had left her. For one instant they looked into each other's blazing eyes and then sprang together with indescribable fury. Round and round the room they struggled, the man cursing, the woman shrieking, both fighting like demons—she to strike him with the dagger, he to strangle her with his great bare hands. I know not how long I had the unhappiness to observe this disagreeable instance of domestic infelicity, but at last, after a more than usually vigorous struggle, the combatants suddenly moved apart.

My father's breast and my mother's weapon showed evidences of contact. For another instant they glared at each other in the most unamiable way; then my poor, wounded father, feeling the hand of death upon him, leaped forward, unmindful of resistance, grasped my dear mother in his arms, dragged her to the side of the boiling cauldron, collected all his failing energies, and sprang in with her! In a moment, both had disappeared and were adding their oil to that of the committee of citizens who had called the day before with an invitation to the public meeting.

Convinced that these unhappy events closed to me every avenue to an honorable career in that town, I removed to the famous city of Otumwee, where these memoirs are written with a heart full of re- morse for a heedless act entailing so dismal a commercial disaster.

From ANTEPENULTIMATA[95]

A Bivouac of the Dead

A way up in the heart of the Allegheny mountains, in Pocahontas county, West Virginia, is a beautiful little valley through which flows the east fork of the Greenbrier river. At a point where the valley road intersects the old Staunton and Parkersburg turnpike, a famous thoroughfare in its day, is a post office in a farm house. The name of the place is Travelers' Repose, for it was once a tavern. Crowning some low hills within a stone's throw of the house are long lines of old Confederate fortifications, skilfully designed and so well "preserved" that an hour's work by a brigade would put them into serviceable shape for the next civil war. This place had its battle—what was called a battle in the "green and salad days" of the great rebellion. A brigade of Federal troops, the writer's regiment among them, came over Cheat mountain, fifteen miles to the westward, and, stringing its lines across the little valley, felt the enemy all day; and the enemy did a little feeling, too. There was a great cannonading, which killed about a dozen on each side; then, finding the place too strong for assault, the Federals called the affair a reconnaissance in force, and burying their dead withdrew to the more comfortable place whence they had come. Those dead now lie in a beautiful national cemetery at Grafton, duly registered, so far as identified, and companioned by other Federal dead gathered from the several camps and battlefields of West Virginia. The fallen soldier (the word "hero" appears to be a later invention) has such humble honors as it is possible to give.

> His part in all the pomp that fills
> The circuit of the Summer hills
> Is that his grave is green.

True, more than a half of the green graves in the Grafton cemetery are marked "Unknown," and sometimes it occurs that one thinks of the contradiction involved in "honoring the memory" of him of whom no memory remains to honor; but the attempt seems to do no great harm to the living, even to the logical.

A few hundred yards to the rear of the old Confederate earth-

works is a wooded hill. Years ago it was not wooded. Here, among
the trees and in the undergrowth, are rows of shallow depressions,
discoverable by removing the accumulated forest leaves. From some
of them may be taken (and reverently replaced) small thin slabs of
the split stone of the country, with rude and reticent inscriptions by
comrades. I found only one with a date, only one with full names of
man and regiment. The entire number found was eight.

In these forgotten graves rest the Confederate dead—between
eighty and one hundred, as nearly as can be made out. Some fell in
the "battle"; the majority died of disease. Two, only two, have apparently been disinterred for reburial at their homes. So neglected
and obscure in this *campo santo*[96] that only he upon whose farm it
is—the aged postmaster of Travelers' Repose—appears to know
about it. Men living within a mile have never heard of it. Yet other
men must be still living who assisted to lay these Southern soldiers
where they are, and could identify some of the graves. Is there a
man, North or South, who would begrudge the expense of giving to
these fallen brothers the tribute of green graves? One would rather
not think so. True, there are several hundreds of such places still
discoverable in the track of the great war. All the stronger is the
dumb demand—the silent plea of these fallen brothers to what is
"likest God within the soul."

They were honest and courageous foemen, having little in common with the political madmen who persuaded them to their doom
and the literary bearers of false witness in the aftertime. They did
not live through the period of honorable strife into the period of
vilification—did not pass from the iron age to the brazen—from the
era of the sword to that of the tongue and pen. Among them is no
member of the Southern Historical Society. Their valor was not the
fury of the non-combatant; they have no voice in the thunder of the
civilians and the shouting. Not by them are impaired the dignity
and infinite pathos of the Lost Cause. Give them, these blameless
gentlemen, their rightful part in all the pomp that fills the circuit of
the summer hills.

1903.

From THE OPINIONATOR

THE CONTROVERSIALIST

The Short Story

"The short story is always distinctly a sketch. It can not express what is the one greatest thing in all literature—intercommunion of human characters, their juxtapositions, their contrasts. . . . It is not a high form of art, and its present extreme popularity bespeaks decadence far more than advance."

So said Edgar Fawcett, an author of no small note and consequence in his day. The one-greatest-things-in-all-literature are as plentiful and obvious, apparently, as the sole causes of the decline of the Roman power, yet new ones being continually discovered, it is a fair presumption that the supply is inexhaustible; and Fawcett, an ingenious man, could hardly have failed to find one and catalogue it. The one that he would discover was pretty sure to be as good as another and to abound in his own work—and Fawcett did not write short stories, but exceedingly long ones. So "the intercommunion of human characters," and so forth, stands. Nevertheless, one fairly great thing in all literature is the power to interest the reader. Perhaps the author having the other thing can afford to forego that one, but its presence is observable, somehow, in much of the work that is devoid of that polyonymous element noted by Messrs. Fawcett, Thomas, Richard and Henry. Having that fact in mind, and the added fact that in his own admirable sonnets (for example) the intercommunion is an absent factor, I am disposed to think that Edgar was facetious.

The short story, quoth'a, "is not a high form of art"; and inferably the long story—the novel—is. Let us see about that. As all the arts are essentially one, addressing the same sensibilities, quickening the same emotions and subject to the same law and limitations of human attention, it may be helpful to consider some of the arts other than literary and see what we can educe from the comparison. It will be admitted, I hope, that even in its exterior aspect St. Peter's Church is a work of high art. But is Rome a work of high art? Was it ever, or could it by rebuilding be made such? Certainly not, and the reason is that it can not all take attention at once. We may know that the several parts are coördinated and interrelated, but we do not discern and feel the coördination and interrelation. An opera, or an oratorio, that can be heard at a sitting may be artistic, but if in the manner of a Chinese play it were extended through the evenings of a week or a month what would it be? The only way to get unity of impression from a novel is to shut it up and look at the covers.

Not only is the novel, for the reason given, and for others, a faulty form of art, but because of its faultiness it has no permanent place in literature. In England it flourished less than a century and a half, beginning with Richardson and ending with Thackeray, since whose death no novels, probably, have been written that are worth attention; though as to this, one can not positively say, for of the incalculable multitude written only a few have been read by competent judges, and of these judges few indeed have uttered judgment that is of record. Novels are still produced in suspicious abundance and read with fatal acclaim but the novel of to-day has no art broader and better than that of its individual sentences—the art of style. That would serve if it had style.

Among the other reasons why the novel is both inartistic and impermanent is this—it is mere reporting. True, the reporter creates his plot, incidents and characters, but that itself is a fault, putting the work on a plane distinctly inferior to that of history. Attention is not long engaged by what could, but did not, occur to individuals; and it is a canon of the trade that nothing is to go into the novel that might not have occurred. "Probability"—which is but another name for the commonplace—is its keynote. When that is transgressed, as in the fiction of Scott and the greater fiction of Hugo, the work is romance, another and superior thing, addressed to higher faculties with a more imperious insistence. The singular inability to distinguish between the novel and the romance is one of criticism's capital ineptitudes. It is like that of a naturalist who should make a single species of the squirrels and the larks. Equally with the novel, the short story may drag at each remove a lengthening chain of probability, but there are fewer removes. The short story does not, at least, cloy attention, confuse with overlaid impressions and efface its own effect.

Great work has been done in novels. That is only to say that great writers have written them. But great writers may err in their choice of literary media, or may choose them wilfully for something else than their artistic possibilities. It may occur that an author of genius is more concerned for gain than excellence—for the nimble popularity that comes of following a literary fashion than for the sacred credentials to a slow renown. The acclamation of the multitude may be sweet in his ear, the clink of coins, heard in its pauses, grateful to his purse. To their gift of genius the gods add no security against its misdirection. I wish they did. I wish they would enjoin its diffusion in the novel, as for so many centuries they did by forbidding the novel to be. And what more than they gave might we not have had from Virgil, Dante, Tasso, Camoëns and Milton if they had not found the epic poem ready to their misguided hands? May there be in Elysium no beds of asphodel and moly for its hardy inventor, whether he was Homer or "another man of the same name."

The art of writing short stories for the magazines of the period can not be acquired. Success depends upon a kind of inability that must be "born into" one—it does not come at call. The torch must be passed down the line by the thumbless hands of an illustrious line of prognathous ancestors unacquainted with fire. For the torch has neither light nor heat—is, in truth, fireproof. It radiates darkness and all shadows fall toward it. The magazine story must relate nothing: like Dr. Hern's "holes" in the luminiferous ether, it is something in which nothing can occur. True, if the thing is written in a "dialect" so abominable that no one of sense will read, or so unintelligible that none who reads will understand, it may relate something that only the writer's kindred spirits care to know; but if told in any human tongue action and incident are fatal to it. It must provoke neither thought nor emotion; it must only stir up from the shallows of its readers' understandings the sediment which they are pleased to call sentiment, murking all their mental pool and effacing the reflected images of their natural environment.

The master of this school of literature is Mr. Howells. Destitute of that supreme and almost sufficient literary endowment, imagination, he does, not what he would, but what he can—takes notes with his eyes and ears and "writes them up" as does any other reporter. He can tell nothing but something like what he has seen or heard, and in his personal progress through the rectangular streets and between the trim hedges of Philistia, with the lettered old maids of his acquaintance curtseying from the doorways, he has seen and heard nothing worth telling. Yet tell it he must and, having told, defend. For years he conducted a department of criticism with a purpose single to expounding the after-thought theories and principles which are the offspring of his own limitations.

Illustrations of these theories and principles he interpreted with tireless insistence as proofs that the art of fiction is to-day a finer art than that known to our benighted fathers. What did Scott, what did even Thackeray know of the subtle psychology of the dear old New England maidens?

I want to be fair: Mr. Howells has considerable abilities. He is insufferable only in fiction and when, in criticism, he is making fiction's laws with one eye upon his paper and the other upon a catalogue of his own novels. When not carrying that heavy load, himself, he has a manly enough mental stride. He is not upon very intimate terms with the English language, but on many subjects, and when you least expect it of him, he thinks with such precision as momentarily to subdue a disobedient vocabulary and keep out the wrong word. Now and then he catches an accidental glimpse of his subject in a side-light and tells with capital vivacity what it is not. The one thing that he never sees is the question that he has raised by inadvertence, deciding it by implication against his convictions. If Mr. Howells had never written fiction his criticism of novels would entertain, but the imagination which can conceive him as writing a good story under any circumstances would be a precious literary possession, enabling its owner to write a better one.

In point of fiction, all the magazines are as like as one vacuum to another, and every month they are the same as they were the month before, excepting that in their holiday numbers at the last of the year their vacuity is a trifle intensified by that essence of all dulness, the "Christmas story." To so infamous a stupidity has popular fiction fallen—to so low a taste is it addressed, that I verily believe it is read by those who write it!

As certain editors of newspapers appear to think that a trivial incident has investiture of dignity and importance by being telegraphed across the continent, so these storywriters of the Reporter School hold that what is not interesting in life becomes interesting in letters—the acts, thoughts, feelings of commonplace people, the lives and loves of noodles, nobodies, ignoramuses and millionaires; of the village vulgarian, the rural maiden whose spiritual grace is not incompatible with the habit of falling over her own feet, the somnolent nigger, the clay-eating "Cracker" of the North Carolinian hills, the society person and the inhabitant of southwestern Missouri. Even when the writers commit infractions of their own literary Decalogue by making their creations and creationesses do something picturesque, or say something worth while, they becloud the miracle with such a multitude of insupportable descriptive details that the reader, like a tourist visiting an artificial waterfall at a New England summer place of last resort, pays through the nose at every step of his way to the Eighth Wonder. Are we given dialogue? It is not enough to report what was said, but the record must be authenticated by enumeration of the inanimate objects—commonly articles of furniture—which were privileged to be present at the conversation. And each dialogian must make certain or uncertain movements of the limbs or eyes before and after saying his say. All this in such prodigal excess of the slender allusions required, when required at all, for *vraisemblance* as abundantly to prove its insertion for its own sake. Yet the inanimate surroundings are precisely like those whose presence bores us our whole lives through, and the movements are those which every human being makes every moment in which he has the misfortune to be awake. One would suppose that to these gentry and ladry everything in the world except what is really remarkable is "rich and strange." They only think themselves able to make it so by the sea-change that it will suffer by being thrown into the duck-pond of an artificial imagination and thrown out again.

Amongst the laws which Cato Howells has given his little senate, and which his little senators would impose upon the rest of us, is an inhibitory statute against a breach of this "probability"—and to them nothing is probable outside the narrow domain of the commonplace man's most commonplace experience. It is not known to them that all men and women sometimes, many men and women frequently, and some men and women habitually, act from impenetrable motives and in a way that is consonant with nothing in their lives, characters and conditions. It is known to them that "truth is stranger than fiction," but not that this has any practical meaning or value in letters. It is to him of widest knowledge, of deepest feeling, of sharpest observation and insight, that life is most crowded with figures of heroic stature, with spirits of dream, with demons of the pit, with graves that yawn in pathways leading to the light, with existences not of earth, both malign and benign—ministers of grace and ministers of doom. The truest eye is that which discerns the shadow and the portent, the dead hands reaching, the light that is the heart of the darkness, the sky "with dreadful faces thronged and fiery arms." The truest ear is that which hears

> *Celestial voices to the midnight air,*
> *Sole, or responsive each to the other's note,*
> *Singing—*

not "their great Creator," but not a negro melody, either; no, nor
the latest favorite of the drawing-room. In short, he to whom life is
not picturesque, enchanting, astonishing, terrible, is denied the gift
and faculty divine, and being no poet can write no prose. He can
tell nothing because he knows nothing. He has not a speaking acquaintance with Nature (by which he means, in a vague general
way, the vegetable kingdom) and can no more find

> *Her secret meaning in her deeds*

than he can discern and expound the immutable law underlying coincidence.

Let us suppose that I have written a novel—which God forbid
that I should do. In the last chapter my assistant hero learns that the
hero-in-chief has supplanted him in the affections of the shero. He
roams aimless about the streets of the sleeping city and follows his
toes into a silent public square. There after appropriate mental agonies he resolves in the nobility of his soul to remove himself forever
from a world where his presence can not fail to be disagreeable to
the lady's conscience. He flings up his hands in mad disquietude
and rushes down to the bay, where there is water enough to drown
all such as he. Does he throw himself in? Not he—no, indeed. He
finds a tug lying there with steam up and, going aboard, descends to
the fire-hold. Opening one of the iron doors of the furnace, which
discloses an aperture just wide enough to admit him, he wriggles in
upon the glowing coals and there, with never a cry, dies a cherry-
red death of unquestionable ingenuity. With that the story ends and
the critics begin.

It is easy to imagine what they say: "This is too much"; "it in-
sults the reader's intelligence"; "it is hardly more shocking for its
atrocity than disgusting for its cold-blooded and unnatural defiance
of probability"; "art should have some traceable relation to the facts
of human experience."

Well, that is exactly what occurred once in the stoke-hold of
a tug lying at a wharf in San Francisco. *Only* the man had not
been disappointed in love, nor disappointed at all. He was a cheerful sort of person, indubitably sane, ceremoniously civil and con-

siderate enough (evidence of a good heart) to spare whom it might concern any written explanation defining his deed as "a rash act."

Probability? Nothing is so improbable as what is true. It is the unexpected that occurs; but that is not saying enough; it is also the unlikely—one might almost say the impossible. John, for example, meets and marries Jane. John was born in Bombay of poor but detestable parents; Jane, the daughter of a gorgeous hidalgo, on a ship bound from Vladivostok to Buenos Ayres. Will some gentleman who has written a realistic novel in which something so nearly out of the common as a wedding was permitted to occur have the goodness to figure out what, at their birth, were the chances that John would meet and marry Jane? Not one in a thousand—not one in a million—not one in a million million! Considered from a viewpoint a little anterior in time, it was almost infinitely unlikely that any event which has occurred would occur—any event worth telling in a story. Everything being so unearthly improbable, I wonder that novelists of the Howells school have the audacity to relate anything at all. And right heartily do I wish they had not.

Fiction has nothing to say to probability; the capable writer gives it not a moment's attention, except to make what is related *seem* probable in the reading—*seem* true. Suppose he relates the impossible; what then? Why, he has but passed over the line into the realm of romance, the kingdom of Scott, Defoe, Hawthorne, Beckford and the authors of the *Arabian Nights*—the land of the poets, the home of all that is good and lasting in the literature of the imagination. Do these little fellows, the so-called realists, ever think of the goodly company which they deny themselves by confining themselves to their clumsy feet and pursuing their stupid noses through the barren hitherland, while just beyond the Delectable Mountains lies in light the Valley of Dreams, with its tall immortals, poppy-crowned? Why, the society of the historians alone would be a distinction and a glory!

1897.

EXPLANATORY NOTES

1. *In the Midst of Life*: From the Book of Common Prayer—The Burial Service: "In the midst of life, we are in death."

Soldiers

A HORSEMAN IN THE SKY

2. salient: A protrusion, in this case a rock jutting out beyond the surface.

AN OCCURRENCE AT OWL CREEK BRIDGE

3. northern Alabama: Owl Creek is in Tennessee, not Alabama, not far from where the Battle of Shiloh was fought.

4. sleepers: Railroad ties.

5. *diminuendo*: Italian; in music a gradual descrease in volume or intensity.

6. æolian harps: Open boxes with stretched strings that play when the wind moves them.

CHICKAMAUGA

7. naked savages: American Indians.

8. civilized race to the far South: Mexicans; the Mexican-American War was conducted from 1846 to 1848; the capital, Mexico City, fell in 1847.

9. "curb the lust for war. . . the loftiest star": From *Childe Harold's Pilgrimage* Canto 3, by Lord Byron (1788–1824).

10. gouted: Clotted.

11. freaked and maculated: Speckled and blotched.

12. "spoor": The trail of a wild animal.

13. "the thunder of the captains and the shouting": From Job 39:25.

14. pillar of fire: In their flight from Egypt, God led the Israelites by a pillar of clouds in the day and a pillar of fire at night (Exodus 13:21).

ONE OF THE MISSING

15. *vis-à-vis*: French; face to face.

16. "Springfield": a breech-loading, bolt-action army rifle, first made at the U.S. Armory in Springfield, Massachusetts.

17. Carpathian Mountains: A mountain system in eastern Europe, forming a continuation of the Alps.

18. dun: Grayish-brown.

KILLED AT RESACA

19. Rincon Hill: In the 1860s, a fashionable district of San Francisco. By the 1880s it had been partially leveled and had become a working-class district. It is located at what is now the base of the San Francisco Bay Bridge.

THE AFFAIR AT COULTER'S NOTCH

20. trick of the cuttlefish: The cuttlefish emits a dark, inky liquid; here the guns likewise emitted clouds of dark smoke.

THE COUP DE GRÂCE

21. *Coup de Grâce*: French; "stroke of mercy."

22. chine: Backbone or spine.

23. unheroic Prometheus: Prometheus is the Greek god who, because he gave fire to mortals, was condemned to have his liver chewed upon eternally by vultures. The comparison here is to the exposed entrails of Sergeant Halcrow; he is "unheroic" because his suffering serves no purpose, not because he was cowardly.

PARKER ADDERSON, PHILOSOPHER

24. haft: The handle of a bladed weapon; with a bayonet it is designed to fit on the barrel of a rifle, though here it is used as a candleholder.

AN AFFAIR OF OUTPOSTS

25. *His Excellency the Fool*: Apparently an invented title.

26. impedimenta: Objects (in this case the persons accompanying the Governor) that impede or obstruct progress.

27. new levies from the line: A levy is one drafted into service; the irony here is that these men are being "drafted" into retreat due to injury.

28. pash: A smashing blow.

THE STORY OF A CONSCIENCE

29. defile in the Cumberland Mountains: A defile is a narrow gorge or valley; the Cumberland Mountains are the western section of the Appalachians and extend along the Virginia–Kentucky border into central Tennessee.

Civilians

THE MAN OUT OF THE NOSE

30. North Beach: On the coast in the northern part of the city; at one time a Bohemian district populated by would-be artists and writers, though here simply a district for the poor. Bierce dramatizes John Hardshaw's fi-

nancial and social descent by his successive moves to ever cheaper and less prestigious parts of the city.

31. Rincon Hill: In the 1860s, a fashionable district of San Francisco. By the 1880s it had been partially leveled and had become a working-class district. It is located at what is now the base of the San Francisco Bay Bridge.

32. that other law which God thundered from Sinai: A nice specimen of Bierce's wry humor; here he conjoins God's commandment against adultery with the law of gravitation.

33. Mission Dolores: In 1776, Father Francisco Palou had a brushwood shelter built in what is now San Francisco and offered the first mass. The present Mission Dolores was dedicated in 1791.

34. Goat Hill: Apparently Bierce's reference is to Billy Goat Hill, in the center of the city in the Noe Valley district.

THE MAN AND THE SNAKE

35. Morryster's *Marvells of Science*: Apparently an invented author and title. Bierce quotes the same author in *The Devil's Dictionary* in the entry for *Tree*. Most of his authorities there are invented and so, it seems, is his citation here.

36. Zola: Émile Zola (1840–1902), French naturalistic novelist, whose fiction was associated in some minds with the vulgar and unseemly side of life, which is the basis of comparison here.

37. *de trop*: French; too much, superfluous.

38. æolian harp: an open box with stretched strings that play when the wind moves them.

39. Memnon's statue: At Thebes, a huge statue of the Egyptian Pharoah Amenhotep III.

40. *ophiophagus*: Greek; serpent eating. A very venomous snake of the East Indies related to the cobra and that feeds on other snakes.

Can Such Things Be?

41. *Can Such Things Be?*: From *Macbeth* 3. iv. After the appearance of Banquo's ghost, Macbeth exclaims to Lady Macbeth:

Can such things be,
And overcome us like a summer's cloud,
Without our special wonder? You make me strange
Even to the disposition I owe,
When now I think you can behold such sights
And keep the natural ruby of your cheeks,
When mine is blanch'd with fear.

MOXON'S MASTER

42. "Herbert Spencer's definition of 'Life' ": Herbert Spencer (1820–1903) was a British materialist philosopher who adapted Darwinian principles to form a comprehensive philosophic system. His definition of life is found in Part One of *First Principles* (1867), though the language there differs a bit from Bierce's quotation.

43. Mill: John Stuart Mill (1806–1873), British philosopher, whose *System of Logic* (1843) stated principles of induction and explored notions of causation.

44. Saul of Tarsus: St. Paul before his conversion. Saul's religious conversion occurred on the road to Damascus. A great light shone round him and the Lord said: "Saul, why persecutest thou me?" (Acts 9:1–4).

45. Lewes: George Henry Lewes (1817–1878), English positivistic philosopher and editor of the liberal journal *Fortnightly Review*. The quotation, which Bierce quotes elsewhere as well, has not been located.

46. pawl: A device on a hinge designed to prevent the movement of a ratchet gear.

A RESUMED IDENTITY

47. "acoustic shadows": This phenomenon was recorded during the Civil War and is now most familiar in ultrasound diagnosis.

48. allocution: Formal address, normally to instruct or advise.

49. the loquacious barber of the Arabian Nights: The barber in the tale "Abu Kir the Dyer and Abu Sur the Barber" from *Tales of the Arabian Nights*.

50. Nineveh: Ancient capital of Assyria whose ruins are on the Tigris River.

51. Tyre: Ancient capital of Phoenicia.

THE NIGHT-DOINGS AT "DEADMAN'S"

52. *flumen*: Latin; to flow. A flume is a channel or gorge.

53. the Adversary: Satan.

THE REALM OF THE UNREAL

54. *prestidigitateurs*: French; jugglers, noted for manual dexterity; sleight-of-hand men.

55. love "*veils her sacred fires, / And, unaware, Morality expires*": / Bierce has altered the subject of the passage from Pope's *The Dunciad* Book ii for his own purposes. Pope wrote:

Religion blushing, veils her sacred fires,
And unawares Morality expires.

Nor public flame nor private dares to shine;
Nor human spark is left, nor glimpse divine!

56. thaumaturgists: Workers of miracles.

THE DAMNED THING

57. *chaparral:* Spanish; a dense thicket of shrubs and small trees generally found in the southwest United States.

58. maculations: Spotted or blotched from the contusions.

59. extravasated blood: Blood forced into surrounding tissues.

60. " 'actinic' rays": Photochemically active radiation, as those produced by the sun.

Soldier Folk

THREE AND ONE ARE ONE

61. sons and daughters of Ham: Slaves; Noah cursed the descendants of his son Ham; they were to be the "servant of servants" (Genesis 9:25).

Negligible Tales

A BOTTOMLESS GRAVE

62. ballot-box with a sliding bottom: That is, the election could be fixed by secretly removing or adding ballots.

63. embracery: Influencing the court through bribery or other corrupt methods.

64. gibbets: Gallows.

JUPITER DOKE, BRIGADIER-GENERAL

65. escutcheon: Originally, an emblem bearing a coat of arms; here one's political reputation.

66. bushwackers: Confederate guerrillas.

67. proxy: A person authorized to act for another.

68. Henry Clay: American statesman (1777–1852) from Kentucky and proponent of the Missouri Compromise and other efforts to avoid dissolution of the Union and ensuing war; nicknamed the "Great Pacificator." In view of the fact that the nation is embroiled in civil war, Clay was hardly the "far-seeing statesman" Doke takes him to be.

69. bolters: Those who have given up their membership in a political party.

70. *countertempus*: Latin; an embarrassing mishap.

71. the 22d ult.: Ultimate; that is, the last or most recent letter, being the one dated January 22.

72. the 2d inst.: Instant; here, the letter now under consideration.

THE CITY OF THE GONE AWAY

73. immortelles: French; immortal; dried flowers that retain their color.

74. *crêpe*: French; a soft, thin fabric; here ironically referring to the black band of crepe worn on the hat or sleeve as a symbol of mourning.

75. full canonicals: Prescribed dress for officiating clergy.

76. necropolis: A large cemetery typically associated with an ancient city.

77. sacerdotal: Pertaining to the priesthood.

78. to take the kink out of a rope: That is, to be hanged.

79. *cadavres*: French; cadavers, dead bodies usually intended for dissection.

80. soaprano: A pun (and not a very good one) on *soap* and *soprano*.

THE MAJOR'S TALE

81. Last of the Hittites: The Hittites were an acient people living in Asia Minor about 2000–1200 BCE.

82. Madagascarene Methuselah: Methuselah lived 969 years according to Genesis 5:27. The connection of Methuselah to Madagascar is unclear, though Bierce did refer to a Madagascarene philosopher in his fable "A Treaty of Peace."

83. "copperhead": A term used by Northern Republicans to label Northern Democrats. They called themselves Peace Democrats, but their opponents called them copperheads because many of them wore copper pennies as a party badge.

84. Sanitary Commission's: The United States Sanitary Commission was organized in 1861 by civilians who wished to assist the Union army by providing humanitarian aid for wounded soldiers.

85. Turveydrop: A character in Charles Dickens's *Bleak House* amusingly devoted to correct conduct.

CURRIED COW

86. Timotheus, who "raised a mortal to the skies": "He raised a mortal to the skies; / She drew an angel down," from "Alexander's Feast" by John Dryden (1631–1700).

87. *dot*: French; dowry.

A REVOLT OF THE GODS

88. Sardasa: Perhaps meant to be reminiscent of Sardis, an ancient city in Asia Minor.

The Parenticide Club

MY FAVORITE MURDER

89. *sobriquet*: French; a nickname.

90. *tendo Achilles*: Latin; Achilles tendon, the large tendon running from the heel bone to the calf muscle.

91. *crescendo*: Italian; in music a gradual increase in volume or intensity.

92. *diminuendo*: Italian; in music a gradual decrease in volume or intensity.

93. *coup de grâce*: French; "stroke of mercy."

OIL OF DOG

94. "walloping": Boiling noisily.

95. *Antepenultimata*: Those things that are second from the last.

The Controversialist

A BIVOUAC OF THE DEAD

96. *campo santo*: Spanish; a sacred field.

GLOSSARY OF MILITARY TERMS

adjutant-general: a staff officer who helps commanders of a unit having a general staff

aide de camp: a confidential assistant to a military officer

assembly: the bugler's call for troops to gather together for a common purpose

battalion: a military unit usually consisting of a headquarters company and four infantry companies

battery: the basic artillery unit; a six-gun battery was commanded by a captain and had as many as 170 men

bivouac: a temporary encampment

brigade: a military unit composed of combat battalions and support services

caisson: a horse-drawn vehicle designed to carry ammunition

canister: a container that when fired explodes and scatters the shot

cannonade: an extended and heavy discharge of artillery

cannoneer: artilleryman

cartridge: a metal casing containing powder and primer

casemate: an armored compartment for artillery

cavalcade: a ceremonial procession

columns: a formation of troops in which the constituent groups follow in lines behind one another

company: a subdivision of a regiment or battalion, usually under the command of a captain

covert: a covered and hence hidden shelter

division: three brigades

dressed: to put ranks of soldiers in proper adjustment and relation to one another

embrasure: an opening in a wall or embankment for a gun

fatigue-party: a group of soldiers deployed for designated clean-up duty

field officer: an officer above a captain and below a brigadier general

field-piece: a field gun

flank: the right or left side of a military formation

fusilade: a rapid, often simultaneous discharge of firearms

grape: a cluster of small iron balls used in cannon; they resemble a cluster of grapes, hence the name

haversack: a canvas bag with a single strap for carrying supplies on the shoulder

infantry: foot soldiers

lanyard: a cord with a hook attached used to fire a cannon *lever*: a metal rod used to adjust the elevation of a cannon

limber: a two-wheeled horse-drawn vehicle for carrying ammunition; a field gun might be towed behind it

line officer: a commander of infantry, typically a lieutenant or captain

parapet: a protective, earthen embankment

phalanx: a formation of infantry

picket: *n.* a detachment of one or more soldiers to warn of enemy approach; *v.* to post with a picket guard

provost-marshal: an officer in the military police who would take a soldier prisoner for subsequent court-martial

quartermaster: a military officer responsible for food, equipment, and clothing for troops

rammer: a rod or staff used to force the charge into a cannon; often the rammer head was at one end of the staff and the sponge was at the other

redoubt: a temporary fortification

regiment: a military unit consisting of at least two battalions

siege guns: heavy cannon and mortars that accompanied a field army

skirmisher: a participant in a relatively minor military encounter

spiked: to render a gun useless by driving a spike into the vent where the fuse was inserted

sponged: to clean and cool a cannon barrel by inserting a large staff with a wool covered sponge at the end into the bore of the cannon

vidette: variant of vedette; a mounted sentinel in advance of the army

BATTLE SITES AND BATTLE LEADERS

Buell, Major General Don Carlos (1818–1898). Commanded the Union Army of the Ohio. His army supplied the badly needed reinforcements at the Battle of Pittsburg Landing, sometimes called the Battle of Shiloh. After a fierce but inconclusive encounter with the Confederates under Gen. Braxton Bragg at the Battle of Perryville in October 1862, Buell was severely criticized and relieved of his command.

Carrick's Ford (or Corrick's Ford). On July 13, 1861, after the Union victory at Cheat Mountain, Gen. Thomas Morris (leader of Bierce's Indiana Brigade) chased the retreating army of Gen. Robert S. Garnett. Garnett was shot and killed at the ford, and, without proper leadership, his soldiers fled.

Cheat Mountain. The Cheat Mountain Campaign was a five-day campaign in September 1861 in Virginia. Gen. Robert E. Lee's forces mounted an attack against Union troops led by J. J. Reynolds. Bad weather and rugged terrain thwarted Lee's success.

Chickahominy Valley. From a few miles north of Richmond, Virginia, the Chickahominy River flows southeast until it empties into the James River. In May 1862 the Chickahominy River became an important factor in the defense of Richmond because heavy spring rains had made the normally slow river a torrent and difficult to cross. The swollen river effectively bisected the two wings of McClellan's army that was closing in on the city.

Chickamauga. The Battle of Chickamauga Creek, Tennessee, was fought on September 19–20, 1863. It was one of the bloodiest engagements of the war, without a clear victory for either side. Confederate General Bragg forced Union General Rosencrans's army to retreat, but Union General Thomas stood his ground and prevented a decisive victory for the Confederates. Confederate losses numbered more than 18,000 killed, wounded, or captured; the Union lost more than 16,000.

Corinth. Confederate General Johnston began concentrating his forces at Corinth, Mississippi, where he hoped to take the offensive and destroy General Grant's Army of the Tennessee. The Confederate engagement at Pittsburg Landing (Shiloh) was successful until Johnston was killed. A delay in the fighting enabled Union reinforcements to bolster Grant's army. With the arrival of Buell's Army of the Ohio, the Confederates, who had made military gains, were forced to march back to Corinth.

Gaines's Mill. The Battle of Gaines's Mill was part of the "Seven Days' Battle" in Virginia, as part of the unsuccessful effort of the Union army to take Richmond. On June 27, 1862, Gen. Fitz John Porter, commanding around 35,000 troops, held off a Confederate force of about 55,000 men. The Battle of Gaines's Mill was the last of the battles to be fought on the north side of the Chickahominy River.

Grant, General Ulysses S. (1822–1885). After his successful campaigns in Tennessee, President Lincoln made Grant commander in chief of the Union armies. Grant led the Army of the Potomac against Gen. Robert E. Lee that eventually led to Lee's surrender at Appomattox. As one can tell from his comments in these stories and elsewhere, Bierce did not regard Grant very highly and believed him to be too intent on self-promotion.

Greenbrier River. A river in western Virginia and the scene of a minor engagement at which Bierce was present on October 3, 1861. Union Gen. Joseph Reynolds failed to outflank Confederate Gen. Henry Jackson, and both sides withdrew.

Halleck, Major General Henry Wager (1815–1872). Union general. In July 1862 he was appointed general in chief of the United States armies. In preparation for the battle that eventually took place at Pittsburg Landing, Halleck ordered General Grant to advance up the Tennessee River and to await the arrival of General Buell's Army of the Ohio from Nashville.

Hazen, General William B. (1830–1887). Union officer who led the 19th Brigade of the Army of Ohio at Shiloh. He was promoted to brigadier general in November 1862 and served at that rank in the Battles of Stone's River, Chickamauga, Missionary Ridge, Resaca, and others. He was promoted to major general in December 1864. Bierce personally admired Hazen and served on his personal staff for a time.

Hood, General John Bell (1831–1879). Confederate general and commander of the Army of Tennessee. His aggressive tactics resulted in early military successes but he was decisively defeated by Union Gen. George Thomas at Nashville, Tennessee, in December 1864.

Kennesaw Mountain. The Battle of Kennesaw Mountain, Georgia, occurred on June 27, 1864. It was a defensive victory for the Confederates because Sherman's forces could not break General Johnston's lines and because Union casualties were far greater than those of the Confederates. Sherman lost some 3,000 men (killed or wounded) with nothing to show for it. The engagement delayed but did not prevent his march through Georgia.

Missionary Ridge. A mountain ridge in Georgia and Tennessee, where, against orders, Union Generals George Thomas and Philip Sheridan ascended the ridge and defeated Confederate forces led by Gen. Braxton Bragg on November 25, 1863. As a result, Bragg's army was forced to retreat deep into Georgia.

Nashville. The Battle of Nashville was a decisive battle on December 15–16, 1864, in which Union General George Henry Thomas succeeded in driving Confederate General John Bell Hood back from his position outside Nashville, Tennessee.

Philippi. Site in western Virginia of a surprise attack of a Confederate encampment on June 3, 1861.

Pickett, General George Edward (1825–1875). Served in the U.S. Army during the Mexican War. At the start of the American Civil War in 1861 he joined the Confederate forces and was commissioned a colonel; he soon rose to the rank of major general. He is best known for his bold but unsuccessful charge on July 3, 1863 ("Pickett's Charge"), during the Battle of Gettysburg.

Port Royal. Port Royal Ferry, South Carolina, is near Hilton Head and about 70 miles south of Charleston. On January 1, 1861, Federal troops attacked Port Royal Ferry. The attacking force included four gunboats, a ferry boat, and four large launches, each carrying twelve-pound howitzer cannons.

Resaca. The Battle of Resaca, Georgia, occurred May 13–14, 1864. As part of Sherman's march to the sea, this was the first major battle in his advance to Atlanta.

Rich Mountain. On July 11, 1861, Gen. William Rosencrans overran the Confederate-held Rich Mountain, helping to secure western Virginia for the Union.

Sheridan, General Philip (1831–1888). Rose from captain at the beginning of the war to major general by 1864. He commanded the Army of the Potomac and the Army of the Shenandoah in his drive through the Shenandoah Valley. He effectively cut off Gen. Robert E. Lee's retreat from Appomattox, thus forcing Lee's surrender to Grant on April 9, 1865.

Sherman, General William Tecumseh (1820–1891). Served under General Grant at Shiloh and later replaced Grant (after Grant became commander of the Union armies) as Commander of the Union Army in the West. Known for his devastating "march to the sea" through Georgia.

Shiloh. Site of the Battle at Pittsburg Landing, Tennessee, on April 6–7, 1862. It was a very costly battle on both sides. The Confederates lost some 13,000 men, the Union more than 10,000. Under the command of Gen. Albert Johnston, the Confederates attacked Grant's army. Johnston was killed in the conflict, and his successor, Gen. Pierre G. T. Beauregard, ordered the fighting suspended a few hours later. With the arrival of General Buell's forces by steamboat, the Union was able to attack the next day, and the Confederates withdrew to Corinth, Mississippi.

Stone's River. The Battle of Stone's River, Dec. 31, 1862–Jan. 2, 1863, sometimes called the "Battle of Murfreesboro," was a particularly fierce battle between Union and Confederate armies over Nashville's supply lines at Murfreesboro, Tennessee. Union Maj. Gen. William Rosencrans and Confederate Gen. Braxton Bragg fought to a stalemate, resulting in more than 20,000 casualties.

Thomas, General George Henry (1816–1870). Popularly referred to as "Pap Thomas." A Union general, also known as "The Rock of Chickamauga," because, at the Battle of Chickamauga, his army withstood a Confederate charge and prevented a rout of Union troops. Thomas was instrumental in several other battles, including Stone's River, Lookout Mountain, and Missionary Ridge.

Printed in the United States
by Baker & Taylor Publisher Services